AN ACCIDENTAL WOMAN

Books by Richard Neely

Death to My Beloved
While Love Lay Sleeping
The Plastic Nightmare
The Damned Innocents
The Walter Syndrome
The Smith Conspiracy
The Japanese Mistress
The Sexton Women
The Ridgway Women
A Madness of the Heart
No Certain Life
Lies
The Obligation
An Accidental Woman

An Accidental Woman

RICHARD NEELY

Holt, Rinehart and Winston • New York

Published by Holt, Rinehart and Winston,
383 Madison Avenue, New York, New York 10017.

Published simultaneously in Canada by Holt, Rinehart
and Winston of Canada, Limited.

Library of Congress Cataloging in Publication Data
Neely, Richard.
  An accidental woman.
  I. Title.
PS3564.E25A64   813'.54   80-26126
ISBN 0-03-058623-2

First Edition
Designer: Jacqueline Schuman
Printed in the United States of America
10 9 8 7 6 5 4 3 2 1

To Lauri, Lisa, and Matthew
with love

Book One

1

AT 4:00 P.M. Sara Vardon was back in her room, stretched out on the high bed in her scratchy, breeze-bottomed hospital gown and staring blind-eyed at an equally blind television set bolted to the ceiling. The nurse, impressed only dimly on Sara's mind as an angular assortment of bones and a voice that suggested the chattering intimacy of a hairdresser, had just squeaked away on her gum-soled shoes, pausing at the door to assure her that the important thing right now was to relax and not to worry.

Sara Vardon was not worried. She was terrified.

Routine tests, her internist, Dr. Monroe Corbett, had said, but necessary to rule out any possible organic basis for her seizure. And certainly the taking of her blood pressure, the beaming of pinpoint lights into her eyes, even the X ray of her head, all done that morning, had seemed routine enough. But not the probings from which she had just returned. Not the removal through a wicked-looking needle of fluid from inside her skull. Not the injection of some opaque substance into the arteries of her neck. Not the electrodes stuck to her scalp and wired to an unearthly machine.

Obviously the thing that had to be ruled out was some horror too appalling even to contemplate, and which she refused to consider.

No, what she had experienced, what she must somehow adjust to and will herself to surmount, was an emotional breakdown. Exactly the same diagnosis Dr. Corbett had intimated months ago when, after stepping from her brownstone apartment on a beautiful fall morning, her vision suddenly blurred, her knees liquefied, and she collapsed against a sidewalk tree. A woman walking a toy poodle had helped her to her feet, accompanied her to her door, and left after being assured that the cause of the accident was a rebellious high heel. She had gulped down three aspirin, then phoned Dr. Corbett and taxied to his office.

"Hold your arms out in front of you," the doctor had said, after checking her heart, blood pressure, and reflexes.

She held out her arms, each weighing a ton.

"Now, with your left forefinger, touch the tip of your nose."

She touched her nose, the fingertip invading a nostril.

"Now with your right forefinger."

Her fingertip landed on her upper lip.

"Hmm," said Dr. Corbett. "Now walk in a straight line to the door, placing one foot in front of the other."

"Excuse me, doctor, but do you think I'm drunk?"

Big grin. "This early in the morning? Of course not. But it's the same drill."

She made the walk, faltering twice. "I'm pretty nervous," she said.

"Sure, you're still shaken up." He sat her down, placed his right haunch on the examining table, and peered at her intently. "Has anything like this happened before?"

"No." She dismissed from her mind the occasional dizzy spells. Nothing alarming about those: maybe low blood sugar, or perhaps she'd gotten up too quickly.

"How did you feel, just before you fell?"

"I don't remember exactly. It seemed like I was, well, like I was going insane."

"You're not, so forget that. You work for an advertising agency, right?"

"Yes, as a copywriter."

"Lots of pressure?"

"Some, off and on. Nothing I haven't been able to handle."

"What about your private life? Any family problems?"

"My parents live in Ohio."

4

"I was thinking of a husband."

"I'm not married."

"You live alone?"

She gazed at his white smock and the stethoscope dangling from his pocket—symbols of confidentiality. "I have a roommate." She dropped her eyes self-consciously. "A man."

"Great." He smiled.

"We don't like to broadcast it."

He appraised her. Dark hair curving over smooth white cheeks. Childlike, indigo eyes. Snub nose, faintly freckled. A full-lipped mouth made for smiling. Long, rather prim body, appearing awkward because it seemed to cringe.

"It troubles you that you're not married?"

"Not really. Not here in New York. But it would if I were back where I was brought up." She sighed ruefully. "I guess there's still a lot of small town in me."

"Good. The country needs it. Look, I've got to ask you an intimate question. Okay?"

She took a breath. "You're the doctor."

"Have your relations with this man been satisfactory?"

"We get along beautifully."

"Including your sexual relations?"

She shifted her gaze to a glass-fronted cabinet. "I'd say he finds them very pleasurable."

"And you?"

"Me? Well, naturally I enjoy being close to him, being held. But I'm not really an erotic woman. A lot of women aren't, as I'm sure you know."

"Mind telling me how unerotic you are?"

"I don't see . . ." She swallowed and stared at him, a man in his early thirties, with curly black hair, outdoor complexion, friendly brown eyes. "I'm afraid I don't get quite the high that he does."

He nibbled at his lower lip for a moment, then stood up. "I guess that answers it. Does he know that you don't respond the way he does?"

"I doubt it. I've never told him."

"You've got lots of company. Have you tried getting help?"

"You mean Masters and Johnson, that sort of thing? No, I just can't see me—"

"Or psychotherapy?"

"No again. I know some people who go. They're all miserable."

"That's why they're going. Eventually most of them improve, some remarkably. I'd consider it."

"For my sex life or for what happened to me this morning?"

"Both."

"You're saying it's all psychological?"

"I'm saying it could be. On the other hand, it might be something as simple as pinched nerves, or a cutoff of circulation that will never happen again. How do you feel now?"

"Better." She smiled wryly. "It's like a toothache that stops hurting the minute you reach the dentist's office."

"It could just be the talking. Takes off the pressure. That's why I suggest a psych—"

"Let me think about it."

He had given her a prescription for Librium and told her to call him immediately if there was a recurrence.

As she left, she wondered what he would have said if she had confessed that never in her twenty-four years had she experienced an orgasm.

She had not called him. Even though, weeks later, she had bolted awake at 3:00 A.M., Rick sleeping blissfully beside her, to find her whole body thrashing and her arms and legs flailing the air. Even though she often had difficulty remembering a name or the day of the week. Even though she sometimes pulled a page of copy from her typewriter and read gibberish.

Nerves, nerves, she told herself, and reached for the Librium.

Then, for a long while, she felt fine—clear-headed, coherent, coordinated. In the office, she was once again "Little Sara Sunshine," never complaining, never questioning an assignment, never asserting herself. The perfect female employee—self-effacing, respectful of authority, dependable.

Then that night with Rick. Coupled in the dark bedroom. Her

legs clamped around him, her hips bucking in disciplined rhythm. Suddenly, an explosion. Not in her loins. In her head. It seemed to shatter her skull and blow her eyes from their sockets. She blacked out.

"Sara, Sara, are you all right?"

Rick, sitting beside her, a shotglass of whiskey in one hand, a glass of water in the other. She took the whiskey, straight.

"I guess I fainted." She looked down, saw her length of naked flesh, and drew up the sheet. She smiled. "Too much excitement."

She suppressed an impulse to describe the intensity of her trauma. He'd think she was going crazy. She was too unsure of him, too insecure, to risk it.

She had called Dr. Corbett's office the next morning. He was vacationing in the Bahamas and wouldn't return for ten days. She declined a substitute, feeling a dependency on Dr. Corbett because of the intimacies she had confided. Besides, she felt okay again, proving it by hatching a clever idea for a television commercial. But she was determined to call Dr. Corbett the first day he got back.

Again, she didn't. Why should she? There had not been another seizure, she was functioning well in her job, and there was the scent of premature spring breezing down the avenues. And why do anything to upset Rick? She was fine, just fine.

Fine. Until a month later, when she was struck by repeated nausea followed by violent visceral quaking. Oh, no, she thought, please *no*!

"Rick, I think I may be pregnant."

A flicker in his eyes. Barely perceptible. But enough to illuminate his shock. He took her in his arms, held her close. "Don't let it worry you. We'll work it out. We'll do whatever you want."

"I could be wrong. But I'm four or five days overdue and I've been getting sick in the mornings."

"Why not wait a few more days and see what happens."

Salvation! Her period arrived the next week. So great was her relief that she ignored the recurrence of vomiting. Nervous stomach, that was all. She thought too much, repressed her feelings, let worry and guilt tie her into knots. She was slightly neurotic, nothing worse. She hadn't yet adjusted to the pace and excitement and freestyle living of New York. The Librium helped, the dosage a little larger than before, but not hazardous.

Yesterday. The streets brazen with April sunshine. Store windows flaunting summer clothes. A look of expectancy on the faces rushing past at lunchtime. She bought a sandwich at a deli and went to Central Park. She sat on a bench beside the pond, gazed at the budding trees, fed crumbs to the ducks, felt wistful and strangely far away. Leaving the park, she wandered aimlessly, ending up at Bloomingdale's, surprised to find herself fondling lacy black lingerie.

"May I help you?" the saleswoman asked.

"Well, I . . ." And suddenly she was unable to speak. She had forgotten language, forgotten her name, forgotten where she was. She gaped in bewilderment, gasped for breath, shook convulsively. Then something big and clawing seemed to grab her brain and give it a vicious yank. A phosphorescent light burst through her skull, streaked down her neck. It was as though she had been slammed senseless by a falling tree.

She swam up to the edge of consciousness in a screaming ambulance. She heard a male voice say "epilepsy" before awareness again vanished. She came to in the emergency room, a black cone covering her nose and mouth, faces pinwheeling above her. Out of a stream of incoherence she found the name Dr. Monroe Corbett, felt it tremble from her lips.

And then he was there, bending close, a blur of geometric features, like a Picasso painting. She was wheeled to intensive care, wrists lashed to the bed, flesh sprouting tubes hooked to bottles and machines that whirred and hissed.

She slept, her mind consorting with leering monsters.

She woke in a pale green room ribbed with sun, a nurse taking her pulse.

She wept.

Now, the sinister tests completed, her mind medicated to a precarious rationality, she waited for Dr. Corbett to appear.

To tell her, in an oblique, euphemistic way that she was insane. Probably the resident psychiatrist would be at his side.

But he came in alone, his smile thin and somehow apologetic. No professional manner. No well-now-how's-the-patient-feeling. Head-on:

"Take a breath. We found something."

Her bated breath seemed to swell and congeal. "You did?"

"Yes." From a manila envelope he drew a sheet of film, an angiogram. He stepped close, squatted, and held it up to the light. Turning her head, she squinted and saw the white, fragile outline of a skull, looking no larger than a monkey's. It was crisscrossed with a network of blood vessels and arteries, one—the carotid—massively dominant.

He pointed to an area just behind the forehead, a space that at first seemed blank, but on closer inspection revealed a faint tracery, a tangle of wormy squiggles.

Then she saw the shadow, a veinless, bloodless mass the size of a walnut.

"Oh," she said. And for a moment, that was all she could manage. "What is it?"

"A tumor. It's been growing. Your brain has been trying to accommodate it. But now the pressure's too much."

She groaned. Whimpered.

"It's called a meningioma. But don't let that scare you. It's not *inside* the brain, only on the surface. Right temporal lobe. And it doesn't look malignant."

"How . . . how did I get it?"

"We don't know. No one does. What we do know is that it's the easiest kind to get rid of."

"How?"

"We'll go in and get it."

2

THE NEUROSURGEON was brought in and introduced: Dr. Vance Kloster, a rangy man in his early sixties, with fierce dark eyes that glowed and sparked, and lines like calipers bracketing a wide, mobile mouth. Shaking his hand, she gazed at the long fingers with their short-clipped nails, noticed the strong, dry grip, the smooth, pink palm—imagined that hand stealing through an aperture framed with bone to carve a poacher from her brain. She commanded herself to trust that hand—her bridge to life.

He did not talk like the remote, dignified brain surgeons who appeared in books and films. "A pushover. The stupid damned thing's a pushover. I'll have it out of there in the time it takes you to enjoy a short snooze. Believe me, if you've got to have one of the stupid damned things, this is the kind to have. Nothing to worry about, nothing."

"You're sure?"

"Sure I'm sure. All it is is tissue. No major blood vessels, no nerve cells, nothing that affects the brain, except the pressure. So far, the pressure's done no damage."

"Is there some way to, well, just shrink it?"

"Wouldn't work. This guy's ambitious. He wants to be a big boy. I've got to stop him."

"And if you don't?"

"He'll take over."

"Kill me?"

"Right. But against me, the stupid slob doesn't stand a chance."

Dr. Kloster stared at her forehead, grinning wolfishly, as though eager to get inside. "And once I've nipped him, you'll feel absolutely terrific."

She attempted a smile but felt it crumple. "When will you—"

"Day after tomorrow. Eight A.M."

Alone, she lay jackknifed on her side, battling the fear that engulfed her like a suffocating vapor. She tried to concentrate her thoughts on Rick but his face was distant and unfocused, just as it had been the evening before, when she had been in intensive care and he had been allowed to see her only briefly. His words had been like a litany, squeezed dry of meaning by time and use: Don't worry, you're going to be fine, hang in, I'll be thinking about you. He must have assumed, as she did, that her mind had snapped and that all their loving, laughing, carefree days might now be over.

How relieved he would be to learn that she had been assaulted by nothing more than a stupid "slob" of a tumor, a "pushover" for the infallible hands of Dr. Vance Kloster. Her fear receded.

But it returned, masked as anxiety, when she thought of her parents. Should they be notified? The answer was instant. No. Why derail their rigid lives with something that sounded so threatening but wasn't? When it was done with and she felt well, she would phone them, trivialize it, laugh away any suggestion that they rush to her side. Her mother, pretending reluctance, would agree, secretly thankful that no time need be sacrificed from her multiple crusades. Her father? He would do as mother said— quietly, without a sign of emotion.

But inwardly he would be distressed. If she were there, he would squeeze her hand, touch her cheek; his bemused gray eyes would declare his anguish. Since she wasn't, he would sneak his hidden bottle of brandy to his workshop out back, and there, amid the tools and wood shavings and smell of shellac, sip the day away lost in thwarted dreams. He would appear at dinner silently smashed, her mother observing his condition with a smile of condescension that camouflaged her ambivalence: contempt for his weakness, satisfaction in the dominance it assured her.

Her poor, dear father. An accountant for the railroad, forced into early retirement, but privately an inventor with visions of wealth and glory. Both were within his grasp when he had developed a device for increasing the efficiency of farm tractors, then lost to a huge, devouring company in a patent litigation that had gone on interminably until, facing defeat, he had yielded to her mother's insistence and settled for twenty thousand dollars. Sara recalled her mother's triumphant smile, retained even when it became known that the invention had brought millions of dollars to the company.

Always the smile. Pasted on that plump, pink, self-satisfied face as a deterrent to criticism, an emblem of righteousness, a coverup for cruelty.

"Sara, this morning I asked you to put the dishes away. Apparently you forgot." Smiling.

"I'm sorry, mother. I'll do it now."

"Yes, do that. And do try to remember things."

Passing by, she thrust her hand playfully at Sara and gave her arm a brutal, bruising pinch. Still smiling.

That smile had carried motions at the PTA, won variances from the planning commission, preserved landmarks for the historical society, provided God with a new altar in the Baptist church. That smile was the symbol of a way of life, a model that her daughter would be wise to emulate.

"You mustn't look gloomy, Sara. You must learn to smile, even when there is nothing to smile about. People like a person who looks happy."

"Yes, mother."

"You do want to be liked, don't you?"

Oh, yes! So she smiled. At the girls and boys thronging the high school corridors. At the teacher who said she was a near-genius, then patted her behind. At the mailman, the garbage collector, the police officers, the store clerks, the librarians.

And particularly, fluorescently, she smiled at Gordon Badgely.

Gordon, who preferred books to basketball, contemplation to convertibles, rebellion to regimentation. Gordon, who looked like his partial namesake, Lord Byron, but disdained his poetry in favor of Rimbaud and Baudelaire and the novels of Joyce, Lawrence, Miller. Gordon, whose IQ was as high as hers, but who, unlike her, saw it only as the key to self-discovery.

He watched her intently as she sat in his living room reading a scatological passage from *Tropic of Cancer,* which he had marked.

"Yuck," she said, her face hot with shame. "Why on earth do you want me to read such . . ."

"Filth?"

"Well, it certainly isn't Elsie Dinsmore."

"It's truth. I wanted to see what my reaction would be when you blushed."

"And?"

"I feel big, dominating, older and wiser than you."

"Is that important?"

"No. What's important is to know how I feel."

"Oh. For when you write books?"

"Maybe. Or maybe so I can understand people through myself. So I can manipulate them."

"You're not manipulating me, are you?"

"Of course I am. Everybody's a manipulator. Here, try this one. It's about love, sort of."

She took the heavy volume—*Ulysses*—and read a portion of the erotic ravings of Molly Bloom. Closing the book, handing it back, she didn't speak to or look at him.

"Like it or not," he said, "that's literature."

She stood up. "I think I'd better go. My mother—"

"Sure. Want to bring her the book? She could put it next to her Bible."

"Really, Gordon! Well, I'll see you. Bye."

Guilt flooded through her like a sickness. If her mother knew what she had read, Sara would be on her knees for a week praying for absolution. And Gordon's parents would be smilingly informed that their son, for his own good, might have to be reported to the juvenile authorities. Forget it. And forget Gordon.

But she couldn't. Especially when it finally occurred to her that he might have been trying to seduce her. Terrifying. And fascinating.

The next time his parents were away she again accompanied him to his house, ostensibly to study. The Punic Wars were halted by the abrupt intervention of kisses. Then Gordon's hand insinuated itself under her dress, an invasion she scarcely noticed until her panties were below her knees. The glimpse of a condom brought her upright. But before she could protest, Gordon spoke:

"I guess that proves it."

She followed his downward gaze and saw his shriveled penis.

"Apparently I'm a homosexual," he said.

She never saw him again, except passing in the halls, his eyes appearing introverted, as though probing his brain. It took weeks before she could look in the mirror without wanting to smash the image.

When her conscience finally relented, she realized that the kisses with Gordon, the pressure of bodies, had aroused no sensual feelings in *her*. Yet she had admired him, romanticized him, thought she was in love with him—a combination of emotions far more compelling than those that incited so many of her peers to joyous promiscuity.

Was she incapable of physical love? No, she decided, just not ready; not yet, at seventeen, in bloom. She should be thankful—it made it easier to endure the sepulchral shalt-nots that issued daily from her mother's lips (awe for the Scriptures pinching away the smile, fanaticizing the eyes). To her, life offered but two choices. Good or evil. God or the Devil. Eternal bliss or everlasting agony. Sara had heard it from the time she could comprehend words. She no longer believed it, but the echoes of the words were recorded in the anterior, silent area of her brain, where complex mental processes took place, processes no one really understood.

Her brain. It was a marvel of perception, of deductive reasoning, of creative thought, of empathy and judgment and intuition and reflexive response. It was a brain that, later, at Ohio's Kent State, had won her an unbroken four-point grade average, a Phi Beta Kappa key, and the uneasy envy of her professors. It was a brain that, socially, among her classmates, must be used with discretion, its capabilities deliberately dimmed lest they annoy and discon- cert, lest she not be liked. The dazzle must be limited to her smile and her eyes, the insight to determining the qualities that pleased and to employing them with subtle dexterity.

All of this was automated by her brain without conscious direction. She pushed no mental buttons, calculated no cause and effect. She simply adjusted, the way a furnace adjusts to the varying commands of a thermostat, just as since infancy she had adjusted to her mother's confining sanctimony and her father's lonely frustrations.

There was of course no way she could hide her academic accomplishments. She could only minimize them, smile ruefully when called The Brain, as though the epithet implied an affliction, then turn the conversation to commonplace subjects like sports, movies, record albums. Still, the aura of intellectualism persisted, perversely enhanced by her diffidence (often interpreted as an Olympian remoteness), evoking admiration but precluding intimacy. Especially with men.

To the big men on campus—the jocks, the charmers, even the scholars—Sara's brain was seen as a threat, an instrument that could peel away their cultivated surface sophistication and expose the uncertainties beneath. Rarely did she go out alone with a man, and then it was to a lecture, a concert, a school play. At parties or picnics, or gatherings at restaurants and bars, she was always part of a mixed group, committed to everyone and to no one. In the spring of her senior year, she was still a virgin.

That hallmark of innocence was shattered during a stupefying encounter on a warm evening in early May.

The two young men (boys, really) in their beat-up Chevy looked like college students. Faces fresh and only faintly acned, outgoing manner, Levi's and T-shirts. She didn't hesitate when they offered her a lift. Nor did she feel any qualms when the driver said he had to make a stop before dropping her at her dorm. But when the stop turned out to be a stretch of woods outside of town, every circuit and nerve in her brain crackled an alarm. But it was too late. A big hand was clamped over her mouth, she was wrestled from the car, dragged through a thicket, hurled to the ground, and brutally raped twice.

Staggering back on the deserted road where they had dumped

her, she finally reached a market and phoned the police. The two officers who picked her up drove her to the station, questioned her, then took her to the hospital. An hour after the humiliating examination, she learned that the stolen Chevy had been discovered on the Ohio side of the Pennsylvania border. The rapists were never caught.

Her name was withheld from the news story and, aside from the police, she did not tell anyone, not even her parents. (Especially not her parents. Her father would be devastated and lapse into drinking. Her mother would feel shamed, as if Sara had been tainted by the Devil, and would haul her home and place her under virtual house arrest.) Her fear and rage, her sense of worthlessness, her lust for revenge, remained locked inside her, barricaded by a vague perception that revelation would constitute social suicide. After several months these emotions ostensibly disappeared—but only on the surface. They simply seeped from the conscious core of her brain to lurk unrecognized in her inner psyche, infusing her with apprehension, churning the guilt instilled in her since infancy. She was beset by strange dreams and fantasies: huge shadows shaped like beasts pursued her; male classmates and teachers leered at her as she lay naked; handsome, golden-haired suitors changed into monsters. And sometimes she would wake in the night panting, heart pounding, flesh feverish, her whole being shocked into sensual awareness by a figment that she frantically erased from her mind.

None of this inner drama was revealed on the surface. Outwardly she became again the gentle, understanding, somewhat shy Sara Vardon who, in her quiet way, tried so hard to please.

When she graduated from college she decided at last to please herself. Over her mother's dire warnings, but with her father's clandestine support, she took a job as a junor copywriter in a Cleveland department store.

She was free.

Free to live and act as she wished.

Free to permit her incandescent brain to light the way to the future.

Her brain.

Now this pink-gray, puddinglike mass, housed in a globe of thick bone, was being pushed and compressed by a vacuous but relentless intruder, whose monstrous presence was signaled by a rhythmic throbbing that reverberated in her ears.

She heard someone in the corridor speaking to a nurse. A man's voice.

She smiled. It was Rick.

3

"A BRAIN TUMOR!" Rick's sky-blue eyes, usually calm and carefree, popped her a look of dismay.

"I know, it sounds terrible. But it's not, not really. They, the doctors, are sure it's not malignant. And it's on the outside of the brain, easy to get at. The operation will be over in no time. So please don't worry."

"What about you? Aren't you worried?"

"A little. But not because I'm afraid everything won't turn out fine. I just don't like the idea of someone poking around inside my head."

He took a breath, absorbing the shock. "I don't either. I like that head. It's a beautiful head."

He had recovered and was smiling his wide smile, his tanned cheeks (courtesy of the Racquet Club) relaxing to descend from his prominent cheekbones into twin hollows. She felt herself, as always, admiring that face, its golden darkness dramatic against the razor-cut blond hair. Looking at it, she forgot all the offenses committed against her body since she had been sirened into the emergency room. Now, her hand held and stroked, she felt secure and loved and indestructible.

"I guess they'll shave off all my hair," she said. "Do you think you can stand making love to a bald woman?"

"I've got a fetish for bald heads. The balder the better. I'll call you Scarlett No'Hara."

"No, I'll wear a wig. Lots of wigs. Every morning you can pick out the one you like best."

"Make it every night. You'll be a one-woman harem."

Tears suddenly spurted from her eyes and washed down her cheeks. "Oh, Rick, Rick, I'm sorry."

He swung from the chair to the bed and clasped her in his arms. "Nonsense. You deserve to cry. If you didn't, I wouldn't think you were human. Just let it all out."

She did, sobbing convulsively, seeing herself lying dead on the operating table and Rick facing Dr. Kloster, who was sadly shaking his head and saying something about "complications." Then the vision was whispered away by Rick's voice in her ear, filling it with endearments. She quieted, drew back, dried her eyes with the hem of the sheet, and smiled.

"Just a little spillage," she said. "I'm fine now."

"Sara Sunshine," he said, his tone gently mocking. "Right now we could use some of that at the office."

She seized the chance to change the subject. "Tell me what's happening. What's today's crisis?"

"The usual. Regal Foods wants to kill their campaign. The president says the fatigue factor has set in. I told him that when he's fatigued, the public's just starting to notice. He doesn't buy it. So we'll be working nights."

"You too?"

"I'm afraid so. But I'll be visiting you every day."

"Good. We can talk about a new campaign. Maybe I'll have a terrific idea."

"No, give that brilliant mind a rest. You may need it for bigger things."

"Like what?"

"Like Transcon Airways may be up for grabs. That's the rumor. If it's true, we'll pitch for it. Then we'll need every terrific idea we can get."

"When do you think we'll know?"

"Maybe next week. Our leader's flying to the Cannes Film Festival tomorrow. That's where Harry Dalton is. As you probably know,

Dalton not only runs Transcon, he's also into film production."

"Plus hotels in Vegas and other places."

"Right. They feed on each other. The airline provides free junkets to the casinos for high-rolling superstars. The superstars drop a bundle and that gives him leverage—a write-off if they agree to appear in his showrooms and movies. Dalton's a slick operator."

"And a very tough client, I hear."

"Uh-huh. A freewheeling maverick. He belongs back with the robber barons—Gould, Fisk, Vanderbilt. I think Brooks is making a mistake, barging in on him unannounced. Dalton will be too busy dealing with film exhibitors. That is, when he's not boozing and bed-hopping. Besides, he delights in making idiots of Mad Avenue Merlins, which is what he calls people like us. In my opinion, the fact that Brooks Madden is our esteemed president won't make him an exception."

"You told him that?"

"I did, gently. That, of course, settled it. He decided to go." He grimaced. "Look, I'm boring you. Right now you can't possibly be interested in—"

"But I am. And it takes my mind off things. Tell me everything you've been doing since my great blackout scene at Bloomingdale's."

As he talked, she only half listened. She was more aware of the warm rhythm of his voice, the confidential tone that seemed to make her the center of his universe. Her mind spun back to the first time she had seen him, presiding over a Plans Board meeting in a conference room that appeared designed for a shah. She had been at Madden and Associates less than a week, a tremulous rookie copywriter from a Cleveland department store, who had been banging out hyperbolic prose for dishwashers and lipsticks and underwear and sofa beds, until finally she could stand it no longer and in a spontaneous rush of courage decided to try for a bite of the Big Apple.

Hearing him relate incidents in the office and at lunch, she thought proudly of how everyone respected Rick, sometimes held him in awe, captivated by his ironic humor, his empathy, his emotional stamina and quiet self-assurance that enabled him to make hard decisions. No one seemed to resent that he was a product of Andover and Yale and the Harvard Business School, and not even his male colleagues felt diminished by his almost theatrical good looks that attracted covetous female stares. He was too unselfconscious, too regular, too concerned with solving problems rather than with enhancing his image, for anyone to fear for long that he was other than a strong ally. Unlike the other senior vice-presidents, who affected a Pentagonian remoteness, Rick made a point of mingling with the troops, usually descending to their cramped cubicles to discuss an assignment rather than summoning them to his plush office. Often, too, he would stop in after hours at the downstairs bar, the Elysee, and drink on equal terms with the aspiring young men and women from traffic, copy, art, media, and production.

It was at the Elysee that she had met him; he had introduced himself as though she had never heard of him. When he learned she was from Cleveland, a newcomer to New York and to the firm, he put her at ease by saying that writing copy for a department store was the best possible experience for working in an agency because you had to do it fast and under pressure, and the customer response, good or bad, was quick, so you found out very quickly what worked and what didn't. She felt understood and, for the first time, important, and when he left her—reluctantly it seemed—she felt as though she'd got a promotion and raise.

After that she stopped at the Elysee every day after work, and whenever he was there he would seek her out to tell her he'd heard something good about her from a copy supervisor, an account executive, an art director. Walking alone to where she then lived—the Barbizon Hotel, women only—her step was buoyant, and the avenue, rosy with spring twilight, appeared, as it supposedly did in the dreams of immigrants, paved with gold. She woke in the morning with a sense of expectancy, an awareness that in this most complex and eclectic of cities she would be touched by exciting, unprecedented happenings. This sensation was heightened by the milling, well-dressed throngs, the indignant horns of the Yellow taxis, the aroma of coffee drifting from breakfast bars, the underground rumble of speeding trains, and the thought, the hope, that at day's end she would drop by the Elysee and see the tall, elegant figure of Rick Bradley.

Her brain did not hide from her the fact that she was in love with him. She faced that, accepted it, just as she faced and accepted the almost simultaneous message that he was unattainable. It was like being in love with Paul Newman or Robert Redford or Al Pacino—fantasy figures to be shared, without rancor or jealousy, with millions. Like them, he had been married to an actress (not a star, but often seen in movies and television dramas as a stylish supporting player) from whom he had recently been divorced, depriving him, except on weekends, of a three-year-old son. That marriage, coupled with his spectacular good looks and charm and the nature of his business, had placed him, so she imagined, in the glamorous mainstream of what she had once heard him refer to as saloon society. To her, it was unthinkable that a man so sophisticated, so important in the agency hierarchy, and at thirty-four, ten years older than she, could possibly have more than a paternalistic interest in a shy, small-town, neophyte copywriter whose off-hours were largely spent amid strangers in museums, on tour boats, at Radio City Music Hall and the Statue of Liberty.

She was astonished when, after a couple of drinks at the Elysee, he asked her to dinner. (Astonished but not hopeful—he had an empty evening on his hands, that was all.) He took her to Elaine's, and immediately afterward, as if to confirm his lack of romantic interest, he taxied her home to the Barbizon, where he bid her an appreciative but physically distant good night. That was it, she thought, her one-night stand as Cinderella. But it wasn't. Again and again he took her to dinner, switching now to obscure restaurants in Greenwich Village or on the Upper West Side, always returning her early, unkissed and unspoken for.

She was perplexed, uncertain whether she was the object of a seduction or simply a convenient companion. Either role seemed absurd when she thought of all the really fascinating women who would be delighted to accommodate him whenever and however he desired. But the fact that he was living at the Yale Club, and had been ever since leaving his wife, seemed to imply a determination to lead a fairly austere life, devoid of entanglements, erotic or otherwise. She could only conclude that his divorce had hurt him deeply and that she was merely a temporary emollient for his wounded ego—soothing, but with no danger of addiction.

And then one evening he took her, not to a restaurant, but to a long iron-railed walkway overlooking the East River in the upper Sixties. They strolled for a while in silence under a pink-splashed sky, eyes turned from each other to gaze down at the sluggish tugs and barges, at cars whizzing past on the bordering expressway, at the jammed-together apartment houses across the water in the sprawling borough of Queens. Then he sat her on a bench and, speaking quietly, proceeded to stun her.

He began by telling her how perceptive she was, how understanding, how lucky for Madden and Associates it was that she had chosen to work there. He explained that the reason he had taken her to out-of-the-way places was to get to know her better, know her as she truly was, which would not have been possible amid the posturing clientele of the celebrity zoos.

So, she thought, he had simply been conducting a project for the agency, evaluating her, as no doubt he had evaluated others, perhaps as a candidate for the elite creative group then being formed to experiment with bold, innovative advertising. Any other copywriter would have been grateful and proud to be given such an opportunity. But she, feeling about him as she did, was disappointed and a little resentful, as though she had been exploited.

Then, looking south at the Queensboro Bridge, he said that he was boring her with all these things only because he wanted her to believe that what he was about to say was not based on impulse or on anything superficial.

She waited, impatient for it to be over with, impatient to accept the offer in a businesslike manner and quickly plead a headache and return to her small, spartan room.

Then he told her how lovely she was, told her at length, in a voice she thought should be accompanied by a string orchestra.

She gazed down at her hands locked in her lap and wondered

why he felt this compulsion to win her acceptance with such transparent flattery.

Then he told her he loved her.

She gasped, stared at him, flabbergasted, and burst out, "You *do*?"

"I do," he said solemnly.

She was speechless, unaware of her huge smile or that her eyes were damp, aware only of a euphoric glow and a commotion in her head.

"Any comment?" he said, smiling.

She just shook her head in wonder.

"It's customary for the lady to say something."

She flung her arms around him, kissed his right eye, his ear, his cheek, slid her face across his, found his mouth, clung there until she was empty of breath. Regaining it, she whispered what to her had never been customary, repeating it over and over: "I love you."

"It looks like I made one of my better presentations," he said.

"A magnificent presentation. But it wasn't necessary. I was presold." Behind him, she saw the river barges become yachts, Queens an enchanted land.

He regarded her seriously. "I wanted you to know that it's a lot more than sex."

Sex. She hadn't thought of it, not in its ultimate sense, hadn't had time. She looked at him, feeling wary, her brain flashing images of a long-ago intimacy aborted by impotence, of a nightmare in the woods, of her mother's smiling piety that could accuse, judge, condemn.

"But it's the natural place to start." He was smiling unashamedly. "I think the Barbizon management might object, so let's make it my place."

"At the Yale Club?"

"The other day I moved. I'm at the Waldorf Towers."

"Oh."

"That's all—'Oh'?"

She mustn't lose him. "I've never been to the Waldorf Towers." She managed a look of eagerness. "Let's go."

It was far better than she could have hoped. The huge square room was semi-dark when she slipped beneath the pale blue sheet, clad in bra and panties. He was gentle with her, as if sensing that her experience was limited and conventional. He didn't rush, but held her for a long time, caressing her and murmuring all the intimate words that she had not dared imagine. Her body felt flushed and yearning when finally he entered her, and it moved reflexively in rhythm with his. And when she felt him surge and his body go rigid, she responded in the same way. But she achieved no orgasm. Pleasure, yes, but no wild, earth-shaking ecstasy. Perhaps this pleasure, the pleasure of being miraculously joined to the man she loved, of giving him such sighing delight, perhaps that was enough. All that really mattered was that Rick Bradley, this treasure of a man, this debonair Mr. Manhattan, was hers and she was his.

But later she brooded about her sexual deficiency, concerned not with her own deprivation but with his. Surely he would prefer to have as a lover an uninhibited, wildly aroused woman. If only she could destoy the inner censor that cringed at erotic thoughts, that accompanied her to Rick's bed and, like a perverse voyeur, watched in anguished disapproval. Perhaps all she needed was time, time to adjust to this sudden splendid upheaval in her life. But instinctively she knew that was not the answer, and she doubted that there was one. Meanwhile she could simulate, pretend to be swept up by the passion depicted in R-rated movies and best-selling novels. Whatever it took to hold Rick, she would do.

She did not hesitate when he suggested they live together, but not at the Waldorf Towers, which was too expensive for his alimony-decimated income. They found a ground-floor furnished apartment with huge, high-ceilinged rooms and tall windows in a brownstone on Sixty-third Street near Third Avenue. Her only request was that they keep their arrangement quiet, not for her sake but because it might compromise his position at the agency. When he assured her that Brooks Madden wouldn't give a damn, she replied, "No, I mean the others, the young ones who think you're a sacred totem. Which, of course, you are." So it was never mentioned, except to a few confidants whom they sometimes entertained and who would have known anyway because of the two names on the mailbox.

At first she was concerned that Rick's relationship with his legal wife—the divorce decree would not be final for another nine months—might be a problem. But Rick handled that in his usual direct way. He simply explained the situation to Janice Powers (her professional name) and relied on her good sense to prevent any interference with his right to visit his adored son, Scott. She did not protest, in fact wished him well, and thus Sara was able to join them openly on weekends to picnic in Central Park, go to the zoo and the aquarium, cheer the Yankees, drive in a rented car to Coney Island or Jones Beach. Far from being bored, as she had feared, she found herself thoroughly enjoying the company of this fair, blue-eyed three-year-old, intelligent beyond his years, bursting with energy and enthusiasm, idolatrous of his father.

She was careful not to act the surrogate mother, affecting instead the role of indulgent aunt. But, in time, she began to feel a maternal closeness that aroused wistful daydreams of someday having a child with Rick. Accompanying that was the thought of eventual marriage, a notion instantly suppressed lest it exacerbate the guilt, instilled by her mother, for the sin of "immoral cohabitation." She told herself, convinced herself, that in the context of this permissive metropolis—indeed, of enlightened societies everywhere—her life was just as it should be. If there was a flaw, it was Rick's Sunday-night sadness after returning his son to Janice, a mood that could quickly be changed with a smile and a suggestive stroke of her hand. It was a glorious world.

And then this thing, this hideous, burgeoning, unexplainable blob of a thing had attached itself to her brain, like an evil messenger sent by God to punish her for some terrible disobedience.

She clung like a terrified cat to Rick when he kissed her goodbye. But when he paused at the door to look back, to say that she'd soon be home and he'd ice a magnum of vintage champagne, she gave him her well-trained smile.

Then she plunged back into her fear.

What if something went wrong?

What if she became, like a victim of stroke, a helpless paralytic, crippled in speech, movement, and visceral functions?

What if all that remained viable was her ability to love, but Rick could no longer return that love except through pity?

She got out of bed and dropped to her knees. For the first time since she had left her mother's house, she prayed.

4

TRAILING THE PORTER into the lobby of Cannes' Carlton Hotel, Brooks Madden felt like a man who, anticipating a quiet gentleman's club, finds he has stumbled into a whorehouse. The sight of the sedate white façade, when he had approached in the taxi, had not prepared him for an interior that, though architecturally elegant, was thronged with loudmouthed characters clad in Levi's and T-shirts, cutoffs and halters, slacks and pullovers, most of whom would seem more at home in the Bronx.

There were exceptions, he noted, as he went to register at the desk—a number of sleek men in well-cut business suits who might plausibly have graced a Manhattan boardroom, and several stunning women, actresses perhaps, who would appear, vanish, then reappear, like so many flashing ornaments.

Observing him, the thin, sad-eyed clerk, who wore an ascot, said dryly, "You may find it more to your liking on the terrace, Mr. Madden."

Brooks smiled amiably. A desk clerk, like a cabdriver, could be a source of all kinds of information. "You suppose that's where I'll find Mr. Dalton? Harry Dalton?"

The clerk's black eyebrows rose in faint surprise. Brooks knew the reason. The man had assumed that anyone wearing a Wilkes-Bashford suit and who, according to the reservation, was the chief executive officer of an enormous multinational advertising agency would speak in a quiet, well-bred voice, not in the rasping nasal tones associated with New York movie gangsters. As a young man, just starting to deal with advantaged clients, Brooks had tried valiantly to iron out the accent, but with only partial success. Now, at sixty-three, he no longer cared. In fact he thought it was often an attribute, combining with his botched Irish face to produce an impression of street-smart judgment and relentless honesty—an impression his clients had found to be accurate.

"Mr. Dalton left the hotel an hour ago," the clerk said.

"Did he leave word when he'd be back?"

"Sorry, he did not." He glanced down at Brooks Madden's reservation card, which stated his position. "You are a friend of Mr. Dalton's?"

"No, we haven't met."

"Ah. Perhaps I can be of help."

"In what way?"

"If you wish, I can telephone you should I see him come in."

"Fine. I'd appreciate it."

"Just one caution, Mr. Madden. Mr. Dalton is extremely protective of his privacy. With all respect to your position, you would find it impossible, I think, to see him unless it concerned something very important."

Brooks looked at him. The clerk had turned things around—now he was the one soliciting information. "It's important," Brooks said.

Broad smile. "Ah, big business. Every year at this time, for two weeks, Cannes is the big-deal capital of the world."

Brooks returned a short version of the smile but said nothing. He slipped out his wallet and started to remove a bill.

The clerk held up a stiffened hand. "Please, Mr. Madden, I would prefer you didn't. Later, after you have seen Mr. Dalton, if you feel—"

"Okay, later then."

"My name is Josef."

"Glad to know you, Josef. I'll be in my room for the next couple of hours, in case you spot Dalton."

"I will call you immediately."

Brooks's room was large, square, and tastefully decorated in pale pastels, but it offered only a minimal view of the harbor. Though he would be quick to approve more lavish accommodations for other agency executives, he shunned such trappings for himself. He would have felt uncomfortable, showy, even a bit corrupt, as though he had traded a part of his substance for a false image. It was all right that for business reasons he invested in fancy-labeled clothes, all right that he must occasionally entertain clients at extortionately priced restaurants, but alone, with no one to impress but himself, he chose to remain closer to the elementary qualities that he knew were his strength and the basis of his success.

Chief among them was self-denial, enforced in childhood and adolescence by the fact that he was the elder son of a janitor, an Irish immigrant content to wear overalls, shovel coal, act as lackey to tenants, and raise his family in three basement rooms infested with roaches and rats. The five-story apartment building stood in a row of similar structures on the northern tip of Manhattan, where the island ascended to its highest point, a section called Washington Heights. Brooks was Sammy then—he had been christened Samuel Brooks Madden (the Brooks in honor of an uncle)—a name he detested and dropped on the day he left the neighborhood. Among the middle-class juveniles who hung out on street corners, Brooks and his brother were known contemptuously as "the janitor kids," social outcasts unworthy of inclusion in such tribal sports as stickball, ringolevio, steal-the-flag.

Though he smarted under the exclusion, it had no practical effect on his activities. He was much too busy earning his keep: selling subscriptions door-to-door to *The Saturday Evening Post, Woman's Home Companion, Delineator;* delivering groceries for Gristede's and the A&P; gathering castoffs and peddling them to the "I cash clothes" man; fishing for coins lost in sewer and subway grates; shoveling snow from merchants' sidewalks, and, in the spring, taking to the thick woods that flanked Snake Hill down to Dyckman Street, where he harvested flowering dogwood, selling it cheap to delighted apartment dwellers.

His only self-indulgence, undiscovered by his father, came on Saturday afternoon, when, for a penny, he bought three licorice whips at Corbin's Stationery, then hurried down St. Nicholas Avenue to sit in the enchanted darkness of the Majestic, the Gem, or the Empress and escape from his loneliness into the glamorous worlds inhabited by Douglas Fairbanks, William Haines, Rod la Rocque, Colleen Moore, Billie Dove, Gloria Swanson.

His monastic existence continued after he graduated from George Washington High School and left home to hole up in a rooming house on West Twenty-eighth Street, a move made possible by a fifteen-dollar-a-week job selling classified ads. He was a good salesman largely because he made more calls than anyone in the history of the newspaper. On rainy or snowy days, when his colleagues had sneaked off to the twenty-five-cent morning matinees at the Capitol or the Paramount, Brooks Madden, wrapped in a frayed overcoat and a mile-long muffler, was mounting the slick steps of brownstones to coax a few lines of agate type out of impoverished and generally irate landladies. The reward came a few years later when, having worked on almost every major classification—furnished rooms, real estate, help wanted, used cars—he quit to start his own classified advertising agency.

Success was almost immediate, and soon, in addition to classified, he was handling the display advertising of small specialty shops, restaurants, nightclubs. Retaining that portion of the business, he sold the rest of the agency to a competitor, realizing a substantial profit and at the same time allowing him to concentrate his tireless energies on the acquisition of even larger accounts. By the mid-1950s he had offices on Madison Avenue, a staff of sixty, and had earned a reputation as a hard-working, no-nonsense ad man who knew how to move merchandise into and out of the stores. As the bigger advertisers grew bigger, powered by the development and introduction of new products, mostly convenience foods, Madden and Associates got more than their share of the business, earning a reputation as package-goods specialists. By the late seventies Brooks Madden, the janitor's kid, presided over an agency billing almost half a billion dollars and employing some three thousand people in offices located in New York, Chicago, Los Angeles, Mexico City, London, Paris, Frankfurt, Tokyo.

Now, sitting at a French Provincial desk, reviewing notes of what he would say to the head of Transcon Airways, Brooks began to feel uneasy about his self-assigned sales pitch. After all, what did he know about airplanes except that they provided you with cramped seats, questionable food, movies you had seen, delayed departures and arrivals, and the ever-present fear of a fiery death? All of his experience had been focused on things people eat and drink, use to wash and clean, spray under their arms, swallow for headaches and allergies, rub into their hair and skins, dust between their toes.

Face it, he thought, he was primarily a merchandiser, a store man, a specialist in supermarket promotions, discount couponing, boxtop premiums, tie-in sales, sampling—a front-line marketing soldier who fought for floor displays, shelf position and frontage, who scouted the aisles and the checkout counters to observe firsthand what Momma was buying. He had no true feel for what Harry Dalton was no doubt looking for: imaginative and intricate creative work that would give Transcon a superior image; consumer and market research that would define the targets of opportunity; smart media buying that would squeeze maximum effectiveness out of every advertising dollar spent. Brooks understood the functions and responsibilities of these departments but rarely became personally involved and left their execution to the vice-presidents who managed them.

In different circumstances, he would have brought these men with him. But his hunch was that here, at the Film Festival in Cannes, Harry Dalton, far from being flattered, would deeply resent being gratuitously descended upon by people he reputedly viewed as little more than parasites living off other people's accomplishments. It would have been great if Rick Bradley could have joined him as planned. Rick was a master at presenting every aspect of the organization, speaking as creative director, as a shrewd buyer of time and space, as an authority on consumer motivation, as the account supervisor that he so skillfully was— all the while making his points quietly and with deference and charm.

But, at the last minute, Rick had been forced to cancel the trip because a girl Brooks had never even heard of, a copywriter working for his own agency, who lived with Rick (which upset Brooks only because he so liked Janice and had been saddened by the divorce), had been struck down by, for godsake, a brain tumor. Of course there had been nothing to do but sympathize, wish the girl—Sara?—the best of luck, and agree that Rick had no choice but to stay.

Deprived of his support, Brooks had about decided to forget the whole thing, until he recalled an impulsive flight he had made some years ago. Two hours after he learned that the country's largest cigarette manufacturer had fired its advertising agency, he was on a plane to Miami Beach, where the chief executive officer was vacationing. Brooks met him when he came in from fishing, introduced himself, bought him a drink, which turned into several, and, over dinner and brandy, progressed to a handshake that certified Madden and Associates as the new agency. This while the rest of the Madison Avenue biggies filled conference rooms with smoke, sent out for sandwiches, and worried over what charts and graphs and exhibits would be the most effective for winning the account.

Brooks did not envision such a coup with Harry Dalton. But he hoped that the similarities in their characters and careers—both hard-driving individualists, both inclined toward bold action (such as this flight to Cannes), both products of poverty who had risen to command huge enterprises—would spark an affinity that would give Madden and Associates an advantage in subsequent presentations. He would be satisfied if he left Cannes feeling that the personal chemistry was right.

The phone rang. Josef must have got a fix on Harry Dalton.

But it was the pleasantly articulated voice of a woman. "Welcome to Cannes, Mr. Madden."

"Thank you." He assumed it was a courtesy call from the hotel's official greeter.

"I saw you at the desk and asked Josef who you were."

"I see. You work for the hotel?"

"I'm a guest of the hotel." She laughed lightly. "If you call paying such an outrageous rate being a guest."

"Have we met before?"

"Regrettably, no. I'm a friend of Janice Powers, Rick Bradley's former wife. They always said the nicest things about you."

Brooks found himself grinning. "They're all true. Listen, who are you?"

"Forgive me. My name is Maria Corliss."

"What! The actress?"

"How dear of you to remember." Said in a wry tone.

"Remember! Listen, I used to—"

"Why not save it, Mr. Madden? For over a drink? I thought it only proper that I initiate you into this madhouse."

"Fine, but—"

"Does right now seem like a good time?"

"I wish it were, but unfortunately, I'm waiting for an important call."

"Ah, too bad."

"But later, possibly. Can I call you?"

"I'm in room three-fifteen. If I should be out, you might leave a message at the desk."

"Count on it."

"I'll do that. Goodbye for now, Mr. Madden."

Maria Corliss! He had admired her since back in the thirties when he bought his theater tickets cut-rate in the subway arcade at Times Square. For fifty-five cents he would sit high in the balcony, up with the bats, and see stars like Ethel Barrymore, Nazimova, Tallulah Bankhead, Katharine Cornell . . . and Maria Corliss. But she hadn't been a star when he first saw her, as a Georgia sexpot in *Tobacco Road,* before word got around that the play was a dirty shocker and took off on a run that went on for years. He'd gone back again and again just to see her, and when she left the cast for Hollywood, he followed her ascending career on film, feeling an almost personal relationship because he'd seen her live in a theater before anyone else knew her name. He'd tracked her as a glamour girl, an experienced woman, a stylish matron, then lost her after her third marriage, to an Argentine businessman who whisked her away to Buenos Aires. Occasionally he'd seen her name in the columns—most notably when her Latin spouse had divorced her—and sometimes he caught her movie reruns on TV, but otherwise she existed for him only in nostalgia, along with the songs of Gershwin and Porter.

He thought back and decided that she must be almost as old as he—at least grazing sixty—too old to be staging a comeback in the movies. Then why was she in Cannes, at the world's biggest film festival? Probably because she was now married to an agent or producer who was too busy hustling a film to pay much attention to his wife. That would explain the phone call. She was so bored that she jumped at any chance for diversion, even if it meant soliciting the company of an aging huckster known only by hearsay.

Listen, he told himself, let's forget the aging bit. He still wore a size thirty-nine jacket, still maintained a thirty-three-inch waist, still retained a ruddy complexion, lined, sure, but the face lean and alert. And he still had his hair, maybe not the pale-orange cloud it once had been, but thick enough to cover, and nicely toned down by a sprinkling of gray. Friends he hadn't seen in forty years would still recognize him as the guy they said looked a bit like the formerly Honorable James J. Walker, New York's "midnight mayor," or the young James Cagney.

He was still massaging his ego, smiling in self-mockery, when the phone rang again. This time he anticipated correctly—it was Josef.

"Mr. Madden, I have just learned that Mr. Dalton flew out earlier for Dubrovnik."

"Dubrovnik?"

"Yes, in Yugoslavia. A seaside resort."

Brooks groaned. "Then I guess I won't get to see him."

"But yes. He took rather a large number of guests with him. Many of them must be back in Cannes by noon tomorrow. He, of course, will be among them."

"Unless he decides to stay."

"I doubt that. He used his private plane—a Learjet—and he is the pilot."

"Well, then—"

"I will phone you tomorrow, Mr. Madden, the moment I hear he has arrived."

He felt a strange sense of freedom. Without hanging up, he dialed Maria Corliss.

5

ALL OF HIS assumptions about her proved wrong.

She looked not sixty, but no more than forty, her figure svelte in a lime-colored pantsuit, her skin smooth and firm, her eyes sparkling—a look, he thought, for which a cosmetic surgeon could take only partial credit.

She was no longer dark and exotic. Her hair was tawny blonde and cut fairly short, she wore little makeup and no jewelry, and she moved with a lithe grace that seemed to belong on a California beach.

And she was not married, the Argentine having been her "last roll of the dice."

All of this absorbed before they had finished one drink at a table on the terrace.

"Have you made a new movie?" he asked. "Is that why you're here?"

"Oh, no." She smiled suggestively. "I came here because of a man."

He tilted his glass. "Can't think of a better reason."

"He's a lot younger than I am, a mere thirty-two."

"Great. I hear that's all the thing these days."

Her smile broadened. "He happens to be my son."

He laughed, surprised at his relief, wondering if it showed.

"Eric's a director, a very good one, I think. He's here with a so-called work in progress, a film that's about two-thirds finished. It seems he's over budget and the financial backers have closed the till. To them, it's a tax shelter—they'll make out better writing it off. Eric hopes to get the money he needs here, from distributors and exhibitors."

"Well, good luck to him."

"He'll need a ton of it, or whatever half a million weighs. He has no important credits, the film has no well-known actors, and the festival will be over in three more days."

"That's a tough one. Would you like him to join us for a drink?"

"He's not staying here. He and a lovely friend—she's in the movie—are at a hotel just out of town. The Cap d'Antibes. Very, very elegant. Eric thinks that if he lives like a rich moviemaker, he'll become one."

"He could be right. I've seen it work in my business."

"I suppose that's why you're here—on business?"

"Yes. But it's my good luck that it's been delayed. The man I'd hoped to see today flew off on an overnight excursion. To Yugoslavia, of all places."

Her eyebrows arched. "That sounds like Harry Dalton."

"Right. You know him?"

"Yes, in a way. A couple I know—he's an exhibitor—went with him. You could call the trip a fund-raiser. I understand Harry is involved with several film properties and is looking for more financing."

He nodded. "I haven't met him yet. I'll try to catch him tomorrow."

He ordered them another drink, then began telling her what a great fan of hers he'd always been, documenting it with detailed memories of her roles. She listened for a few minutes, smiling but with an expression almost of regret. At first he thought it was regret at having left all those exciting days behind. But then, as her eyes seemed to study his face, he suspected there was nothing wistful about it, that she was simply uncomfortable at being reminded of how long she'd been around. He felt sure that was it when she abruptly turned the conversation to Rick Bradley and Janice Powers. They talked briefly about them, mostly to bewail the breakup of two such fine people. Brooks did not mention the girl Rick now lived with—why go into it?—but the thought reminded him that her operation had been scheduled for the next morning. He must remember to call Rick afterward.

It was past five when they finished their second drink. The terrace was crowded now with people shaking hands, slapping backs, pulling up chairs. Strident voices spoke of deals, of up-front money, of percentages, of promotion tours. Names like Zanuck, Bergman, and De Laurentiis were being shouted into staring faces vivid with greed. Brooks wanted to leave, but it was too early to suggest going to dinner, and besides, she was probably joining her son and his companion. Still, he didn't want to lose her.

"Listen," he said, "there's a lot of daylight left. Suppose I rent a car and you show me around Cannes."

"Why don't we just walk? The festival's only three blocks long."

They jostled their way to the hotel entrance, where starlets with pneumatic breasts were striking poses for a swarm of paparazzi. Laughing, she took his hand and guided him along a palm-lined street to the Croisette, a Mediterranean-style boardwalk, along which paraded thousands of dreamers—producers, directors, agents, distributors, exhibitors, actors, writers, some of whom had made it, most of whom had not—all lured to this carnival of cinema by the hope that here, somewhere, was the elusive key to untold riches and international fame. They were not, thought Brooks, too different from himself, except that in his case failure to find the magic key would be damaging only to his ego.

But it was certainly good for his ego to be with this delightful woman, whom he plied with questions for no other purpose than to hear her voice. Though all else about her may have changed, that voice, a trifle throaty, tinged with amusement, remained as he had first heard it projecting warmly up to the last row of the balcony from stage and screen. Somehow it brought drama even to the impressive festival statistics—five hundred films screened every twenty-four hours, perhaps forty at this very moment, ranging from hardcore porn to children's tales. Its melody took precedence over the blare of rock music from a nearby yacht, over the drone of a plane trailing a banner emblazoned with a movie title, over shrill voices exclaiming, "Look, there's . . ."

He had not truly enjoyed the company of a woman since his wife had died almost two years ago. And, during her last year, he would hardly have called her presence an enjoyment, so ravaged was she with cancer, so stoic and grim in her pain. Now he was intrigued, fascinated, and at the same time at ease, uninhibited, like a much younger man on vacation who—and the thought produced a pleasant shock—was on the threshold of a summer romance. He mocked the notion, put it from his mind, only to have it surface as a tingling of his skin, a feeling of weightlessness, a sense of anticipation. And it shone from his eyes, must have, because looking at him her eyes flashed back and her lips curved in an expression of recognition. He could not believe it, simply could not believe it. And yet, why not? Even without his wealth and position, he would not be considered an unattractive man. And she—she was a mature, sophisticated woman, three times divorced, an inhabitant of the permissive theatrical worlds of New York and Hollywood, a woman temporarily lonely—why would she turn away from an affair, however fleeting, if it would provide pleasure without penalty? The answer was she wouldn't, especially when the man was respectable, responsible—and eligible.

They were walking the beach near the waterline, oblivious to the recumbent, bikinied bodies still on display, when he told her about his wife. He made it brief, but a graininess came into his voice that suggested the depths of his emotion. She stopped, a breeze ruffling her tawny hair, and touched his shoulder.

"I'm glad you told me," she said. Her tone implied not so much sympathy as relief that he was unencumbered.

He was moved to boldness. "There's been no one since."

She was silent for a minute, then smiled as if to herself. "There will be," she said.

And they continued their tour—to the Blue Bar for a cold Beck's beer; to canopied sidewalk markets; to the Festival Palace, where they inspected the gaudy exhibition booths; then back to the chaotic Carlton lobby, where they gazed at each other without speaking.

He glanced at his watch. Past seven-thirty. He had the feeling that she was drifting away, vanishing like an iridescent bubble.

"I guess you're having dinner with your son," he said.

"He'll be screening for most of the night."

"Well, then . . ." He hesitated.

"'Well, then' is fine. But first I must freshen up. Will you call me in a half-hour? Then we can talk about dinner." She was smiling, knowing that he liked her assertiveness, so long as she was asserting her interest in him.

They went to their rooms. He showered, shaved, lotioned, changed to a tan linen suit. He was about to pick up the phone when it rang.

"It just occurred to me," she said, "we have no dinner reservation. We'll have to wait forever."

"Never thought of that. And I'm supposed to be a good manager. You must think I'm a fake."

Her voice lowered. "That's not at all what I think." Then, in a practical tone, "Why not have dinner here? I have a living room and we can be quite comfortable."

"But the dinner's on me."

"As they say in Cannes, you got it. But I'll supply the libations."

She met him at her door, dressed in a flowing, floor-length coral gown that appeared diaphanous but wasn't. Softly glowing lamps shadowed their faces, added richness to the deep-pile carpeting, enhanced the grandeur of the brocaded French period pieces. Looking about, he had the illusion of being transported back to another time, to another set of values. She led him to a narrow, high-backed sofa, sat him down, then went to a tiny kitchen and returned with a tray bearing a bottle of the finest scotch, flanked by crystal glasses and a silver bucket of ice. She sat beside him and they drank slowly, eyes over the rims of the glasses conducting ambiguous meetings, hastily adjourned and as quickly reconvened.

She left him but once, to switch on the stereo and softly flood the room with old show tunes—George Metaxas celebrating "You and the Night and the Music," Gene Kelly "Singin' in the Rain." He was entranced, delightfully estranged from the machinations of business and his reason for coming to Cannes, the knowledge that some girl was facing a brain operation, and that he was sixty-three years old and should no longer be susceptible to romantic excitement. He forgot the time, forgot to order dinner, forgot everything but the perfumed presence of this lovely woman, who, in the midst of a Libby Holman vocal, suddenly moved her face close to his and murmured:

"You're a very attractive man, Mr. Brooks Madden."

He assumed the kiss would be casual, friendly, a glancing New York party kiss, not a Maria Corliss movie kiss, as this one was, lips moist and parted, tongue-tip penetrating, breath warm and slightly frantic.

He was astonished, but only for the instant it took to become an eager collaborator. It went on and on, gaining momentum, the pressure of their bodies increasing, until it became evident that the ceremonial sofa could no longer contain them.

She drew back, caught her breath, smiled weakly, and whispered, "You haven't seen the rest of the suite."

"It's time I did."

In the bedroom, lit only by the glow from the street, there was no awkwardness about it. She unfastened her gown, let it drift to the floor, exposing her taut nakedness; then, while they stood, she helped him out of his jacket, hung it on a chair, followed it with his trousers, and was in bed, the satin sheet pulled down, when he came to her.

She was as experienced as he had thought, but she didn't flaunt it, instead used it almost ingenuously and with a sense of discovery, as though her hands and her lips were drawn to his body by a force more compelling than anything she might calculate. Stroking her, joining her in all the ways, caught up in her lubricity, he found himself losing control. It had been so long. But she restrained him, gripping him hard, then stretching out beside him in breathless quiet. Soon they resumed, and finally, when they could bear it no longer, when he was half sitting up and bolstered by a pillow and she faced him, straddled him, guided his entry, the climax came quickly, in a mutual frenzy, and seemed to last for a very long time.

Then, when they lay limply together, her head tucked against his chest, she said, "It was a magnificent dinner, Mr. Madden."

And he laughed, tears wetting his eyes.

He returned to his room at ten the next morning, head and eyes clear, feeling young and vital, though he'd had but five hours' sleep. His mind was a record of scented skin, jubilant breasts, golden thighs, the dizzying curve of a hip, and of her eyes, touch, and voice, which, over coffee, confirmed that it was all real and would be, must be, relived.

She had invited him to join her that evening to have dinner with her son and later view his film. And then? "And then," she said archly, "we can see if we overlooked anything last night."

Opening his door, he was surprised to find half a dozen envelopes scattered on the carpet. He gathered them up, went to the desk, and glanced through them. All were handwritten, all were invitations—to lunch, cocktails, dinner, private screenings. Most of the names sounded foreign—French, Italian, Swedish, God-knows-what. How did these men, obviously film people, know he was in Cannes? Perhaps his arrival had been reported in one of the daily trade papers, which would have noted that he was president and chief executive officer of a high-powered American advertising agency. In any case, the purpose of the invitations was clear: Brooks Madden was on the hit list for movie money.

He brushed the letters aside, thinking that he had better things to do, fantastically better, than suffer the blandishments of unctuous hustlers, the kind he'd seen on the Carlton terrace. Besides, it was time he started to move on Harry Dalton.

He phoned the desk. Josef did not come on duty until noon, but the answering voice said that Mr. Dalton had apparently not returned—his mailbox was stuffed with messages. Hanging up, Brooks got a sheet of his firm's letterhead, which included his name and title, and wrote a brief note:

Dear Mr. Dalton:

I have flown here from New York for only one reason—to meet you.

You'll find, I believe, that what I have to say could be of great benefit to your future plans, as well as to the people I represent.

I'd appreciate it if you'd arrange a meeting at your convenience. I'm staying here at the Carlton, room 626.

Signing his name, he wondered if he should have said more. No, he decided, best to save it for when they were face to face. He went down to the lobby and had the note placed in Dalton's box. He hoped now that Dalton would not call before the next morning—it was intolerable to think of business interfering with his newfound pleasure. The thought incited him to phone Maria from the lobby. Perhaps they could meet for lunch. There was no answer.

Back in his room, he again reviewed the notes for his discussion with Harry Dalton. There would be no fancy charts or exhibits, just straight talk, unvarnished, pragmatic, factual—the only way he knew how to talk—and that he hoped would make him appear an exception to Dalton's scorned Mad Avenue Merlins.

By eleven o'clock his stomach was protesting that it had not been fed since getting off the plane. He ordered up soup and a cheese sandwich and ate at the desk. As he was finishing, the phone rang. It was Josef, his tone apologetic.

"Mr. Madden, I just came on duty. Otherwise I would have notified you that Mr. Dalton arrived more than an hour ago."

"Thank you, Josef. I'll stop by to see you later today."

"Very good. I trust your meeting will turn out as you wish."

Josef, he was sure, sincerely meant it. Success, even a modest success, would earn him a handsome reward. Brooks debated whether to phone Dalton now or wait until he could assume the man had finished lunch. He stalled, thinking about it, decided to wait.

The phone rang again. Maria, he thought, and picked it up.

"Mr. Madden?"

"Yes."

"This is Thea Roland, Mr. Dalton's secretary."

"Oh, yes, I wrote—"

"Mr. Dalton has received your note. He would like to see you. Would four P.M. today be convenient?"

"That would be fine."

"We're on the fourth floor."

"I'll be there. What's the room number?"

"If you'll just wait by the elevator, I'll be out to meet you."

"By the elevator?"

"Yes, we have the whole fourth floor."

Brooks wished again that Rick Bradley could have come. The thought caused him to look at his watch. Considering the time differential, he figured that Rick's girlfriend must now be in the operating room.

6

DR. VANCE KLOSTER'S eyebrows, thick as pelts, rose in a look that he hoped appeared benign. He said to the draped figure on the cart, "Think happy. Nothing to worry about." He unconsciously held up his hands and spread the long, bony fingers. "Done hundreds of 'em. No problems, no problems at all."

Which was not entirely true. What he meant was that he'd never lost a patient to death. To maximum-care nursing homes, yes, but never to death.

Sara Vardon smiled wanly up at him, triggering in Kloster the same pang that had struck him during the workup. She reminded him, in her sweetness, her reticence, her vulnerability, of his daughter, who at eighteen had been hurled into the dashboard of a careening Porsche, fatally crushing her skull. This girl, this Sara Vardon, even looked a bit like his daughter—the porcelain-white skin, the large, luminous eyes, particularly the glossy black hair. On impulse he had ordered that the hair not be totally shorn, only a section extending from the right temple to just beyond the mastoid projection and up to the crown. The thick hair that remained could later be artfully arranged to cover the affected area.

He stood there, dressed in his green, pajamalike surgical clothing, and watched as the orderly wheeled the cart through the double doors of the operating room. He knew that despite the layers of tranquilizing medication that held panic at bay, Sara Vardon would feel an excruciating sense of abandonment the moment she was lifted onto the table to stare up at the cold, glareless light. He would like to go to her now, hold her hand, touch her cheek, continue to reassure her. But he could not; he would be in the way. Right now the anesthesiologist and his assistant, the anesthetist, were at the head of the operating table, screened from where the patient would lie, testing their machines. The scrub nurse was setting out instruments—knives, clips, forceps, elevators, mallets, spreaders, steel drills, syringes, sterile water, sponges, electric coagulators, suction tubes. The circulating nurse was checking out the medicine cabinets and X-ray equipment and doing odd jobs. Interns and residents were gathering, primarily to observe the awesome Dr. Vance Kloster at work, but also to render assistance in case of emergency.

Kloster glanced at the wall clock. Ten past nine. He started to move toward the doors, as though drawn to the operating room by gravity. A voice interrupted.

"Afraid you'll be late for golf, doctor?"

He swung around. It was Dr. Peter Bower, the resident neurosurgeon, who would be assisting. His round, chubby face wore a jocular expression.

"Golf?" he said blankly. "What's that? Anyway, I plan to be out of there in under three hours. Just in time for you to line up a nooner." Bower was known in the hospital as a conscientious womanizer. He was young, twenty-eight, and had the stamina for it.

They bantered until a nurse pushed through the doors and said, "We're ready, Dr. Kloster."

They entered. Sara Vardon lay illuminated on the operating table in the center of the room, her head clamped by steel pins, her body punctured by intravenous needles that connected to tubes running to blood-pressure gauges and devices that delivered dextrose solution and blood. She was no longer breathing. It was being done for her by a ventilator, a puffed-up rubber lung attached to more tubes, these thrust down her throat. She was unconscious, blacked out by sodium pentothal and nitrous oxide, narcotized by sublimaze, rendered limp as a slab of raw beef by the paralyzing drug curare.

Bower now stood beside her, holding an electric razor. He turned to look at Kloster, eyes inquiring whether he should go ahead. No, Kloster would do it himself. He would do it all, right down to the closing of the flap, when Bower could handle the skin sutures and the cleanup, which Kloster called the "artwork." Kloster strode forward, tall, big-boned, somehow ferocious, his cap pushed back from his forehead, his surgical mask strung loosely about his neck.

He grasped the electric razor and ran it over the stubbled area of Sara Vardon's scalp. Finishing, he took a straight razor from the nurse and shaved the scalp completely clean. Then he scrubbed it with soap and water, fingered its smoothness, gently applied antiseptic solution. Stepping back, he peered up at the X rays in a luminous viewer rack and saw, inside translucent bone, the round little monster he had come to slay. He picked up a sterile pin and scratched deep in the flesh an outline of where he would make the incision. Using a Q-tip, he applied a bright blue stain to the scratch.

Then he and Bower left to scrub.

Returning, they were helped into sterile overgowns and, their hands talcumed, into cream-colored rubber gloves, two pairs each lest an outer glove be punctured. They were now "untouchable," physically inaccessible to the unscrubbed, hands and bodies allowed contact only with sterilized instruments and the operating field around the surgical wound.

As they moved back to the operating table, the room was suddenly flooded with the modulated sound of big-band music playing a song made famous by Frank Sinatra. Behind his mask, Kloster smiled. Other surgeons could have their Chopin and Bach and Debussy instrumentals; he'd stick with Old Blue Eyes. The thought of his resonant, romantic voice evoked in a part of his brain not connected to the work at hand a soothing mood of nostalgia that helped to control the zealotry with which he always approached his task.

He went to the head of Sara Vardon, first circling his own with a steel ring to which was fastened a headlight. She was now enshrouded by pale green sterile drapes, exposing only the shaved section above and beyond the ear. Quickly he sutured thin towels to all four sides of the area, then covered it all with an adhesive sheet of transparent plastic that stuck to both the towels and the skin. The scrub nurse handed him a syringe, and at intervals along the blue scratch line he injected epinephrine, a blood retardant.

Now the knife. Kloster felt a slight soaring sensation as he gripped the flat-handled instrument no longer than a toothbrush, with a blade no larger than his fingertip. He stroked it forward, making an arcing cut through the plastic, along the scratch line. Blood spurted, flowed thickly, like a rich, dark syrup. He and Bower quickly cleared the field with gauze sponges, then with suction tubes—"suckers"—finally with an electric coagulator that passed a current through the small blood vessels and "cooked" them closed. A sweet odor, not unpleasant, rose from the wound.

Kloster held the knife poised for an instant, then, wrist stiff, forced the blade down through skin, flesh, muscle—down to the bone. He peeled back the curved flap, revealing the skull, then clamped the flap and laid it back. He scraped the residual flesh from the skull, flushed it with water, then sponge-dried it until it was a gleaming white.

Turning his head toward the anesthesiologist, he said, "She's had the Mannutol?"—a drug that shrinks the brain, giving him room to move about.

"Yes, of course." The voice behind the screen was faintly indignant.

Kloster picked up an electric drill. He set himself to exert the heavy pressure required to penetrate hard, resilient bone and at the same time maintain extreme care not to let the drill bit push into the brain. He made three burr holes—the bone curling up on the drill like wood shavings—forming a rough triangle, which he flushed with water. Into one hole he inserted a small flat blade—a Freer elevator—slipping it between the skull and dura, a thin gristly lining, to make sure they were not stuck to one another. Satisfied, he replaced the drill bit with a fluted steel blade, which he used as a saw to connect the three burr holes. The small round disc of bone popped out. Now the membrane, which he cut quickly and pinned back. Sara Vardon's brain, a three-and-a-half-pound, gelatinous mass of ridges, folds, and crevices, pulsing like a beating heart, was now laid bare.

Kloster backed off to don magnifying glasses, the lenses barrel-shaped like those used by a jeweler. He moved close to peer in at the brain, fascinated as always by the sight of it floating in the cerebrospinal fluid, which cushioned it, protected it, nourished it. One micrometric slip of the blade, he thought, and Sara Vardon—this girl who reminded him so much of his daughter—could lose speech, or senses, or mobility, could become a vegetable. All that had made her human would cease to exist, the body becoming merely a blood-pumping machine.

The thought did not unnerve him. Rather it strengthened his already massive ego, added drama to his role as hero come to rescue the distressed maiden. Here in this theater dedicated to the ultimate theme of life against death, Kloster was the superstar— aggressive, fearless, infallible. He wished that the handsome blond man who had sought him out late yesterday afternoon could be present. He had appeared so poised, so very much in command of himself, and yet, the sudden huskiness of his voice, the darkening blue of his eyes, was so revelatory of his anxiety, of his love for this woman, this girl, who seemed so much to deserve being loved, who had spent the interminable day in silent terror, smiling, always smiling, while everything inside her goaded her to shriek. He had sent the young man away reassured, he thought, and himself so charmed that he had impulsively promised to have a nurse call as soon as the operation was successfully concluded. Oh, yes, he wished that the fine, sensitive blond man could be here right now, not only to witness a master at work, but also to see how simple it was to excise this demon of death clinging to Sara Vardon's brain and thus to be totally convinced that never again would she be placed in such jeopardy.

He straightened, adjusted his barrel-shaped glasses, which gave him a crazed look, then bent down, headlight beaming into the open skull, and began delicately to probe the labyrinths of the pulsing brain. It was a technique not so much of penetration as of avoidance. He must bypass vessels and arteries, which, if pierced, could cause fatal hemorrhage. He must be wary of disturbing the almond-shaped thalamus, which receives incoming sensory nerve fibers and interprets their messages. He must not offend that most complex of structures, the hypothalamus, which, though weighing less than an ounce, controls breathing, regulates and coordinates the internal organs and supplies them with blood, and which, most remarkably of all, commands the emotions. Wires implanted in the hypothalamus of a docile cat and sparked with an electric current could transform it into a spitting, snarling predator. Other areas, when electrically stimulated, could produce orgasm in females, erection and ejaculation in males, could incite laughter or tears, hunger and thirst.

All this and a hundred times more Kloster knew, as others knew the workings of a television set or of a sophisticated computer, which was primitive indeed compared to the astronomically intricate circuitry of the human brain. He possessed all the knowledge that had accumulated since ancient man had sought to purge demons by scraping a hole in the skull with a stone knife.

But there were things he did not know, that no one knew. He did not know, for example, where memory was centered, or even whether it had a center or, as many thought, was scattered by billions of neurons throughout the brain. In particular, he did not know what occurred in the area he was now so cautiously approaching, the anterior "silent" area, situated just back of the prefrontal lobe, and called silent because it had yet to reveal its secrets despite the most skillful urging. True, it was hypothesized that this mysterious region was involved with such mental activities as thinking and planning and maintaining attention. But no one really knew—there was no empirical evidence. It was simply a medical *notion*, as suspect as the notion that it might contain the key to the most baffling enigma of all—the existence of conscience, of moral sensibility, of what civilized people proudly proclaimed as the most significant distinction between themselves and the beasts of the jungle.

Still, Kloster felt no discomfort, no qualms at proceeding through this silent realm. He had been there many times before, and knew every pathway, every fissure, every ridge—just as he knew when he must replace one instrument with another, when he must pause for a nurse to wipe his brow or to change his gloves or to verify the clarity of his glasses—knew precisely when to make the flick of the knife that now revealed the disgusting, pulpy ball of tissue that was contesting for the life of Sara Vardon.

Oh, you're a wretched thing, he thought, ecologically unjustified, a parasitic son of a bitch, with a hideous past, and now, thank Christ, no future. "Goodbye, you miserable slob," he said, and touched it with the blade, and as he did so an odd sensation, like a valve opening and closing, occurred inside his head and he felt a numbness crawl down his arm and produce a tremor in the fingers that pinched the knife.

He withdrew the knife, straightened, inflated his lungs, let a nurse mop away sweat, heard Bower say, "You okay?" jerked a nod, and felt the sensation subside. Emotion, he thought, nothing else, a tenseness—no, it was more than that—a physical loathing, a revulsion that always accompanied the first sighting of a monstrous tumor. And with a baleful grimace that creased his mask, he returned to the assault.

Now the blade probed, picked, cut, separated; Kloster maneuvered it pitilessly because the brain has no feeling. And as the plum-sized tumor broke loose, the sensation again erupted in Kloster's head, this time clouding his vision, jolting his arm, jerking his hand, thrusting the knife with its lethal blade forward into forbidden territory. As the tumor popped out to the tray, a sudden effusion of dark blood engulfed the cavity it had vacated. Kloster snapped back, gave his head a vicious shake, reached to snatch sponges from the nurse, but found that Bower, intervening, was already throwing sponges into the open skull, tossing them in like laundry into a chute.

And as Bower continued to take over—replacing, then discarding sponges, working the suckers and the coagulator—Kloster stood stunned and staring, unable to speak.

Then Bower's voice, as though from far away: "All under control, doctor. You go ahead. I'll close," said somberly, regretfully, the way one speaks of a fallen idol.

At the bar down the street, his rangy figure now encased in a three-piece suit, Kloster sipped his scotch on the rocks and meditated over what had happened to him. Physically he felt as fine as when he had first stepped into the hospital early that morning. Mentally he was depressed, but his thoughts were clear.

Clear enough to understand with certainty that what he had suffered was a trauma not unexpected at his age: the bursting of a tiny blood vessel in his head, what doctors liked to call a small stroke.

Nothing drastic, nothing that threatened his life, only something that would terminate what his life was all about—the ability, the artistry, the virtuosity, to operate with sureness and precision on the human brain. Soon, perhaps, as more blood vessels self-destructed, he would become forgetful, his reflexes would slow, his eyes would dim—he would become, *had* become, a neurosurgeon fit only for consultation. Later he would discuss it with his friend Amos Loring, a cardiologist.

Right now that was not important. What was important was the condition of Sara Vardon, who now lay in the recovery room, swimming up to consciousness from the depths of anesthesia. He had left word that he was to be notified by beeper as soon as she was fully aware and had been returned to her room. Then he would visit her and try to discern what if any damage his straying knife might have inflicted.

A horror story, celebrated in medical annals, sneaked into his thoughts. It concerned Phineas Gage, whose skull Kloster had seen on display at Harvard. Gage was a railroad worker who in 1848 had an inch-thick, four-foot-long iron bar blasted through his head, destroying much of his front brain. Miraculously he survived, with thought and memory intact. But he was, the medical report said, "no longer Gage." He had turned from a mild-mannered, efficient, godly man into an erratic, foul-mouthed, irreverent creature unfit for employment. He had lived for twelve years with what was described as an imbalance "between his intellectual faculties and animal propensities."

But nothing like that had happened to Sara Vardon's brain; Kloster was sure of it. The prefrontal area had not been invaded, the fibers therefore not severed. There had been no accidental lobotomy, to which modern medicine ascribed the strange behavior of Phineas Gage.

But there had been penetration of the silent area, how incisive he did not know. Whether this might in some way influence her thought processes was beyond his knowledge to predict.

Two hours later he was walking aimlessly down Fifth Avenue when his pocket beeper sounded.

"You were absolutely right," Sara Vardon said, smiling happily. "I feel terrific. A little woozy, but aside from that, fine."

Kloster felt an immense relief. "No headache? No strange thoughts?"

"No pain at all. Strange thoughts? Should I be having strange thoughts?" Automatically she touched her bandages, then ran her fingers to the other side, where her remaining hair swooped down in dark splendor.

"Sometimes that happens. Not often, though. Well, I'm glad you're feeling so good. You should be out of this jail in a few weeks."

When he left, a nurse came in, the one with the novocaine smile like her mother's, and gave her something to help her rest.

From under half-closed lids Sara watched her disappear into the corridor. Then, without warning, she gasped as a sudden sharp sensation burst through her brain. Vaguely surprised, she semiconsciously shook it away, then dozed off quickly.

When she awoke several hours later, immediately her thoughts turned to Rick. She imagined them in bed together, bodies taut, buttocks pumping. Her hands slipped beneath the sheet, crept down her body, and lingered between her legs. Unconsciously at first, then with knowing abandon, she committed what her mother would have denounced as an act of the Devil, an obscenity against God.

The orgasm, the first in her life, was explosive, earthshaking, prolonged.

She was astounded. But she felt elated.

7

THEA ROLAND met Brooks as he stepped from the elevator. She was tall, honey-blonde, thin as a mannequin but with full, upthrust breasts accentuated by the cleavage of a glossy white, pearl-buttoned blouse. Her handshake was firm, her voice cultivated, crisp, and self-assured.

"I'll see if Mr. Dalton is ready." She excused herself and moved briskly to a French phone that sat on a corner table. She spoke, hung up, and walked back, her body as erect and mobile as a model's, then glanced at a platinum wristwatch set with diamonds. "In three minutes," she said. She didn't smile. She seemed too preoccupied with timing their entrance to the split second.

They waited in silence. He felt a need to break it. "Have you worked for Mr. Dalton long?"

"Two years," she said.

"An exciting job, I imagine."

"Yes." Her expression remained stolid.

Silence.

Again she consulted her watch. There must have been a few seconds left because she said, "I'll be present at your meeting. Please don't let that inhibit you. I'm Mr. Dalton's *confidential* secretary."

He grinned. "Great. It'll add some beauty to the scene."

Even as he said it he knew it was a mistake—a butter-and-egg-man remark, the kind you hear in the rag business on Seventh

Avenue. Her expression verified the error—a sardonic flicker in the brown eyes, a slight disdainful curl of the lips.

"We'll go in now," she said.

As she led him down a broad corridor, he heard the click of typewriters and male voices speaking intensely from several rooms. He guessed that Dalton had transported a part of his New York headquarters staff to Cannes—typical of a man who liked to conduct staff meetings aboard a 747 cruising at thirty-five thousand feet above the North Atlantic coast. Like almost everyone else, Brooks's knowledge of Harry Dalton embraced little more than what he had read in news clippings and articles in *Business Week* and *Fortune*. The latter publications had dealt in depth with Dalton's exploits as a bold entrepreneur but had offered few human insights. Perhaps the writers felt that his personal record spoke for itself: ace fighter pilot in the Korean War; leader of an unauthorized flying group ferrying anti-Castro Cubans from Central America to fight at the Bay of Pigs; pilot of an unofficial transport that evacuated Vietnamese employees of the American consulate from Saigon; married twice, both times to wealthy socialites, each of whom had divorced him within two years; now single but often linked to internationally famous beauties. The picture that emerged was a stereotype of the driving, ruthless, independent corporate executive, but showed almost nothing of what made him tick.

Thea Roland stopped at the end of the corridor before a pair of double doors. She opened one, glanced inside, then motioned for Brooks to follow. He entered a dark-paneled room big enough to hold a banquet. Lounge chairs were lined up ten deep to face a gold curtain covering the far wall; off to the side, a speaker's stand was mounted on a low dais.

Thea Roland gazed toward the opposite end of the room and said, "Mr. Madden is here, Mr. Dalton."

At first Brooks saw no one. Then, from a back corner, a figure rose from a desk and came forward, hand outstretched, mouth smiling, but the gray eyes looking hard as slate. He didn't speak.

"Glad to meet you, Mr. Dalton," Brooks said, and grasped a hand that seemed the size of a catcher's mitt.

Harry Dalton was big all over—big head, strewn with thick, curly black hair; big face, with a beak of a nose and jaws that looked like they could pulverize granite; big shoulders, chest, legs, arms, feet—and tall, perhaps six foot three. But he wasn't *lazy* big, not the cliché character that admen liked to portray lying in a hammock, ecstatically drinking iced tea or beer. Even standing still, Harry Dalton appeared to be in motion, his stance thrusting him forward, his muscles seeming to strain against his patterned sport shirt and wide leather belt, his tanned skin suggesting sweat, through it was dry and smooth. A bull of a man, thought Brooks, who at forty-eight was giving time one hell of a licking.

His voice, too, was big, but modulated as if by effort. "Glad you could come, Madden." He gave him an up-and-down look. "You don't seem to belong in this crazy town. That's in your favor." He motioned toward the front row of chairs. "Let's get comfortable."

Dalton sat facing the curtain. Beside him was a console dotted with buttons. Thea Roland angled two other lounge chairs so they more or less faced him. Though Brooks was physically comfortable, psychologically he was not. The room was too big for intimate talks, the furnishings alien, both unsettling reminders that this was very much Harry Dalton's turf.

He started to speak but Dalton cut in. "I like your approach, Madden. No bullshit. No staff of paper-pushers. Just hop a plane, fly over, go straight to the head honcho. Smart. We start with something in common."

Brooks smiled. "I don't like to waste time."

"Good. Neither do I. So let's get right to it. You've got a proposition for me, right?"

"Right."

"Okay. But before you make it, let me give you a rundown on where I am and what I see down the road. I think you'll find that this operation is a hell of a lot bigger than you thought. So you may want to consult with your people before jumping in."

"Fine, I'm listening."

Dalton plucked a cigarette from his shirt pocket and stabbed it between his lips. Thea Roland quickly leaned across and lit it with a flaring lighter. Brooks looked at her. The way she snapped the lighter shut, then jerked back to a rigid posture, reminded him of a robot.

"First," Dalton said, "let's go to the movies."

He jabbed two buttons on the console, the room darkened, and the gold curtains parted, revealing a large screen. Brooks and Thea Roland swung their chairs around to face it.

"What you'll see," said Dalton, "are just excerpts, dramatic highlights. Later, if you want, I'll set it up for you to see everything that's been filmed so far."

Brooks nodded and sat back, alerting himself to appear interested in scenes of Transcon planes taking off and landing, happy passengers strolling about wide-bodied interiors, pretty flight attendants serving drinks.

Dalton hit another button. The sound burst out—traveling music—and the screen filled with a closeup of a young man hunched over the handlebars of a speeding motorcycle. Next a pullback to show he was being pursued by a police squad car. The film cut back and forth, then held on a medium long shot as the biker reached a high, sheer cliff, sailed through the air, arced and twisted, then plunged (cut to closeup) into white-water rapids below. Dissolve to softly lit bedroom and shot of same man and a gorgeous blonde woman making strenuous love in a king-size bed. Dissolve to two-shot of same couple, woman threatening man with gun. . . .

And on it went, shots of violence, soft-porn sex, black comedy, dramatic confrontations, all well acted, imaginatively directed, and produced with a high gloss.

Dalton punched off the film and brought up the lights. He looked inquiringly at Brooks.

"Great!" Brooks said. "It looks like a winner." All right, he thought, the man had shown off his new toy and was now ready to settle down to business. The movie scenes provided an easy transition. "Looks like you'll be as successful in movies as you are running Transcon Airlines."

Dalton's eyes brightened. "They're only part of it." To his secretary he said, "Let's have coffee."

She sprang up as though electrified, and darted off.

"Just hang in," he said to Brooks. "I want you to get the whole picture."

"That's why I'm here."

Dalton smiled. "Good, very damned good." He stood up and began to pace, a hand tangling his black curls. "I'll start with the airline. We'll get back to the movie. Right now Transcon ranks number four in the U.S. But that's about to change, change fast. Right this minute I've got men negotiating to take over a competitor, I can't say which one. But when I get it, and I damned sure will, Transcon will be within smelling distance of United and Pan Am. For now, that's confidential information."

"Of course." Brooks calculated that the account should bill half again as much as he'd expected, not the twenty-two million dollars in advertising expenditures reported in *Advertising Age*, but upwards of thirty million.

Thea Roland came back with mugs of steaming coffee. As she handed one to Dalton, her masklike face was suddenly animated by a quick smile and a warm flicker in her eyes. Brooks surmised that her confidential status went beyond that of secretary.

"So much for Transcon," Dalton said. "Now about the hotels. There are six, one each in Miami Beach, Puerto Rico, Reno, Las Vegas, Acapulco, Honolulu. But that's nothing to what I've got on the boards." He took a gulp of coffee, the steam seeming to jet from his nostrils. "Madden, I intend to make Club Med look like a string of overnight rooming houses. The Dalton resorts will have everything. And I mean *everything*. They'll be palaces. Huge rooms. Gold-plated fixtures. Sunken bathtubs you can swim in. Rolls-Royces and yachts for cruising around. And they'll be all over the world—the West Indies, Tahiti, Samoa, Sri Lanka, Singapore, Crete, Dubrovnik, Kenya, you name it. And of course all of them will be served by Transcon Airlines."

Brooks let out an audible breath while shaking his head in awe.

"What I'm talking about, Madden, is not millions of dollars. I'm talking about *billions*."

In Brooks's mind the potential worth of the account doubled, tripled, rose to approach the billing of Procter & Gamble, which in the previous year had an advertising outlay of close to half a billion dollars.

"All right, now let's get back to the movies. The clips you saw are from a film budgeted at six million. Photography has begun on another, budgeted at ten million. So, as you know, that's one reason I'm here, to lay off a big chunk of the financing on qualified investors. But that's just a start. What I'm a hell of a lot more interested in is to raise capital for a related venture, the production of movies for cassettes. Think about it. A dozen or so movies a year, made with top talent—writers, producers, directors, stars—movies you can rent or buy outright to view at home or in a motel, even at a campsite. Movies—and here's the kicker—that you can rent on cassettes in our hotel lobbies, and better yet, on our planes, planes that will be rigged so that an individual or a couple or a family can have their own private showing—maybe twenty or more different movies running simultaneously on a single flight. Imagine it! Every hour, every day, a captive audience of bored passengers, aggregating millions, who for a few lousy bucks can be entertained by the best Hollywood has to offer. And the profits, everything over the nut, not split with anyone—not with distributors, not with exhibitors—all of it flowing into my coffers!"

He swigged his coffee, then spat it back. It was cold. Thea Roland jumped up and snatched the cup, but he waved her off. "Now, Madden, how does that grab you?"

"Great! Terrific! And I'm grateful you told me about it." His mind was busily revising his sales pitch to capitalize on Dalton's grandiose plans. "But I don't have to consult with my people. I have the authority to make any decision I think is right."

Dalton halted his pacing and moved to stand in front of Brooks. "You're sure of that? Even if it requires a much bigger commitment than you'd expected?"

Brooks smiled confidently. "Whatever it is, we can handle it."

"Look, Madden, I'm talking about eight or ten million bucks, and that'd be just a piece of it."

Brooks hid his disappointment. "No problem. Naturally we'd like it all, but—"

"You'd like it *all*?"

"Sure, why not?" His smile stretched to a grin. "But I guess we'll just have to work up to it."

Dalton looked puzzled. "I don't get it. You fly over here to invest maybe a million or two in a movie. Then I tell you it's not just a movie but a huge leisure industry and it will cost you people maybe ten million. You not only don't flinch, you want to go for broke. Just who are you talking for, Madden—the U.S. Treasury?"

Brooks suddenly felt sick.

Dalton spoke again, his voice edged with suspicion, "Perhaps you should tell me who it is you represent, Mr. Madden."

Brooks stared at him, eyed the screen, then said, "I represent the people who work in my advertising agency. I thought—"

"They're the *investors*?"

Brooks felt like the biker plunging off the precipice. Clenching his jaw, he said, "Mr. Dalton, apparently there's been a serious misunderstanding. I didn't come here to invest in a movie or anything else. I came here as what I am, an advertising man. I came here hoping to convince you that we're the best agency to handle the advertising for Transcon Airlines."

Dalton gaped in disbelief. "Well, for Christsake!"

Brooks tried for an ironic smile, the kind that came so easily to Rick Bradley, a smile expressing wry amusement at this comedy of errors. But he felt his lips twist into an apologetic grimace, felt his eyes become furtive, like someone caught peddling phony goods.

Thea Roland said, "That's not the way we heard it, Mr. Madden."

"I don't understand. What was it you heard?"

"I'll answer that!" Dalton's dark eyes now looked like an erupting storm, his face had contracted into taut muscle. "What I heard was that you'd come here representing a group of your wealthy clients who wanted to buy into the movie business. It wasn't something I picked up at a bar or from some hanger-on outside the hotel. Hell, no. It came in writing, checked out by Thea on the phone, from reputable people I do business with. There's no way that story could have gotten around if it hadn't first been planted. And who else would—"

"Hold it now. Just a minute. If that's what happened, you can't think *I* planted it."

Dalton gave an ugly smile. "Madden, I can't think of a single other person."

"Now listen, why would I—"

"Because you knew that I wouldn't see anybody who wasn't an investor, ready to come up with big bucks. So you spread your bullshit around, gave it time for the smell to drift my way, then wrote your little come-on note saying you could be of great benefit to my future plans."

"That's absolutely untrue! Listen, I'd have to be an idiot to pull a trick like that!"

"Idiot? No, I wouldn't say that. You probably figured I'd get a bang out of it. A misunderstanding, a fuckup you had no control over. We'd both get a big laugh out of it and right away we'd be buddy-buddy."

"That's wrong! Absolutely wrong! You've got to believe—"

"The only thing I believe is that you heard Transcon might be restless and you decided to make a grandstand play for it. Well, Madden, that could be another mistake. The decision to open up the account hasn't been made."

"I'm aware of that. I had no intention of making a presentation at this time."

Dalton fixed him with a hard look. "Or any other time."

"Listen—"

"The hell I'll listen. This meeting's adjourned."

Dalton strode from the room.

Brooks started to follow, then gave it up. Turning, he was aware of Thea Roland's eyes regarding him with contempt. He seemed to read her thoughts: How dare this little huckster with his New York voice think he could con the god-giant she so humbly served.

"I think you know your way to the elevator," she said.

Mindless, murderous rage was still seething through him as he entered his room. When it abated, leaving behind a sense of deep humiliation and the feeling he had disgraced all the people at his agency, he was standing at the window staring at a blimp bannered with the name of a movie.

My God, he thought, the hustle—the conniving, the maneuvering, the exhibitionism—it was all here in Cannes, concentrated, relentless, inescapable.

And worst of all, for him, was the poisonous grapevine of rumor, of speculation quickly escalated to fact. It was the only way he could explain his transformation from advertising man to movie entrepreneur.

Where could it have started? With the possible reporting of his arrival in the daily press? That might account for the invitations stacked on his desk, but it was preposterous to think that such an innocuous item would have spawned the enormous fiction that had won him an audience with Harry Dalton.

He recalled his actions since leaving New York. Except for a few idle remarks, he had spoken to no one on the plane. After arriving, he had taken a taxi, entered the hotel, checked in at the desk. . . .

Josef!

Josef, the desk clerk, who spoke provocatively of big business, big deals. Who knew Brooks was eager to see Dalton. Who doubtless could think of no other reason for such eagerness than a desire for a piece of the movie action. Who had probably passed the word to others that a rich and vulnerable angel had landed, thus multiplying his chances for reward. And the others, perhaps needing allies, had given impetus to the rumor, each adding bits of embroidery, until, by the time it reached Dalton, Brooks had become the spokesman for an investment syndicate.

Josef. It had to have been Josef who planted the mischievous seeds.

Brooks was controlled as he picked up the phone and dialed the desk. Immediately the respectful voice answered.

"Josef? This is Mr. Madden. I wonder if I could see you in private." He spoke in a tone of friendly conspiracy.

"Certainly, Mr. Madden. I will be on my relief in ten minutes."

"Could you come to my room?"

"Of course. I shall be there promptly at five."

There was, thought Brooks, a note of avarice in that smooth voice.

"I'm ready for a drink, Josef. Why not join me?"

Josef considered it, his heavy lower lip clasping the thin upper one. "I shouldn't while on duty. However, if this is an occasion . . ."

"That's exactly what it is, Josef, an occasion."

Josef's thin, dark face creased in a smile. "So. Am I correct that you met with Mr. Dalton and that it went well?"

"Just came from seeing him. For that, I have you to thank."

"I am pleased I could be of service." His sad eyes were no longer sad.

Brooks poured brandy, motioned his guest to a chair by the window, and sat facing him. Josef sniffed the brandy, registered pleasure, then sipped.

"You know," Brooks said good-humoredly, "if you lived in New York, I think I might hire you as my press agent."

Josef's smile was tentative. "Why do you say that?"

"Because you helped open doors for me. I came here as an absolute stranger and within hours I was getting invitations from important movie people."

Josef gave him a noncommittal look. "News travels fast in Cannes, Mr. Madden."

"But it has to start someplace." Brooks managed a grateful smile. "I'm assuming you dropped a good word here and there. Believe me, I appreciate it."

Josef fingered his ascot. "As you say, you were a stranger here. It seemed only hospitable to acquaint you with people who might be of assistance."

"Well, you certainly did that."

Josef no longer looked cautious. His smile was now expansive. "Then you and Mr. Dalton reached an agreement?"

A lie, thought Brooks, would only encourage Josef to expect a sizable broker's fee. And a lie wasn't necessary; his suspicions had already been confirmed. "Unfortunately, we didn't. But perhaps there will be other meetings."

"Ah, too bad." His eyes were again sad. Then, abruptly, they brightened. "But perhaps you will have better luck with Mrs. Corliss."

Brooks's hand twitched. The brandy glass clicked against his teeth. He felt a wild urge to fling it in Josef's face. "Mrs. Corliss?" he said stupidly.

"Yes. Maria Corliss, the former actress. When I told her about you—"

"You, uh, told her about me?" Something slimy and snakelike seemed to be twisting through his innards.

"She didn't mention it?"

"Oh, yes, now I remember." He felt cold all over now, as cold and hard as a corpse.

"When I suggested you might be interested in her project—"

"Her project?"

"Of course I mean her son's project, his unfinished film. Seeing you together in the lobby yesterday, I hoped that something would come of it."

Unable to speak, Brooks knocked back his brandy. The sudden jolt helped bring him to his feet.

Josef rose. "Are you all right, Mr. Madden? I hope I haven't offended you."

"Not at all. I'm fine. Josef, you've saved me a great deal of"—he groped for an ambiguous word—"of difficulty."

He did not call Maria Corliss to withdraw from dinner and the screening of her son's film. He was too afraid that he might lapse and confess that he despised women who bartered their bodies, even if motivated by maternal devotion.

Instead, after hastily packing his bags, he wrote her a note:

Dear Maria,
    I've been unexpectedly called back to New York on urgent business. Sorry to spoil your plans. I'll never forget you.

He handed the note to the bell captain as he followed his luggage out through the lobby to a waiting taxi.

On the plane, thrusting skyward, he did not look down. He vowed that never again would he so much as fly over the French Riviera.

8

FOR SEVERAL DAYS Sara felt as though she had been inducted into heaven. First there was the glorious relief that seemed to radiate from her now-pristine brain to every cell in her body. She had foiled death or—even worse—mindless paralysis, and was buoyant with a sense of life everlasting. If, when waking from her frequent slumbers, there was doubt, she had only to touch the bandages that swathed her head to confirm her miraculous resurrection.

Then, too, there were the angels, dressed in starched white and hovering about her to minister to her every need. And the acolytes, handsome young men who monitored her vital functions to make sure she was never in jeopardy.

And, of course, God, or at least his surrogate, Dr. Vance Kloster, who appeared daily at rounds to smile encouragement, inspect her chart, and explain to his reverent disciples how the miracle had been accomplished. And there were also Dr. Kloster's private visits, during which he seemed more like a watchful analyst than an exorcist of hostile brain tissue.

Finally, and most heavenly of all, there was Rick, who materialized promptly at five o'clock to join her for dinner, his consisting of a brown-bagged sandwich and a carton of milk. It did not matter that he vanished at seven to attend to his earthly duties at the agency—there was always the delicious anticipation of his return.

More than that, there were also the erotic fantasies he conjured in her brain and that later, in the hushed darkness, she unabashedly exploited.

A week passed before she became conscious of a gnawing restlessness. By then she was allowed to roam the corridors, lounge in the sun room, mingle with other patients. She was, she told Dr. Kloster, feeling fine, wonderful, terrific. If he objected to her going back to work, why couldn't she at least go home, employing a daytime nurse if he thought that necessary? Not yet, he said. When asked why, he replied that he wanted her under routine observation simply as a precaution. She murmured "Goddamn it," and was perversely pleased to see him arch a thick eyebrow.

A few days later, escorted by a nurse, she was permitted to tour the streets adjacent to the hospital. Kloster had cautioned her that she might feel a touch of agoraphobia, but instead she felt immediately at home amid the whizzing traffic, the soaring buildings, the rushing crowds. Everything in her told her that she was ready not just to go home, but also to return to work, for which she was beginning to long.

The feeling became acute when, watching television, she found herself more interested in the commercials than in the programs. Some were more fascinating than others because, months ago, she herself had conceived them. Now, with the perspective of time and isolation, she was able to view them objectively and conclude that they were fresh and arresting and original. Which led to the question: Was the agency giving her the recognition she deserved? Probably not. She had come in as a hungry young woman copywriter whose only television experience had been the production of cheapie commercials employing local announcers, who generally presented the product by holding it next to their ears. Then suddenly she had become the writer of glossy productions, often mini-extravaganzas, employing seasoned actors, top directors, sophisticated optical effects, the bottom line running in many cases to a hundred thousand dollars or more. And not one of these commercials would have been possible were it not for an idea illuminated by a single brain. *Her* brain.

But how many people knew that? Very few in the agency, none among the clients whose products she extolled. Even Rick was only vaguely aware of her achievements. How could it be otherwise? Hadn't it been hammered into her that women must be modest? That pride was a sin? That respect, admiration, affection could be won only through humility? All this, ironically, from a mother who was boastful, haughty, arrogant!

How often those precepts had deprived her of glory: countless times when writers had picked her brains, then claimed her ideas as their own; when the commercials she had written were credited to others—to the storyboard artist, the producer, the director—one of them winning a Clio, the most coveted creative award in advertising. She remembered the many compliments tacitly accepted by slick operators at plans review board meetings for work she had done but was too timid to present, as well as the filmed commercials, conceived by her, spliced into the sample reels of lesser contributors for the acclaim of some future employer.

Always she had shrugged it off. Why complain? Why hassle? Besides, she had told herself, it didn't really matter, so long as the agency looked good and the clients were happy.

But it did matter. It had mattered then, but she had suppressed her resentment, sublimated it, because it was so contrary to the person she had become convinced she was—the sweet, agreeable, demure girl who refrained from asserting herself for fear she might not be liked.

Now she was furious with herself. How could she have been so naïve, so gutless, so self-demeaning! Sara Sunshine, the girl—not woman, *girl*—who so willingly served the ambitions of others. A mark, a pigeon, a pushover. Contemptible!

Why this sudden rebellion? Because she was away from the battle? Because she was in an impersonal sanctuary where nothing was demanded of her, nothing known of the person she was supposed to be? Perhaps that was part of it. But there was a far more dramatic explanation, her triumph over a monstrous tumor, making her more conscious of herself, aware of her own value.

Had Kloster's scalpel truly liberated her? There was no way of knowing until she was again confronted by the expectations of her associates.

Meanwhile, she would discuss her new attitude with Rick. He, more than anyone, would know how to move toward center stage without stumbling. But when he appeared that Sunday evening, after returning Scott to his mother, she decided not to mention it. He seemed distant, melancholy, a mood she attributed to what she had come to call his Sunday-night syndrome, a mild grief at leaving his son. A mood she could magically banish with a smile and a touch of her hand. But this time the magic did not work, produced only a mechanical smile, a shifting of the eyes, a somewhat forced and vague explanation that he must prepare for a Monday-morning meeting and could stay but a short while. He left in ten minutes, his parting kiss perfunctory, his manner almost formal.

The next evening was similar. Asked about his meeting, he acted as though he'd forgotten it, then ad-libbed something about a new marketing strategy for Regal Foods. Again he left early, this time for a night session at the office. Still she did not doubt him. Why should she? Hadn't he told her day before the operation that Regal Foods was demanding a new campaign that would require him to work overtime? Naturally he'd appear remote—his mind, quite understandably, was preoccupied with what might be a defecting client.

But that did not prevent him from having a clandestine discussion with Dr. Vance Kloster, a fact she learned from a talkative nurse. When she mentioned it to Rick, he seemed disconcerted, then said he simply wanted to make sure she was progressing satisfactorily. Very plausible, but was it true? Or was he seeking to gauge her emotional stamina, determine whether she could withstand the shock of hearing that he wanted to return to the free-and-easy ways of bachelorhood? That, as his withdrawal became more pronounced, was her first suspicious thought.

Then it was replaced by a thought far more terrible. Had he become involved with another woman?

There had been plenty of time for Rick, faced each night with an empty apartment, an empty bed, to venture out where nubile women were on the prowl for just such a man. It would not be, she thought miserably, someone like herself, innocent and guileless.

There would no longer be novelty in that. This new woman would be worldly and calculating, an unscrupulous bitch who would know exactly the right kind and amount of bait that would lure him into her web.

As she sat brooding in the sun room, the unknown woman suddenly became herself, thrashing about naked with Rick in lavender light, and she felt a fierce urge to be back in bed where, as so often before, she could surreptitiously gratify this awesome erotic craving. Often, she marveled at the miracle of it, ascribing it to a combination of psychological factors: an overdue umbilical severance, association with sexually liberated New Yorkers, elimination of the seizures and thus of anxiety, and above all, her enforced celibacy due to Rick's sexual inaccessibility.

She had a lot of catching up to do, and she would start the minute they got home. Another woman? There couldn't be, certainly not one who could threaten the love she and Rick shared, the physical connection that soon would become spectacular. It was all a paranoid delusion, induced by her own sexual craving.

She was dressed, her suitcase packed, and was sitting in a comfortable chair when she heard footsteps approaching down the corridor. Her hand rose and smoothed her sleek hair, now combed to the other side to cover the patch of stubble. She knew she was much better looking than when she had come in, having in her boredom experimented with ways to glamorize herself, deciding finally to leave her white skin untouched but add a gloss of color to her lips and darken the setting for her large eyes. Automatically she put on her best smile as she glanced up expectantly.

But instead of Rick, the tall, thin figure of Dr. Kloster appeared in the doorway. His face wore a grin that combined with his ferocious eyes to produce the look of an amiable madman, one who sported a three-piece suit.

"Sara, I stopped by to commiserate. You must be heartbroken, having to leave this joyful establishment."

She affected a sad look. "You're so right. I've spent my happiest days here. In fact, *all* my days, the way I feel."

He chuckled and came in and sat on the bed.

"You really feel up to the rat race?"

"I can't wait." She grinned. "I may even try for head rat."

A line between his heavy eyebrows deepened slightly. "Looking back, to before the operation, do you notice any changes in yourself?"

"Changes?"

"Well, sometimes there are side effects. Personality changes maybe. Not bad ones necessarily, and they usually don't last for long."

She nodded thoughtfully. "I guess I have changed. For one thing, I feel a lot freer."

"You should. You got rid of that stupid slob in your head."

"It seems like more than that. I feel a lot more sure of myself. And more outgoing."

"More aggressive?"

"Well, yes. At least my thoughts are."

"That's interesting. Can you give me an example?"

"Let's see. Most are about my job. Others are—" She paused and smiled mischievously. "Here's one that should grab you. It's a thought I had just before you came in. But you mustn't tell anyone."

"Scout's honor."

"I was thinking that as soon as I get home I'm going to rape Rick."

Kloster stared at her, then burst into laughter.

"Does that shock you?"

"Sure. It also delights me. Shows you're in excellent health."

And then Rick walked in.

In the taxi she had wanted to fling her arms around him, tangle her legs with his, assault him with her breasts. But he had forestalled that by immediately grasping her shoulders, gazing intently into her face, and insisting she give him the details of her routine pre-release checkups. Arriving at the apartment, chaste and impatient, she went on ahead while he got her suitcase and said something to the driver, which, if she'd overheard correctly, seemed reason enough to make a scene right there on the sidewalk.

She confronted him as soon as they entered the living room. "Did I hear you tell the driver to *wait*?"

He smiled uneasily, his tan seeming to fade. "I'm sorry, Sara, but it can't be helped. A gang of people are in my office right now."

"Suppose I'd been delayed at the hospital. Would you have waited or just taken off?"

"Waited, of course. You know that."

"Fine. Then why not pretend that's what happened? You're stuck at the hospital and the meeting's postponed until morning."

He stared at her as though asking himself, who is this pushy woman? "I can't . . . Sara, this is nonsense."

"You're damned right it's nonsense. Here I come home after having my skull sawed open and spending weeks in the hospital and you say, sorry, old thing, I haven't time to kiss you or talk to you. I've got to blast off and figure out how to peddle more pudding mix. My God!"

He was forced to smile, looking for a moment like the man who had declared his love on a bench beside the East River. "It's not a pudding mix. It's an airline—Transcon. Dalton's finally asked for agency presentations."

Surprise checked her anger. "And *we're* invited? After Brooks's fiasco in Cannes?"

"Not exactly invited. But I talked to the ad director and he sneaked us in. Maybe Dalton agreed so he wouldn't look petty. Anyway, Brooks was against a big dog-and-pony show, but he's going along."

"And right now I'm the dog."

"Look, Sara, I'm sorry but—"

"Rick, I'm asking you to dismiss that taxi. Please."

He looked at her grimly. For the first time she noticed that his cheeks were haggard, his eyes glazed with fatigue. He ran long fingers through his blond hair in what seemed a gesture of futility.

"All right," he said. "And I'll postpone the meeting, but only for a couple of hours."

She smiled. "That should be time enough, for now."

He regarded her curiously—warily, she thought—then turned away and went out to the taxi.

She darted into the bedroom, stripped off her clothes, and wrapped herself loosely in a sexy silk dressing gown.

She sat on the sofa while, across the room at the drum table, he talked on the phone. Her suspicions receded as it became clear that he had not faked the meeting, but in fact headed the group assigned to the presentation for the Transcon account.

She glanced about, wondering whether to snap on some lamps, then decided that the late-afternoon sun slanting through the tall windows provided exactly the right ambience. Crossing her legs, she parted the dressing gown just enough to offer a glimpse of white thigh.

"The meeting's now set for seven," he said, turning from the phone.

"You see? The troops love to cooperate with their commander."

"The troops are cursing my name."

"But *I'm* not." She moved her hips slightly, as if to make room for him. He started for a chair that faced her. "Let's have a drink," she said. "It's almost five." She laughed. "Who cares about the time? This is a *reunion.*"

He hesitated, then said, "Right," and went to the small bar beside the bookshelves. Pouring vodka on the rocks, he said, "I'll have to go easy because—" then stopped as she came up behind him and clasped her arms around his waist.

She felt his body stiffen but refused to be deterred, sliding her hand below his belt to begin a circular stroking with her palms. He turned, leaving the drinks on the bar, and her hands resumed, now on his buttocks. She raised her face, parted her lips, and kissed him with all the lush interior of her mouth. She heard his breath, like a whispered exclamation, felt his mounting response, his beginning hardness, then arched back, parting her gown, wriggling from it so that the upper part fell to overflow the sash. Then quickly she returned to him, breasts rising and pressing, projecting and drawing heat, loins burrowing into his until she felt a warm dampness, and then, suddenly, a dizzying prolonged spasm, becoming more acute as he abruptly broke away.

"Oh, no," she said, "no."

"We'd better sit down," he said, and she, thinking he meant to complete it more comfortably, reeled to the sofa where she yanked off her gown and sank to the cushions, head thrown back, eyes closed, legs splayed to welcome him in any way he wished.

"*Stop it, Sara! Stop right now!*"

For an instant she thought of her brain, thought that something had gone wrong, that it had misunderstood, that he really had said, "Do it, Sara! Do it right now!" But when her eyes blinked open and she saw him standing before her, shocked and perplexed but resolute in his rejection, she knew that her brain had made no mistake.

She did not move, did not change position. There was no feeling of shame, only an overwhelming despair so paralyzing that she could do no more than utter a wounded whimper.

"There's something we've got to talk about, Sara."

Oh, God, how often she had heard that line in very bad movies. Something we've got to talk about. You see, there's this girl . . . nothing that was planned, it just happened, we couldn't help ourselves. Believe me. . . .

She felt a need to regain her dignity, but all she could manage was a sardonic tone. "Yes, Rick, quite obviously there's something we've got to talk about. I simply can't imagine what it is."

"Look, you've got to talk sensibly."

She sat up. "No, I don't. I prefer *in*sensibly." She rose slowly, donned her dressing gown, and went to the bar. The first glass of vodka scorched her throat, startled her nose with its fumes. The second one didn't. Then she poured a third, and brought it back across the room and stood facing him.

"All right, Rick," she said, "explain why it is I'm so loathsome to you."

He stood very still but seemed to recoil. "Sit down, Sara, please."

She did, on the edge of the sofa. A tremor shook her arm and she placed the glass on the coffee table. He took a chair, tensing forward, hands fisted on his knees.

"Sara, I didn't intend to tell you this right now, but—"

"When *did* you intend to tell me?"

"Later, when you had a chance to settle in."

"You mean after your meeting? After I'd bathed and put on perfume and my sexiest clothes—is that when you were going to tell me that I turned you off?"

"I didn't see it that way. You never seemed overly eager for sex."

"I've changed."

He eyed her as though she were some strange sort of specimen. "Yes, you have."

She felt compelled to become a supplicant. Softening her voice, she said, "Now that you know, why not enjoy it?"

"Because it wouldn't be fair to you."

"Meaning you'd leave me anyway—is that it?"

He flexed his jaw. "Yes, Sara."

She had known the answer, sensed it since stepping from the hospital, but hearing it stated, firmly, unequivocally, was as devastating as total surprise. Her hand jittered to her drink. She splashed some on the table before getting the glass to her mouth and draining it.

"I've got to tell you about it," he said.

She was appalled. "Tell me about it! You find yourself a new bedmate and now you want to *tell* me about it!"

He waited until she gained control. Then he said quietly, "You're wrong, Sara, it's not a new bedmate."

"Oh, come on, what's the sense of lying?"

"It's my wife."

She thought she might faint. His wife! But she wasn't his wife; they were divorced. No, they weren't, not legally, not yet. They were still married, Rick Bradley and Janice Powers. And they had a son, Scott. A loving and lovable little boy who . . .

She was not aware of speaking, yet she heard her voice, choked and bitter: "Yes, I see now, you've got to tell me, all of it."

He heaved a breath, massaged his cheeks, then, superficially composed, began, "It started more than a week ago. It was—"

"A Sunday afternoon," she said dully. "You'd just brought Scott back to his mother."

He showed no surprise. "Yes. It was his birthday. I hadn't told you because I didn't want you feeling you should do something. Janice had planned a special dinner for him—the cake-and-candles bit—and asked me to stay. I said I couldn't because—"

"Because you had to see someone you sort of kind of knew who was in the hospital." She knew she was being bitchy, but didn't care, didn't care about anything. Nothing mattered except venting this awful inner pressure.

"It wasn't like that, Sara. She knew about us and understood it."

"You mean she understood you were shacking up with a dumb little broad from a one-street town in Ohio?"

"That's enough!" His voice was harsh, peremptory. "I'll get back to us. But right now, just listen. I owe you this explanation. I owe it to everyone involved."

Her bitterness, she saw, had served only to elevate him from supplicant to man-in-charge. Now she felt small, ineffectual, trapped into listening without protest to the story of her fall from grace. She brought the glass to her lips, sipped at it, then stared into the clear liquid, fancying it as a pool designed for drowning.

He went on, speaking quietly now. "All right. Yes, I said I had to go to the hospital. Then Scott asked if I couldn't come back later, they'd wait dinner for me. Naturally, that's what I did."

"Naturally." She said it to herself.

"Later, when he was in bed and I was about to leave, Janice asked me to stay. There was something she wanted to talk about. I assumed it concerned Scott." He paused, blinking. "It didn't. Janice said she felt we'd made a big mistake. She asked me to come back."

She visualized it. The little family birthday party. Paper hats, jokes, reminiscence. The blowing out of candles—four, plus one to grow on—while a wish was made. The pride, mutually shared, in their only begotten. And later, the glow still warm: "We need you, Rick. Scott needs you. *I* need you." And Rick, so lonely for his son, so long without a woman's body, yielding.

"I was stunned. I'd totally believed that we were finished for good. I tried to put her off, saying she was just being impulsive, that it was the reunion, Scott's birthday, that made her feel as she did. No, she said, she'd been thinking about it for a long time and was sure it was right. She said that all our problems stemmed from the kind of people we'd been running around with, people who represented what she called 'schlock chic.' She said she was through with all that, hated it, and wanted only to be close to her family."

"Farewell to acting?"

"No, but she said she'd never again let it interfere with my, our"—his eyes shifted from her face—"happiness."

It all seemed clear now. Janice Powers had prepared the scenario in advance, rehearsed her role, probably even prompted Scott to plead with his father to attend his birthday party. Happiness. The word, spoken in that contrived context, was obscene.

"That's bullshit," she said. She saw him wince but went recklessly on, driven by desperation. "She set you up. She knew that the way to get to you was through Scott. And you fell for it." She felt a surge of confidence. "You don't love *her*, Rick. You love your son. He's the one you really want. But that's where it gets confusing. Loving him, you think you also love her."

He nodded. "I've thought of that. And you may be right. I just don't know. What I do know is that there's only one way to find out."

"You didn't get a clue when you slept with her?"

He was silent.

"You *did* sleep with her?"

"No, I left. I said I had to think about it."

"But you've been sleeping with her since then."

"Yes."

Again, the wild, uncontrollable fury. "And you found out she's a much better lay than I was!"

"Goddamn it, Sara, I don't have to listen to that kind of talk!"

"Yes, you do! You started this!" But she subsided, ravaged by the thought that he might have been immune to persuasion if only she, Sara Vardon, had been able to lavish on him the rampant sexuality that had so astonishingly been released.

He seemed to be making a heroic effort to control himself. Finally, speaking evenly, he said, "Yes, I started it. And now I'll finish it." His voice softened. "Sara, you know that what you and I had was no shackup. I care about you very much."

"Oh, yes, certainly. It's tearing you into little pieces having to walk out on me."

"Yes, that's true."

"And, as they say in the romance novels, in a special corner of your heart you'll always love me."

"That's also true." He smiled ruefully. "I hope I can keep it cornered."

She melted. "Oh, Rick, why must you do this? Why don't you give us a little time together? A week. That's not asking very much. Then see how you feel."

"I'm sorry. It wouldn't change anything."

"But *I've* changed. You know I have."

He contemplated her for a moment, then said in a tone that seemed to imply some deep significance, "I liked you the way you were, Sara."

"Then that's how I'll be."

His eyebrows rose slightly, as though in skepticism. "And that's how I'll think of you." He stood up. "I'm leaving now. It's senseless to prolong the agony."

"Not yet, please not yet." She thought of once again slipping off her gown.

But he was implacable. "Most of my things are packed. I'll pick them up tomorrow, when you're not here, and leave the key."

"Rick! Rick! For godsake . . ."

He brushed past her, awkwardly touching her shoulder.

She heard the front door quietly open, and even more quietly close.

She ranted. She threw things. She wept.

Then she lay flat on the bed, hand stretched out to where he should have been, and listened to the promptings of her brain.

He still loved her. She had not lost him, not forever. She would get him back somehow. No matter how long it took.

Nothing could stop her.

9

SARA LEFT the hospital on Thursday, so she decided to postpone her office debut until the following Monday. She left the apartment early on Friday to shop at Bloomingdale's and Bergdorf's where, heedless of expense, she charged enough elegant clothes for a fashion show. By two she was at Elizabeth Arden, submitting for the next few hours to the full treatment, hair to toenails. She arrived home at five-thirty, arms piled with packages, and paused in the living room to glance at the coffee table. Rick's key was there.

Prepared for the sight, she was able to stifle a moan. But in the bedroom, she dropped the packages and entered the walk-in closet, her knees suddenly gave way and she grasped the door for support. On one side her clothes hung in neat rows, and below them her shoes rested on an angled platform. The other side was empty, a void also expected and steeled against. But what she had not anticipated, the invisible thing that struck her with an almost physical force, was the subtle scent of him, of his after-shave lotion, the polished leather of his shoes, the mingled odors of cashmere and tweed and camel's hair.

She lurched back, tripped over a package, fell across the bed, and lay there staring at the ceiling while she battled with panic. Triumphing, she went to the bar, downed a drink, went back, stripped, and took a long hot shower. By the time she had tried on her new clothes and approved of the ravishing woman in the full-length mirror, she felt more insulated against fear and depression.

Saturday was a minute-by-minute, hour-by-hour struggle to maintain her emotional balance, a struggle fought with books and magazines and television. Sunday she woke early, exhausted by baleful dreams, sensing the approach of walls, convinced she must escape or go mad. She dressed, gulped some coffee, all but ran to the deserted street, then turned west and began an aimless walk. At Fifth Avenue she veered south, meandered past the greenery of the park, followed it along its southern border until it ended at Columbus Circle. Stopping at the low-walled corner, she began to comprehend why she had unconsciously taken this route. Directly to the north, only a few blocks away on Central Park West, was Janice Powers's apartment.

Having come this far, she could not resist going the full distance. Nor, when she was opposite the address, the tall building rising orange in the morning sunlight, could she resist backing off into the park, half concealing herself behind a thick tree, to watch and wait.

An hour must have passed before she saw them—little Scott in the lead, bouncing out of the iron-grilled door, followed by Rick, wearing pale slacks and a blue blazer, and Janice in a clinging white pantsuit. It was the first time Sara had seen the actress in person and she found herself grudgingly admiring the slim, rounded figure and the silky chestnut hair that spilled down her shoulders. They were laughing as they caught up with their son, each taking a hand and at times swinging him off his feet, much to his delight. Perhaps, Sara thought, they were on their way to some hotel like the Plaza, where all of them, this happy nuclear family, would devour a huge breakfast.

When they had disappeared, she crossed the street and hailed a passing taxi. Inside, she sat up straight on the cracked vinyl and stared at the picture of the driver framed on the back of the front seat. She forbade her mind to function, ordered her senses to remain numb.

But when she stepped into her apartment and was assailed by its silent emptiness, she broke down.

Monday, and suddenly she was resurrected from her tomb. She had been given a new, larger office, the windows facing Madison Avenue instead of an airshaft. (Rick's doing? A way to ease his guilt?) People dropped by, some she hardly knew, saying, hey, we missed you; the place went to hell without you; buy you a drink at the Elysee tonight; and—most often—you look terrific; my God, just gorgeous; that dress! I've got to know where you got that dress! (a beige "creation" that did everything within decency for her hips and her breasts and enhanced her lustrous hair). And then everyone abruptly scattered.

Brooks Madden stood in the doorway.

He came in smiling his broad Irish smile, thin pink face thrust forward, hand outstretched from his buttoned cuff, New York voice rasping but warm: "We're awfully glad you're back, Sara."

She had met him only once, and then in a group, but the way he looked at her, she might have been a favorite niece. Shaking his hand, thanking him, she wondered if this presidential visit was another of Rick's consolation offerings.

"I hear you've had a rotten time of it," he said. "Not that anyone'd know it, looking at you."

She gave him her Sara Sunshine smile. "I'm fine, just fine."

"Sure you are. But why not break in easy? Come in a little later, go home a little earlier."

"Thanks, Mr. Madden, but I know I can cut it now."

"That's the way to talk. Still—"

"Look, Mr. Madden, would you mind sitting down for a minute? There's a question I'd like to ask you."

"Glad to. It's like a vacation to get away from my office."

They sat, facing each other across her desk.

"Let's have it," he said pleasantly.

"I'd like to work with the Transcon group."

A shadow seemed to cross his face. "Hmm. Maybe I shouldn't say this, but the odds are that'll be just an exercise. I think you'll be a lot better off sticking to your regular assignments." He smiled. "Which I hear you're very good at."

"Thank you. But I think I can do something better for an airline."

"You've got some ideas?"

"Not yet. I haven't had time to think about it. But I'd like the chance."

He shifted uncomfortably. "Well, things are pretty well along and . . ." His face twisted in a look of mild self-disgust. "Look, who am I kidding? The fact is, and I thought you knew it, the Transcon group is headed up by Rick Bradley."

She didn't blink. "I do know it, Mr. Madden. But I don't see why that should matter. Rick Bradley is a professional. I like to think I am, too."

He studied her for a moment. "Listen, *I* have no objection. If you—"

"But you think he has?"

His manner seemed to cool. "I don't know. We didn't discuss it. Rick's running this show and I'm butting out. You'll have to talk to him."

She sensed his annoyance. Part of it, she knew from talking to Rick, arose from his humiliating experience with Harry Dalton in Cannes. Another part, perhaps more crucial, sprang from his affection for Rick's wife, which automatically made Sara "the other woman," susceptible to all sorts of ugly suspicions.

"Of course," she said. "I shouldn't have bothered you with it."

"No bother." He stood up, again smiling. "My advice is to stand pat. As I figure it, Harry Dalton will never see our presentation. His ad director, yeah. But that's as far up as it'll go."

"Is that unusual? Won't it be the same for the other agencies?"

"You don't know Dalton. He's got his nose into everything, *especially* his advertising. But I'm afraid we won't get his personal attention. We're trying to get to him through the back door, but I don't think we'll make it past the servants."

"Rick must find that pretty discouraging."

"Not him. He thinks we'll find the rabbit in the hat. Well, if anyone can, he's the man. So forget what I said."

He welcomed her again and left.

She sat there idly thumbing through a stack of conference reports, which would bring her up to date. But her mind was preoccupied with finding some way to break into the Transcon group. Certainly not by confronting Rick directly. He had to have considered her and, for obvious personal reasons, rejected her. He might have arranged for this new office and nudged Madden to visit her, but there his charity had stopped. No, she would have to manage it some other way.

Wait a minute. Who said that an account executive, even one as lofty as Rick Bradley, ran the creative department? Each department was supposedly autonomous, guided by the plans review board but accountable only to the executive committee, which in practice meant Brooks Madden.

She got up and headed down the corridor to the corner office, occupied by Lou Kahn, vice-president and creative director. She paused beside the railing that isolated the typing pool and peered through Lou's open door. He was animated as usual, weaving about the room, waving his long skinny arms as he "woodshedded" a TV storyboard held limply by a hapless art director. Swinging around, black pointed beard stabbing the air, eyes enormous behind thick lenses, he spotted Sara and froze. "Baby!" he shouted. "Come in, come in! Sweet Jesus Christ—choosing a name at random—how I've needed you!"

She grinned and went inside. Lou seized her, pressed her against his gangly frame, smeared a hairy kiss on her cheek, then stood back and gave her a look of adoration.

"Beautiful! Right off the cover of *Cosmo*! Who the hell would ever think you had a brain?"

"My neurosurgeon."

"Dr. Kloster, right?"

"Right. How did—"

"I checked him out when I heard he was the guy making the forced entry. He's to brain surgery what I am to advertising. Anyway, you look fantastic, like a respectable hooker."

"Thanks—I guess."

The art director, a short, stocky man with a load of black hair, said, "Hi, Sara, glad you're back." He glanced darkly at Lou Kahn. "And I'm glad you came in when you did."

"Hi, Tony." She knew him slightly, from meetings. "Lou giving you a hard time?"

"He hates Italians. Be glad you're not Italian. Italians he throws out of windows."

"Give me a minute," Lou said to Sara. He took the storyboard from Tony, skipped to his desk, and, with a grease pencil, sketched several stick figures on a drawing pad. He numbered them, then looked at Tony, who stood glumly beside him. "Okay, Eye-talian, these aren't exactly right—my arthritis—but they give the idea. The numbers coincide with the ones on your frames, where I think you've jumped the track. Mostly, it's a question of tighter closeups, not just of the product but of the *faces*. It's got to look like the stuff produces orgasm. And we've got to see it on a little half-ass tube, not Cinemascope. Got it?"

Tony sulkily inspected the stick features. "They'll never make it in an art show, Lou. But yeah, I got it."

"Sensational. If you've still got complaints, phone the Vatican, collect."

Tony left, muttering but half smiling.

"Storyboards," Lou Kahn said. "God, how I hate 'em. You try to get it on film and it's like making love while reading a sex manual." He perched on the front of his desk, pointed to a chair, said, "Put it there," and as she sat, "Hey, how do you like your new office?"

"I'm delighted. That's one reason I'm here—to thank you."

"Don't thank me, thank McCann Erickson."

"McCann?"

"Yeah. Sam Harlow had that office. He's now on McCann's payroll, seduced by buckets of bucks. If they come after you, talk to me first."

"I'm very happy here, Lou. But you could make me even happier."

"Try me."

"Assign me to the Transcon group."

"You a masochist? That one's got me pulling people off the window ledges."

"You see? As you said, you need me."

He fussed with his beard. "What we need is an act of God." He hopped up and strode to a wall-length cork bulletin board pinned with layouts. "Here's some of the stuff we've got." He moved to an oblong table stacked with more layouts. "And here. Also, we've got some rough commercials on film, plus slides with soundtracks."

"All that? But I thought you'd just started."

"We've been breaking our picks for weeks."

She felt a small shock. Two weeks ago Rick had reconciled with his wife. He had known then about the Transcon solicitation, but had kept it to himself lest Sara expect to be included. Only when he was leaving her did he mention it, and at that point it didn't matter. She could only assume that Rick Bradley was determined to exclude her from any project he was associated with.

Lou was saying, "And we still haven't got it. Sure, a lot of it's bright and clever, but the ingredients are the same as for the other airlines. Toothy stewardesses. Pilots who belong in Marlboro Country. Passengers who look like they just hit a jackpot in Vegas. We could run one of our commercials and half the viewers would think it was a nice pitch for United or American."

"So we'll have to do more digging."

"Where else to dig? We've ridden their planes, checked out their maintenance shops, talked to their people, interviewed airport personnel, passengers, travel agents. My God, the bucks we've blown on research! And you know the absolutely astounding thing we came up with?"

"Transcon's not number one."

"Well, yeah. So how do they get there? By giving passengers what they want in an airline. And you know what that is? They want safety. They want on-time takeoffs and arrivals. They want low fares, decent food, good service. For Christake! I could have figured that out dead drunk in a bar."

"So you're looking for something else?"

"Hell no. That's what the people want, that's what we say we've got. Okay, the first thing is to make 'em look and listen, right? Right. And that we can do. But once they're inside the tent, we've got to convert 'em into *believers*. And that's where we lose our wheels. Maybe what we need is a hypnotist."

"Looks like I timed my return perfectly."

"You did if you brought your magic kit. Sure, the other agencies have the same problem, but they've also got a leg up. They got invited to this party and we had to crash. That means our stuff's got to be so much better that even a blind imbecile could see it. You still want in?"

"I'd like a go at it."

"So okay. But you don't have to be assigned to the group. You, anybody, can throw an idea into the pot."

"That wouldn't be the same, Lou. If I'm not on the inside, I won't have the chance to present my ideas."

His eyebrows rose above his glasses. "You're now a *presenter*? What'd they do to you at the hospital, give you self-assertion hormones? I never even heard you clear your throat at a meeting."

She laughed, sharing his surprise. Who'd ever have thought that the meek Sara Vardon could be so bold? "They did *something*. I used to be afraid I'd step on someone's toes. Now I don't give a goddamn."

His eyes popped. "They also taught you blasphemy. Keep it up and you'll take over my job. Okay, you're in." He sprang to the phone, about to pick it up. "I'll tell Rick."

"Lou, please don't."

"Why not? It'll show I go all the way when he makes a suggestion."

"He suggested me for Transcon?"

"No, for the new office. He figured it'd be a nice welcome-back gift."

She kept her voice steady. "But why not just surprise him? Bring me to the next meeting." She knew that once she was observed there by others, he would not risk embarrassing her or himself by later having her removed.

"A deal." He flung a hand toward the layouts. "Okay, go through the riffle pile and see where we are. I'll route you the preliminary report on strategy and research and all that crap, also copies of their current print ads and those of their competitors, and reels of their commercials. You'll have it all in twenty minutes."

"Thanks, Lou. I'll move on it fast."

"You'll have to. A week from tomorrow we're on. Just keep in mind what we're after. Something more than a gimmick or a device, something—a core idea—that will pull together everything Transcon's got to offer under one umbrella. Jesus, I sound like a bullshit account man."

"But it's true. We need to come up with something that gives Transcon a unique image, separates them from the pack, and that's very believable."

"Honey, you find it and Rick Bradley will kiss you."

She smiled. "That's quite an incentive."

By four o'clock she had read the reports and reviewed all the print stuff—newspapers, magazines, outdoor billboards. Every ad, however brilliant, seemed to her like a one-shot—nothing that could be developed into a cohesive campaign. To achieve any cumulative impact, they would have to rely heavily on mechanics—uniform layout, identical typeface, similar artwork—all easily obtainable from design specialists. But that would simply be a coverup—apparent to a practiced eye—for the lack of a single forceful idea that would, like fingerprints, belong to Transcon alone.

She went to the drugstore across the street, ordered coffee at the counter, and sat and thought. When Mary Wells had landed Braniff, she'd hired a fashion designer to paint the planes in gaudy colors. (Later she married Braniff's president.) The resultant publicity had been far more valuable than the advertising. An airline in California—PSA—had painted a huge smile under each plane's nose. So forget paint, glamorous or cute.

What else? Something dramatic. Something personal. Something unique. Something flexible enough to embrace all of Transcon's activities. Above all, something the flying public would believe.

She sat there for an hour, had three cups of coffee, and left stumped.

Back at the office, she closed herself in the screening room and viewed the commercials, both Transcon's and those of its competitors. All of them were good. All of them, except for the slogans, could have been run by any of the others. All had a deadly sameness.

Her mind was a blur.

Then suddenly it was penetrated by a vision so graphically vivid that it jolted her head back.

"Well, I'll be damned," she said.

It was so beautifully simple. And so absolutely *right*.

But there were problems. Big problems.

She would have to develop the idea entirely on her own. That she could do, working nights and over the weekend. But then, God help her, she would have to be the lone presenter. Only once before had she made a presentation—to the plans review board—an ordeal preceded by vomiting and accomplished in a whispered stammer accompanied by cold sweat and spastic hands. Never again, she had vowed.

Worst of all, her big idea wouldn't have a chance unless it was presented directly to the man who had said he wouldn't be there— the ferocious Harry Dalton.

10

"RICK? Lou Kahn. I think we've found the rabbit in the hat. Most beautiful goddamned rabbit you ever saw."

"Great! Want me to come down?"

"We're not ready to spring it. First we need your charm, your prestige, the power of your great office."

"That and forty cents will buy you a cup of coffee. All right, what can I do?"

"You can call your buddies at the networks—NBC and CBS should be enough—and tell 'em we want to rifle their film libraries."

"No problem. What is it you want—old shows, movies?"

"No, news clips. Current and past, maybe going back five years or more."

"That might be tougher. I doubt if they'd release their news films for commercial use."

"It won't be commercial. Not a single frame will be shown outside our offices. We'd use it only for demonstration."

"I think I can swing that. You've got me damned curious, Lou."

"Good. So I'll make you curiouser. Rick, I think this idea is dynamite. But it'll fizzle if it's just *told* to someone. It's got to be seen and heard right off the tube. That means we can forget it if we can't meet one condition."

"Which is?"

"Which is that Harry Dalton has got to be at the presentation."

"Now look, Lou—"

"It's the only way. If he gets it secondhand, you can count on it being a dud. The ad director knows we don't rate high with Dalton, so chances are he'll ho-hum it, maybe ridicule it."

"What makes you think Dalton won't?"

"Trust me."

"I trust you, Lou. But I'll have to wait till I see it. I can't even try to get at Dalton unless we're all pretty sure that the idea will interest him."

"You're wounding me. But okay, you'll see it in a few days. You'll call the networks?"

"As soon as I hang up. Who are you sending?"

"The one who hatched the idea. Come to think of it, maybe that new office helped incubate it."

"Who is it?"

"I was going to surpise you at our next meeting. But now it can't wait. Imagine, she's back one day and, bang, she slugs the first pitch over the wall."

"You mean it's—"

"Yeah, your protége, Sara Vardon."

After calling friends at the two networks and making the arrangements, he sat back with a feeling of entrapment. He had thought that the separation by three floors, the exclusion of her from his accounts, and the avoidance of the Elysee bar would preclude a confrontation, except perhaps in a crowded elevator. He had also hoped that the new office and the contrived welcoming visit from Brooks would be seen by her as no more than friendly gestures intended to ease the finality of the break, as well as his guilt. Instead she seemed to have interpreted them as signals to continue their relationship, even if it meant a furtive affair.

He could think of no other reason why, immediately upon her return, she would involve herself in a project that she must have been told was a loser. And now she had come up with an idea that she had sold to Lou Kahn as a winner. But there was a catch. It must be presented personally to Harry Dalton, who she knew had refused to attend. In that case, she would be invulnerable to personal failure:

she would be in the position of casting pearls before swine. Meanwhile she would have reopened communications with the lover who had left her.

It pained him to think she could be so devious. In others, that was often a trait to be cynically prized, to be managed, directed, exploited for the benefit of the agency. But not with Sara. Not with the girl who had so appealed to him with her honesty, her humility, her sense of propriety.

But that Sara seemed to have vanished, only to be replaced by a woman who, to his astonishment, had practically assaulted him in a frenzy of uninhibited lust. It was as though some unknown recess in her brain had been plugged by the tumor, which, once removed, had released a coven of primitive emotions.

Now, about to call Lou Kahn back, he was surprised to discover himself strangely intrigued by this new Sara Vardon. He tried to dispel the thought but it persisted, accompanied by contradictory terms: innocent sophisticate, wanton virgin. And that helped to clarify it. The trauma of the operation, the hammering fear of death or mental impairment, had aroused her repressed animal instincts, freed them to engage in open warfare with the puritanical restraints instilled by a strict upbringing. But his personal prognosis was that eventually Sara would revert to the shy, compliant girl who had arrived wide-eyed from the boondocks of Ohio.

He punched the phone's buttons to connect with Lou Kahn's extension.

"Hello." A brisk feminine voice.

It was Sara. Unconsciously he had, as so often before, punched her number.

"Sara?" He recovered quickly from his surprise. Why not deliver the message to the one assigned to the job, the one in fact responsible for the alleged breakthrough?

"Oh, it's you, Rick." Said without emotion.

"Yes. Congratulations. Lou tells me you've come up with a great idea."

"Well, it might not win any awards, but I think it's perfect for Transcon." Then, suspiciously, "He didn't tell you what it is, did he?"

"No. He was very mysterious."

"Good, I expect to present it to you on Friday."

"Fine. I'll look forward—"

"If you and Brooks buy it, I'd also like to present it to Harry Dalton."

He was startled. "You mean you *personally*?"

"Yes, me personally." Her tone was brusque.

"But you've never made a presentation in your life."

She gave a short, harsh laugh. "Then you'll agree it's time I expanded my talents."

He felt a stab of anger. "No, Sara, I don't agree. At least not in this case. Dalton would eat you raw."

"You think you should do it?"

"I don't know. Maybe Lou Kahn."

"You mean someone with a title, not a lowly copywriter?"

"I don't mean that at all. It's just—"

"Because I'm a woman?"

"No. Because it takes someone with enough experience to handle the beast."

"I say that this idea takes a woman. Namely, Sara Vardon."

He exhaled a controlled breath. "Look, Sara, I'm not going to argue about an idea I haven't even seen."

"Right. You can decide on Friday, after I've auditioned. Now, did you get clearance from the networks?"

"I did." He gave her the information.

She thanked him and hung up.

He stared at the receiver, not quite believing the voice it had transmitted, cool, assured, with an inflection of superiority. Was it an act? Or did she now hold him in disdain, having decided that she had squandered herself on someone unworthy?

He felt challenged, a reaction regrettably callow but nonetheless poignant. His impulse was to deflate this imperious young woman, then recast her in the image that he had once found so pleasurable.

If she had remained as she was, if there had been no operation, no long nights without her, would he have reconciled with Janice? Perhaps not. Absolutely not if there had been no Scott. His son had been the catalyst, so transcendent of mere obligation, so loved by his parents that all three were locked into a love inseparable from the feelings the father and mother might have for each other. Exactly what these feelings were had yet to be fully resolved. Respect, yes. Mutual interests, partial. Sexual attraction, moderate. Beyond these, he was compelled to turn wistfully to the past.

She was the second girl from the end of the chorus line, to his right from where he sat alone in the third row of the small Greenwich Village theater. His eyes had fastened on her from the moment she high-stepped from the wings, dressed like the others in a white V-necked sweater and a short pleated skirt. "Good news," they caroled in this satirical romp from the famous old musical comedy. They flashed bright teeth at the sparse audience with all the verve of Rockettes. Her smile, he thought, was the most dazzling, her body the most supple, her kick the most enticing. As they danced off the stage, he imagined that she paused for an instant to fix him with a look.

He was back the next night, again forsaking his two fellow grad students who had come down from Cambridge with him, ostensibly to see the shows but in fact preferring the singles bars of midtown Manhattan. And this time he knew the look was not imagined. It came flaunting out to where he sat, bold as the brass accompaniment, her smile as incandescent as the spotlights. Then, as the line danced away, she threw him a backward glance and seemed to give a little nod.

He went to the stage door and sent her a note. He admired her. So much that he had been drawn back for a second performance. Was it possible she had seen him in the third-row seat? He was the blond one with the worshipful expression. The man at the stage door came back, eyes glinting wickedly. Yes, Miss Powers would see him, but only for a few minutes. She had an engagement.

She met him outside the noisy dressing room, wearing a pale green dress that enhanced her long chestnut hair. She looked different than she had on stage, more serious, more mature, but no less attractive. He repeated and expanded his compliments, which she accepted modestly.

"And now you're about to wreck my evening," he said.

"How?"

"By leaving for another date."

"That was a precaution. I thought I'd better talk to you first."

"Do I pass?"

He got a closeup of that wonderful smile. "Oh, yes!"

They went across the street to a small bar jammed with members of the cast. She introduced him around, her cheeks flushing when a number of girls started to come on to him. After one glass of wine, he suggested they go someplace more private.

"I suppose you mean your hotel," she said, her eyes cynical.

"No, my two roommates might object."

She looked chagrined, and relieved.

She took him to Julius on West Tenth Street. The bar was crowded but there was an available table in the small back room. He ordered a liter of wine.

"I think this is the same Julius where my father used to hang out," he said. "That was before I was born. He was a student at NYU."

"It probably is. I think this is the oldest bar in New York. Where is your father now?"

"In Boston with my mother and sister. He's a doctor, an internist."

"And that's where you live?"

"In Cambridge. Harvard. I'm in grad school, business administration. I get my master's in three months."

"Heavens! A college boy. And Harvard. And he's going to be a business tycoon sitting at a huge desk in a fancy glass office." But she smiled to soothe the sting.

So he told her about it. He had wanted to be a playwright, perhaps also write novels, but despaired of his talent. Why not, then, go for something related, managing the affairs of people who were talented?

"You mean an agent?"

"Partly, but a lot more. Their accounting, their investments, their relations with the trade and the public."

"You sound like a good candidate for MCA or William Morris."

"As a starter. Eventually I'd like to run my own show."

She regarded him closely. "I think maybe you will. As for talent, you're loaded with it."

"Ha! But keep talking."

"Not writing, I wouldn't know about that. But with people, that's something else. There you're a star."

"With you?"

She put down her glass and gave him an arch, purposely stagey look. "You're shining brighter every second, Mr. Bradley."

He grinned. "Well, enough about you. Now let's talk about me."

She said, through a laugh, "You see? You make people feel good. All right, my turn. Don't bother to take notes."

She had been born and raised in Maplewood, New Jersey, and had been stagestruck ever since she had played a witch in a seventh-grade play. Her vacations had mostly been spent painting scenery and doing walk-ons in summer theaters, the last at Ogunquit, Maine. She had performed in several television commercials, two off-Broadway disasters, and a feature movie filmed in New York ("I had one line: 'No! Don't, please!'—and then was fatally stabbed"). She had an audition for a role in a TV soap opera the following week. If she landed it, she hoped to save enough money to study with Lee Strasberg.

"What about *Good News*?"

"It closes tomorrow night. I'll be, as they say, at liberty." She paused, and when he didn't reply, said, "I was hoping you'd pick that up."

"I got it. But I've also got to be back in Cambridge tomorrow."

"Oh, dear," she said sadly.

"But after exhaustive analysis and considerable thought, I've decided to temporarily delay my education. Tomorrow night, look for me. I'll be in the audience."

"Wonderful! I'll throw you a garter."

"In that case, I'll also be at the stage door. I'll be the suave one with the top hat, gold-headed cane, and a dozen red roses."

"We'll go to Rector's or Delmonico's. Maybe we'll see Diamond Jim Brady there with Lillian Russell. And Stanford White with Evelyn Nesbitt."

It was all so nice and easy, so comfortable. And glamorous. Rick Bradley, man about Manhattan, great and good friend of a stunning actress. An actress he must now lose, as the hands on the bar clock moved toward 4:00 A.M.

"I'll get a taxi," he said.

"We can walk. I'm only a few blocks away."

But he insisted, went out, and found a taxi parked across the street. During the brief ride—she lived in a basement apartment on Waverly Place—she sat away from him and, deliberately it seemed, confined her conversation to facts. She was his age, twenty-six, her parents still lived in Maplewood, she had two older brothers, both married, one living in Los Angeles, the other in Miami. Etcetera, etcetera.

Leaving the taxi, he said, "You filled out the form just fine. Now all we need is your social security number."

She laughed. "Okay, I'm guilty. But I was afraid something might happen in that cozy back seat."

"Something? You thought I might attack you?"

"Or vice versa." She walked quickly ahead, down the three stone steps to her door.

She had partly opened it when he reached her. He grasped her elbow and gently swung her around. His hands moved to her shoulders and he looked intently into her face, her cheeks dark hollows, her eyes liquid in the glow of the streetlamp. When he bent to kiss her, her mouth, still damply touched with wine, reached to meet his. Her lithe body arched and curved against him.

"Janice," he said.

"I know," she said, then, as he remained stationary, went inside, turning to give him a look of mock anguish, and quietly closed the door.

He stood in the shadows and watched her as she came out the stage door and looked around for him. Then, when the other cast members had passed by and she was alone, he stepped into the pale light. Her reaction was exactly what he had hoped for, mouth dropping open, eyes expanding to full moons, voice whispering in awe, "Good God."

He tapped his silk top hat, gave his black Inverness cape a flourish, and produced a dozen red roses. Then he beckoned grandly toward the horsedrawn hansom, complete with uniformed driver, parked at the curb. "At your service, madam."

"You're insane."

He stroked an imaginary mustache, bestowed the roses, kissed her lightly. "Agreed."

"You're also rich."

"No, but I *think* rich. Please enter. The meter's running."

They were inside the cab before her astonishment erupted into laughter. She fell helplessly against him, body quaking, eyes streaming tears. He wrapped her in his cape and addressed the elegant figure that sat rigidly above. "To Fifth Avenue, Thomas."

Thomas gave a snap of the reins and the horse strutted away.

Rick raised her chin as she emptied an exhausted breath. "You're in critical condition. Calls for resuscitation. Mouth to mouth."

The kiss was longer, deeper, more urgent than the one at her door. But again she drew away.

"Where did you ever get that outfit?"

"In a phone booth. Belongs to a fellow named Clark Kent."

"Probably some fly-by-night."

"My dear, *I* am in charge of the jokes."

"You're in charge of everything. Oh, what a wonderful way to close the show!"

"And to bid farewell to New York."

"You mean—"

"If I fail to report to academe before five P.M. tomorrow, I'll get the rack, the wheel, and be hanged by the thumbs in a smelly dungeon."

"I don't like that at all!"

He looked at her and spoke in his normal voice, sincerely, "I don't either, Janice. I wish it could go on and—"

Her mouth silenced him. And this time she did not withdraw.

They rode to Fifth Avenue, the trip orchestrated by squeaking wheels, the clop of hooves, flatulent equine explosions. They paraded across Fourteenth Street, their passage marked by gawking pedestrians, and then turned back to wind through crooked streets, silent now at midnight, finally to pull up in front of Julius Restaurant.

He peered at her radiant face, at the roses clutched to the breast of her white fleecy coat. "It seemed like the right place," he said.

She nodded. "Do you suppose they'll serve the horse?"

"No way. He's not wearing a tie. Besides, he's now a mouse and the cab's a pumpkin. This is the last stop."

They got out, patted and thanked the horse, and bid a warm farewell to Thomas, Rick adding a generous tip to what he had already paid. Inside the restaurant, they passed the conscientious drinkers at the bar, none of whom blinked an eye at Rick's costume. Reaching the back room, they found a couple just leaving the table they had shared the night before. They smiled at each other, as though a small miracle had been performed, then she abruptly shivered and said, "I'm freezing."

"I should have got a hansom with a heater."

She stood there, gazing at him through her lashes. "I have a fireplace," she said softly.

He felt his breath suspend. "Funny thing, I was just wondering if you had a fireplace."

They walked to her apartment without speaking, communicating all that was necessary through pressures of their hands.

Her apartment was small—living room, alcove for the bed, kitchenette, bath. The living room was sparsely furnished with pieces she claimed were made from genuine antique peach crates. But there *was* a fireplace—beautiful if you liked gas logs, which he was suddenly crazy about—and, facing it, two chairs. "You can see they're overstuffed chairs," she said, pointing to where the innards had burst through.

She squeezed into the kitchenette and brought back glasses and a bottle of wine, a cheap white sherry that suddenly tasted like a vintage import. They sat in silence, gazing at the darting flames, adjusting to their sudden seclusion. Then, as he poured more wine, the silence became tense and he had the feeling that they were fast becoming strangers.

He got up, went to the wall switch, and snapped off the two lamps. When he turned back, she was sitting stiffly on the edge of the three-quarter bed in the alcove. He went to her, kissed her, lingering over it until their breathing became shallow and fast and their hands began to glide and explore. They rose, still entwined, and she kicked off her shoes, instantly becoming shorter, then reached back for her zipper while he squirmed from his jacket and fumbled with shirt buttons. Then they laughed quietly, self-derisively, and stood back and in the ghostly light watched each other undress.

She was not at all like the girls from Vassar and Smith and Wellesley, who were either fiercely aggressive or mutely inert. She was more like a superbly graceful ballroom dancer who anticipates her partner's every movement, synchronizing every muscle, every region of flesh, all the while murmuring words of admiration and joy. And when it was over, when the orchestra had reached a crescendo and the cymbals had crashed, the music played on, softly now but with the promise of new and more meaningful melodies.

"You'll stay all night?"

"Certainly. I just quit school."

But he was on a plane to Boston the next afternoon, totally exhausted, totally broke, totally in love.

11

IT WAS A frantic time, those last few months in Harvard Business School. The course itself was enough to erode the stamina of a long-distance runner—which he had been at Yale—but to combine it with a frenetic bi-city love life was to invite self-destruction. But he hung in, shuttling between Cambridge and New York, transferring from her bed to a taxi to a plane, sometimes dosing himself with uppers, catching a few hours' sleep, appearing zombie-like in class, willing his mind to function, his hand to take notes, and later, often while wolfing a sandwich, translating the notes into long, pretentious papers.

She had failed to get the soap-opera role—it called for a flighty type and she appeared much too rational—but a day later had been signed for another off-Broadway production that she thought had a lot going for it. Constant rehearsals kept her grounded in Manhattan, but twice on weekends she was able to fly up, once to join him in a motel, the other time to meet and stay with his family in Boston. (They had taken to her instantly, his father's interest seeming a bit more than fatherly, his teenage sister practically deifying her—a New York *actress*!) Somehow he survived to get his degree in January and almost immediately went to work for the William Morris Agency, to whom he'd applied soon after the night she had mentioned it. Work and love, he thought, could now be conducted in a more orderly fashion.

He was wrong. The off-Broadway play had proved to be a sleeper, transformed by word of mouth into a must-see, and soon it was moved uptown to a theater near Times Square. At first Rick thought his enforced routine was fun: home at six to his one-room apartment on Tenth Street (they had decided it would be more exciting to live near each other but apart); a quick dinner followed by a three-hour nap, a shower, change of clothes, a subway rush to meet her as she emerged from the theater, then drinks and snacks at Sardi's. Always Sardi's. Because that was the hangout of actors and playwrights and producers and directors—from Hollywood as well as New York—and there was always the chance that someone with clout would exclaim, "Janice Powers! The part I've got, you were made for it!" (And it could easily happen because, though she appeared only briefly in three scenes, she'd been singled out for good notices.) But soon the relentless sameness began to pall, the brutal schedule to debilitate, and in time he was openly yawning at the caricatures of celebrities framed on the walls, and stifling his yawns when in the presence of flesh-and-blood models. On the night he failed to look up when Neil Simon came in, and later ignored a greeting (actually addressed to Janice) from David Merrick, he decided to revise his scenario.

So, once home from the office, he stayed there, Janice skipping Sardi's to come to his bed, or he to hers. The only full day they had together was Sunday. And by then they had too little energy left to do more than read the hefty *New York Times*, perhaps stroll to Sheridan Square for a couple of Bloody Marys, watch television, and of course make love. Well, what was wrong with that?

"What's wrong," she said, "is that we're not really *together*. We should be facing each other at breakfast. We should be using the same bathroom. You should be yelling at me for hanging things on doorknobs. I should be making sure you've got enough clean socks."

"Are you proposing holy wedlock?"

"No, I'm not. But I'm proposing we share the bad with the good—to make us closer."

"We were pretty close last night."

"Yes, true. But then, this morning, you had to leave early to go to your place and change clothes for the office. And all that time you could have been lying right beside me, or better still, all over me."

"Unshaved?"

"I want you unshaved."

"You're saying we should live together."

"Yes, that's what I'm saying."

They took a furnished place on Barrow Street, this one with a bedroom, and he found that she was right: there was a greater unity to their relationship, a sense of commitment bonded by a multiplicity of small sharings. After her show closed, their lives became almost normal, most of her jobs—modeling, commercials, an occasional role in a television drama—occurring in the daytime. Meanwhile, his job had brought him into contact with executives at Madden and Associates and eventually with Brooks himself, who one day invited him to lunch, and there persuaded him, with big money and straight talk, to join the agency as a senior vice-president. Soon after, she got her first offer from Hollywood, a supporting role, and was gone almost a month, keeping in touch with impassioned daily phone calls. Their reunion was tempestuous and he was almost glad she had gone, because for a while she was once again the girl who had flirted with him across the footlights.

But a change came over her as the trips to Hollywood became more frequent and more lucrative. It wasn't that she had a craving for stardom—she seemed quite satisfied to play the good and loyal friend, or the strong, level-headed wife of the hero's earthbound brother—it was simply that she became enamored of the celebrity way of life, the star-studded parties, the mandatory appearances at the Hollywood Bowl and the Dorothy Chandler Pavilion, the gossip at The Bistro and the Polo Lounge, the Sunday poolside drinking with actors whose names were emblazoned on the nation's marquees. Returning to New York, she was restless and often moody, a condition that could only be alleviated by joining trendy new friends at celebrity showcases like Elaine's and Studio 54.

Finally he protested. His ambition didn't allow for this amount of hedonism. He was tired of people energized by snorting coke from silver spoons or laid back by smoking grass, who constantly lived in a world insulated from reality. He wanted to stay home, and if they did go out, why not just the two of them, the way it used to be? They fought, recriminated, sulked, then, perhaps at four in the morning, reconciled in a sexual storm of released tensions that left them physically together but no closer in attitude. They were edging toward the precipice when they were yanked back by an unexpected intervention—she was pregnant.

They were married quietly in City Hall, the only celebrity present being Mayor Koch, whom they had come to know when Janice had appeared at a political benefit. After that, everything changed. She became subdued, serene, content to remain at home and contemplate the miracle of motherhood. When Scott arrived, they became even closer than in the beginning, their lives revolving around formulas and child-care books and concerns like maybe the back of his head was a bit flat and should he be taught to sleep on his stomach.

And then just about the time Scott was taking his first steps, it began again, slowly at first, then insidiously. They were back on the same old whirligig, spinning from party to party, event to event, punctuated by more of her absences in Hollywood and, once, a pre-Broadway tryout in New Haven of a sick dog of a play that died after five performances. Naturally they had a cook and a nursemaid for Scott, who must have thought that the entire world consisted of the Central Park Zoo and the lake and benches nearby, occupied by old people with despairing faces. Of course, by then they had moved uptown, into an East Side co-op apartment that looked more like a gallery than a home, where it was more convenient for friends to drop in, which they did incessantly, so that by the time Rick arrived from work he could count on being just another member of an impromptu party.

He stood it until the day she announced she was going on a roadshow revival of *A Chorus Line.* She would be gone six weeks, leaving the cast after its run in San Francisco. He was furious.

"You've already inked the contract?"

"Yes, right after lunch."

"Then *un*-ink it. Get on that phone right now and tell them you can't do it because you're opposed to divorce." He had never before even thought of the word.

"What! What are you saying?"

"Look it up. It means dissolution of a marriage."

"You're not being fair. I'm an actress. That means I act, whenever and wherever I get the chance."

"You're also a wife and, if you'll pardon the expression, a mother. Scott needs you. Ma Bell's not enough."

"Are you saying I don't love him?"

"Only according to schedule. He's a doll that you take out at certain times, then put back in its box. I know—I'm in the box next to his."

"Oh, what a terribly rotten thing to say. I adore Scott and you know it."

"Fine. Then you'll cancel the road trip."

"I won't!"

But she did, after shouting that he was a macho monster, a relic of the Dark Ages, a smug Boston Brahmin with a Harvard degree for paper-pushing, and then finally dissolving in tears. They patched it up, but the patches showed and they were uneasily aware that some sudden strain might rip them apart. She tried to avoid that by suggesting they vacate the milieu that seemed to be the real cause of their friction. So they moved to Central Park West, into an apartment not quite so large, which she was careful to furnish with pieces that looked like they were supposed to be sat on or leaned against. But Rick Bradley and Janice Powers were a sought-after couple now, and their escape proved illusory. The drop-ins were fewer but the invitations burgeoned, and once again they became caught up in the addictive pursuit of pleasureless pleasure.

No big happening, no sudden clash precipitated the end. It was arrived at simply by a cumulative discontent, a weariness of spirit, an escalating sense that life together had become an armed truce, a recognition that their attitudes and needs had become polarized— irrevocably, they decided. They ended it with neither a bang nor a whimper, but quietly, decently, generously.

And then, for Rick, in the depths of loneliness, cut off from friends, miserable in his role of weekend father, along had come Sara Vardon—lovely, shy, intelligent, a low-key version of the original and idealized Janice Powers who had introduced him to the wonders of being young and romantic and intensely alive. Sara, whose whole being had been centered on him, who wanted no other presence, no other stimulant, only his allegiance, which he had then been forced to withdraw. But he had not been able to withdraw his feelings for her, not yet, and he was tortured by the thought that he was bound to two women, more so perhaps to the one he had abandoned.

But now the phone on his desk rang, and it was Janice, speaking in the warm voice of long ago:

"Hi, am I interrupting anything?"

"Yes. I was thinking about you."

"Ah, you lovely man. Now I hate to tell you why I called. But you can just say no and that'll be fine with me."

"What is it?"

"I just got a call from an old friend. And before I knew it, I'd invited her to dinner tonight. But I can call back and say—"

"Someone I know?"

"Yes. And you always said you liked her. Maria Corliss."

"Maria! Great. Invite all the Marias you like, anytime. I thought she was in Europe."

"She was, with her son. He's been trying to make it as a film director. Well, he has this unfinished project, most of it shot, but the financing dried up. Maria finally got some more in Munich, from some German tax-shelter group. Now, she has decided to come home. I don't think she'll stay long—tonight, I mean."

"I hope she does."

"Well, I don't. I have some very interesting plans for us."

Ringing off, he thought for a minute about Maria Corliss. Not as a former movie star, but as Janice's good friend, the one person she had met in Hollywood who seemed to have her head on straight. It had been Maria who guided Janice through the cinematic thickets, advising her when to take a stand and when to yield, steering her clear of the lechers and the hustlers and the shoestring operators, always providing a sanctuary where Janice could simply be herself. Rick had been introduced to her on the phone, and when she came to New York he made a point of cultivating her, hoping to bring her even closer to Janice as a counterbalance to the exhibitionists who crowded their lives.

He recalled hearing somewhere that she had been rejuvenated

since their last meeting via cosmetic surgery in Switzerland and a beauty spa in Arizona. He only hoped that she had not permitted some guru to tamper with her inner self.

That she had not was evident the moment she entered their door. The same easy grace, the same girlish optimism, the same refreshing candor.

And the same self-mocking humor: "Please feel free to comment on my new face and figure. They cost a fortune and I'd like to hear I wasn't cheated."

The compliments were as sincere as they were lavish. With her tawny hair, taut creamy skin, and svelte body, she looked like she had stepped out of one of her movies from the late forties.

She played with Scott, delighting him with imitations of Big Bird and various Muppets and telling him a story about a mouse who kept an elephant for a pet. Then, with Scott off to bed, they settled down over martinis, reminisced, and brought each other up to date. She referred to their reconciliation only once, and briefly—"I'm glad you both recovered your sanity"—then quickly switched the subject to her travels in Europe in pursuit of movie dollars.

"Which brings me to the Cannes Film Festival," she said, looking at Rick. "I suppose you heard that I met Brooks Madden there."

"You did? He didn't mention it. But then, that was a quick business trip and he had a lot on his mind."

Maria lit a cigarette. "The fact is, for about twenty-four hours he had little else on his mind but me."

"You're joking," Janice said. "You mean you two actually—"

"Let's just say I found him very attractive."

"And it had to have been mutual," Rick said.

"It was—that is until he suspected that my only interest in him was as a backer for my son's film. Oh, it was all a stupid misunderstanding, started by a desk clerk at the Carlton. I won't bore you with it."

"Go ahead, bore us," Janice said. She was smiling mischievously, scenting a choice bit of gossip about her husband's saintly boss.

"All right, but only because I wish it could be straightened out. Josef—that's the desk clerk—phoned me one afternoon to say that the president of a big worldwide advertising agency had just arrived. According to Josef, the man represented a syndicate planning to invest in films. Naturally, I was interested—*extremely* interested when I heard that the man's name was Brooks Madden. I'd often heard you two speak of him, so I figured I had the perfect entree— mutual friends, welcome to Cannes, that sort of thing."

"So you called him," Rick said.

"Yes, and we had drinks, toured the festival, had dinner. And I found him a delightful companion, warm and real."

"And lonely," Janice said.

"We were both lonely," Maria said quietly. "Anyway, the next day we were supposed to have dinner with my son and then screen his film. My intention then was to ask Brooks quite frankly if he thought it would be a worthwhile investment. Believe me, at that point I was much more intrigued by him than by his capital."

"He must have known that," Rick said. "He's a pretty perceptive guy."

"He'd have known it, I think, if I'd had the chance to talk to him. But I couldn't. About an hour before we were to meet, he had a note delivered to me. It said he was sorry but he had to rush back to New York on urgent business. Later, I talked to Josef. From what I gathered, I could only surmise that Brooks thought I'd cold-blood-edly pursued him for money."

"Did you write and explain?" Janice asked.

"I couldn't see what good it would do. It was true that my original purpose was to persuade him to invest. Knowing that, he'd go on believing that what happened between us was designed to serve that purpose, especially when it all went so fast."

Rick said, "Does he still interest you?"

"Yes."

"Then let me see if I can help."

"Thanks, Rick, but I'd rather you didn't. He'd surely suspect me of more connivance. Someday, perhaps, we'll meet again and we'll talk about it."

There was a silence. Then Rick said, "You found out, of course, that his trip had nothing to do with buying into movies."

"No, isn't that why he wanted to see Harry Dalton?"

"God, no. He went there to pitch for Dalton's airline, Transcon. Dalton had about decided to move it to another agency and Brooks was jockeying for the inside track."

"Well, I hope he was successful."

Rick smiled ruefully. "Look, I shouldn't let this out. Brooks told me in confidence because it's so damned embarrassing to him. But all right. The fact is, you weren't the only one who misunderstood why he was in Cannes. Dalton was right along with you, but for much bigger numbers."

"You mean Harry thought—"

"The same as you, that Brooks was fronting for a movie syndicate. The rumor had really traveled. Dalton got hold of Brooks and spilled all his wild plans, which included a lot more than movies. When he finished and Brooks revealed why he was really there, Dalton flipped. He told Brooks that he'd have nothing to do with him or his agency and then stomped out."

"Oh, this is too much. It's like one of those awful old comedies of mistaken identity."

Rick regarded her curiously. "You sound like you know Harry Dalton."

She bowed her head. "Guilty."

Janice exchanged a look with Rick, then said, "How well, Maria?"

Maria affected a demure smile. "Are you asking me to bare my lurid past?"

"She is," Rick said.

"To quote Louella Parsons," Maria said, "I was his 'constant companion.' That was a long time ago. Now we're simply friends."

Rick squinted an eye. "Friends enough to ask him a favor?"

Maria said, "If the favor was for you, yes."

Before dinner was served, Maria had agreed to ask Harry Dalton to attend the agency's presentation. She answered Rick's thanks with a wistful smile, then said, "But I'm not doing it for you, Rick. I'm doing it for a very fine gentleman named Brooks Madden."

Late Friday afternoon Sara made her presentation to Brooks Madden, Rick Bradley, and Lou Kahn. When she finished, the hush in Rick's office seemed to vibrate.

Finally Lou Kahn said, "Do we flip for who leads the snake dance?"

Rick looked at him, then at Sara, standing straight beside the television set. "It's terrific," he said.

"Absolutely," Brooks said. "No question about it. It's the kind of thing that would give us a big edge."

"But," Sara said.

Rick nodded. "But, as you said, it won't mean a thing unless Harry Dalton sees it."

"Right. The other day you seemed optimistic."

"I still haven't gotten any word."

"Well," said Kahn, "you've got till Tuesday. Meanwhile, I'll get the other stuff together in case Dalton's a no-show."

Sara gave Rick an acid smile. "At least I can use this for a sample when I look for another job."

There were more compliments, then Sara and Lou Kahn left.

Brooks said, "Listen, Rick, I hope she didn't mean that, about another job. The girl's sensational."

"I know."

The phone rang. As Rick picked it up, Brooks moved to the window and stared gloomily down at Madison Avenue. He turned abruptly when he heard the receiver slam and Rick exclaim, "By God, she did it!"

"Who did what?"

"A friend—it doesn't matter. That was Transcon's ad director, Jim Westbrook. He's astonished to inform us that the great Harry Dalton has consented to come!"

"Hey!"

"He'll give us thirty minutes, no more."

"That's enough. We'll go with this one idea." Brooks snorted a laugh. "Maybe Sara Vardon can wipe out my dumb performance in Cannes."

Sara wouldn't have had the chance, thought Rick, but for Maria Corliss. He wasn't ready yet to tell that to Brooks Madden, at least not until after the presentation.

12

SARA VARDON's first impression of Harry Dalton, as he strode into Rick's office, was of an overgrown boy forced to attend his kid sister's birthday party. His big tanned face was sullen, his manner remote, his appearance careless (suit wrinkled, tie askew, black curly hair looking finger-combed). In contrast, his advertising director, Jim Westbrook, a plump, scrubbed-pink man flashing enormous eyeglasses, appeared serene and ingratiating, and dapper enough to satisfy the brothers Brooks.

Confronting them, Sara felt a twinge of fear. For an instant she imagined herself the girl she had been in school, refusing the offer of class valedictorian because she knew she would collapse while facing her peers and their parents, rejecting the drama society—though she yearned to join—because the only role she could have played would have been that of a mute idiot. She dismissed the thoughts, assuring herself that she was simply reacting reflexively to the remnants of a discarded personality that would vanish once she took charge. Please, please, let that be true!

Rick and Westbrook handled the introductions. Dalton honored Sara with a slight smile, a handgrip, and a look of mild curiosity. Lou Kahn and Rick got half-salutes. Brooks got a cool stare and a nod.

"Where do I sit?" Dalton said to Rick.

"There, if that's agreeable." Rick indicated a green leather easy chair in front of his desk, facing the twenty-four-inch television set. "Jim, if you'll take the one next to it."

They sat, Westbrook leaning back, pudgy hands folded across his vest, Dalton making a trough of the chair's edge, his body thrust forward, thick arms planted on his thighs. He twisted a hairy wrist and stared at his watch.

"It's now exactly three thirty-two," Rick said, smiling. "That leaves us twenty-eight minutes."

Dalton grunted.

Westbrook chuckled. "More like twenty minutes, Rick, by the time we walk to the conference room and you set up all the goodies."

"We're doing it here, Jim. All on that box, plus live commentary." He looked at Dalton, whose glance swept past Brooks and Lou Kahn, both seated off to the side, and fastened on Sara standing beside the television set. "Mr. Dalton, I won't waste time telling you what clients we serve, the number of offices we have, how many people we employ, and so on. Jim has all that sort of information."

"Do I ever!" said Westbrook.

"You just lost another minute," Dalton said. He rubbed impatiently at his heavy jaw.

Rick contemplated him for a moment, then turned to Sara. "You're on," he said.

Sara picked up the remote-control unit from the top of the television set, stepped to the side, and pressed a button. The screen burst from black to a color shot of a soaring plane. Ecstatic voices rose in singing accompaniment: *"Fly the friendly skies—of United!"*

She let it run for ten seconds while she gazed directly at Harry Dalton. His eyelids flickered and his body seemed to stiffen. Jim Westbrook adjusted his huge glasses, then flicked at a lapel.

"Music," Sara said.

She pushed a button and the scene cut to another plane in flight. More singing voices: *"We're American Airlines, doing what we do best!"*

Dalton's jaw flexed. Westbrook gave a dry cough.

"Music," Sara said.

She punched to a Pan Am plane. Voices: *"Pan Am-m-m-m!"*

"Music," Sara said.

To a Delta plane. Voices: *"Delta's ready when you-u-u are!"*

"Music."

TWA. Voices: *"TWA-A-A-A!"*

"Music."

And so on, a dozen planes from as many airlines, floating aloft against cloudless blue skies, all seemingly powered by big-band rhythm and proud voices proclaiming their majesty.

"Music, music, music," said Sara, and snapped off the set. "And good music—all of it happy, most of it memorable. We're not against it." She smiled. "But we do seriously question whether it's the best way to persuade people to fly a particular airline. If that were true, why not just hire the number-one composer, the number-one band, the number-one singing group, and battle it out at Carnegie Hall?"

Dalton appeared fascinated, but not by what he'd seen and heard—he was staring at her cleavage, his eyes seeming to penetrate the aqua silk cinching her breasts.

Westbrook gave a knowing laugh and hunched forward. "But of course music's only a part of it," he said. "A signature, for memorability."

"Right," Sara said, widening her smile. "The battle's fought with a number of other weapons." She snapped the remote-control button. "This, for example."

The screen came alive with beautiful stewardesses strolling about the plane, handing out pillows, serving drinks, chatting with children.

"Now that's the airline to pick. Terrific companions all the way. Glamorous, efficient, but also very human. The only problem is"—she hit the button, cutting to an almost identical scene—"the competition's got flight attendants that look just as good, maybe better if you prefer the uniform." Now she pushed the button at three-second intervals, producing a montage of smiling beauties coddling passengers. Then the screen went to black.

"Confusing, isn't it? How can you create a preference when every airline begins to look the same?" She paused. "Well, how about food? That's the way to the heart."

Now a series of fast cuts, alternating lifts from TV commercials with page ads from glossy magazines, all portraying sumptuous gourmet meals.

"Again, why make a choice? No matter whose planes you fly, you'll think you're dining at Maxim's." Another pause. "So let's try something else. Comfort. People hate to be cramped, some even get claustrophobic. Well, not to worry . . ."

Shots of spacious interiors. Passengers blissfully stretching out, roaming the aisles, conversing in groups.

"Those wide-body planes are great. It's just too bad that every long-distance airline has them. Oh, well, there's always the movie . . ."

Shot of passengers wearing headsets and observing a small screen.

"Damn! Already seen it! Why must they show month-old films?"

Fade to black. She snapped off the set.

Dalton was now eyeing her legs. Westbrook was regarding her indulgently, as though she were a precocious child.

She was suddenly struck full force by the doubt that had merely threatened during all her hours of preparation, while digging out the right film, viewing it on a large screen and then on the Movieola, while editing, cutting, splicing, writing. What she was showing them was too simple. They—Westbrook anyway—were accustomed to presentations that included slide projections of charts defining share of market, competitive expenditures, demographic analyses, the whole arcane *schmeer* designed to show expertise and called by some agencies "positioning the company." Then there would be a dizzying display of proposed TV commercials, print ads, outdoor billboards, folders, special promotions—a total "package" right down to lapel buttons to be worn by ticket clerks.

Sara had none of that, not a single chart or ad or gimmick. What she did have was a unifying idea, dependent for acceptance on the ability of Dalton, and perhaps Westbrook, to visualize how it could be directed into a forceful advertising vehicle. What's more, her presentation now seemed much too brief—no longer than twenty minutes. It would be forgotten if only because it had been given too little time to penetrate.

All this was transmitted by her brain in the fraction of an instant. But before it could cripple her will, before it could destroy her self-assurance, another series of mental impulses evoked a meeting still talked about along Madison Avenue. A creative director stood before the principals of a company that manufactured an electric razor. He drew from his pocket a ripe, fuzzy peach. Holding it aloft with one hand, he reached with the other for the electric razor that was the pride of everyone assembled. Then he shaved the peach. "Gentle," he said. Next he produced a hairbrush and proceeded to shave the bristles. "But tough." He sat down and said, "Gentlemen, I have just presented your new advertising campaign." Standing ovation.

Brief. Simple. Dramatic. She felt a surge of confidence. And of wonder. Was this really she, standing firmly, speaking clearly and positively, totally unintimidated by the mighty Harry Dalton?

"I'm sure that I've demonstrated nothing you don't already know. Most airline advertising is look-alike advertising, me-too advertising, advertising that, except for certain showy effects, makes it all but impossible to distinguish one airline from another. But that's not the worst of it. The worst of it is that the people you're out to convince too often simply don't believe you. I hope that doesn't offend you. It shouldn't. This lack of belief applies to the advertising of almost any product you can mention."

"I gather you people know how to make us sound like the word of God," Dalton said.

She looked at him amiably, feeling now like a ringmaster about to confront the most recalcitrant tiger. "Would you settle for one of His temporal representatives?"

At last he seemed to smile—a small hook at the corner of his mouth—but it could have been a sneer. "Don't tell me you've turned the video saint into a huckster?"

"Who?"

"Walter Cronkite."

She gave a light laugh. "Well, we *do* propose that your advertising have a spokesman. Not Cronkite but—"

"An *actor*?" Westbrook said, frowning. "They're all over the tube—Hope, Garner, Olivier, just about everybody but Redford. Now if you could get *him*—"

"We recommend someone better than Redford, Mr. Westbrook. Better, that is, for your purpose, which is to create belief. The man we—"

Rick cut in gently: "I think it's time they met him, Sara."

She nodded, smiled at Dalton, and pressed the control.

The screen erupted with a scene of carnage—smoke swirling over a landscape littered with uprooted trees, overturned vehicles, burning buildings, ragged men and women milling about in panic. The camera, obviously hand-held, moved in on a large man clad in a jumpsuit, surrounded by a pleading mob. The man's lips were moving but there was no sound, just as there were no background sounds.

"This man," said Sara, "had a difference of opinion with certain American bureaucrats in Saigon. It seems he had the effrontery to actually believe that our Vietnamese allies should be rescued."

Sara gazed at Dalton. He was no longer interested in her endowments. He had jerked straight up, eyes riveted on the screen. Westbrook's reaction was identical.

Sara snapped on the audio. The room became strident with shouts and wails, the roar of engines, the crackle of distant gunfire. Then the voice of the man in the jumpsuit was picked up, harsh and impatient, but controlled:

"I don't give a goddamn about the ambassador. And that goes for his flunkies. They're not stopping me. I'm getting these people out. For Christsake, they worked for us, trusted us. Now our government is saying, so sorry, but fuck you. Go ahead, quote me. But also get the hell out of my way."

Sara said, "That was telecast, with a few bleeps, in 1973." She paused for comment. There was none. Both men were transfixed by the picture on the screen, now silent and frozen.

Sara went on: "About a year later, there was an interesting exchange of views in our nation's capital."

She flipped to a stop-action scene of a large hearing room packed with newsmen, spectators, five senators, and a witness.

"For once," Sara said, "a United States Senator was allowed to hear what one American citizen really thought."

She brought the scene alive as it cut back and forth between a dour senator and an equally dour witness:

WITNESS: Senator, you say my discount plan is unfair to the competition. The fact is, if they match me, they'll make more money because they'll get more customers.

SENATOR: Your competition thinks otherwise.

WITNESS: My competition also thinks the earth is flat. But the hell with my competitors. How about the *people*? I thought that's who you're supposed to represent.

SENATOR: You're being contemptuous.

WITNESS: You catch on fast, Senator. Right now I'm the most contemptuous man in the United States. So fine me, throw me in the slammer. That way you'll be telling the American people that you're in favor of price gouging, that you don't give a damn that they're being robbed blind so long as the fat cats get fatter.

Now Sara did not pause. (Dalton and Westbrook looked as though they'd hardened into concrete.) She flipped to a scene of a large banquet.

"Then there was the address to the Commonwealth Club of San Francisco. The affluent diners received some unexpected—and many thought rude—views on business morality."

She cut to the rostrum, then zeroed in on the scowling speaker. His voice was accusing:

"We've gotten to the point where the only question businessmen want answered is, will it sell? Why worry if a house starts falling apart in ten years? Why give a damn if a car breaks down the day after the warranty expires? Why tell the diner that the fresh trout he ordered is really prefrozen? Don't conduct research to make things better—do it to make sure that razor blades and shoes and washing machines and all kinds of gadgets wear out fast. I say it's time we started thinking of that old cabinetmaker who'd constructed a desk and was finishing off the inside of the drawers. A kid watching said, 'Why bother with the inside? Who'll ever know?' The old man, a proud man, looked at him and said, 'I will.'"

"And," said Sara, "I'm sure you recall the interview by Mike Wallace on '60 Minutes.' There was a rumor, said Wallace, that his subject might run for public office. How about it?" (Tight closeup of subject, eyes pained, lips curled.) "This was the response."

"Look, I won't work with people unless I can believe what they say. That eliminates politicians. Besides, most of 'em haven't got the brains of a turkey. I wouldn't hire one to stuff cotton in pill bottles."

Freeze frame.

"And finally," said Sara, "another question from Wallace." Live action.

WALLACE: We're always hearing that the key to success is hard work. Granting there's some truth there, is that really the secret of making it?

SUBJECT: No.

WALLACE: Then what is?

SUBJECT: Giving a buck's worth of value for a buck.

Sara hit the button that froze the image on the screen, a face that in its strength, its determination, its defiance of opposition suddenly reminded her of Karsh's famous "bulldog" portrait of Winston Churchill.

She hoped that Harry Dalton, staring at this portrait of himself, had the same impression.

"Mr. Dalton," Sara said, "I saw that show on the night it ran. And when you said, 'a buck's worth of value for a buck,' you came across as the kind of man who would deliver just that. But I can't expect you to take my word for it—after all, we're trying to get your business. But I do ask you to accept the findings of a survey we conducted yesterday afternoon and last night."

"A telephone survey?" Westbrook asked.

"A very live survey. We rented a theater and offered free admission to a feature film. The only condition was that the audience also view excerpts from certain TV news films, then fill out a questionnaire. The films you just saw were included, along with others portraying well-known people who had something important to say. We even used a segment from an old interview with Einstein. More than two hundred people attended the afternoon performance. Almost five hundred were there in the evening."

Westbrook glanced at Dalton, who was still staring at his screen image, then gave Sara a skeptical smile. "You couldn't possibly have processed and tabulated the opinions of seven hundred people in that short a time."

"We had researchers working all night. But you're right, we haven't tabulated them all, only about a quarter, a random sample of almost two hundred viewers." She stepped to Rick's desk and came back with a small stack of photocopies. "Tomorrow we'll send you the complete survey. But the preliminary results are so over-whelming as to seem conclusive. Here are a few. Ninety-eight percent of the respondents scored Mr. Dalton as being exceptionally truthful—second only to Einstein, who scored a ninety-nine. Ninety-six percent or better scored Mr. Dalton as being the most fearless, the most determined, the most conscientious, the most enterprising, the most . . . but I won't go on lest"—she grinned at Dalton—"we turn you off out of sheer embarrassment."

Dalton shifted his eyes, gave her a deadpan look, and growled, "Who's embarrassed?"

Laughter. Rick got up and handed copies of the preliminary survey to Dalton and Westbrook.

Sara said, "It's enough to say that this is an incredible perfor-mance. Is it any wonder, then, that we enthusiastically recommend that Mr. Harry Dalton be featured in the media as the spokesman for Transcon Airlines?"

Westbrook darted a look at Dalton. Seeing no reaction, he said, "All well and good, but Mr. Dalton is a very busy man."

"We're keenly aware of that. So we'd schedule shootings accord-ing to Mr. Dalton's convenience, taking the print photos at the same sessions. We'd also provide a private dressing room—a large, well-furnished trailer, equipped with every type of communication device, so that other business could be conducted."

Westbrook smiled. "Oh, I'm sure the studio could provide an office."

"Except that we don't want the usual studio setup. If the commercial dealt with plane maintenance, we'd want Mr. Dalton talking while touring a maintenance shop. We'd want him inside a plane, or standing on the tarmac, or maybe even at a ticket counter. The image we'd want to convey would be the true image—a man who cares enough about his company and the people who ride his planes to involve himself personally in every phase of the operation. Not a manicured, Gucci-dressed executive in an ivory tower, but a man ready to pull on coveralls and get grease under his fingernails if it will better serve the flying public. The employment of this one believable, highly respected man in television, radio, print, billboards, would integrate your advertising, adding greatly to its impact. It would make it unique, separate and distinct from all other airline advertising, and much more persuasive. It would—"

Her mouth snapped shut. Harry Dalton had stood up and was consulting his watch.

Dead silence.

Dalton gazed straight through her and gave a nod. "You did a good job. Sorry, but now I've got to leave." He turned his big head and seemed to address the room. "Thank you. You'll be hearing from us."

He strode out, followed by Westbrook, who smiled rather dazedly and murmured an inclusive goodbye.

13

"YOU WERE sensational," Lou Kahn said.

"Sara, you amazed me," Rick said.

"Damned proud of you," Brooks said.

She looked at them, her mouth twisted in a small, cynical smile. "Thank you. Now let's say what we're all thinking." Their eyebrows rose inquiringly. "We won't get the business."

"Oh, come on," Brooks said, "there's no reason to say that."

"I hope you didn't think they'd decide right on the spot," Rick said. "They've got to talk it over."

"It bombed," Sara said. "Weren't you watching that big moose? First he ogled me like I was about to do a strip. When I didn't, he acted like I was reading him the phone book."

"Not when you showed the film clips," Lou said.

"Certainly not. He loves to look at himself. The guy's a ham."

Rick smiled. "Let's hope so. Here's his chance to ham it up all over the tube."

"That's another thing," Sara said. "He probably thinks we don't really believe in this campaign, that the only reason we presented it was to hook him through his vanity."

"I'm sure that wasn't his impression."

"Well, if it wasn't, I'm sure his smart-ass friend will suggest it. In Dalton's book, that will make us whores."

She saw Brooks wince. Probably, she thought, because he feared this was a repetition of the Cannes disaster.

"Listen," he said, "there's no sense trying to predict it. You gave a fine, honest presentation. Now let's all go into my office and have a drink on it."

It was a few doors away, the corner one. Six windows, Sara noted, aware that the number of windows, like military stripes, was a measure of rank. (She was a two-window person.) The decor was austere, Colonial-style hard maple, including the large desk uncluttered by papers. (Everyone knew that Brooks Madden disliked memos, preferring face-to-face talk.) He went to a tall cabinet and dropped the front panel, revealing a well-stocked bar complete with small refrigerator. He insisted on pouring the drinks himself, the three men taking scotch, she a vodka and tonic. Lou Kahn drank his quickly and left, saying he had to look at an experimental campaign.

Brooks pressed another drink on them, then began talking nostalgically about the old days of radio, before television, when the agencies, not the networks, controlled the shows. "Better shows," he said, and cited "Fibber McGee and Molly," "Amos 'n' Andy," "The Great Gildersleeve," "The Goldbergs," "Lux Radio Theater," and stars like Jack Benny, Bob Hope, Fred Allen, Eddie Cantor, Edgar Bergen and Charlie McCarthy. Listening, Sara thought how rooted he was in another era, one totally unlike the present, with its sex and violence, instant replays, satellite transmitters. Was Brooks Madden really qualified to be chief executive officer, the final decision-maker, of a modern advertising agency? All she had to do was look at Rick Bradley to get the answer. Now *there* was a man who was with it.

The thought produced a vague yearning sensation, sharpening as Rick rose to leave. She beat him to it, thanking Brooks and smiling away further compliments as she backed out into the now-deserted secretarial area.

She went to the reception lobby, picked up the phone on the unattended desk, and dialed the time. She listened to the mechanical voice for two minutes and nine seconds before Rick appeared.

She gave him a nod, kept an eye on the illuminated numbers above the elevators, and, when one approached, hung up and joined Rick. They rode down in a silence shared by three other occupants.

On the street, Rick said good night, then walked to the curb and hailed a taxi. She came up beside him as the door sprung open.

"How about a lift?"

He swung around, startled. "Well—"

"You can drop me at Fifty-ninth Street. It's an easy walk from there."

"Sure. Get in."

As soon as they settled inside, he began to speak. But not about her. About anything *but* her: the crowded avenue, the shortening days, the fall fashions in the store windows. And Brooks—Brooks was good for almost five crawling blocks. A fine man. A lonely man. A man whose home was really the office. Why, right now he was probably wandering from floor to floor, awed by all he had. . . .

"You've decided you're just not going to talk about it," she said.

He stared at her, then spoke gently. "I thought it had all been said, Sara."

She said, without recrimination, "Your side, Rick. Not mine."

Empathy saddened his eyes. "I think I understand your feelings."

"You mean that I'm outraged and bitter?"

"Yes, and you should be."

She smiled. "Well, I'm not."

He looked at her with surprised relief. "I'm glad of that, Sara."

"The day you left, I hated you. And the day after. Then I began to see there was nothing else you could do. You'd had only months with me, but years with her." She paused. "And then there was Scott."

"Yes, it gets complicated."

"It would be a lot less complicated if you could convince yourself of one thing."

"What's that?"

"That you no longer love me."

His head went back, then turned as he gazed out the window. He said nothing.

"*Are* you convinced?"

"Of course not." His tone was now harsh, almost savage. "But that's not the point, is it—to convince myself I don't love you?"

"What is, then?"

"To get over it. To reach a point where we can still be friends but—"

"But nothing else?"

"Nothing else would work."

She lurched forward as the taxi braked to a sudden stop. Looking past Rick, she saw her own apartment building.

"I gave him this address," Rick said. "I didn't want you to have to walk."

She felt a ripple of triumph—he was concerned about her. "Why not come in?" she said. "We'll have a drink to friendship."

He helped her out before saying, "Thanks, Sara. But I'll have to take a rain check."

"Until when?"

"Until I can be sure that's all we are—friends."

He smiled and got back in the taxi. She stood there as the door slammed, then watched as the taxi gunned away.

Pouring the vodka, she was suddenly struck by a spastic shaking. She jittered the glass to her mouth, emptied it, shook another drink from the bottle, grasped the glass in both hands, and paced erratically around the room, pausing only to gulp the stinging liquid. She was afraid to sit down, afraid that if she relaxed the muscular tension too quickly she would scream.

Her first thought was that some area of her brain, weakened by Dr. Kloster's probings, had given way. But then, as the alcohol began its sedation, freeing her mind to think, she realized she was suffering no more than a nervous reaction to a week of constant pressure. The trauma of Rick's sudden departure. The day-and-night and weekend work on the presentation. The presentation itself, only a short while ago, before two men who had a clock on her and who had practically sat on their hands.

All of that had loaded the inner gun. It needed only Rick's presence beside her as they taxied up the avenue in twilight, as they had done so often before, to squeeze the trigger. And there was something else, an incendiary something that enveloped her body and now began to gather in her loins. The feeling had teased at her for a week but had been sublimated by the creative demands of her work. No longer could she deny it, nor did she wish to.

She poured another drink, then, with rising anticipation, took it to the bathroom and set it on a corner of the tub. She ran the hot water full force, added bath oil, and, as the room clouded with steam, stripped off her clothes. Slipping into the scorching water, she gasped, as much from pleasure as from pain. For a while she simply lay there, her skin tantalized by the mass of sensuous bubbles. Then she reached for her drink, sipped at it, deliberately willed Rick from her mind, and replaced him with a shadowy, anonymous figure perceived only as an obscene voice with overpowering genitals. She was lost in fantasy, her hands became his hands as they stroked her breasts, bringing her nipples erect, then descended to the convergence of her thighs.

And suddenly there was a splash and a heaving wave of bubbles and she was sitting up straight, moaning plaintively, "Oh, no, no, not tonight, not like this."

What she needed, lusted for, was a real live man, a partner with strong arms and legs, a ravenous mouth, chest coarse with hair, muscles ridged in his belly, genitals hard and relentless. Not this. Not this ghostly confection that would vanish even before the last drop of passion had been spent.

She stood up, water and bubbles spewing to the floor. Getting out, she wrapped herself in a white terry cloth robe, then went to her bedroom closet and examined her wardrobe.

Her eyes searched for something lascivious. She hoped not to linger very long at the singles bar before the action began.

His name was Eddie, he said. Eddie Baron. He was dark, thick-haired, muscular, and wore a pale-blue, European-cut jacket over a white shirt unbuttoned far enough to display a hirsute chest.

"I'm Jennifer," she said. "Jennifer Ralston."

"Nice name," he said, hiking up the stool beside her. "You made it here before?"

"This is my first time."

"Thought so. I'd of noticed." He glanced at her satin shocking-pink dress that bared her white shoulders and midriff, the skirt drifting in folds to her ankles.

"I'm supposed to be here with a man," she said.

"He's late?"

"No. At the last minute, he got sick. There I was all dressed, so I decided to come anyway. Just for one drink."

"Let's try for two." He smiled at her as he signaled a green-coated man behind the circular bar.

"Coming up, Mr. Baron," the bartender said. So she knew he had given his true name.

"Just one more," she said. "Then I really must go."

His eyes, looking like licorice drops in the pale-blue light, glinted sardonically. "Funny thing. That guy who got sick. Well, he called me, and you know what he said?"

"What?"

"He said that a beautiful girl named Jennifer Ralston was coming in here and I was to take care of her and show her a really good time."

"And you said?"

"I said, what the hell, anything for a friend."

They both laughed, and the drinks came—which he paid for with a fifty-dollar bill—and she knew that everything would work out just fine.

It had all been so easy. The moment she walked through the door the blow-dried heads swung around as though she'd fired a pistol. As soon as she sat down, the eye contact began—the eager stare, the blasé scrutiny from beneath heavy lids, the stony macho inspection, the furtive leer. But this one, this Eddie Baron, had simply skipped the ocular preamble. With a white grin and a tilt of his glass, he had jumped up, stalked around the bar, and staked his claim.

And, she thought, he had the credentials. The man reeked of sex. It flashed from his eyes, dripped from his lips, rose from his pores. He came on like a ram in rutting season, aroused by the scent of venereal heat, ready to lock horns with any challenger.

"My God," he was saying, flinging out a hand, "I just met you and already you're driving me crazy!"

"Please, not in public."

"To hell with public. Take off your shoes and I'll kiss your feet.

Stretch out on the bar and I'll give you a massage. How are you for Rolfing? Or peacock feathers? Yeah, that's it, peacock feathers. Let's go buy some peacock feathers."

He was laughing, laughing her toward a bed. And she was laughing too, her thoughts rushing in the same direction. And inside her was this astonishing urge, insistent, demanding, threatening at any moment to erupt.

"It's getting so crowded," she said.

"Too crowded."

"And so noisy. That music!"

"You want to go where it's not crowded?"

"That might be nice."

"And where the music's any way you want it?"

"Fine. But where?"

"I know just the place."

The place was a second-floor walkup apartment on West Forty-ninth Street, with white shag carpeting, art deco furnishings, and an elaborate stereo setup that surrounded them with sultry, slow-beat rhythms. Little time was spent on preliminaries—a drink, a cigarette, a long experimental kiss, soon accompanied by hands frantically searching and finding.

While still in the living room they all but ripped off each other's clothes, and when they reached the bed, a king-size playground of purple sheets and brass-barred headboard, she had gasped through her first orgasm. From then on, it was she who was in control. She became like an enthusiastic and admiring coach putting a star athlete through his paces to see how far he could extend himself. *There, right there, oh, that's wonderful. Oh, no, no, don't stop, keep doing it, yes, like that, ahhhh. . . .* And on and on through the night, punctuated by brief intervals of shallow sleep. Innovative, vora-cious, insatiable, a compendium of all the libidinous acts perpe-trated in mutual hostility and euphemized as "making love."

And when, in the milky dawn, she slipped from the bed, pausing to observe Eddie Baron's gaunt, stubbled face and his body—now flaccid in what appeared to be terminal sleep—she enjoyed a deli-cious sense of victory. Out on the deserted street, seeing the born-again sun glinting from the spire of the Chrysler Building, striding toward a slate-colored sky turning blue, her whole being felt charged with energy and a sense of exhilaration.

She picked up a taxi on Broadway, the driver eyeing her as though she were a neophyte whore from Minnesota, and twenty minutes later she was again immersed in hot water, her flesh garnished with bubbles. But this time the purpose was therapeutic, to bring her down from the manic high that kept prompting her to streak through the streets shouting joyous obscenities.

Oh, thank God, she thought, at last she was truly free. Not free of Rick, any more than he was free of her, but liberated from inhibitions and shame and guilt—all the artificial barriers that so often denied access to pleasure and personal gain.

She cared not how it had happened. It was enough to know that she could indulge herself outrageously and not suffer pain.

She arrived at the office a half-hour late and was greeted by the ringing phone.

"Oh, you're there, Sara," Rick said.

"I just walked in." Why try to cover her lateness?

"Then you're still standing?"

"Yes. Does it matter?"

"It might. Better sit down."

She rounded the desk and sat. "What is it? Are you demoting me to the mail room?"

"I just got a call from Jim Westbrook. I thought you should be the first to know."

"Oh, that. Don't spare me. After all, I watched it go down the tubes. Remember?"

"Well, look again. Transcon Airlines is now a client of Madden and Associates."

"What! Oh, no, I can't believe—"

"It's a fact. We take over immediately."

"But Dalton—the way he acted, like he wasn't there."

"Jim explained that. Dalton was stunned. He couldn't understand why he'd never thought of beating the drum for his own airline. And it's more than the airline. If he can establish himself with the public as the guy in the white hat, he'll swing a lot of support for his other projects. The more he thought about it, the higher he got. He called Westbrook at seven this morning and told him to hire us."

"Maybe I should go downstairs and get drunk."

"Sure. Hang it on the company. Anyway, you were the star and you can be damned sure you'll get the recognition you deserve. Look, Brooks just walked in. We'll get back to you."

The news sped swiftly. Ten minutes later, people started dropping in—copywriters, art directors, account executives, secretaries—bubbling with congratulations. ("Imagine! Wordwoman knocks over Harry Dalton!") Lou Kahn appeared, solemnly stroked his beard, then dropped to his knees and salaamed. Brooks Madden, his face one big Irish grin, slipped quietly to her side, gave her a fatherly pat, and announced, "She showed the old pros how it's done. Champagne at five, outside my office."

Then the phone started ringing. *Advertising Age* wanted an interview. So did *Business Week* and *Time* and *Newsweek* and *The New York Times* and the *Wall Street Journal*. (She took the reporters' names, said she'd call back.)

And then, after a Bloody Mary lunch with Lou Kahn, after collapsing from exhaustion at her desk, a final phone call:

"Miss Vardon?" A woman's voice, precise and cool.

"Yes."

"One moment. Mr. Dalton is on the line." Was there an inflection of displeasure in the woman's voice?

"Sara? Harry Dalton. I wanted you to know personally that you gave one hell of a presentation. But you know that. Otherwise you wouldn't have got the business. I hope Madden appreciates you."

"Thank you, Mr. Dalton, you're very thoughtful. As for Mr. Madden, he's always generous about giving credit."

"In your case, he'd better be. Okay, just wanted you to know. I'll see you in San Francisco next week."

"San Francisco? Next week?"

"For the first shooting. At S.F. International. So! *That* they didn't tell you. Well, I will. I gave your agency the account on one condition—that Sara Vardon be there every time a commercial is shot."

"I'm overwhelmed." It was true.

"I also told Jim Westbrook to pass on something else. It may interest you."

"I'm sure it will."

"I said that you should be running the joint."

Later, she thought about his words, tried to laugh them away, but they stuck in her brain.

Book Two

14

HARRY DALTON, dressed in coveralls, climbed down from the wing of the 747, peered into the glaring lights, and said, "Don't print that."

The director, a young man in T-shirt, blue jeans, and sneakers, ran a hand through his close-cropped hair—the first sign of the exasperation that had been building all afternoon. He spoke in a restrained voice. "It looked right on from here, Mr. Dalton."

"Kill it." Dalton squinted beyond him to where Sara stood several yards behind the camera. In her teal-blue designer jumpsuit, she struck Dalton as being ridiculously out of place in the cavernous maintenance hangar. "Kill it all," he said.

She smiled and said to the director, "Let's wrap it for today, Steve."

In front of her, Thea Roland sprang from a canvas chair and fetched a towel to wipe the sheen from Dalton's face. He waved her away and stripped off his coveralls, exposing gray slacks and a dark sport shirt.

"But you were wonderful, Harry," Thea said.

"Bullshit." He strode past her, shook his big head at the camera crew, growled, "It's me, not you," and came up to Sara, who continued to smile.

"It *is* bullshit, isn't it?" she said.

He scowled at her. "You sound like you expected it."

She nodded and said to the director, "I'll call you later, Steve." Then, to Dalton, "I think we'd better talk about it."

Thea joined them, her face stolid as she contemplated Sara. "*Wasn't* he good, Miss Vardon?"

"Please call me Sara."

"Sara, then. Wasn't he—"

"No."

Dalton exploded a laugh. "Well, Thea, you can't say she's evasive."

Thea's eyes sparked. "No, Harry, just wrong."

Sara ignored her, saying to Dalton, "Let's go to the trailer. I think I know how to fix it."

"I'll take notes," Thea said.

Sara put on her sweetest smile. "Thea, that's part of the problem—too much writing."

Thea's eyes appealed to Dalton. He shrugged and made a palms-up gesture, as though he were powerless. In fact, he relished Thea's discomfiture. Rarely did anyone, except himself, seek to frustrate his beautiful alter ego.

"Go to the hotel," he said. "I'll call you."

Her overripe lips thinned. "When?"

"When I've finished with Sara."

She stared at him for a moment, then gave her long blonde hair a toss, turned on her heel, and stalked toward the limousine parked outside the hangar.

"You've got her very well trained," Sara said with mock approval.

He found the remark oddly disconcerting, felt a need to retaliate in some perverse way. "Glad you appreciate it. You should see her when I throw a stick or tell her to play dead."

"Or roll over?"

He had to grin. "Jesus Christ, you don't seem to realize I'm your *client*."

"My deepest apologies, Mr. Dalton."

"Harry."

"Okay, Harry. Now suppose I start earning my salary."

The silver trailer, fifty feet long and twelve feet wide, sat in the shade next to the hangar. The interior looked like the private room in a men's club—thick oyster-white carpeting, buttery-leather chairs and wall seats, hunting prints on the walls. There were two telephones, a telex machine, a tape recorder. And a small, completely equipped kitchen, which Dalton immediately entered and began to make drinks.

"Not for me," Sara said, dropping into a leather chair. "But you go ahead."

He came to her with two bourbons on the rocks. He kept one and set the other on a small table beside her.

"I heard," he said. "Not while you're working, right?"

"Right."

"That's for when you quit working. In five minutes."

"It may take longer."

"So the booze will age a bit." He lowered his bulk into a matching chair opposite her and massaged his powerful jaws. "I feel like I've been yelling underwater. Why the hell did I get into this? I'm no actor."

"That's exactly the problem."

His eyes flashed belligerently. "*Now* you tell me. But when you were making your big pitch, you told me I was Oscar material."

"I didn't say you were an actor. I said you came across as honest, direct, dynamic."

"Just now I came across like a dummy."

"It's the idiot board—the cue cards. You're not talking, you're reading. From now on, we throw out the cue cards, throw out the scripts."

"Then what do I do—imitations?"

"Yes. Of Harry Dalton. The real Harry Dalton. The man who told off a senator, who leveled with Mike Wallace."

He shook his head, black curls falling to clutter his brow. "That was different. The senator pissed me off. Wallace asked questions that hit a nerve. I didn't bother to think, just let go with my mouth and to hell with cameras and recorders."

She was silent, unconsciously picking up her drink and sipping. Then she looked at him, curled her lips in disgust, and said, "Maybe the real problem is those guys you're fronting for—the maintenance workers. From what I saw, they looked like a bunch of bums."

He glared at her, knocked back his drink, heaved to his feet. "Well, I'll be goddamned! You! What the hell do *you* know? Look, those bums know more about airplanes than anyone in the business. That's why I hired 'em. They know every bolt, every rivet, every gear. They know exactly what every component is supposed to do and they know how to make 'em do it. And they didn't learn it from us. They learned it from their fathers and grandfathers. They're not just working for bucks. They're working because they give a shit about what they're doing. They're master mechanics, not grease monkeys. To them, an airplane's like the family car. They're proud of it. They want it to run right. They want it to be the safest thing you can put in the sky. They—"

He was interrupted by her applause.

"Now you've got it," she said.

Comprehension flooded his face. He picked up his glass, went into the kitchen, brought back another drink.

"With a little editing," Sara said, "we could put that on the air."

He sat down, pulling reflectively at his beaklike nose. "No, you couldn't. If I had to play it back, I'd sound as phony as I did out there."

"Right. So here's what we do. You memorize nothing. Instead, I stand beside the camera and needle you with questions and put-downs. You answer spontaneously."

"It won't work. I'll know it's a setup. I'll be uptight."

"At first, maybe. But after a while, I think you'll be coming on the way you did just now."

"It'll be all mixed up. You'll have hash."

"Uh-huh. Lots of footage, lots of hash. But not after we edit. We'll get rid of the onions and potatoes and have nothing but prime beef."

He gulped his bourbon, lit a cigarette, gazed at her through curls of smoke. "You're a pretty bright girl."

"What makes you think I'm a girl?"

"Okay, *woman*." He smiled at her. "Now hoist your glass. It's quitting time."

"Not quite. I have one more suggestion. You know how we plan to end every commercial with a long interior shot of the passengers?

And then—surprise, surprise—the camera zooms in on you in a middle seat?"

"Sure. That line I can handle: 'Even ride 'em myself.' Pretty cute."

"It stinks."

"What!"

"You almost said it yourself. It's cutesy. Every commercial on the tube is tagged with some cutesy scene or remark, usually between a dumb wife and her slob of a husband. Sometimes it's fine. Mostly it's for throwing up."

"Wait a minute. Are you saying—"

"I'm saying it's hokey. Here we've got this big strong airline president laying it on the line. Sincere, no bullshit. Then all of a sudden he switches to a slick ha-ha traveling salesman—a Willy Loman who's really only a performer after all. Presto, you've zilched your credibility. Why not just end with your Churchillian look and something like, 'That's another reason we think you should fly Transcon'?"

"Christ, why'd you people come up with the idea in the first place?"

"We didn't."

"That's right. It was my ad director's idea."

"I suggest we let Mr. Westbrook keep it."

"He'll hate your guts."

"But *you* won't. That's more important."

Dalton laughed, then fixed her with a speculative look. "You let Westbrook think he'd come up with a dynamite idea, but all the time you figured to kill it when you got me alone. Is that it?"

"That's it. I'm a devious woman. But not with Harry Dalton. With you I level—provided, that is, you level with me."

"A deal. That's just what I'll do. First, have a belt. Work's over."

She raised her glass and drank, eyeing him inquisitively over the rim.

"Sara, there's something on my mind I've got to get off. But it's got to be confidential, just between us."

"Cross my heart."

"Okay, it's this." He put down his drink and gazed at her as though he were the lens of a camera. "I think you should jump out of that jumpsuit and jump into bed."

She didn't laugh, didn't appear shocked or surprised. She just looked at him steadily, with a flicker of regret in her big eyes.

"I'm damned serious," he said.

"I know you are, Harry. And I'd like that."

He thrust forward, extending his huge hands to lift her to her feet.

"But it's no go, Harry. I guess we'd better get that clear right now."

He withdrew, his face hardening. "You'd like it but you wouldn't like it. Now there's a girl who really knows where she's at."

"That *is* where I'm at. I'd like it because you're an attractive man. But I wouldn't like it because I can't afford the price."

"Price? Jesus, not 'I'll hate myself in the morning.'"

"Never. The fact is, it wouldn't mean anything to you. I'd be just another lay. I'd lose my value, and so would the agency, if I started acting like—" She stopped, picked up her glass, and took a drink.

"Like who? Thea?"

She nodded.

"Thea's happy."

"Lots of masochists are. They like the taste of their wounds."

"Christ, you know everything."

"Enough to survive." She stood up. "You're supposed to call her, remember?"

"I'll get around to it." He eased back and looked at her lazily. "I'll also get around to you."

She shook her head, smiling.

"And when that happens, you can be damned sure of one thing."

She raised an eyebrow.

"You won't be just another lay."

True, he thought, sitting alone with his drink. Sara Vardon might not be the most versatile sexual performer—too much the lady—but he was sure he wouldn't confuse her with any of the multitude of bodies that had blunted his lust since he was an oversized kid of fourteen. There was an energy there, a roiling, combustible energy only barely contained, which, once detonated, would probably rattle the windows.

But even that wouldn't satisfy him for long. He would then have to harness that energy, direct it, make it as responsive to his will as the fingers of his hand. The way it had been with Thea. Two years ago, applying for the job as his secretary, she had been much like Sara Vardon—self-absorbed, shrewd, coolly professional. And wary, oh so wary. Three days later, when they'd boarded his Learjet at JFK for a flight to Vegas, she made a big deal of telling him about the fine young man she was planning to marry. Great, he said, wonderful, let's drink to it. By the third round, somewhere over western Pennsylvania, she was back in his compartment, stripped to her honey-blonde skin and providing him with the very best of in-flight entertainment. Then she burst into tears of remorse. Then they did it again. More tears. Then they settled down and she fucked and wept all the way to touchdown.

That was the end of the fine young man. In the casinos and the showrooms, where Harry Dalton got the boss treatment, where he was surrounded by suck-ups, many of them movie idols and TV personalities and big-time politicians, the tears in Thea's eyes were replaced by stars that shone only on her master. From then on, aside from her work, at which she was very efficient, she became a figure in what the shrinks liked to call an adolescent fantasy, but which, Harry suspected, excited the minds of all men until the day their juices ran dry.

In his case, the fantasy quickly became reality. Struck by a sudden carnal urge while in the office, he simply gave a nod, got up, snapped the lock on the door, and by the time he turned around, she had converted to a naked nymph. A fast learner, always eager to add new techniques to her repertoire, applying them as though she had been granted a privilege. And adaptable, ingeniously managing to circumvent the limitations of a chauffeured limo or a cocktail party or a stretch of foreign beach, easily adjusting to whatever physical posture the circumstances seemed to require: standing, sitting, squatting, or jackknifed on her side. A true virtuoso of sex, thought Harry, but even so, not enough to sustain their relationship for long without the inclusion of one other faculty vital to his well-being. The girl seemed to possess preternatural perception, a sensory radar that could almost infallibly identify a cheat, a hustler, a pretender—anyone with motives other than the aggrandizement of Harry Dalton.

Of course that perception also applied to himself. She didn't need to scent another woman's perfume or discover a pink smudge on a shirt collar to know when he had shared someone else's bed. She just knew. But she mentioned it only once, the very first time it happened, right after they returned to New York and he was late arriving at the office.

"You were with a woman, weren't you, Harry?" Spoken gently, plaintively.

"No."

"You were, I know it. But go ahead, lie to me. Maybe I'll start to believe it."

"Why the hell should I lie to you? I told you I wasn't with a woman."

"Really?"

"I was with *two* women. Stewardesses. But not Transcon stewardesses. You know how I like to fuck the competition."

"Oh, Harry."

"Close the door. Then sit down."

She obeyed, eyeing him anxiously as he loosened his tie, planted his elbows on the desk, and rested his face in his hands.

"Take a memo. Head it 'confidential.'"

She flipped open her shorthand book and began to write.

"This is to notify you that, effective immediately, any questioning of Harry Dalton's private activities is cause for instant dismissal. Even a remark or a suspicious look will result in severe penalties."

He heard the pencil snap but continued:

"The reason for this should be made clear. Harry Dalton is a practicing lecher, an avocation he considers to be natural, respectable, and, in his case, essential. He is unable to work at peak efficiency unless he gets laid at least twice a day. While he generally prefers to do this with the same woman, there are often times when he feels a need for change. When this occurs, the woman who is his steady companion will be expected to accept the situation as though it didn't exist. She will welcome him back with affection and understanding, and will not let it interfere with her own sexual performance." He paused and looked at her. "Have you got that?"

She had dropped the book and the pencil and was staring at him. She gave her head a hard shake, saying, "My god, you really mean it."

"Every word. Disagree and you've got an easy alternative. You just get up, open the door, walk through it, and keep right on walking. Tomorrow you'll find a check in your mailbox for services rendered."

"Harry, I just can't believe, after the way we've been . . ." Tears spurted down her cheeks.

"That's another thing. Crying's out. I had enough of that on the flight to Vegas."

She wiped her eyes, took a last sobbing breath, and straightened in her chair.

"Well?"

"Oh, Harry."

He stood up.

"All right, Harry, all right. However you want it."

He sat down. "You just made a worthwhile decision. From now on you'll be paid a vice-president's salary. That will get you out of that cave you live in and into a place where I don't feel I'll be mugged every time I enter the door."

They ratified the agreement with a horizontal ceremony on the leather couch.

A few days later she was ensconced in an East Side apartment, only a block from the hotel where Harry kept a suite for the nights he spent in the city. On weekends, when he was in town, he retired to his twelve-acre estate on the outskirts of Greenwich, Connecticut, a showplace he'd built for his last wife—*absolutely* his last, he vowed—who, like her predecessor, had failed miserably to accommodate to Harry's satyriasis. Generally he brought Thea with him, but sometimes not, in which case she would appear in the office on Monday morning smiling valiantly, displaying lots of cleavage, and suggesting a noontime liaison at her apartment. Harry, a busy man, usually precluded that by simply locking the door.

Now, two years later, Thea Roland, at twenty-seven, was probably the highest-paid executive secretary in the world—sixty thousand a year, plus an annual bonus. She had handled her income wisely, investing regularly in blue-chip stocks and plowing back a substantial sum into the improvement of her personal assets, courses that spanned everything from physical fitness to international finance, elocution to advanced psychology. For Harry, who had estimated the relationship in terms of months, she had become in effect his corporate as well as concupiscent partner, respected and feared by his associates.

Meanwhile, she had adjusted to his tomcat life-style in a way he would never have thought possible. Not only did she come to accept his promiscuity, she seemed actually to encourage it, in fact often introducing him to susceptible young females who, she could be sure, would waste none of his precious time in boring preliminaries. For a while Harry was puzzled, thinking that Thea's passion had cooled, but after returning several times from one of her protégées to find her more ardent than ever, he figured it out. In every instance, the girls were as empty-headed as they were fully endowed. Thea had simply decided that if he must have other bodies, they might as well belong to women who had no brains and who therefore posed no genuine threat to herself.

But that did not quite explain Thea's voracious sexual appetite that greeted his return. Then, vaguely, intuitively, he began to comprehend. While he was indulging himself elsewhere, she was alone in her apartment, fantasizing herself as a witness, an absentee voyeur torturing herself into a frenzy of jealous desire that could be gratified only by the man who held her in thrall. It was, thought Harry, a very neat arrangement. The more he fornicated with others, the more wildly inventive Thea became. Without any effort, he had achieved nirvana.

But he knew instinctively that her reaction would be quite different if the other woman was as intelligent and clever and ambitious as Sara Vardon.

15

CLAMBERING DOWN from the wing, Harry glared at Sara. "It still doesn't work," he said. He gazed past her at Thea, in her canvas chair, and thought he detected a smug look on her face. When he had reported Sara's suggestion for shooting the commercials, Thea had grimaced and said, "It's obvious the girl doesn't know what she's doing."

Sara drew him aside and faced him calmly. "You're right. You're still not relaxed. Your answers still sound prepared."

"Okay, let's pack it in. Get yourself a pro with a sincere face and a voice to match."

She shook her head. "No, it's got to be you. That's the whole idea. Otherwise we forget it."

"Fine. Forget it."

From beside the camera, the director called wearily, "Do we wrap it, Sara, or what?"

Harry watched as she studied the director's face, then turned to observe the crew, whose expressions ran from skepticism to resignation. "Take ten," she said. "Then we'll try again."

"Not with me you won't," Harry said. "I'm burning my Guild card." He started to unzip his coveralls. "There's an old saying: 'Shoemaker, stick to your last.'"

"Stay zipped, Harry. I think I know what's bugging you. When you're up there talking, where are you looking?"

"At the goddamned camera, where else?"

"No, you're not. You're looking just to the right of the camera and beyond it."

"For Christsake, what difference—"

"You're looking at Thea."

"So?"

"What does she think of this ad-lib approach?"

"She thinks it's shit."

"Uh-huh. Now you figure it out. You're smart."

He thought for a minute, then gave her a grudging smile. "You think I'm hamming it for her, trying to prove she's wrong. And that makes me uptight and phony. Right?"

"As I said, you're smart."

"Then you want her out of here?"

"Yes."

"She'll be after your ass."

"I'm good at covering ass."

He grinned. "So I've noticed. Okay, exit Thea."

He turned and saw that she was watching them intently, eyes glittering. Strolling over, he explained that her presence was distracting him, causing him to act unnaturally, implying that he alone was the source of the complaint.

She looked at him, not rising. "Is that what she just said, Harry?"

"*I* said it."

"But she planted it. I think I'd better talk to her." She stood up.

"Sure, talk to her. Talk your head off. But not till we finish shooting."

"Harry, don't you see what she's doing?"

"Yeah. Her job."

"No, she's trying to cut me out. She thinks if I'm not around, she can really come on to you."

He looked at his watch. "There's a Transcon plane leaving S.F. in two hours, nonstop to New York. If you don't get the hell out of here right now, you'll be on it."

Her face tightened. She stared past him at Sara. Their eyes clashed. "I'll be at the hotel," she said. "It'll be interesting to hear how she screws up this time."

But this time there was no screwup. Standing on the wing, sitting on it and waving a hand, Harry began to forget there was anyone in the hangar except himself and Sara. She became an adversary, but not a hateful one, not one who was seeking to belittle him or make him look foolish, but rather a concerned citizen determined that this Transcon airplane had been checked out to the last nut before she would venture aloft.

He found himself responding to her questions and remarks— some friendly, some stinging, all knowledgeable—even before they were fully articulated. Once again—and this thought didn't surface until later—he was a seventeen-year-old kid, working the assembly line at the General Motors plant in Detroit and taking a break to answer the inquisitions of time-and-motion experts whose job was to cut labor costs while increasing production. His purpose then had been to convince those tough, icy men that certain procedures were absolutely essential to the creation of a quality automobile and that to skip them or skimp on them would risk not only reputation but also lives. He had been charged-up then, eloquent in a gruff, positive, almost possessive way, as though the steel bodies crawling down the line were his children, into which must be built integrity, dependability, character. And he was like that now, giving a damn about his company, caring about his planes, immodest in his conviction that they were the most looked-after machines that had ever flown the skies.

When he was done, after giving his bulldog look and—as a result of Sara's prompting—growling that sure, this was a hell of a good reason to fly Transcon, he was as exhilarated as an actor who'd just knocked 'em in the aisles. Shaking his big head, curls lying damp on his sweating forehead, Harry heard the director shout "Boffo!" He looked around and saw a crew suddenly happy in their jobs, then turned his gaze on Sara, who was grinning, head thrown back. In that instant he felt that no one else on earth could have evoked in him such a gut response. He laughed, they all laughed, and when Sara said, "Let's keep going while you're hot," he was delighted to oblige.

They shot in the plane's interior, shot on the tarmac, shot, surrounded by gawking throngs, in the baggage room, the main rotunda, the concourse. By the end of the day there was enough footage for a feature-length movie, from which would be extracted two minutes of air-quality film to produce four thirty-second commercials.

"Christ, that's all?" Harry said, as he and Sara relaxed in the trailer over a drink.

"All? Harry, that's sensational. We got one more commercial than I'd expected. And we did it in two days instead of the three I'd planned."

"Great. So you can take tomorrow off."

"Not exactly. I'll fly back in the morning. This time I'll go commercial. Transcon, of course, if you'll have someone arrange it."

"The hell with that. You'll fly with me."

She smiled. "I'm afraid it will be too crowded."

"Oh, for godsake." He laughed, picked up a phone and dialed.

"Now look, Harry—"

He waved her to be quiet. "Thea? Just finished shooting, all of it. So we'll take off at noon tomorrow. This may surprise you, but it was terrific. . . . Well, fine, I'm glad you're glad. Then you'll also be happy to hear that, to show my appreciation, I'm taking Sara to dinner."

Sara gave her head a negative shake. Harry ignored it.

"Thea, you still there? . . . Thanks, we'll do that. See you in the morning."

He hung up and smiled innocently at Sara. "She hopes we'll have a good time."

They did. Part of it, Harry thought, was because they ran into so many of his old acquaintances: jazzman Turk Murphy, who joined them for a drink at his club, Earthquake McGoon's; columnist Herb Caen, Mr. San Francisco, who regaled them with tales of the city before the high-rises; financier Bob Lurie, owner of the Giants, who seemed undaunted by his team's fourth-place standing; lawyer Mel Belli, king of torts, who was celebrating a huge judgment in a damage suit; restaurateur Enrico Banducci, who now ran a sidewalk café in North Beach but preferred to reminisce over his old club, the hungry i, where he had introduced performers like Mort Sahl and Lenny Bruce; football star O. J. Simpson (with a gorgeous blonde), whom Harry cautioned against running through airports. And now Trader Vic, who had just marched away on his wooden leg after ordering an exotic after-dinner drink sent to their table.

That was all part of Harry's enjoyment. But a bigger part, by far the more fascinating, was the company of Sara Vardon, this unfathomable creature of paradoxes, who looked like an angel and sometimes talked like the Devil, who was girlish and mature, comfortable and exciting, acerbic and gentle, vulnerable and tough, sensual and virginal. Intrigued, he had sought to draw her out as they rolled over steep hills in a chauffeured limo, sat at smoky bars and outdoor tables, danced under flashing lights, but he had learned little more than that she was originally from Ohio, lived alone on Manhattan's East Side, and was deeply committed to her career. Always, through some artful transition, she had turned the conversation back to him and he was surprised to find that he had revealed emotions he had never before discussed: his love and admiration for his father—a fearless labor organizer who had been shot to death outside a steel plant; his rage and elation as he plunged his Saber jet toward a MIG interceptor in the skies over Korea; his sense of triumph in merging small airlines into a company that now challenged the industry's giants.

Now, on impulse, he said, "You know, you should be working for me. We'd make a hell of a team."

"I *am* working for you, and we *are* a hell of a team."

"I mean on my payroll."

"As Thea's assistant?"

He pretended a look of pain. "No, no, you'd hardly ever see her. With Westbrook, in advertising. He's mostly an organizer, a detail man. He needs someone like you to do his thinking."

"Thanks, Harry, I'm flattered. But I wouldn't be happy. At Transcon, advertising's the tail of the dog. At Madden, it's the whole animal."

"That stops me." He sipped thoughtfully on Trader Vic's pink concoction. "Ever think of starting your own agency?"

"Sure. I've also thought of marrying Prince Charles."

"Seriously. Hell, you're the only reason I went with Madden."

"You mean you'd give me Transcon?"

"Right now, I think so."

"Right now, you're hearing the voice of I. W. Harper."

"It'll fade by morning. We'll talk about it then."

She laughed. "And Brooks likes to say we have no hip-pocket accounts. But no, Harry, much as I appreciate it, I'll stay with Brooks. I like the people."

His eyes narrowed on her. "People? Or someone special—a particular man?"

Her lips thinned as she hesitated, then said, "No, there's no particular man. Look, the main reason I'm against it is that I'd be dominated by a single account. I'd practically be a house agency, which means I'd have to kiss ass." She smiled. "For that I prefer to choose the time and place."

He didn't pick it up. Strangely, at this moment he was less interested in her body than in her mind. He wanted to possess it, use it as a sounding board, merge it with his soaring ambitions, which, to be realized, would need all the Sara Vardons he could get.

He said, half-jokingly, but only half, "Then I guess the answer is to make you head honcho at Madden."

She gave him an amused look. "Now I know you're crazy."

He thrust out his glass and clicked it against hers. "To the achievers," he said. "The crazy people."

He made no attempt at intimacies as they returned to the airport hotel, but not for fear of being rebuffed. It was simply that, at this moment, his feelings ran more toward friendship than desire, a unique experience he was loath to disturb.

But outside her door, seeing a new, softer look in her eyes, aware of a note of affection in her voice, he impulsively grasped her in his arms and kissed her. She accepted the kiss, and for a few seconds that was all she did—accept. Then, as though some inner control had suddenly snapped, her body quivered, her lips parted, and her mouth yielded all that it could possibly give.

Then, just as suddenly, she stiffened, broke away, gasped a good night, and was inside her room, door closed, before he could protest.

He smiled as he walked down the corridor. It was a beginning. Tomorrow, on the flight to New York, he would court her. And when they arrived, she would welcome him to her bed.

The note was delivered to him at ten the next morning, just after Thea had gone into her bedroom to pack. It was brief:

Dear Harry:
I'm catching the 9:00 A.M. Transcon flight. It was all so delightful. Too delightful, as you must have known when we said good night.

Sara

His anger, explosive and consuming, told him that never before had he wanted a woman as much as he wanted Sara Vardon.

16

IN THE WEEKS that followed, Sara did not see Harry Dalton, but there were constant reminders of him—mentions in columns, items in the business pages concerning his various projects, comments by Jim Westbrook at meetings. Once she was startled into an eerie feeling that he was actually present in her office, so close and intimate did his voice sound when he telephoned from Paris to insist she fly over for the weekend.

"You're stoned," she said.

"No. I'm just goddamned lonely."

"Thea's not there?"

"She's around. But it's you I want. Christ Almighty, I want you."

"What you want, Harry, is to own me."

"Maybe. But you wouldn't allow it. You're tough. We'd be an even match."

"I'm not so sure. Anyway, I'm not taking the chance." She quickly changed the subject. "By the way, next week you'll be all over the tube. Tune in."

"I'll do that. All right, I'll back off. But I'll be at you again. So stay warm."

Harry Dalton came off the tube like a composite of Churchill, Cronkite, and John Wayne, causing as much stir in the insular advertising community as the series of ads Wayne had done for a savings institution. Added to Sara's role in landing the account, a feat trumpeted by headlines in *Advertising Age*, the commercials elevated her to the status of instant genius, envied and acclaimed over martinis in the huckster hangouts of Madison Avenue.

Though pleased and excited, Sara was by no means overwhelmed. She knew that in a business dedicated to superficiality, where flash was honored more often than substance, where glibness dominated thought, genius led a precarious existence, ever vulnerable to the constant arrival of new geniuses. So she set about gathering more laurels—a glamorous campaign for a line of cosmetics, amusing yet hard-sell commercials for a soft drink, an ingenious idea for demonstrating the superiority of a laundry detergent. And now, with her sudden fame, she was no longer the anonymous copywriter. In fact, rival agencies and their clients often credited her with campaigns in which she'd played no part, the same as had happened to certified geniuses like Mary Wells, Bill Bernbach, David Ogilvy, once they'd set up their own shops. Meanwhile, campaigns that Sara had conceived months earlier took on a fresh aura of success as it became known that she was the author. Suddenly she was being referred to simply as Sara, the last name redundant for an instant celebrity like herself.

Little of this escaped the notice of Brooks Madden and Rick Bradley—particularly Rick, who was a far more frequent visitor to the gathering places of advertising people. He was also present on the morning Brooks called her into his office.

Sitting in a rung-backed Colonial chair, she wondered why she had been summoned. Not, she thought, to be given a raise—she had been given a fantastic one the day after the Transcon acquisition. More likely it was simply a stroking session designed to neutralize the overtures of other agencies, of which she'd had many.

Brooks, behind his cleanswept desk, and Rick, sitting close by him, were smiling benignly at her. Here it comes, she thought, the snow job.

Brooks reached across and handed her a sheet of paper. It was a memorandum addressed "To the staff." She read the first sentence: "I am sure you are all aware of the great contributions made to the agency by Sara Vardon. In recognition of this, effective immediately, the executive committee has elected Sara . . ."

She let out a yelp. Brooks and Rick laughed.

"My God," she said. "You mean it? I'm now a V.P.?"

"That's what it says," Brooks said. "Vice-president in charge of special projects. You've earned it, more than earned it."

She knew that agencies had as many vice-presidents as they had doorknobs, but still she was impressed—and stunned. "The only thing I can think to say," she said, "is that I don't know what to say. Except thank you."

"That'll do nicely," Rick said. He glanced archly at Brooks. "It seems to me there was something else."

"Oh, yeah." Brooks cleared a rasp from his throat. "With the title goes another raise, ten thousand a year. Also, we're making you a stockholder."

She caught her breath. "Oh, this is too much!"

Rick gave her a mock frown. "Don't say that. He might take it back."

Of the largess so unexpectedly bestowed on her, Sara knew that the most prized was the ownership of stock. Madden and Associates was a private corporation, and thus only its employees were eligible to become stockholders. Less than ten percent of the staff were so favored, with Brooks holding the majority of shares. It was the company's most potent weapon against raids on key personnel by competing agencies.

As Sara expressed her thanks, she was struck by an odd feeling of cynicism. Despite all her acclaimed work, would Brooks Madden have been nearly as generous if she were not so outspokenly admired by Harry Dalton, a man over whom neither Brooks nor Rick exerted any influence? The thought gave her a sudden sense of power, the feeling that she was now in a position not only to further her own ambitions, but also to manipulate the ambitions of others. Why should that occur to her? Hadn't she achieved, just now, all that she could have hoped for? A thrill ran through her as she realized the answer was no.

She was walking—almost dancing—down the hall when Rick caught up with her.

"I'm very happy for you, Sara."

"Thanks, Rick." She smiled up at him. "I don't suppose you had anything to do with this."

"Only as cheerleader. Lou Kahn made the pitch for the title and the raise. He was afraid you'd be seduced by another agency. After the hype he gave you, practically chewing the carpet, Brooks decided to add the stock deal."

She felt a twinge of disappointment, wishing that it had all been promoted by Rick. But no, of course not. Personally it would probably have suited him just fine if she'd been lured to another agency. But not professionally. He would then have to worry that the Transcon account might follow her. Again, the sense of power, this time sharper and more meaningful—she now had the leverage to influence her former lover.

"I'll thank Lou," she said, "and recite my pledge of allegiance."

"Good. It'll mean a lot to his ulcer. Incidentally, now that you're part of management, you may have some questions. If I can help, just call on me."

"As a friend?" She had not meant to sound sardonic.

His voice lowered, lost its casual tone. "Yes, Sara, as a friend."

"Is it easy for you, just being a friend?" she pressed.

He started to speak, then responded with merely a quick shake of the head—involuntary, Sara thought.

"Well, it's certainly not easy for *me*," she said, stopping and turning her eyes on his face.

He touched her shoulder—again it seemed involuntary—said quietly, "We'll get there," then turned and headed back toward his office.

It was the closest they had come to an intimate exchange since the day of the Transcon presentation three months ago, when he had taken her home in a taxi. Since then she had seen him only at meetings, some of them small, with only an art director or another writer present, most of them large and including members of all major departments. In the small meetings she sensed in him a feeling of strain, a tautness, a rigidity of speech, as though he feared that by some word or gesture he might reveal a disturbing secret. But at the large meetings he always appeared relaxed, outgoing, and friendly, and when he asked her for an opinion, his manner was no more intimate than that of a teacher calling on a precocious student.

The very fact that he still felt the need to manufacture an attitude toward her implied his failure to escape from the emotions that had bound them. Perhaps now, looking back, those emotions were gaining in strength, their love becoming ever more idyllic, enhanced by the editing of memory. Surely his reconversion to "family man"—one now pledged to the quiet life, a life of punctuality and sameness and calculated good humor—must often evoke yearning for carefree days with a woman always eager to adapt to his wishes, adjust to his moods.

Now, watching his tall, graceful figure as it moved away, she was swept by nostalgia for this man who had so gently, so understandingly, so romantically, inducted her into womanhood. He was the first real love of her life, discovered not in adolescence, when it might easily have been discarded or outgrown, but at the beginning of maturity, when her mind and her heart were united in judgment. He was her considered choice. There could be no other. Until he returned—as she was determined he would someday—there could be only her work and her autoerotic nights, her compulsive forays to singles bars, always a different one, always using a different name, always returning at dawn, renewed by the catharsis of joining with masculine flesh.

Returning to her office, she felt her euphoria fade and she was absorbed by a growing discontent. How long, she wondered, could she endure the emptiness in her life, the part of her life that was separate from her work, the life without Rick? At only twenty-five, she was a highly paid officer and stockholder of a great advertising agency, a woman admired and emulated by members of her profession, but a woman achingly alone, with no one to whom she could bring her prizes, with whom she could share her joys, her frustrations, her bed. What if she was deluding herself about Rick? What if he longed, not for the new Sara Vardon, polished, self-possessed, aggressive, but for the straight, hesitant, self-effacing Sara Sunshine who had at first attracted him?

Oh, she had changed, all right, she knew that, and not merely on the surface. There was a driving, visceral energy to her now, uninhibited by concerns for what others might think, a relentless ambition that was often harsh, always insatiable. She had Rick to credit or blame for that, for creating a vacuum, a void in her life, that somehow must be filled. And what other material could she use but the dynamic energy produced by her brain?

Her brain. Yes, that too was part of the change. Her brain, released from its hideous oppressor, and thus from thoughts of disability or death, had responded with the message that there is really no natural sense of sin, that it was something invented and then imposed by sanctimonious, juiceless people like her mother, who forever lived in fear. And so, she rationalized, her brain had banished sin, destroyed its power to produce anxiety that paralyzed the will, thus freeing her to celebrate her desires and assert her intellect.

Was she not now a far more interesting person than the one Rick had abandoned? Surely he must be suffering from the realization that he had lost her before he could enjoy the passionate and purposeful woman she had become. Eventually his resistance would crumble and . . .

Eventually? That could mean a long, long time, a year, maybe longer. She must find a way to speed the process.

A grinning office boy was putting Brooks's memo on her desk when a possible solution flashed through her brain. Somehow she must maneuver herself into a position where Rick would become more dependent on her, where she could play an active, perhaps even decisive, role in his carer.

She thought for a while, then phoned the executive offices of Transcon Airlines, identified herself, and asked to speak to Mr. Dalton. Sorry, Mr. Dalton was now in Hawaii en route to the Orient, and would be gone for at least two weeks. She left a message for him to call her when he returned.

Two weeks, she thought, would be fine. It would be stupid to act before that, wise to wait even longer.

Harry Dalton called her three days later, from Tokyo.

"What's up—another shooting session?"

"No, not just yet. Harry, I've got to talk to you."

"You are. Keep going."

"I mean in person. Privately."

"Just talk? For something more exciting, I could fly back today. I won't even need a plane."

"Talk, that's all. But there's no hurry, it can wait a couple of weeks. Will you call me when you get back? I'll buy you lunch."

"Lunch? Why not dinner and then—"

"Lunch is safer, Harry."

Two weeks later he strode through the door of the restaurant she had selected. He was tanned, though it was late November, and his suit looked unpressed, as though it had wearied of trying to accommodate his bulk. He gave her a smile and a quick hug, then surveyed the scene, a darkly lit eatery with a vinyl floor, a scattering of maroon-topped tables in front, and a number of scarred booths in the rear.

"How'd you find this joint? Christ, we'd do better getting a chili dog from a pushcart."

"Just a precaution. I don't want us seen together."

"Looks like a setup for a killing. Let's take a booth. I'll face the door."

When they were seated and had ordered drinks, she asked what he'd been doing. Too much, he said. Since he'd last seen her in San Francisco, he'd been to a dozen countries, arranging reciprocal airline agreements, assigning exhibition rights to his movies, negotiating for the acquisition of another resort hotel, discussing with the Japanese the production of cassette equipment.

"Okay," he said, "you're caught up. And so am I. Right now I'm the most available guy in America. Want to make something of it?"

"Up to a point. I need your help."

"*My* help? You seem to be doing great on your own. Westbrook tells me you've practically been voted huckster of the year."

She smiled. "That's why I think the timing's right."

He brushed impatiently at his dark curls. "Let's cut the cloak-and-dagger. You ask me to take a taxi instead of the limo. You bring me to a greasy spoon next door to Hell's Kitchen. Now you sound like you're plotting a heist. Just lay it out."

"First a question. In San Francisco, you suggested I start my own agency, saying you'd give me your account. We'd been boozing, so I'm not holding you to that. But I've got to ask—"

"Hold me to it. It still goes."

"Thank you, Harry."

"It's my gain. After we've gagged down some food, come back to the office. We'll call in Westbrook and work out the details, including the announcement."

She gave him a direct look. "That's not what I had in mind."

He arched an eyebrow. "I should have figured that. With your mind, it couldn't be anything so simple. All right, clue me in."

She told him. And as she talked, quietly and confidently, she saw his eyes begin to glint, then look far off. When she finished, he ordered another drink and, saying nothing, stared thoughtfully into the glass.

"Do you think it would work, Harry?"

He looked at her. "Tell me something. Are you my friend?"

"Of course I'm your friend. Why?"

"Because I'd sure as hell hate to have you as my enemy. Sure, it will work."

"Then you'll go along?"

He took a pull at his bourbon. "On one condition."

She gave an elaborate sigh. "I was expecting that."

"You're wrong—what you're thinking. I don't accept bodies as chips. When you're ready for that, you'll let me know. And it'll be for free. The condition is business, nothing else."

"What?"

"That once this works—and we'll make it work—you agree to listen to another proposition."

"That's all—just listen?"

"Yes, but very intently."

"Why not tell me now?"

"Because first I want to see how you handle this one. Sara, you're moving into the fast lane now, and how do I know you won't crack up? Most people do, and the corporate world is strewn with their corpses. I know. A lot of 'em are covered with my tire marks."

"I'm getting very good at twisting through traffic."

"I'm sure of it. But it's not enough to be shrewd and clever. This is a power trip you've started on. So you've got to be tough, sometimes coldblooded. You've got to be willing to wreck some decent people if they're blocking the road. Could you do that?"

"If the prize was important enough to me, yes."

"You wouldn't be hung up by remorse?"

She grinned. "What's remorse, daddy?"

She waited almost two weeks before approaching Lou Kahn.

"Lou, this is a tough one for me. I guess the only way is to give it to you straight."

He scratched at his beard, then yanked off his glasses and breathed on the thick lenses, eyeing her suspiciously. "Sure. Hit me."

"I'm leaving the agency."

He fell back in his chair and clutched his chest. "Please, my angina! What the hell did you say? Say it again. I'm a little deaf."

She said it again.

"Ouchamagoucha! What the hell gave you that idea? You unhappy here? Tell me who makes you unhappy and I'll cut off his balls. Or hers. I'm no sexist."

She laughed. "Lou, it's nothing like that. It's just that . . ." She paused.

"Don't tell me you got a better offer. Offers, yeah, but a *better* offer? Jesus, Sara, no more than a month ago you made V. P., got a fat raise, got stock, got to head up a freewheeling group of all-stars. You mean to tell me another agency's topping that?"

"I'm not going with another agency. That is, I'm not—" She bit her lip.

"Not what?"

"Not going with an agency that now exists. Lou, that's all I can tell you. I can't say anything until the others involved are ready to announce."

He rested his beard on his flimsy chest and raised his arms horizontally. "You're crucifying me."

"I'm sorry, Lou, really I am. I've enjoyed working with you."

He flung himself halfway across the desk, body tensed. "Look, suppose I parley about this with the big chiefs. You mind if I do that?"

"I'd rather you didn't mention it to Brooks. I'll do that myself in a day or so."

"Rick Bradley, then. Maybe he'll come up with something. He usually does."

"That's okay, I guess. But I'm afraid it'll be a waste of time. I'm sure he won't change my mind."

Lou grabbed the phone and dialed. "Rick? Lou Kahn. Something's popped that needs your great wisdom. Can I come up? . . . Yeah, okay . . . I'll be in your office at two-thirty." He hung up and said, "He's on his way to Transcon. Westbrook wants to take him to lunch. That's a switch—a client springing for the tab."

And at that lunch, thought Sara, Jim Westbrook would tell Rick Bradley that perhaps what Transcon needed was a smaller, more flexible agency, one better tailored to the fast-moving style of Harry Dalton. Nothing definite, of course, just passing on what seemed to be in Dalton's mind, just leveling.

The next afternoon Sara was again summoned to Brooks Madden's office. This time she was quite sure of what to expect, and she was prepared for it.

17

THIS WAS A new one on him, Brooks thought, as he waited for Sara. Usually the squeeze was easy to figure, easy to handle. Sometimes it was an employee passing the word that he was unhappy—so you either loaded on the dough or let him seek happiness elsewhere. Or a hotshot who used an offer from another outfit as a gun to hold you up—again, you either surrendered the money or called his bluff. Or, fortunately the most common variety, the straight-shooter who simply walked in and put it on the line—no sulking, no threats, just a direct, clean hit for more money, a bigger job.

But this! If it were anybody but Sara Vardon—open, direct, honest—he might suspect a conspiracy. God knows, you could make a *prima facie* case for that. First she tells Lou Kahn she's quitting, reluctantly confiding she's about to join some mysterious agency that's just getting organized. Then Kahn tells it to Rick Bradley, who just came from lunch with Jim Westbrook, who dropped a lot of broad hints that Transcon was thinking of switching to a smaller shop that would be more adaptable to Harry Dalton's convoluted operations. Put it all together, and anybody but an idiot would have to conclude that Sara Vardon, whom Harry Dalton considered a genius—rightly, no doubt—was setting up her own agency to serve Harry Dalton.

But that didn't make it a conspiracy. The whole idea was probably Dalton's—an outgrowth of his need to dominate everything he touched—with Sara having no part in the decision except to say yes.

He couldn't blame her for that. My God, a woman in her mid-twenties heading up her own show with instant billings of at least twenty million! When he was that age—even when he was forty—he, Brooks Madden, would have jumped at the chance.

Losing Transcon would be a bitter blow, not because of the loss in billing—hell, that would be less than five percent of the agency total—but because they'd had the business for only a few months and the competition would imply, perhaps to his own clients, that Madden and Associates had committed some gross offense. Even that wouldn't be so bad—big advertisers heard that kind of crap all the time—except that a lot of those same clients had begun to think of Sara Vardon as a miracle worker. Time and again, Madden's own executives had come into his office to beg him to assign Sara to their accounts, saying their clients demanded it—and why wouldn't they? Weren't they spending enough to entitle them to the best the agency had to offer? Which meant that if Sara left, a number of those clients would follow, and along with them would go some of his most valued people.

This was no ordinary defection, not something that he could shrug off because he knew there was always some creative star he could pirate from another shop. Sara Vardon was a very special person, right now irreplaceable. She really had the company by the short hairs, assuming, as he must, that the question of her staying or leaving was still negotiable.

He was standing when she came in, her dress, dark and lustrous as her hair, looking carefully chosen, her makeup subdued but nevertheless eloquent, her smile set just so, friendly but a bit aloof—all very much the glamorous young businesswoman celebrated in *Cosmo* and the Sunday newspaper supplements. Greeting her, he felt a sudden mental imbalance, as though it were he who had come to supplicate for her favors, and he couldn't help thinking back to earlier times when, except for secretaries and receptionists, agencies were populated by eager young men in well-tailored suits and white broadcloth shirts and shiny shoes, men who never reached beyond their assigned jobs and who, if they were in the creative department, almost never so much as saw a client. But all that had changed, he supposed for the better, and now there were women fresh out of college who had liberated themselves into important executive positions that seemed to interfere not at all with a vigorous and publicized social life.

As he seated her and took his place behind his desk, he had the feeling of growing a little older, a little less sure of himself, a little less in command of his huge enterprise. He lowered his head, feeling a flab of flesh bunch against his chin, then looked up from beneath his gray-orange eyebrows and gave her a wry smile. "You know, Sara, a guy in my job gets a lot of good news and a lot of bad news. Yesterday I got the worst news I've heard in a long time. Believe me, I was shocked. Sara Vardon leaving us? Listen, I said, I'll believe it when I hear it from her, not before."

Her eyes glimmered with contrition. "I'm sorry, Brooks, sorry you had to hear it from someone else. I'd planned to tell you about it personally. Tomorrow, in fact."

He raised his head, his expression now bemused. "Then it's true? After all the success you've—" He cut it off with a slice of his hand. "It must be one hell of a good offer."

"It is. It would have to be, or I wouldn't think of leaving. Brooks, I can't tell you how much I appreciate all you've done for me."

"You earned it, every bit of it." He leaned forward, cufflinks clicking on the desktop. "This offer, did it involve signing a contract? I mean, how firm is it?"

"Nothing's signed. But I'd say it's firm. In the next day or so I'll have the letter of agreement."

That confirmed Brooks's surmise. A letter of agreement was the standard covenant between an agency and a new client. "So you're setting up your own shop?"

She blinked and gazed down at her hands. "Sorry, I didn't mean to—" Her eyes came up, direct and honest. "Look, I wish I could talk about it, but I can't. Not until all the business is settled."

"Sure, I understand." He eased back and made a tent of his fingers. "I just thought—*hoped* is the word—that there was still time for me to come up with some sort of proposal. If it's a question of money, I'm sure we could work it out."

"I appreciate that. Of course, money's part of the reason I'm leaving. But it's the smaller part. I want—well, I guess I feel the way you did when you started this agency—I want to call the shots, have an influence on everything that's produced."

"Yeah, why not? You're ambitious and have every right to be. That's why we made you head of the special projects group. But I guess that's not enough."

"It was, believe me it was. But after this offer came along—" She broke off, shaking her head. "Don't think I didn't try to turn it down. I spent hours, days, trying to think of some way—some job I might feel qualified for—that would keep me here."

"And you couldn't think of any?" He grinned. "Aside from *my* job, that is."

Her smile flashed on his remark, then became self-deprecating. "Oh, I thought of one. But it's too absurd to mention. You'd laugh me right out of this office—or throw me out."

"Listen, Sara, right now I'm not for laughing or throwing. So let's hear it. Maybe it'll give me a new slant on the agency."

"Well, all right, but I warned you. It's not an original idea. I'm sure I wouldn't have thought of it if I hadn't heard that something like it had been set up at McCann years ago. They formed what was sort of an agency within an agency, all creative people, but I guess with a couple of account executives. It was headed up by, let's see—"

"Jack Tinker, an art director and also a writer"—and suddenly Brooks saw the whole picture, a way out, but at a price that at that moment, despite the loss of Transcon, despite the threatened defection of other clients and key personnel, he was not prepared to pay. His voice became more rasping, issuing from the side of stiffened lips as he added, "An elite group. And you're right, an agency within an agency. Even went by their own name: Tinker and Associates, I think. Now it's Tinker Campbell-Ewald, a separate agency but still part of the Interpublic Group, same as McCann."

"I don't know that much about the agencies. Anyway, when they were with McCann, they were pretty much autonomous."

"Not quite." His breathing was coming harder now, as she sat there cool and self-possessed, her pulse probably beating at a comfortable seventy-five, reminding him that, God help him, this had become more than ever a business of youth. "They had to be responsible to McCann's executive committee."

"Yes, that's what I thought. So I guess Tinker was a member of the committee."

He stared at her in silence, feeling his jaw flex, his saliva thicken. Maybe he was wrong to feel as he did, angry and exasperated and defensive—after all, she was a talented kid who'd suddenly been showered with praise and promotions and money, and it was only natural that she'd try to see how much she could squeeze from her success—but he was sure, now, that she was playing him, manipulating circumstances into a situation that would put his back to the wall. Ten minutes ago it would have been inconceivable to think that he could ever have disliked Sara Vardon, that sweet, easygoing, unsophisticated girl who everyone said was a ray of sunshine. But now, sensing that before coming in she'd had it all figured out—the leverage given her by Transcon and her own magnetic brilliance that could attract other clients and people who serviced them—he was helpless against the resentment and rage that flooded through him. This was his agency, bearing his name, and here was this girl, no older than a lot of trainees, proposing—oh, it was a proposal, all right, not just an absurd notion—that she be welcomed into the topmost clique of the management hierarchy, the executive committee.

Somehow he managed an outward control that permitted a tight smile and a quiet tone of voice that sounded undismayed. "And you thought if you could have something like that, you'd forget about this other thing?"

"Well, of course, who wouldn't?" Her smile was broad now, bubbling into a small laugh as she appreciated her joke. "But I live in the real world where things like that don't happen." She uncrossed her legs and started to get up. "I've taken enough of your time. I'll just say thank you again and—"

"Sit down, Sara. Maybe we're not quite finished."

She dropped back, looking surprised.

"I'd like some time to think. Can you hold off on this new proposition?"

"I don't know, Brooks. They *are* pressing me."

"Twenty-four hours?"

"Oh, sure. But I don't see—"

"Frankly, neither do I. But I can't just dismiss it. I'll get back to you tomorrow afternoon."

In Rick's office, with just the two of them present, he reported it all calmly, masking his indignation lest it influence Rick's judgment of the facts. (No, it was more than that. He was also concerned that his reaction might, in Rick's eyes, place him way back with rolltop desks and green eyeshades and bosses who treated their employees like serfs.) He paced the floor slowly as he spoke, but when he finished he sat on the leather couch, stiff and straight, and rubbed at the deepening lines in his lean face.

"Of course," he said, "there's always the chance she's bluffing."

Rick, leaning back at his desk, said, "No, she's not bluffing." He shifted his weight and the chair sprang forward. "Just before you came in, I got a call from Jim Westbrook. Supposedly it was about a change in schedule. But then he hit me with a question. Dalton, he said, had a couple of private business meetings with Sara, and he, Westbrook, asked if I knew what was going on. I said it was probably about arranging a shooting session, and he let it go. But I know and he knows that we're not even close to making new commercials."

Brooks squinted an eye. "Rick, this is beginning to smell like low tide. If Dalton's setting up Sara in her own agency, why wouldn't Westbrook know about it?"

"That's not too surprising. Jim's not much more than an errand boy for Dalton. He's never let him in on the big thinking."

"Maybe so. But only yesterday, at lunch—a lunch he suggested and paid for—he told you that Dalton was thinking of a smaller agency for Transcon. Now he plays innocent and wonders what his boss and Sara are up to. Rick, I don't like it. It begins to look like Dalton assigned Westbrook to do exactly what he's doing."

"Which is?"

"To worry us. To establish beyond doubt that Dalton's ready to back Sara in starting her own shop. If we buy that, he figures, we'll do just about anything to hold on to Sara."

"Apparently *she* buys it. Otherwise she certainly wouldn't be giving notice."

"Right. And I think he'll go ahead with it if we don't give Sara what she wants. And what she wants, I think, is the same thing Dalton wants—a say in the management of the company. We know he's a manipulator. We know he's the kind of guy that's got to be pulling the switches. So what better way than to get Sara Vardon, who's come up so fast, who's suddenly got muscle, to build her own private empire inside the agency and back it up with a seat on the executive committee?"

"But why? No one person, excepting yourself, could possibly control the actions of the committee."

"Okay, I agree. But I'm not saying he wants control. What he wants is just to be damned sure he's got someone in there looking out for his interests. He doesn't trust corporate chiefs. We know that. That's why he's a maverick, always against the big wheels in his own business. He's paranoid. Unless he's on the inside, he figures he's getting shafted. Also, with him I think it's a game, a power game that he plays like it's a hobby."

"Then you think this whole thing is exclusively Dalton's idea and Sara's just going along?"

"That's one side of the coin. Sara the innocent, who just happens to be in a position where she can't lose. Either she gets what amounts to a piece of this agency or she gets an agency of her very own. But there's the other side, and it's damned ugly. It shows Sara as the evil genius behind the whole scheme, working on Dalton, who she knows thinks she's the greatest thing since chopped liver." Brooks jumped to his feet. "That, dammit, is the Sara Vardon I thought I saw sitting in my office. Now tell me I'm wrong."

Rick said gently, "I think you are, Brooks."

"But I could feel it in my gut. It was like she'd written the whole scenario."

"Well, naturally she'd thought about it." He paused, running his fingers through his blond hair. "Brooks, there's another way of looking at this that we're not even considering."

Brooks sat down. "I'm listening."

"The obvious way. Suppose she was being totally honest. She'd had this offer, as she said, and didn't see how she could pass it up. But she loved working here and tried hard to think of something that would induce her to stay. The idea of heading up an agency within an agency occurred to her because she'd heard it had been done at McCann. But she laughed that off as being out of the question for her. The only reason she even mentioned it to you was to show the lengths she'd gone to in the hope of offsetting Dalton's proposition. She was genuinely astonished when you indicated that you wanted time to consider it." Rick paused again, as though waiting for the new image to form. "Now what do you think of her?"

Brooks barked a laugh. "As a candidate for sainthood. But what about Westbrook's part in this?"

"It could be no more than I thought at the time. He'd heard Dalton say something about getting a new agency. He felt left out and thought I might have some information."

"And Dalton himself? You don't think he wants to plant Sara into our top management?"

"It's possible. But it seems to me a lot more probable that he'd want an agency that his account created. That way he wouldn't be just an influence on a committee. He'd have almost total authority, just as he insists on having it in everything else he's involved with."

Brooks took a big breath, then whooshed it out. "I guess your way makes more sense. And that's a relief. It's not good for my blood pressure to think Sara could be so damned ruthless and devious."

"She couldn't be, Brooks. Not the Sara I knew. She's changed, yes—the operation, the success. But a coldblooded conspiracy? Never. If nothing else stopped her, her conscience would."

"Thank God for conscience." Brooks rose, smiling, now feeling relaxed. "Rick, I won't ask your advice on what we should offer Sara, if anything. I'll sleep on it and get back to you in the morning."

"I think that's best."

Leaving the office, Brooks wondered about Rick's sympathetic defense of Sara. Was he still in love with her? Brooks hoped not. That could be hell on Janice.

A light, feathery snow was falling as Brooks stepped out on Madison Avenue and headed north. Somehow, he thought, a way must be found to avoid a repetition of this sort of squeeze, which, however innocent the motivation, amounted to no less than an assault on the agency. Apparently it was no longer enough to reward deserving employees with ten-percent raises and titles and stock and pension plans. The competition had become too fierce, too cutthroat, particularly in the scramble for creative people, whose work, after all, was the only visible product an agency had to offer. God, the stories he'd heard. It was nothing for some kid, only a year out of college, to be pulling down fifty thousand a year. There were presidents of agencies—the "creative boutiques"—who had not been old enough to vote in the last presidential election. And as more and more of these boy and girl wonders entered the scene, as agencies proliferated—there were now almost eighty, billing anywhere from thirty million to over one billion dollars—the bidding became furious, job-switching epidemic, the challenge to maintain stability overwhelming. All because of a crazy logic dictated by dollars: up to $150,000 for a thirty-second pitch on a prime-time show. If it cost that much, then the people who created the commercials must be worth a proportionate amount, even though the mini-dramas, the rigged demonstrations, the phony interviews they produced were so often boring, tasteless, ludicrous. But that was the way they reasoned, the way the game was played, the way the lunatics ran the asylum. And management could only thank God that rates for television time kept soaring, because that meant that the agencies' fifteen- or seventeen-percent commission took bigger and bigger bites, a lot of which could be fed to the geniuses who manufactured the banalities that viewers did their best to ignore.

It was crazy, absolutely crazy. It was nothing at all like this back in the days when there were only print and radio. Sure, writers and art directors were well paid, but not nearly as much as an account executive, let alone a senior vice-president, the men who gave the orders and ran the show. It was inconceivable that any of the present breed could have climbed to the top rungs of the ladder if they'd worked under giants like Albert Lasker, Sterling Getchell, Stanley Resor, Ray Rubicam, Milton Biow, Rosser Reeves, Bruce Barton, men who ran their shops with an iron, though sometimes velvet-gloved hand, men who permitted no nonsense, tolerated no prima donnas, suffered no glory hunters. He himself had run his agency in the same independent, authoritarian way—though, he thought, with a degree of sympathy and a certain rough justice—but even he had changed as the creative people began to rise and the need for sensitive, diplomatic, all-around managers like Rick Bradley became apparent.

Still, there was a limit, and the question he now had to resolve—he alone, not the executive committee—was whether or not Sara Vardon's implied demands exceeded that limit. He was unconcerned about establishing a precedent. In this business, where close to a hundred percent of the inventory was people and thus wildly variant in value, it was not uncommon to pay one person twice as much as another, though they performed the same job. What made the difference, of course, was talent, and it was a shrewd advertiser who understood that he was not really hiring an agency with so many employees, so many floors, so many departments, so many blue-chip clients, but was in fact hiring a very small group of people within that complex, upon whose talents often depended the success or failure of his product. No agency, as such, deserved to take credit for the brilliant campaigns produced for Volkswagen or Sony or Levi's or Pepsi. The ideas behind them had been mysteriously seeded, gestated, born in the brains of individuals, and the only significant contribution made by the agency was in the creation of a climate where inventiveness could flourish.

That, perhaps, was the crux of the matter. Would the elevation of Sara Vardon to a unique creative status and a position in top management act as an incentive to others, or would it be seen as a despicable maneuver to appease a bullying client?

He was, thought Brooks, getting close to the answer. A little more discussion, a good sleep while his unconscious self put his thoughts in perspective, and he would arrive at the right decision. And once that was done, he would turn his mind to devising some system of rewards that would help immunize talented people against temptation.

Approaching his apartment building, his step quickened and his weariness washed away in a surge of excitement. He greeted the doorman with a smile, hummed along with the nostalgic tune piped into the elevator, and took off his hat and straightened his tie as he reached his door. He got out his key, started it into the lock, then decided to ring. But before he could press the bell, the door opened wide.

She stood there for a moment in her see-through saffron gown, eyes glowing, smile inviting, hands half-raised in anticipation. Never, not even in Cannes, had he seen Maria Corliss look so beautiful.

18

MARIA had been staying with him for the past week, as she had twice before, remaining until called away by business interests—a dress shop in Beverly Hills, a condominium development in Phoenix, a small hotel in St. Tropez—and by the need to visit her son. For more than half the year, she had told him, she was free to come to New York and join him on any basis he wished.

For Brooks, there could be no other basis than that she make his home hers. Agreeing, she made it clear that, while wanting only him, she had no thought of marriage. In fact, after three stifling experiences, she could not bring herself even to witness "a ceremony dedicated to mutual bondage."

It was, Brooks supposed, an ideal arrangement—a word distasteful to him because it implied so little commitment. Yet, during her last absence, he had become morose and irritable and begun to wish for a more encompassing relationship. Not marriage, necessarily—he had no moral compunctions—but a year-round union that would allow them to share all of each other's concerns. Such thoughts he kept to himself, silenced by his awareness that she prized her independence and that he was confined to New York by his job. Occasionally he had a wistful impulse to chuck it all and spend the rest of his life wandering about the world with this friend, companion, lover. But always reality intervened, the reality that required him to be loyal to the firm he had built.

Back in July, when he had fled Cannes in bitter disillusionment, he would have considered himself deranged if he had so much as dreamed of sitting here now in his living room beside an affectionate Maria Corliss, enjoying a tall scotch. Indeed, his mind had boggled when, after Transcon had appointed the agency, Rick had informed him that it was none other than Maria who had persuaded Harry Dalton to attend the presentation. *Why?* was all he could say. Because she's in love with you, said Rick. *Oh, come on, it's my money she's in love with.* She's got her own money, said Rick.

In love with him? He had been unable to believe it—until he picked up the phone and heard her voice, rich with promise.

"Of course," Maria said, "I don't know her, but from all I've heard, she'd make a great addition to the executive committee."

"But she's so damned young. If she had about five more years—"

"How old were you when you started your own agency?"

"Just a kid, nineteen, twenty. But that was a shoestring operation, nothing like—"

"But you turned it into a much bigger operation, and did it before you were"—she smiled—"how old? Twenty-five?"

"About that." He sipped his scotch, his second. "What you're telling me is that it's not her age that bothers me, that it's something else."

"I think it might be."

"Like what?"

"Like you think a lot of Janice Bradley. And you find it offensive to promote a woman who lived with her husband."

"That's not it, not at all. Listen, I was happy to make her a vice-president, give her stock, let her run a special group."

"But not a group with her name on it. And not the executive committee. That would bring her a lot closer to Rick and might rekindle the fires. Then goodbye Janice, again."

His eyebrows shot up in surprise. "You know, you may be right. I hadn't really thought about it, but it's probably been sneaking around in my head. Anyway, I can't make a business decision based on whose bed Rick might end up in."

"Of course not. That's why I opened my big mouth. You've got to consider it as though Rick and Janice didn't exist. Now I'll shut up."

She jumped to her feet. "Oh, my, I've got to check the oven. Unless you like your beef Stroganoff black."

He watched her admiringly as she moved to the kitchen. Tawny blonde hair slightly disarranged, as though done deliberately to give her a wanton look. Her figure, faintly outlined beneath the saffron gown, thrusting forward at the hips with the supple grace of a ballet dancer. And her voice—coming to him now through the open door ("Stroganoff lives!")—happy, content, elated. He surveyed the room as he never did when alone, and noted with delight the spectrum of bindings in the ceiling-high bookcase, the whipped-cream look of the deep-pile carpeting, the gleam of silk on chairs and sofa, the burnished beauty of banister and stairs that curved up to a balcony, off which were the two bedrooms, both of them familiar to their bodies, the pillows and sheets endeared by her scent.

Always he wanted her here, the world locked out, the past forgotten, the present alive and suspended in time. But he feared that such isolation would soon bore her; that he, a plain, unsubtle man, could not alone sustain her interest, which, perhaps, would have faded quickly had he not retained so much of his sexual vigor. And so he took her often to the theater, concerts, sporting events, dinners with the Bradleys—shunning, however, the late-night celebrity showcases, which she said depressed her.

He was surprised by her fascination with his beginnings. At her insistence, one Saturday morning they rode the subway to 190th Street and St. Nicholas Avenue, the peak of Washington Heights, where he had not visited since his widowed mother had died twenty years ago. They walked through jabbering crowds to his old address, the apartment building gone now and replaced by a taller, more modern structure. So much of what he had known was also gone—the stationery store, the Greek restaurant, the corner ice-cream parlor, the thick woods where he had gathered flowering dogwood, were stamped out by towering apartments. The hill where in winter he had gone sledding on hard-packed snow, the hummock of city land where General George Washington had commanded a fort and where, in Brooks's youth, the poor had cultivated vegetable gardens, were all lost to bricks and concrete and glass, with only strange kids in jeans playing stickball to remind him of the busy outsider he once had been.

It was a sad visit, an insult to nostalgia, and on the ride back in a taxi—he could not abide another bout with those roaring, tunneling subway trains, once so awesome and now humiliated with sprayed graffiti—he was silent and brooding, a mood that Maria immediately understood, and sought to offset with tales of the horrors that had, since her childhood, been inflicted on Los Angeles.

Now he heard her voice as she came from the kitchen and, his thoughts elsewhere, he asked her to repeat what she had said.

"I said—and *then* I'll shut up—that any girl Rick felt so strongly about must be pretty all right."

He was jarred back to the problem, to his indecision. Smiling, he said, "You're quite a rooter for Sara."

"Not exactly. It's just that, well, she must have been knocked silly when Rick left her."

"I guess." He wanted to get off the subject, annoyed with himself for initiating this intrusion into their privacy.

"I just hope Janice doesn't go bonkers when Rick tells her," Maria said.

"Listen, let's forget it. It's got nothing to do with us."

Aware of his sudden melancholy, she came and curled up beside him, brushing her lips against his cheek. Abruptly he turned, folded her in his arms, and kissed her, lightly at first, then with a passionate hunger. It went on for a while before, breathless, she drew back.

"To hell with Stroganoff," she said.

As she went to turn off the oven, and even when she met him at the stairs, stroking his back as they ascended, his mind was confessing the real reason he opposed investing Sara with more power.

He was afraid of how she might use it.

"And then," said Rick to his saucer-eyed son, "the lion whizzed out of the high grass and headed straight for the hunter. The hunter was terribly frightened and he stumbled back and fell down. And as he hit the ground, he lost his rifle. It just sailed away and landed where he couldn't reach it. And now the lion was leaping at the hunter with his big jaws wide open. And you know what the hunter did?"

"What, Dad? What did the hunter do?"

Rick rose from the bed, made a claw of his hand, and darted it forward. "He stuck his hand down the lion's throat, all the way down through the lion's body to his tail. Then he grabbed the tail, gave it a hard yank, and pulled the lion inside out"—pause—"and that made the lion run the other way!"

For a moment, Scott's mouth hung open, then it spread to a grin and he burst into delighted laughter. Then, sobering, "Really, Dad, really?"

"Well, that's the way my father told it to me. But he liked to make up stories, so I guess that's what it was."

"Tell me another one."

"That's another thing my father told me—only one story a night. After that, he said if I didn't go to sleep, there'd be no more stories."

"Okay, Dad. See you in the morning."

Rick bent down, kissed him, told him he loved him, and left.

Now, he thought, he would have to tell Janice about Sara. It would be stupid to keep it from her. Eventually she would hear of it—from an announcement in the papers, from Maria or Brooks or a remark that he himself might drop—and she would then be upset by the suspicion that there was some ulterior purpose for his silence.

He recalled her reaction when she had read in the advertising notes of the *Times* that Sara had been elected a vice-president. She had smiled a forced smile and said casually—too casually—"I see that one of your business associates has come up in the world." And he had replied in the same too-casual tone, "Oh, you mean Sara? Yeah, she made V.P. Not such a big deal, really. We've got more V.P.s than the Mexican army has generals." And that was the last time Sara had been mentioned. But she was always there, at the breakfast and dinner table, over cocktails, in the quiet of the living room, and, most poignantly, almost visibly, in the bedroom.

It was damned well time that they stopped pretending there was no such person as Sara Vardon, whose bed he had shared, who worked in his office, who now would either move closer to him in the agency hierarchy or would walk out of their lives entirely. He did not want to go the other way and make her a part of everyday conversation, but when circumstances indicated that she be mentioned, they should have no reluctance in doing so.

They had, of course, discussed Sara right after the reconciliation. Rather, Janice had discussed her, Rick interjecting only to make sure that she was not judged unfairly. She had been in the hospital then, and Janice was all sympathy, berating herself for the unfortunate timing of her proposal, but at the same time defending it, saying it was better to have it happen before Sara was in a position to resume their relationship. No, she didn't blame Sara, not in the least. After all, Rick had lived alone, was in effect a bachelor, with all the markings of a free man, and why wouldn't a young girl, or any woman for that matter, consider him fair game and go gunning for him? When she was corrected, Rick pointing out that it was he who had done the gunning, Janice simply shrugged and smiled and said something like, well, that may be, but a woman didn't really have to be too clever to make a man think he had been the aggressor. Rick was annoyed and showed it, and was only partially appeased when Janice quickly said that it really was not a case of one or the other taking the initiative, it was simply circumstance, propinquity, and was the most natural thing in the world for two people who were lonely and unattached. Anyway, it wasn't important now. They were together again, she and Rick and their son, nothing else mattered, and the only thing to do was close the door on that little interlude, forget there ever was a Sara, and get on with living a joyful family life.

The meeting was then adjourned in favor of more sociable pursuits, but it left Rick disturbed and uncertain, words like "gunning" and "clever" and "interlude" remaining to fester in his mind. Didn't Janice realize that Sara had been much more than a fortuitous episode, a frivolity, a Band-Aid for a wounding loneliness? Probably she did, but to admit it would be to feel herself under constant threat, ever vulnerable to any sly advances Sara might decide to make upon him. And so Sara became a nonperson, while Janice became the perfect wife and mother, declining offers from producers, divesting the household of maid and nursemaid and retaining only a semiweekly cleaning woman. She devoted her days to Scott, to shopping, to preparing gourmet dishes, and at night, after television or reading or an outing to a movie or play, transforming herself into a wicked, imaginative lover, enraptured by her handsome husband.

It was, thought Rick, a marriage that most men dream of, but rarely attain. And yet he could not deny his sense of loss, his frequent restlessness, his memories, enhanced by time and distance, that came unbidden in the night. And when he saw Sara, at a meeting or passing in the halls, looking so chic, so poised, so much the purposeful career woman, he was gripped by an intense desire to penetrate that smooth surface and return her to the ingenuous, refreshing girl who had revived in him all the feelings of young romantic love and the brash eagerness of his youth.

He had to remind himself that he was a mature man, with the experience and character to deal with choices. He had made his choice and, if he was to respect himself, he could not compromise it by engaging in a sneaky infidelity, which Sara had more than implied would be quite all right with her.

What the hell had happened to Sara that she could accept a role she once would have scorned as utterly degrading? Where was the sense of propriety, the latent guilt that he suspected had troubled her in their unblessed union and consequently inhibited her sexual response? And, thinking of the latter, what had occurred to produce the brazen, turned-on woman who had all but assaulted him on the day they returned from the hospital? He would have enjoyed making love to her then—who wouldn't have enjoyed a lover so totally abandoned?—but afterward he would have worried. If they had remained together and her strange behavior had continued, he would have felt compelled to go again to Dr. Kloster and, probing more deeply, resisting his bland answers, demand to know if anything, anything at all, had happened during the operation that could be held accountable.

But she was not his worry now, not in a responsible way. His obligation—a cold, unfeeling word, he thought—was to Janice, his wife, the mother of his son, the very pretty woman with long chestnut hair who, as he entered the living room, put aside her book and gave him a warm smile.

"Well," she said, "did you give him something pleasant to dream about?"

"You bet. A ferocious man-eating lion."

"Oh, dear. He'll dream he's being eaten alive."

"Nope. He'll know exactly how to handle the beast."

Dropping down on the sofa, away from where she was curled up, looking very domestic in her white robe, he repeated the story. She laughed and said Scott would now probably drag her to the zoo in search of inside-out lions.

He stretched, rubbed his eyes, said, "I'm afraid I wasn't at my dramatic best."

"Rough day?"

"Not particularly. Nothing big. It was like that description of life: one damned thing after another. I spent half the afternoon commiserating with Brooks."

"Don't tell me that he and Maria—"

"Oh, no. I gather they're still rediscovering their youth. Brooks is worried that we may lose some of our best people to the competition. Today's crisis was Sara. She told him she was leaving the agency."

Janice slowly straightened her legs and sat up. Glancing at her, Rick saw that her eyes had become greedily bright.

"Why?"

He knew the answer she hoped for—that Sara was leaving New York. Or, better still, that she was getting married to someone who lived in Europe or South America. But she seemed no less pleased when he explained that apparently Harry Dalton had offered Sara the Transcon account if she would start her own agency. "That could shake loose a few of our other clients, not to mention some of our more talented people."

She gave him a candid look. "Well, I'd be sorry about that. But not about her leaving."

"That's understandable."

She kept her gaze on him. "Rick, do you still . . . I mean, do you ever—"

"Janice, Sara Vardon is someone I know in business. That's all." It took an effort to keep his eyes from wavering.

"I'm sorry. I shouldn't have asked."

"Yes, you should. We can't go on acting like I never knew her. I'm not saying we should make a point of talking about her, but why work so hard to avoid the subject?"

"I know, and I will try, really I will." She sighed almost contentedly. "It should be a cinch, now that she's leaving."

He felt his face tighten. "She may not be."

Disappointment darkened her eyes. "But you just said—"

"Brooks is considering making an offer she can't refuse."

"Like what?"

"I don't know how far he'll go. Right now he's thinking about it. He says he'll have a decision tomorrow."

"It would have to be something big, after what Dalton offered her."

"Too big for Brooks to stomach, I think. Anyway, whatever he decides, it won't have any effect on me." He looked at her closely. "Or us."

She slid over next to him and dropped her head on his shoulder. "I'm betting she goes with Harry Dalton."

"Why so sure?"

"Woman's intuition. It tells me that she and Dalton have something very heavy going on."

He was startled. For some reason the thought had never occurred to him.

It was almost noon the next day when Sara again sat facing Brooks Madden. He smiled at her, but it was a strange, noncommittal sort of smile that did not extend to his eyes. It was the expression of a man not quite sure if he was dealing with an extortionist, but who, she guessed, was determined not to yield.

"Sara, I've given lots of thought to what we talked about yesterday. And this morning I sounded out a number of people around here, management people."

"I appreciate all the trouble you've—"

"That's my job, my responsibility. The most important thing I can do is make sure that the people we put into top management are not only capable but also absolutely loyal to the company. If I find that anyone high up is an operator, just working for number one, then out he goes. No hearing, no appeal, just *out*."

Jesus Christ, a speech! No, more like an indictment by a public prosecutor. And she was the target. She felt a surge of anger, felt her mouth pinch tight, her eyes go cold. She said nothing. Let him rant. Once she'd set up her own shop, she'd show Mr. Brooks Madden that his faith in certain members of the top brass had been very much misplaced.

"As I said, I've talked to several of our key executives. And what they said confirmed what I felt myself."

Here it comes. Goodbye Brooks, hello Harry.

"I heard nothing but enthusiasm. For your talent, sure, I expected that. But the thing that really got to me was the way they went all out for you as a person. They were one hundred percent behind the offer I'm going to make to you."

"Offer?" She suddenly felt she was at the wrong meeting.

"Right. Listen, Sara, to keep you here, I'm ready to go the limit." He ticked it off on his fingers. "One, your own agency, a subsidiary of Madden and Associates, but with your name on it. Two, your own separate offices on one of our floors. Three, your election to the executive committee at its next meeting." He dropped his hands and sat back.

"Don't stop now, Brooks. You're doing fine." She was grinning, a mere hint of her pounding elation.

His sense of humor had deserted him. "That's it. Now, if you feel you can't accept that, well . . ." He shrugged.

She accepted it, the warning as well as the crown.

She called Harry Dalton from a pay phone as she was leaving the building for lunch. "Harry, it worked! I got it all, everything we talked about!"

"Congratulations. But why so surprised? You had him by the balls. All you had to do was squeeze."

"Hey, how about us having a drink, to celebrate?"

"Fine. But make it in my office, lunch too. Now that you've learned how the system operates, you're ready for your next lesson."

"I don't get it."

"Remember our deal? If this worked out, you agreed to consider another proposition."

"Right." She grinned. "You sound like the devil asking me to sell my soul."

"You're not selling?"

"Only if the price is right."

19

THE RED-HAIRED receptionist hung up the phone and smiled. "Miss Roland will be right with you."

Sara turned away to hide her annoyance. Previously, Harry himself had come striding out to escort her inside. Now it seemed that Thea, excluded from their discussions, was determined to find out just what the hell it was that demanded such secrecy.

Sara waited. And waited. She was about to protest to the receptionist when Thea finally appeared, greeting her with a quick nod, an icy smile, and no apology. She led her through a large open area, the desks deserted now at twelve-thirty, and stopped before the closed door of Harry's office.

She turned to Sara. "Will you be staying long?"

"Long enough for lunch."

A muscle twitched in Thea's cheek. "I see."

"Of course, we'll have drinks first." Sara said it haughtily, enjoying this small revenge.

Thea gave her a cold stare, then turned and knocked on the door. She was about to grasp the knob when the door was flung open to reveal Harry's towering figure. Looking past Thea, he smiled at Sara.

"What'd you do, come by dogsled?"

"No, by taxi." She studied her watch. "But I had to wait in the lobby. Let's see. Exactly fifteen minutes."

"For Christsake! I told the receptionist to send you right in." He scowled at Thea. "Did you—"

"Sorry," Thea said calmly, "I didn't know about that. When I heard she was here, I naturally—"

"Naturally," Sara said. "That's your job—to protect the boss against intruders." She smiled magnanimously. "Don't let it upset you. We all make mistakes."

Thea flushed and looked at Dalton. "Shall we go in?"

Dalton now regarded her amiably, as though enjoying himself. "You run along, Thea. I won't need you until after lunch."

For a moment she didn't move, her breathing audible through flared nostrils. Then she turned abruptly and stalked off.

"I guess I shouldn't have baited her," Sara said, entering the office. "Now she's pissed."

"Not at you, at me. It seems I had her order lunch sent up for two. I forgot to tell her she wasn't the guest. Do her good. Every now and then she needs a little taking down."

"You're a cruel man," Sara said, smiling.

"When necessary, same as you." He motioned toward a couch. "Okay, get comfortable and we'll have a bottle of celebration."

He went behind a bar in the corner and got a bottle of champagne from the small refrigerator. While he popped it and poured, Sara strolled to a glass wall and gazed down on Park Avenue, observing the traffic and the people scurrying about like frightened bugs. She had a strange feeling that she belonged here on the fortieth floor, high above those anonymous creatures, unaffected by the petty problems that drove them into narrow, ordered lives destined for sorrow and frustration. The only escape was in money and power, the ability to control events, just as she, aided by this big man with all his experience, had controlled her spectacular rise at the agency.

The feeling was reinforced as she turned and contemplated the office, a room as big as a squash court, resplendently furnished in rich leather and solid mahogany, with a long table at one end for meeting or eating. The grass-cloth walls were backdrops for Harry's ornaments of success: a scale-model Transcon 747 projecting from a silver rod, honorary plaques and framed certificates, oil paintings of his resorts and his estate in Connecticut, inscribed photographs of him with Presidents Kennedy, Johnson, Ford, as well as famous sports figures, entertainers, and men and women renowned in the arts and sciences. Ability alone, she thought, was not enough to reach such heights. There must also be a singleness of purpose, a ruthless opportunism, a sense of superior destiny. Harry Dalton had these qualities. And so, as she had just demonstrated, did she.

She was seated on the leather couch when he brought the champagne. As they clicked glasses, they exchanged the arch smiles of triumphant conspirators.

"To the beginning," he said, then dropped into a chair and piled his feet on the coffee table.

"Beginning? What more could I want?"

"We'll get to that. Give me the blow-by-blow."

She reported her meeting with Brooks, including his emphasis on company loyalty.

"That's good," Harry said. "Very, very good. Now you've got him scared."

"Of me? Not anymore." She gave a mock salute. "I'm now his most loyal employee."

"That's what he hopes. But he can't be sure. Look, put yourself in his seat. Here's this brainy girl—you—who comes into his office, breaks his arms and legs, and rifles his pockets. He could kick her ass out, but he doesn't because he's afraid she might take some of his backers and troops with her. So he appeases her, gives her every damn thing she wants. But do you think he trusts her?"

"Maybe not at the moment. But he will when I prove myself."

"That may not be easy. Anyway, you jarred the hell out of him. You showed him that he's got a lot more than his competition to worry about. He knows, now, that his clients could be picked off by certain key people on his own staff. So he's got to come up with some way to protect himself."

"He was pretty clear on that. Once he spots an operator, he said, out he goes."

"Yeah, *if* he spots him. Fine in the old days when the agency was small and he could keep an eye on everybody. But now it's so big that no single person could possibly police it. No, there's only one way he can be reasonably sure of loyalty, and that's to buy it. If he didn't completely understand that before, he does now, thanks to you."

"But it cost him plenty. His heart's blood, by the look of him. He's not about to make deals like that with all his top people, just so they'll stick around."

Dalton emptied his glass and set it down. "I say he'll make a better one."

"You mean pay them more money?"

"Yes, but not thousands of dollars—millions."

"Oh, come on. There's not that much net profit. He'd go broke."

"It won't cost him a cent."

She stared at him. "What does he do, rub a lamp?"

"Drink your bubbly. Time for a refill."

As she finished her champagne and he poured more, she was aware of her quickened heartbeat, of a flush of excitement warming her body, coloring her cheeks. The great Harry Dalton was about to make the preposterous seem plausible.

"Okay," she said, "where does Brooks get these millions to throw around?"

"From investors. He goes public. He gets listed on the New York Stock Exchange."

Her excitement receded. She had expected something more grandiose. "It's that simple?"

"It's that simple. The price of Madden stock on the big board would be many times the book value, which is all a stockholder would get if he cashed in under the present setup."

"You're sure?"

"I'm sure. Madden and Associates is a solid, growing company, with a terrific track record. Madden's inner circle would go to bed one night worth maybe a few hundred thousand apiece. They'd all wake up millionaires. Madden himself, the biggest stockholder, would be as rich as an oil sheik."

"Jesus. But if that's the case, wouldn't these instant millionaires cash in, take the money and run?"

"Only the ones who wanted out anyway. The guy aching for early retirement. The dreamer who can't wait to start that chicken ranch in California. None of them threats to the agency. The hot ones, the ones with balls, who really make the business go, they'd hang in.

They'd work their asses off, and everybody else's, to push the stock higher and higher. They'd find out there's no such thing as being rich enough."

She thought a minute. "But what about all those new stockholders outside the agency? Wouldn't they have a say in running the show?"

"Theoretically, yes. But they wouldn't give a damn about anything except how the stock performs and the amount of dividends. So, in practice, they'd go along with the board of directors, which would be expanded to include outside members, people well known in the financial community. The board would be all-powerful. They'd control every move the agency made."

"Which means they'd control Brooks." She shook her head. "That's where the wheels fall off. After all, he built the agency from a hole in the wall. It's his whole life. He'd never give up his authority."

"He'd still be chairman of the board, still the chief executive officer, still the biggest stockholder. He'd have more authority than any one man should really handle."

"But not as much as before."

"That's right. But I think he can be convinced that it's worth that sacrifice in order to hold on to the people he wants to keep. I also think he's ready to ease up a bit. He's worked like a donkey since he was a kid, and he's now sixty-three years old. It's time he started learning how to play."

"You don't know Brooks. The only thing that turns him on is the office."

"Wrong. He's also turned on by Maria Corliss."

"Maria . . . you mean Maria Corliss, the actress?"

"That's the one. You know her? She's a bit before your time."

"I've heard of her." She recalled that Rick had mentioned her. "What makes you think they've got something going?"

"Maria's an old friend. In fact, it was Maria who twisted my arm to attend your pitch for my business. And she did it because she's in love with Brooks Madden."

"I'll be goddamned!"

"I talked to her the other day. She's living at Madden's place right now and has been, off and on, for some time. But she leaves him when she has business to look after or to see her son, which is pretty often. So ask yourself—wouldn't Madden welcome some time off to keep her company?"

She gave a slow nod as her mind replayed parts of their conversation. Where was he heading? Obviously toward some sort of proposition, the one she had promised to listen to intently. Well, she was listening and she was fascinated, but she could see nothing in all this that would involve her.

"All right," he said, "let's assume that Madden, as chief executive officer, is weighed down by too much responsibility, too much work, when what he really wants is more freedom to be with Maria. What can he do? Easy. He simply dumps a lot of his duties on executives he trusts, people like Rick Bradley, say."

The champagne seemed to effervesce in Sara's blood. One of those duties might require her to report to Rick. In essence, they'd be partners.

"The result," said Harry, "would be a diffusion of authority. Whoever shared in it would no longer be chiefly concerned with Madden's approval. A bigger concern would be to please the *real* bosses, the board of directors."

"What difference would that make to you—or me?"

Dalton poured the last of the champagne. Smiling, he said, "I think that, working together, we could control the board of directors."

"Harry, we couldn't!"

"The hell we couldn't. You'd be lobbying the insiders. I'd be manipulating the outsiders. Pretty soon we'd have a majority of the directors seeing things our way. Believe me, Sara, without Madden or any of his executives realizing it, we'd be running the whole operation."

"Wow!" She drained her glass. "But why? To milk it?"

"No, to make it bigger and even more profitable. But we'll talk about that later. Right now, let's concentrate on the first phase, to convince Madden to go public. So now you know where you come in."

"Me, convince Brooks? Oh, look, Harry, after what I just did to him, he'd think I was out to steal the whole damned agency. His next thought would be that you're in on it."

"No question about it. The proposal's got to come from someone else, ideally from the man closest to Madden—Rick Bradley."

She gave a start. "I couldn't push it with Rick. He'd be as suspicious as Brooks."

"Okay, then you grease the other big wheels. Remember, you'll be on the executive committee. You'll have prestige, clout. The other members will listen to you."

"Sure they will. And they'll be so impressed, they'll be delighted to give me full credit—with Brooks."

He looked her up and down. "Not the way you'd handle it. Whoever you talked to would come away thinking it was his idea. You'd be out of it. A couple of charged-up guys, that's all you'd need to get it rolling. You'd choose them very carefully—men desperate for money, or who've been with the agency a long time and would love to quit but can't afford to. Got any of those?"

"I think so. But I'm not sure they're the kind who make waves."

"Try them. There's nothing like greed to grow a little hair on the chest. Besides, they wouldn't exactly be revolutionaries. Over the last ten or fifteen years, just about every big agency has gone public. Madden's still living back in the forties. After the scare you gave him, he may need only a nudge to get with it."

There was a knock on the door.

Dalton stood up, keeping his eyes on her face. "That's my proposition. Are you buying?"

She was silent for a moment, thinking. So this was the way the men played it. The power game, they called it. Hardball. Much too rough for the ladies. Do you hear that, Sara Sunshine?

She rose, smiling, and faced him. "I'm buying."

They shook hands.

"Lunch is served," he said, and went to the door.

Three days later, responding to a decision of the board of directors, the executive committee elected Sara to membership and approved her plan to set up a separate agency unit. Called in to the meeting, Sara gave her prettiest smile as the men rose and applauded. After a brief welcoming speech from Brooks, the meeting broke up and the men crowded around to congratulate her personally. They were charmed to find that she remembered their names, their positions, and seemed familiar with their duties.

They would have been less charmed and quite perplexed, thought Sara, had they been aware of just how much she had learned about each of them.

20

SHE WAS a corner-office, four-window manager now, with a staff of six writers, four art directors, one film producer, three secretaries, and two typists, occupying a section of the floor below the executive suite. Officially they were called The Vardon Group, but were generally referred to, enviously, as Sara's Superstars, assigned to no particular accounts except Transcon Airlines, but engaged whenever a client decided upon a shift in strategy, or introduced a new product, or simply became desperately bored with the stuff that had been running. The Vardon Group were ad-makers, nothing else, dependent on the resources of the agency for such services as media buying, merchandising, research, although, at the behest of account executives, Sara would often present a campaign to a client.

Rick Bradley, though continuing as account supervisor of Transcon, was not Sara's overseer, as she had hoped. Instead, she was to report directly to Brooks Madden. That, thought Sara, would change just as quickly as Harry Dalton's plan could be implemented.

She took a first tentative step in that direction during a lunch at "21" with Lou Kahn. He had invited her ostensibly as a congratulatory gesture, but actually, she thought, to reassure herself that she had no designs on his job, upon which she had already intruded. She decided to meet that concern head-on, knowing that Lou, also a member of the executive committee, could be a valuable ally.

"Lou, I hope you don't feel any resentment about this new setup."

He shrugged and set down his martini. "No, I go with the flow."

But his eyes, behind the thick lenses, were guarded. "Sure, when Brooks first hit me with it—that was before the offer—I got a few complaints from my ulcer. But he calmed me down."

"I hope so. I'd feel terrible if you thought I was trying to move in on you."

A small smile split his beard. "You got to admit it's a logical thought."

"Logical, yes, but wrong. Believe me, Lou, I've already got everything I want. You won't get any competition from me. Just cooperation."

"Thanks, Sara, glad to hear it. Anyway, when Brooks said that's what it would take to put a lock on you, I was all for it."

"I appreciate that." She thought she saw an opening. "I suppose with almost any other agency, I wouldn't even have considered leaving. They'd simply have given me more stock."

Lou cocked an eyebrow. "You'd have settled for that?"

"Oh, no, not at Madden. But with an agency that's gone public, there'd be a chance the stock would take off and I'd end up rich. Being a greedy bitch, I'd probably have stayed."

Lou looked at her sharply. "Did you tell that to Brooks?"

"No. What good would it have done?"

"It might have started him thinking again. Look, the executive committee's gone round and round on this. The last time was maybe two years ago. Everybody waffled on it, taking both sides until they were sure where Brooks stood. Well, he finally told 'em. In a few hundred carefully chosen words, he said no. Since then, no one's let out a peep."

"Then it's a damned good thing I kept my mouth shut."

"I'm not so sure. A hell of a lot's changed in the last couple of years. It's gotten tougher to keep good people. You load on the bucks and the titles and the agency down the street not only tops you, they also sweeten the pot with stock options."

"You're starting to worry me. Here I get my own group and you're saying it could all come apart."

He flashed a grin. "Maybe it's time we gave Brooks another goose."

"Leave me out of it. I'm very happy as is."

"You should be. But there are others . . ." He signaled the waiter. "Anyway, what's to hurt if I have a little talk with Rick?"

It was, she thought, a good beginning.

Guy Romley did not look like the sort of man who could be manipulated. Standing more than six feet tall, he was still, at fifty-eight, lean and hard-muscled, his ruddy cheeks stretched tight across a prominent bone structure. His hair was full, as white as Cary Grant's, and styled in the same way. His usual expression was dogged, almost belligerent, evoking in the beholder a feeling of pleasant surprise when a smile displayed his even white teeth, most of them his own.

In a movie, thought Sara, he would make the perfect gentleman rancher, a cattle king who ran his spread with steely-eyed authority. In fact, he was a cream puff. Ironically, in the tough world of advertising, this gentleness of character was his salvation and the springboard to his success.

The story was well known in the agency. Some twenty years ago, a Brooklyn manufacturer of packaged spaghetti had come to Brooks Madden "over the transom" to offer him their account. He had accepted it reluctantly, the billing being small and the potential for growth seeming nonexistent. Brooks had assigned Guy Romley as account executive, a convenient choice inasmuch as Brooks had about decided that this man whom everyone liked, agreeable, conscientious, totally honest, was in the wrong business. But it was Brooks who was wrong, on both counts. The company, branching out into a broad line of pasta products, became one of the great marketing successes of the decade, the advertising expenditure increasing proportionately until it now stood at thirty-five million dollars annually. Guy Romley rose with it, not because of any unperceived brilliance, but because he stoically suffered the abuse and humiliation inflicted on him by the three Sicilian brothers who owned the company and were inevitably referred to as "the Brooklyn Mafia."

Sara was aware of all this as they sat having a drink in a Brooklyn bar to recover from her first meeting with the Sicilian trio. Guy had beseeched her to come so that his suspicious clients might be convinced that their advertising was receiving the personal attention of a great creative talent. They had struggled to act like gentlemen, but their condescending manner and sly exchange of smirks would have been more appropriate to an approach of a streetwalker.

"You noticed I backed out of their office," Sara said. "I was afraid they'd pinch my ass."

Guy Romley didn't smile. "They're really not bad fellows. They're just not used to meeting women who are successful in business."

"Oh, I'm sure they're good to their wives. Always giving them vacuum cleaners and mops and lawnmowers and providing the best medical care when poppa breaks their bones." She studied his look of discomfort. "Don't mind me. I'm just having fun. But I'd hate like hell to put my career in their hands."

He looked at her defensively. "The way I have, you mean?"

"I wasn't thinking of that. Sorry. But that's right—you've been on the account for a long time, haven't you?"

"More than twenty years."

"My God."

"You get used to it."

"I suppose. Like getting your teeth drilled. After a while, you no longer detest it. You merely hate it."

He finally smiled, his white squared-off teeth seeming to illuminate the darkly lit booth. He was, thought Sara, a man with the temperament to be happy, but he had squandered it on three callous men who had committed him to slavery.

"Well, it's not forever," he said. "Five more years. That's when I'll take early retirement." He raised his glass. "Then it's goodbye to New York."

"Sounds like you have exciting plans."

He told her about them. They centered on a small beach cottage in Nantucket he had owned for the past twelve years. He was eager to enlarge it, adding a studio wing where his wife could paint, and later a guest room or two to accommodate the families of his son and daughter on weekend and vacation visits. All that was quite practical, and even now he was discussing the expansion with an architect. But that was only the tip of his dream. What he wanted above all else was to develop the frontage adjacent to the cottage into a splendid marina presided over by a boat and tackle shop that he would own and personally operate.

"The impossible dream," he said ruefully. "But perhaps by the time I turn in my uniform, I'll have enough to get it started."

She pretended to think for a minute. "Maybe you won't have to wait that long. You may suddenly find yourself in the big bucks."

"No way. I don't even have a ticket for the Irish Sweepstakes."

"This could be better. That is, if you own a good chunk of company stock."

He assumed a blank expression. "Brooks has been pretty generous. But, after all, I've been with the firm for more than twenty years. Still, I don't see—"

"I suppose I shouldn't mention this. But Lou didn't say it was confidential. In fact, he was quite open about it."

"Lou Kahn?"

"Yes. The other day at lunch he told me that a number of executives were talking about the agency going public. I don't know much about the process, but he said that the stock would then be worth a lot more than it is now. Is that right?"

"Well, sure. But Brooks would never—"

"Lou said that Brooks has been against it. But he thinks he may be ready for it now. If not, Lou says, a lot of good people may walk out, and a few of them might take their clients with them."

"Like you almost did with Transcon?"

She smiled. "He didn't mention that, but maybe that's why he pitched it at me. He knew I'd understand how vulnerable some accounts are." She arched her eyebrows. "Come to think of it, you're in the same position with your Sicilian friends."

"Oh, hey, I'd never think of—"

"Of course you wouldn't. But the fact is, you could probably move them to another agency. If that occurs to me, it certainly must have occurred to Brooks. So he'd be dumb not to nail you down. And what better way than to make you rich?"

Guy gave his head a shake. "Unbelievable. Really unbelievable."

"I could be all wrong about this. I suppose what you'd better do is talk to the other members of the executive committee. Then you'll be getting it straight."

His face set in his familiar look of determination. "I may do that." He nibbled his lower lip. "Maybe I'll do more than that."

"Whatever you do, Guy, please don't say you heard this from me. Others might think I was trying to influence you. Believe me, I'm not."

"Sure, I understand. I appreciate your telling me."

She changed the subject, noticing that he scarcely listened. His eyes had turned wistful, as though contemplating a tall, white-haired man in a yachting cap, gazing at a forest of masts swaying in a sun-splashed marina.

Sam Kramer stood framed in the doorway, his sleek, dark head thrusting forward as his eyes rolled over Sara's office. He blinked at the silky, dark-red furniture, pale-blue carpet and walls, the handsome reproductions of paintings by Matisse, Monet, and Corot.

Sara leaned back in her chair, smiling. "Hi, Sam, welcome to the cathouse."

He stepped in gingerly, stood over her, and gazed at her warily. "I'll have a drink with you but I won't go upstairs."

She laughed and waved him to a chair. Sam Kramer, account supervisor and member of the executive committee, handled Blue Grass Distillers, producers of half a dozen brands of bourbon, of which he was an ardent consumer. The result showed in pouched pink eyes and a slight tremor of the hands, job-related afflictions that he sought to compensate for with a sunlamp tan, an energetic manner, and impeccable dress. He was the stereotype of the slick, glib Madison Avenue huckster, an image he cultivated carefully because it so appealed to the officers of his whiskey-making client in Kentucky, who would have felt cheated had they been assigned an ordinary businessman. Years ago he had endeared himself to them with such phrases as "Let's run it up the flagpole and see who salutes," "Let's put it on the train and see if it gets off at Westport." An advertising campaign was a "blitz." Sales meetings were conducted to "stir up the animals." A product didn't merely succeed, it found "its place in the sun." This, by golly, was a real honest-to-God New York adman who could be depended upon to get you looped, laid, and limoed to the airport.

"Keep your head back," Sara said. "I don't want those eyes bleeding on my desk."

"Who's got blood? I left it all in Louisville. Jesus, if those guys paid for the booze they drink, sales would double."

"Well, just relax and tell me your problem. Your client looking for a new idea?"

"You crazy? Give 'em anything but a big bottle with maybe a horse behind it and they'd choke on their tobacco. So okay, why am I here? Don't ask, I'll tell you. I'm here to put diamonds in your navel, butlers in your pantry, a Rolls in your garage."

"Sorry, I just quit knocking over banks."

"You're sitting in one right now. But you don't knock it over. All you do is nod your head and you get the key to the vault. How's that grab you?"

"I don't know," Sara said. "Give it to me in English."

"Okay. I come in here this morning after a red-eye flight from Louisville, and before I can make it to the men's room, three of our top cats land on me with a proposition. Not a new proposition—I'd heard it before and I'd pitched it before and I'd attended its funeral. But maybe, I'm told, we can revive the corpse and put it to work for us. All it takes is for us doctors to work as a team."

"Sam, I love the metaphors. I only wish I could understand them."

So he gave it to her straight. It was like a playback of what she had told Lou Kahn and Guy Romley, but delivered with proselytizing zeal and with no attempt to cloak avarice in sanctimony. Sara sat perfectly still, expressionless, fearful that her inner laughter might suddenly burst out and betray her as the instigator.

"That's it," Sam said, "the Yellow Brick Road to riches." He paused to peer at her blank face. "Look, I didn't expect confetti and noisemakers but also I didn't expect you to look like you'd flunked your Pap test. Speak to me, just one word."

"Fantastic," she said calmly, and smiled.

"Is that good or bad?"

"Good. I think going public is a fine idea."

"Then you're with us?"

"I'm with you."

"Great. If we can swing this, I may even stop hating my former wives. The bloodsuckers—every month they kick me in the groin and roll me. Okay. So you'll give it the hard sell?"

"No, Sam. I'll vote for it but I won't try to sell it."

He squinted a pink eye. "Yeah, I can see why. Brooks just gave you your own boutique. You wouldn't want him thinking you're after the whole store."

Brooks stared across his desk at the papers in Rick's hand as though they were snakes.

"That's the report?"

"Yes." Rick smiled. "I hope neatness doesn't count. I pecked it out myself."

Brooks snorted. "Sure. For security. To keep the lid on. Then it gets leaked to five members of the executive committee."

"Six. Sam Kramer was in yesterday. He was as charged up as Lou Kahn. Going public, he said, would be like giving the agency a new set of balls. You know Sam."

"Yeah, Mr. Mouth. It's a good thing he knows the liquor business like nobody else. Did he say how he got the word?"

"From the others. But I don't think any of them know I've been investigating it. My guess is it was just a natural reaction."

"To what?"

"To the deal you made with Sara. Here are these guys, top executives who've been around for years, and they see a young woman step in, pull a few levers, and hit the jackpot. They had to have asked themselves, what about us? Shouldn't we get a bigger piece of the action? So naturally they talked it over. There's nothing sinister about it."

"I guess not. Dammit, sometimes I wish I'd let Sara take Dalton's account and get the hell out.

"That wouldn't have solved the problem. It would only have encouraged others to try the same thing."

"Don't I know it! She had me boxed. And whether she knows it or not, she's got me boxed again. If she hadn't put the screws on me, this damfool stock business would never have come up."

Rick recalled the day following Sara's triumph, when Brooks had come into his office asking for help in devising some system of rewards that would "bind our key people closer to the company." After some discussion, Rick had gingerly suggested the taboo subject: inflate their stock through a public offering. That had done it. Listen, said Brooks, that had all been settled. Goddammit, he didn't want a bunch of financial analysts and efficiency experts and stuffed shirts who made a career of being corporate directors poking around in something they didn't understand and never would. So who cared if they'd done great things for other agencies. This agency was different. It was still run by the guy who'd founded it. He wasn't about to share control with people who didn't give a damn about anything but money. Then, as quickly as he had erupted, he calmed down and said, okay, give it a look, prepare a report, but he told Rick not to go away thinking he'd buy it. He was just meeting his responsibility to consider everything, even something he was dead set against.

"All right," Brooks said, "let's hear it. Just the highlights. I'll read the whole thing later."

"I talked to people at three Wall Street houses. Based on the information I gave them, they all agreed that our stock would sell on the open market for four or five times its book value. In other words, from a book of eight, it could jump to as high as forty—instantly."

"My God, I'd be surrounded by millionaires."

"A few. But you'd be the richest."

"Forget me. Already I'm as rich as any man has a right to be. So okay, we suddenly have a lot of fat cats. What's to stop them from cashing in and taking a walk?"

"Nothing. They could all just hang in for a year in order to have their profit taxed as a capital gain, no more than twenty-five percent, leaving a million-dollar stockholder with over three-quarters of a million net."

"I'd be the only one left to run the business."

"But I'm assured it doesn't work that way. The only people you'd stand to lose are the older guys, the ones counting the days to retirement. No great loss really, in some cases a blessing. And there'd be little danger they'd move to another shop or start their own."

"That leaves the younger ones. Sure as hell they wouldn't retire.

But what's to stop them from switching to the competition or picking off a client and setting up for themselves?"

"Because their chances of getting richer would be a lot better if they stayed right here, in an established agency with a phenomenal record of growth. They wouldn't be satisfied with the stock remaining at forty. They'd want to double it, triple it, boost the dividends, see it split. Which means they'd work like they never worked before. Everything they said or did would be in the interests of the company, because they'd *be* the company. And they'd insist on the same attitude from everyone they're associated with."

Brooks gave a grim smile. "You've certainly got it figured."

"I'm quoting the men I talked to."

"But you believe it?"

"Yes."

Brooks shook his head, as though in disillusionment. "Sure, you'd be one of the millionaires."

Rick felt a stab of anger. "I don't think I deserve that remark, Brooks."

Their eyes clashed for a moment. Then Brooks's face softened into a look of regret. "No, you don't. I'm sorry. I know you care about the company." He sighed. "Let's go on. So far we've been talking about the big wheels who are loaded. How about the smaller shareholders, our future managers? Even pegged at forty, their holdings wouldn't amount to very much."

Rick wondered if he was thinking of Sara. She had a few hundred shares, which would rise in value from about twenty-four hundred dollars to perhaps twelve thousand dollars—a spectacular gain, but hardly enough to assure her allegiance.

"That would be pretty much up to you," Rick said. "Before going public, you could sell them more stock at book value. They'd pay for it with a low-interest loan from the company, secured by the stock. Of course, as soon as the stock was publicly traded, they'd have an enormous profit. When they eventually sold stock, they could easily pay off the loan."

"Looks like I'd have a money-making machine," Brooks said dryly. "Listen, Rick, that's enough for now. Anything else I'll get from the report."

Rick started to rise, then dropped back. "There's one item not covered. I didn't want to put it in writing. It applies to you personally."

Brooks barked a laugh. "The whole damned thing applies to me personally."

"This concerns your estate. You know, of course, that when you die, whatever you leave will be subject to tax."

"I know it but I try not to think about it."

"I'm afraid you've got to. As things stand now, when the IRS estimates the value of your estate, they'll see right away that your company stock is worth considerably more than book. So they'll place a much higher figure on it and that's the figure they'll tax. Your heirs—your sons, I assume—will have to sell that stock to come up with the huge tax. And they might have to take even less than book because they'll be depending on the present stockholders to buy it. It's quite possible they wouldn't have the capital to swing it. But that wouldn't happen if you went public. Then the estate value of your stock would be established by the market, and that's the figure the IRS would accept. The tax would be paid out of the sale of readily marketable shares, leaving a much larger estate than you could right now."

Brooks stared at him, then burst into laughter.

Rick gave a perplexed smile. "What did I day that was so funny?"

"Nothing. It was something I thought. I decided to cancel my death. It's just not worth it."

That evening, over his second scotch, Maria told Brooks that she must leave the next day for Phoenix. The people who managed her condominiums had quit after a long battle with the tenants and must be replaced. She hoped to be gone no longer than a week or ten days.

"Come with me," she said. "Get out of the slush, make love in the desert."

"Listen, I'd like nothing better. But I've got a problem and it's got to be settled now."

"Let Rick handle it. You're always saying he's your problem-solver."

"Not this one. It's something I've got to handle myself."

He told her about it, keeping his voice steady and noncommittal, curious about her reaction and not wanting to influence her.

"But that's wonderful! You just wave your magic wand and everybody gets rich. That's a problem?"

"You bet it is. I wouldn't have such a free hand. A lot of know-it-all characters would be brought in and they'd start telling me how to run the business. But there's another side to it, and that's what I've got to think about and discuss. Hey, listen, this is your last night. Let's not spend it talking shop."

"I'm with you. Let's just talk about us."

Later, when the talk yielded to desire, and then, in his bed, a bodily sharing, he was surprised and disturbed by how long it took him to climax. She reassured him by saying that it was only natural, he was distracted and upset, and anyway—laughing as she kissed his cheek—she was glad of the protraction because it had prolonged her pleasure.

He lay awake, staring into the darkness, weighing the pros and cons of what seemed to be the biggest business decision he had ever faced. He felt alone and trapped, now seeing his top executives banded against him, imagining wholesale resignations if he failed to fulfill their dreams of wealth. And then there was his estate, threatened with virtual extinction, depriving his sons . . .

He switched his thoughts to Maria, soothing his mind with golden images of them lying beside a desert pool. Oh, God, if only for a while he could chuck it all.

Two days later, Sara returned from lunch to find Rick waiting in her office.

"The executive committee meets in ten minutes," he said.

"I know." She smiled. "My first meeting."

"That's why I'm here. I thought I'd better fill you in on something that's coming up."

"You're very thoughtful. Something important?"

"Brooks has decided to go public."

Her face went blank. She sat down.

"That could mean a lot to you, Sara."

She stared at him. "Rick, I haven't the vaguest idea of what you're talking about."

He explained.

She fell back in her chair. "Well, I'll be damned. When does it happen?"

"In about a week—as soon as Brooks gets back. He's taking off on a quickie vacation."

"Where to?"

"Phoenix."

21

SITTING in her office, separated from Harry Dalton's by his private bathroom, Thea Roland heard his door open, heard his voice, heard Sara's, heard their burst of intimate laughter, then watched as Sara walked, almost pranced, across the carpeted area and disappeared through the glass doors to the reception lobby. Thea's long fingernails bit into her palms as her hands formed into fists.

Another victory celebration, she thought. And inasmuch as it coincided with Brooks Madden's return from Phoenix, it could mean only one thing: the public stock offering, promised before he had left, was now an accomplished fact. Oh, there was no question about it. It didn't matter that Harry had not mentioned a word of it, that he let her assume that their private meetings concerned only his advertising. But if that was so, why had Jim Westbrook never been present? She'd have known even if she hadn't eavesdropped on their phone conversations, or once left the key open on his intercom. Just knowing Harry, knowing the way he operated, would have been enough for her to conclude that he was using Sara to grab a piece of Madden and Associates.

She had seen it happen many times before. Harry picking up a small, tottering airline by practically bribing its bankers, through a huge deposit, to threaten foreclosure. Harry concealing himself behind a front man so he wouldn't have to pay a pumped-up price for shares in a casino. Harry using low-budget producers to bargain with Hollywood agents for movie rights to a novel. Not because he gave a damn about the costs—he certainly didn't run his airline on the cheap—but because it would have offended his pride to think that he had been bested by so much as a dime. And now it was Sara, gifted, beautiful, voraciously ambitious, who was acting as Harry's accomplice, working her wiles from inside the agency, like a "mole" planted by an enemy spy apparatus.

To what final purpose? That hadn't yet become clear, but it must be something big or Harry, macho stud that he was, would never had tolerated a relationship that required him to keep his fly zipped. She was almost certain they'd never slept together. Not in San Francisco when, peeking through the peephole in her door, Thea had seen Sara wrench herself from his kiss and close him out. Not in his office, or she'd have heard the click of the lock. And not in his hotel, unless the night bellman was lying himself out of a fat reward.

It made absolutely no sense, unless you figured she was playing Harry, keeping her legs crossed until he sprung them apart with a commitment that would move her to his Greenwich mansion and allow her a voice in his various enterprises. Now that was a real possibility. That was something to be investigated and—whatever it took—eliminated.

The first thing that had struck her as slightly odd was Sara's phone number—it was unlisted. Was there a special reason, aside from the wish to be inaccessible to solicitors and heavy breathers? Thea went to Sara's apartment house during the day and looked at the mailboxes. Above Sara's were two small frames, one with her name, the other empty. Had a name once filled that blank space? Back in her office, Thea called a friend at the phone company and got a listing for the number. Well, well, well. Sara had once shared the apartment with none other than the account supervisor of Transcon Airlines—Rick Bradley.

It took only an otherwise boring lunch with Jim Westbrook to learn that Rick Bradley had been separated from his wife, an actress, but had reconciled with her shortly before the agency got the Transcon business. It was only natural to ask if a woman had caused the breakup, but Westbrook knew nothing about that, so the question of whether Sara might still have strong feelings for Bradley didn't arise. But that seemed a good possibility, especially when Thea discovered that Bradley had a small son he adored, which made it seem plausible that he had dumped Sara only because he could no longer stand not being a full-time father. Anyway, if Sara was still hooked on the guy, it would help to explain why she was out of bounds for Harry. She'd be scared that an affair with him would reach Bradley's ears and thus kill any hope of getting him back. From what Thea had seen of Rick Bradley, he wasn't the kind of man that Sara could easily get out of her system. Not that handsome bastard, all sleek and blond and beautiful outside, but inside a sharp mind and a hard core of self-assurance that could make a woman surrender every speck of herself, the same as Thea had with Harry. So, sure as hell, Sara must be thinking of ways to reclaim him. Sara Vardon, under all those smiles and charming graces, was a tough, mean bitch who wouldn't just roll over when somebody crossed her. She'd fight back with every trick instilled in females since Eve came on with her tasty apple.

Did Harry know any of this? Not likely. It would be dumb of Sara to tell him, if only because she'd know that Harry would then be afraid she'd leak his plans to her former lover. And that could be disastrous because Bradley was close to Madden—his heir apparent, Westbrook had said—and he'd tip off his boss if he suspected any funny business was going on. Now there was an idea! All that was needed to stop Sara cold, in fact, get her ass thrown out, maybe even ruin her in the industry, was for someone to inform Rick Bradley that she and Harry Dalton were in cahoots to somehow get a handle on the agency.

But that someone couldn't be herself or anyone Harry might connect with her. Just one small suspicion and Harry would send her own ass flying, and not on one of his planes. Sure, she could get another top job, but nothing that paid like this one, nothing with the power and the prestige and round-the-world excitement that came with being the head honcho's number-one woman. And worst of all, she'd lose Harry.

No one had ever turned her on like Harry. She'd felt it that first day in his office as she'd sat there trying to look cool and professional, the way they'd taught her at Katharine Gibbs, while his eyes stripped her and his voice echoed inside her as though her head were pressed to his chest. And that night, when she told her boyfriend Roger Schermerhorn, that she was now employed and he congratulated her and came on strong, she had thought of Harry Dalton and of his palatial office, and Roger Schermerhorn had gotten the wildest fuck he had ever experienced. She tried in her mind to give Roger full credit for it, but she knew better a few days later when she flew with Harry to Vegas.

She had been determined not to let him put a hand on her—after all, she and Roger had already picked out their furniture—but a few drinks wouldn't hurt, and besides, if something did happen, she could cool her conscience by laying it off on the booze. But all of that was forgotten once she was encapsulated with Harry in an aluminum tube traveling four hundred miles an hour at thirty thousand feet. Just sitting there talking to him, she had felt like the target of some invincible force, and mentally she was stark naked before she even started skinning out of her clothes. And then the crying—oh, how she'd cried. Not because, as Harry thought, she'd been unfaithful to Roger Schermerhorn—the hell with Roger Schermerhorn—but because this big, driving, insatiable man, who could in one session produce more orgasms than she'd had in her whole life, would toss her aside as he probably had a thousand other girls. And when they got to Las Vegas and she saw him treated like a god, which to her, by then, he was, she knew that this was the end of the line for her and the rest of her life would be spent asking Roger Schermerhorn, "How was it today at the hardware store?"

But she was damned if she'd lose out for not trying. Like a gourmet cook, she spent hours concocting new ways to titillate and satisfy her lover's enormous sexual appetite. She bought all the how-to literature, including magazines at the Times Square porn shops. At home she invented and practiced positions ranging from the submissive to the acrobatic, and exercised daily, bending, stretching, twisting, expanding, contracting. She memorized a lexicon of words and phrases with which to pay lewd tribute to Harry's remarkable endowments, bought expensive perfumes and provocative clothes, and glamorized herself at chic beauty salons. She took classes to improve her body, her mind, her speech.

But still it was not enough. Nothing she could do would ever be enough. So, in addition to being Harry's confidential secretary, in addition to offering him twenty-four-hour sexual service, she also became his pimp, a role she accepted voluntarily because it enabled her to select broads so dumb that Harry couldn't abide them once the action was over. Oddly, these one-nighters produced in her an almost pleasurable pain, affecting her like an aphrodisiac, inciting her the next day to fantastic depravities.

Thus, for two years, through compromise, training, and constant vigilance, she had maintained a precarious position as Harry's number-one partner in business and in bed. And now she was being threatened in both those areas, not by a stupid broad, but by a gutsy, calculating, brilliant woman—a genius, they called her—who flaunted her sex but did not yield it, using it as a lure to entice Harry into her net. If she succeeded, which seemed imminent, that would be the end of Thea Roland.

Obviously something had to be done, and quickly. She thought for a while, her fist beating a slow rhythm on the desktop. Then she made a decision, got up, and headed for Harry's office. It was a risk, she thought, but she had to take it, even if it meant branding herself as a spy.

His door was open and his back was toward her as he stood at a window. He turned as she entered and she detected an uncharacteristic wistful look in his eyes. Had it been put there by dreams of glory or by Sara, or both? She felt a stiffening of her resolve.

"Did you and Sara get everything settled?" she asked pleasantly.

"I think we know where we're going." Enigmatic as usual, when any reference was made to their private meetings.

"I saw her as she was leaving. She seemed really up." Thea smiled. "Like she was about to get it on with Robert Redford."

He grinned, going along. "Sure, who else?"

Her smile turned mischievous. "Well, now that you ask, it could be she's meeting Rick Bradley."

He looked at her sharply, as though to interpret the remark through her expression. She changed her smile to one of indulgence.

"That could be," he said slowly. "Technically, I guess Bradley's her boss. At least he supervises our account."

"I wasn't thinking of business."

His eyes narrowed. "Okay, now tell me what you *were* thinking."

"Oh, Harry, I'm sure that's obvious."

"It isn't."

"But you know about them, don't you?"

"Know what?" His face now looked like a bronze bust.

"That they used to live together."

His face remained stolid, but his eyes seemed to spark. A few moments passed before he said, "I wasn't aware it was common knowledge."

"Maybe it isn't. I don't know. In fact, I can't even recall who told me. Anyway, he left her to go back to his wife. They have a small son, I think."

"But he's still got Sara on the side—is that what you were saying?"

"I don't really know. It was just something that occurred to me. What difference does it make?"

"None." He went to his desk and sat down heavily. "You and your goddamned radar. But this time I'd say you're wrong."

"Okay, I'm wrong. It just seemed to me that it would be pretty tough to live with a man as attractive as Rick Bradley and then just forget about him. But maybe Sara's the kind who—"

He said suddenly, "Sara told me about them living together."

There was a defensive edge to his voice, a signal that he lied. He could not admit that any woman, and especially Sara, had deceived him.

"Well, Harry, if she told you that, then obviously she's through with him. If she wasn't through with him, she'd keep quiet about the whole affair."

He seemed to give a slight start, his eyes flashing her a hostile look, as though she'd trapped him. His gaze remained on her, touring her body, as though seeking the most vulnerable spot to inflict a wound.

She said, "I really came in to see if you needed anything."

"I do." His look became more intense.

She smiled seductively. "Whatever you want."

"Lock the door."

She did. And then, as she kicked off her shoes, unbuttoned her pale-peach blouse, and unzipped her skirt, she phoned the switch-board to hold all calls. She was down to her bra and panties when she hung up and turned to face him. He had flung off his jacket and was standing in the center of the room, like a massive gladiator awaiting his adversary. She went to him quickly but was stopped by his outstretched hands grasping her shoulders. Releasing her, his hands slid to her bra and ripped it off. They descended to her panties, grabbed the top, knuckles grinding into her navel, and all but shredded them. Then, as she stood there, arms straight at her sides, head thrown back to create a lustrous blonde fall, lungs inflated to swell her breasts, he slowly and meticulously undressed.

When he came for her she knew intuitively that it was not merely to gratify his genital lust, but more to punish her for what she had told him. But what he did to her—practically slamming her to the floor, ferociously roughing her flesh, assaulting every orifice—was not punishment, but instead an excruciating ecstasy that engaged every function of her body. And when he was finished with her and she lay perspiring and whimpering next to a wall, far from where they had begun, she knew with certainty that what she had painfully enjoyed was an expression of his love—for Sara Vardon.

When she had gone, Harry poured a stiff bourbon and sat sipping at his desk. Thea's words, spoken so casually, shouted through his mind: ". . . it would be pretty tough to live with a man as attractive as Rick Bradley and then just forget about him." Living with him, having a heavy affair with him, that was easy enough to accept—hell, he himself had yet to sleep with a virgin—but splitting with him, stepping aside for his wife, and then allowing him to sneak back into her bed, that was something else.

Was it true? If it had been any other woman, he'd have believed it without question simply because it had been suggested by Thea, whose perception he had found almost infallible. But Thea per-ceived Sara as a rival, both sexually and corporately—in the latter instance, accurately—and would not hesitate to invent any lie, manufacture any mischief, that might chop her down. (Christ, the hatred he had felt for that smug blonde bitch, the compulsion to crush her as she stood there glorying in her spectacular nakedness.)

But, putting aside Thea's malice, wouldn't the circumstances alone justify the suspicion that Sara and Rick Bradley were still lovers? And if they were, could she be trusted not to unintentionally tip off Bradley on their plans for the agency? If she did, Bradley would feel duty-bound to pass the word to Madden—his great friend, as Maria Corliss had said—and Sara would be departing the company on the next elevator.

But Sara was too shrewd, too clever, too self-controlled to make that mistake. No, there was nothing to worry about there. In fact, the only basis for concern at all was his feeling of being duped. And that was nonsense. Sara owed him no accounting of her private life. That had been clear in her rejection of him as a lover, and no doubt Bradley could take credit for that.

But to hell with it. Bradley had probably been no more to Sara than a youthful infatuation. Pursuing the affair now meant degrading herself by conforming to the furtive arrangements of a part-time, cheating lover, a situation that a woman like Sara, with so much pride and self-esteem, would not tolerate for long. Then she would come to him, Harry Dalton. She would come because she could no longer resist, as she had unwillingly resisted him that night at the hotel, and he would show her how dynamic love could be.

Until then, he told himself, let it alone. Consider Sara only as what she considered herself—an essential partner in an intrigue dedicated to mutual gain.

With an effort, he turned his mind to business. Now that Madden and Associates had officially gone public, it was time to exercise the obligations of certain influential men on Wall Street.

22

DURING THE first two months that Madden and Associates was listed on the New York Stock Exchange, Brooks had to admit he'd been wrong in his opposition. There was a new feeling running through the agency—a greater self-esteem, an enthusiasm, a unity that Brooks equated with the winning spirit of a football team bound for the Super Bowl. He got a kick out of stepping into an elevator and seeing newspapers folded to the financial section, or dropping by a crowded boardroom after lunch to watch the clicking numbers, or being greeted in the halls like a beneficent patriarch, which in substance he was, so generous had he been in distributing stock prior to going public. ("Listen, as long as we're doing it, we'll go all the way!")

In all his years of acquiring wealth, he had never invested in common stocks, opting for the safety and yield of corporate and municipal bonds and blue-chip preferreds, with all transactions handled by his bank. So he had a lot of catching up to do and he applied himself with his usual diligence, reading books, studying the experience of other agencies, and, most informative, consulting with Wall Street professionals. The latter also made him aware of what could not be learned—a feel for the market, an instinct for gauging public attitudes, a talent for prophecy. One man, who had made himself always available, giving unsparingly of his time and knowledge, seemed to stand above all others in meeting these abstract criteria. He was a financial analyst who had helped organize many successful companies, author of a number of erudite tomes on the philosophy of investment, a man generally revered by his professional peers. His name was James Jacoby.

At first glance, Jacoby was anything but attractive. He was short, wirily thin, his nose too large for his gaunt face, his polished scalp fringed by lackluster graying hair that hung raggedly to his starched white shirt collar. But the gnomelike appearance, which seemed to associate him with an underground chemistry laboratory, was quickly forgotten once he was engaged in conversation. His voice, deep and resonant, articulated his views with a calm authority that seemed an echo of God, belied by an expression of humility that confessed that he was but an earthling. And not only did he speak well, he listened well, listened intently, according the most stupefying banalities the attention one would give the pronouncements of a seer. And always there was the empathy, glowing from the depths of his large brown eyes, and the benign little smile, intimate and confidential. Though a lifelong bachelor, he had conducted ardent affairs with many attractive women, invariably retaining them as friends, partially because he invariably left them with fatter bank accounts. Much as he enjoyed sensual indulgence, his one ruling passion was the accumulation—by artful but legitimate means—of money.

Brooks had taken to him immediately, predisposed to like a man who wore an elegant midnight-blue homburg, and whose vest was ornamented by a heavy gold heirloom watch chain—items that in his. impoverished youth, Brooks had envied as symbols of the rich and wellborn, and now thought of wistfully as relics of an age when people understood value instead of merely knowing the price.

After a number of meetings, during which James Jacoby became "J.J.," Brooks was convinced that, now that he had plunged into the erratic world of securities marketing, what the agency needed was just such a man, one who would provide wisdom but would seek no authority. Would Jacoby consent to a seat on the board of directors? Jacoby, appearing surprised, replied that he felt honored but really should decline. He was involved in so many enterprises, not to mention his writing and his lectures. Still, if he could clear himself sufficiently to do a responsible and conscientious job—the only basis on which he would accept—why, then, well, could he think about it for a few days? When, three days later, he called to accept, Brooks felt that he had scored a major triumph. He also felt an immense relief. Now he could concentrate his energies on running the agency and not have to worry whether his decisions would have a good or bad effect on the stock. James Jacoby, a director of the company, would be right there beside him to advise and protect.

Meanwhile the stock, performing contrary to the sharply declining Dow Jones averages, had spurted ahead eight points. Brooks, though delighted, was baffled. He could find nothing to account for such an advance. He discussed it with the company members of the board: Charlie Quigley, the treasurer, who had been with Brooks since graduating from NYU forty years ago; Pete Sanchez, marketing director, a swarthy chunk of a man, hired some thirty years ago from Procter & Gamble; Ed Jamison, media director, a big, rumpled, gregarious fellow who had worked for Hearst, Luce, Paley before joining the company twenty-five years ago; and Rick Bradley, senior vice-president, a nine-year man previously with the William Morris Agency. All had cautious theories—none had answers based on facts. At the next formal meeting of the board, Brooks put the question to Jacoby.

The little man's head stretched up from his crisp white collar like a turtle's emerging from its shell. "I have made some inquiries," he said quietly. "It seems apparent that the stock is simply reflecting an excess of optimism."

"You mean," said Brooks, "the buyers think our next earnings report will show a big increase in profit?"

Jacoby gave his small, charming smile. "I would doubt that." He gazed respectfully at Charlie Quigley, the treasurer. "Your projections are generally known to investors. Am I correct that the next quarterly report will show only a modest increase?"

Quigley flicked a strand of white hair from his seamed forehead. "Very modest. You can say the same for the quarter after that."

Pete Sanchez, the marketing director, yanked off his dark glasses—his eyes were sensitive to light—and as quickly reset them on his squat nose. "It's all psychological," he said, waving a hand.

"We're new in the market. We've got a good reputation. So maybe they think we're a sleeper."

Jacoby rewarded him with a nod of agreement. "You've put your finger on it, Mr. Sanchez. But I'm sure you'll agree that there must be an underlying reason for this attitude. A stock does not jump twenty percent in such a short time, and in a soft market, simply on the basis of blind faith, particularly for a company that is not well known to the general public."

Rick smiled at him. "You sound like you know the reason."

Jacoby smiled back. "I believe I do, Mr. Bradley. And I believe you do, too. I'm sure your professors at Harvard at least touched on it."

Rick glanced at Brooks in surprise. Brooks grinned, pleased that this distinguished financial expert had apparently acquainted himself with the backgrounds of his top executives.

"Rumor," said Jacoby. "There is a rumor on the Street that Madden and Associates is anticipating significant growth."

"Now who the hell started that?" Brooks asked.

Ed Jamison, the media director, said, "It could have come from the media reps. They're rumormongers, all of 'em. And they all hang out together. After a few martinis, they're apt to pass the word that the new editor of the *Washington Post* is Richard Nixon."

They all laughed, Jacoby leaning back and jangling his watch chain.

"Maybe they know something I don't," Brooks said. "What could be on their minds?"

"The word I heard most frequently was 'acquisitions.' "

"What do they mean by acquisitions? Buying up other agencies?"

"I had not interpreted it that way." Jacoby paused, frowning in thought. "But now you mention it, that would be something to ponder." He shook his head, dismissing it. "I assumed the reference was to the acquisition of new accounts."

"Well, sure," Brooks said, "we're always looking for new accounts. So's everybody. But right now there's nothing we're optimistic about."

"I gather the optimism was not generated by any specific account.

It had more to do with the quality of your personnel. One person in particular was cited as a reason for the agency to attract new business. Her name is Sara Vardon."

The others exchanged questioning looks, as though doubting that Jacoby was as wise as he had been billed. Brooks grimaced and shook his head skeptically.

"Listen," he said, "you mean to tell me that one woman—I don't care how terrific she is—one woman can make those Wall Street pros so bullish?"

Jacoby chuckled. "Sometimes the bulls need very little to start a stampede. They are optimists by nature. As I said, in this case the optimism appears excessive. Nevertheless, to answer your question, I am convinced that Sara Vardon is largely responsible for the advance of the stock."

"J.J., I just can't buy it."

Jacoby inclined his head in deference. "I may of course be wrong. But with your permission, I'd like to develop the thought."

Brooks smiled apologetically. "Sure, sure, please go ahead. We're here to listen."

Jacoby now had their complete attention.

"First, about Sara Vardon herself. I have not met her, but I understand that she is as brilliant as she is charming. Perhaps there are many people in advertising with those qualities, but none has received such publicity, a good deal of it through the trade press, but mostly by word of mouth. She is looked upon as a creative wonder, a view the agency itself has fostered through an unprecedented action. I refer, of course, to the setting up of what amounts to an elite associate agency bearing her name, The Vardon Group."

"That's just a small part of the agency," Brooks said. "A fraction."

"In billing, yes. But psychologically it is of incalculable importance."

Rick said, "You're talking about image."

Jacoby gave a soft cluck of regret. "Yes, image, Mr. Bradley—the American form of sorcery. But I am not speaking only of Sara Vardon's image. There is also the image she brings to the agency as a whole, of energy and youth, of innovation and great creativity, even of glamour—all the elements that companies seek in their advertising but too seldom get. Granting this, it is easy to understand why analysts foresee a favorable future."

Brooks smiled ironically. Here he had been practically blackmailed into meeting Sara's demands and now he was being told by this financial wizard that he had made one of the wisest decisions of his career. He looked at Rick, who was regarding Jacoby with alert eyes and a small smile, an expression Brooks recognized as agreement. His glance swept on to Quigley, Sanchez, Jamison. Their faces also registered agreement but, unlike Rick's, it was manifested by sagging chins and brooding eyes, images that were the antithesis of the one Jacoby had described. My God, thought Brooks, they're becoming old men and they know it and they're scared, scared of the energy and youth they were just reminded of and that they sense could blow them away.

They had wanted to be very rich, and now they were, but in getting rich they had sacrificed some of their influence to outsiders—anonymous men in Wall Street whose only concern was profit and who therefore didn't give a damn about a man's loyalty and years of service and past performance because those things contributed nothing to the bottom line. And now he himself was aware of an unsettled feeling, as though some vital part of him was slipping away under the relentless pressure of age and an inability to adapt to change. No, that wasn't true, he was different, he was the boss, he still had the vigor and flexibility of youth—especially now, since Maria—and he would still be going strong long after the others had yielded their lives to golf and gardening and grandchildren.

He ended the meeting by saying to Jacoby, "Well, it looks like we'll have to hire someone to hold Sara's hand when she's crossing the street. Anything happens to her and the whole outfit would go right down the tubes."

He managed a grim smile, and only that because Jacoby seemed so amused. The others, including Rick, showed no expression, none at all.

He was wrong in thinking that Jacoby's presence on the board would allow him to concentrate on purely agency functions. There were the constant appearances before top Wall Street men to hustle the stock, an assignment he could not help but enjoy because he was, after all, a salesman. There were sessions with brokers, accountants, SEC officials. There were discussions with the board to initiate a painless stock-purchase plan for employees. There were options, dividends, earnings reports to consider. Most time-consuming were the almost daily meetings with the management consultants whose job was to increase agency efficiency. They had been brought in at the suggestion of James Jacoby, who assured Brooks that their function was not so much to recommend drastic changes as to reassure the Street that the agency was being kept abreast of the most modern business systems.

But that was not how it appeared to Brooks. The consultants, smooth, sharp-eyed men in impeccable three-piece suits, were all over the place, armed with their leatherbound pads and thin gold pencils, quizzing everybody from the mailroom crew to Brooks himself. Then, later in the day, they would convene in Brooks's office to tell him that he must cut here, cut there, consolidate jobs, crack down on expense accounts, curtail travel, revise the cash flow, check employees' arrival and departure times, require them to fill out forms itemizing the hours spent on each account—recommendations that had Brooks muttering "For Christsake!" with increasing frequency. He had always run a loose, relaxed shop—deliberately, because, almost totally, his assets were human beings, not, for Christsake, machines—a shop where people could feel free to express themselves, which was the only way to get good advertising. Sure, there was some fat, and there were times when people were in the conference room watching Mike Douglas on TV, or drinking three-hour lunches, or splitting early to catch a twi-night doubleheader, but what the hell, these were the same people who worked all night to lick a crisis or meet a deadline. Observing the consultants during these outbursts, Brooks sensed that they regarded him as a corporate Neanderthal who really should be playing shuffleboard in Florida.

Still, he made a few belt-tightening changes, if only to justify the huge consulting fee. The board rubber-stamped them, as expected, but he was sure there would be protests from the executive committee, whose members would have to police the new procedures with the rank and file. He was astonished to find that the committee not only accepted them, but did so with enthusiasm, even offering suggestions for further austerities. The reason was clear: if this was what Wall Street wanted, if this would make the company more attractive to investors, well, sure, why not work a little harder, spend a little less, shuffle a few more papers?

They were saying, thought Brooks, that what was good for the stock was good for the agency (failing to mention that, as major shareholders, they would reap the greatest benefit), an equation he felt it his duty to question. So he wandered about the various departments, talked informally with people on all levels, took a number of them to lunch, and was beset by a rising apprehension. The conversations seemed less concerned with advertising than with finance—the rise in the discount rate, the imbalance in foreign trade, the money supply, the latest action of OPEC—anything and everything that might affect the stock's performance.

Ironically, the only reassurance he got came from Sara Vardon. Taking her to lunch at The Four Seasons, he commented on the stock's exceptional performance.

"Yes, I hear it's doing well," she said.

"You hear? Don't tell me you're not following it."

She looked embarrassed. "I'm sorry, I guess I should."

"Well, you did get a pretty nice chunk before we went public."

"I know, and I'm very grateful. But I find the stock market a bore, probably because I don't understand it." She gazed at him seriously. "Besides, that isn't what our business is all about."

"Well, right now, it seems like it is."

"Yes, and I think that's too bad. The only thing we should be concerned about is creating the best advertising in town. Then the stock will take care of itself."

His estimation of Sara's character rose several notches. "I wish everyone had that attitude," he said. "It would sure help if you let others know how you feel."

"Oh, I have. At least I have with my own group. But I'm not in a position to have much influence with the rest of the agency."

He looked at her, recalling Jacoby's remarks about her influence on the financial community. Apparently she was not aware of it. He decided not to enlighten her.

The written report of the management consultants contained two major recommendations that they thought important enough to underscore.

First, the report said, it was unsound, even dangerous, for an agency of this size to vest so much responsibility in one man, no matter how capable he was. While of course Brooks Madden should continue as chairman of the board and chief executive officer, it was recommended that he be relieved of certain administrative duties and whoever was appointed to handle them be given an appropriate title.

Second, in the opinion of the consultants, the company's board of directors was handicapped in making decisions by the absence of a representative of the creative department, which performed the agency's most important function. Therefore, it was recommended that the board be expanded to include a top creative executive, preferably one who had risen from the ranks and had a record of achievement.

Much as he wished to disagree, Brooks saw immediately that the proposals were irresistibly logical. Overburdened as he was, he had been forced to give only token attention to many problems, and there were others he had simply ignored in the hope they would solve themselves. Fortunately, there was a simple solution. Rick Bradley, whom he had come more and more to depend on, both as friend and associate, would be given additional responsibilities and his position formalized by the title "executive vice-president." Later on he would be named president, a title Brooks had been reluctant to bestow, not only because it had been his for so many years, but also because it seemed to confuse his own authority as chief executive officer.

The second proposal was equally right; in fact, it hit at a problem that for a long time had caused him feelings of guilt. Certainly the creative department should be represented on the board. It was pure hypocrisy for him to proclaim that the creation of bright, arresting, convincing advertising was the name of the game, and at the same time deny its creators participation at the top level of management. But who was he to choose except, dammit, Lou Kahn? Lou was a great creative director, inspiring people, exciting them, getting them to love him or hate him, whichever worked, steering them in the right direction with a mind that cut through the nonessentials to the core of a creative problem. But a member of the board of directors? His flamboyance, his positiveness, his disdain of tact would have the other directors aching to cut his throat. Besides, Lou didn't give a damn about rapping with a group who were, he was once overheard to say, "as important to the agency as parsley is to a lamb chop." He had also said many times that all he wanted out of this business was to run the best creative shop in the country.

So it wouldn't be Lou Kahn. Which left only one other choice—a thought too unnerving to be brooded over alone. Brooks decided to get Rick's thinking.

"I think it's a great idea," Rick said.

"Just like that? Without even discussing it?"

"In a way, we discussed it at the last board meeting; rather, Jacoby did. If you accept just half of what he said, you have to agree she'd make a good addition."

"He was talking about her effect on investors. This is something different."

"Is it, Brooks? Look, among other things, Jacoby talked about energy and youth and innovation. No one can dispute that Sara's got them all." He raised an eyebrow. "Wouldn't you say we could use a little more of that on the board?"

Brooks stirred uncomfortably in his chair. "You think the others are over the hill?"

"Of course not. They're damned good in their jobs and the agency needs their experience. But maybe we're all getting a little out of touch with what's going on. By appointing Sara, you'd be recognizing the importance of youth and you'd be demonstrating your belief in providing new opportunities for women. Gloria Steinem will love you."

Brooks eyed him curiously. "It doesn't bother you that the young woman happens to be someone you once lived with?"

"A little. But there's no reason it should. Thanks to her, we've managed to remain friends. She accepts what happened and has made it clear that she feels no bitterness."

"Very mature. I suppose that's another point in her favor."

He tried it on Lou Kahn, summing up the reasons.

Lou gave his hairy grin. "Brooks, you have my permission. The stock will probably triple. I'll sell mine and buy a yacht."

"You don't feel it would be unfair to you?"

"Hell, no. Sara's got her side of the street and I've got mine. On hers, the sidewalks are bigger, but that's okay, she deserves the room. Besides, I figure all you directors do is play poker."

And on James Jacoby:

"An excellent choice. Good for the agency, good for the stock."

He felt himself bristle. "I wasn't thinking of the stock."

"Nevertheless, may I make a suggestion?"

"Sure."

"If she is appointed, I would give it all the publicity possible."

"You mean," Brooks said dryly, "so we can polish our image?"

Jacoby chuckled. "Now you've got it."

And on Maria:

"Are you sure you want her to have that much power?"

"She wouldn't have power. The Old Guard would keep her in line. But we might profit from her input."

"*Input.* How you admen talk. Anyway, I'm sure you can handle her. Look how you handle me, and I'm a very independent woman."

"Sometimes too independent. That's why I had to drop everything and fly off to Phoenix."

They smiled at each other, remembering the elegant hotel nestled in the mountains overlooking Phoenix in a town named Carefree, the clear dry air that seemed to bathe the lungs, the lazy blue days on divans beside the pool, the spontaneous lovemaking that did not wait until dark, the sense of being utterly free and young.

"What I'm really delighted about," she said, "is Rick. Now you can unload on him and play hooky more often."

"I hope so. But right now—"

"Remember skinny-dipping in the pool in the middle of the night?"

"Do I! You were beautiful."

"The most beautiful body money can buy."

A week later, Sara phoned Harry Dalton from the drugstore across the street. She spoke in a tone of breathless excitement:

"Harry, you're not going to believe this, but you will when you see my picture in tomorrow's *Times*."

"Uh-huh, first page of the business section."

"You mean you *know*?"

"I know. You were just made a director. Congratulations."

His voice sounded controlled and impersonal, just as it had for some time. Had she done something to offend him?

"Okay, Harry, you're psychic. Isn't it terrific? I was so goddamned surprised, I almost crashed on the carpet!"

"It was implicit in the situation. Except for Bradley, and maybe Madden, the board's made up of has-beens. They needed someone young and bright, a star, and that person had to come from the creative side. I knew the consultants would see that right away. But to make sure, I gave them a nudge."

"*You* talked to the consultants?"

"Hell, no. I'm out of it."

"Then who—"

"Jacoby," he said.

23

THE CONCIERGE explained that Madame Corliss and Monsieur Madden had planned to go to the beach, then to the market, but should be arriving back at any moment, and *oui*, he would see that the message to call was delivered immediately.

As Rick hung up, his vision of Maria's hotel in St. Tropez was as clear in his mind as Brooks's postcard: a sprawling pink structure with a red tile roof, surrounded by green lawns and majestic palms. Soon, thought Rick, he would have quite a pictorial collection; already he had scenes of Phoenix, Beverly Hills, La Jolla, Acapulco, Cuernavaca, San Francisco, and now St. Tropez. They covered a period of almost three months, beginning soon after he had been officially crowned executive vice-president. Most of Brooks's trips had been brief—the shortest, to Phoenix, lasting only a few days, the longest, to Los Angeles and Mexico, extending for ten days. In between, Brooks would reappear at the office, his usually pink face burned brick-red, his orange-gray hair bleached silver-blond, his whole being radiating youthful energy.

He seemed pleasantly surprised that the agency ran so smoothly during his absences, praising Rick lavishly, but at the same time crediting himself for the presence on the board of James Jacoby and Sara Vardon. The two, he said, had rejuvenated the management, Jacoby with his experience and wisdom, Sara with her enthusiasm and suggestions that reflected the concerns of the average employee. The fact that two sizable new accounts had been acquired—both directly attributable to Sara—removed his last doubts about his decision to establish The Vardon Group and, later, elevate Sara to the agency hierarchy. "Now we've got a hot team," he said, adding archly, "so why shouldn't the boss go out and play?"

Rick, despite his increased work load, begrudged Brooks not a moment of it. The man had more than earned it. In the almost ten years of their association, Brooks had rarely taken a real vacation—none in the two years since his wife had died. And now here he was closing in on sixty-five, an age when most men retired, and he was only beginning to discover that life was a lot more than work and worry, that out there in the great beyond there was joy to be shared with a lover and he'd better grab it before his term on Earth expired.

Besides, the burden was not all that heavy. Brooks was right—Jacoby and Sara had been invaluable: the first quietly counseling, pointing out opportunities, warning of hazards; the second over-flowing with ideas for moving the company forward. Had it been she or Jacoby who first suggested that they consider expanding through the acquisition of other, smaller agencies? No matter, it was Sara who pushed it the hardest—Jacoby, as usual, objectively weighing the pros and cons, advising caution and careful study. Sanchez and Jamison were quick to endorse the idea, perhaps because they feared adding more wrinkles to their aging images if they failed to demonstrate enthusiasm. Charlie Quigley, the treasurer and one of Brooks's first employees, was implacably opposed, resentful, in fact, that anyone should seem to care about being the biggest rather than simply the best. Brooks, his thoughts off in some romantic elsewhere, tabled the proposal, later saying to Rick, who had been neutral, "That'll be the end of it, so forget it."

The phone rang. It was Brooks, his voice buoyant:

"Don't tell me we've landed another account."

"I wish that was it. Then I wouldn't mind bothering you. It's mostly about Charlie Quigley. He just left my office. Brooks, he's resigned."

"What! Charlie *resigned*? Why, for godsake, he's been with me for more than forty years!"

"I know, but—"

"And only a few months ago I told him I wanted him for another forty. He was so grateful, I was afraid he'd kiss my hand. What is it with Charlie? Is he sick? In that case, we'll just put him on paid leave of absence."

"It's not that kind of sickness—he's sick of the advertising business. He says he's become too old for it. He says if he doesn't quit now he'll end up on the funny farm playing with his toes."

"What the hell brought this on?"

"It took a while to get it out. It seems the agency's changed so much, he thinks he's working someplace else. I gather that going public started it. He remarked that maybe we should move to the corner of Wall and Broad streets so we'd be close to the men running our business."

"Yeah, that's Charlie. He hates the Street, thinks the market's just a big crapshoot. But that shouldn't be enough to—"

"That isn't all. What's really got his blood up is this pressure to expand."

"Hell, we've been expanding like a balloon ever since he started as a forty-buck-a-week accountant."

"I mean through takeovers. That's where we're getting the pressure."

"From where?"

"From everywhere. From people poking their heads into my office. From the executive committee. From the consultants and the financial analysts."

"For Christsake! All this in the two weeks I've been over here?"

"Apparently it's been building for some time. Now it's out in the open. Somehow the word's got around that if we start buying up other agencies, the stock will soar."

"Yeah, and we could collapse from the weight. Have you discussed this with the board?"

"Yesterday. Just a routine meeting, I thought. Then Jacoby told us he'd heard of an agency that might be on the block at an attractive price. Thornley and Babson. You know them?"

"Sure. They bill about eighty million. Mostly institutional stuff. Almost nothing we'd handle."

"Jacoby thought that was a great advantage. He made a good case for it."

"He wants us to go ahead?"

"No, just to consider it when you get back, if it's still available. You know Jacoby—no hard sell, simply the facts."

"What'd the others have to say?"

"Jamison and Sanchez and Sara are all for it. In fact, they suggested flying over there and laying it out for you. I said no, but I agreed to phone you. I was about to place the call when Charlie Quigley came in. He said he was sorry he couldn't do this face to face, but he's written you a letter. I don't know what it says, but you can be sure that yesterday's meeting, this whole acquisition bit, was the last straw for him."

"Listen, you get hold of Charlie. You tell him you talked to me and that I don't accept his resignation. You tell him that if it's this damned takeover business that's eating him, to forget it. And the reason he can forget it is that I won't stand for it. You got that?"

"Got it."

"Then you tell Charlie to get the hell home, take Martha out to a good dinner, and I'll talk to him tomorrow. But before that, I'll talk to the members of the board and I'll kill this goddamned foolishness once and for all. So get 'em together, say, for eleven A.M."

"Right. I'll set up a conference call."

"Like hell. I'll be on the next plane I can get."

Brooks arrived at JFK at nine the next morning. He took a taxi to his apartment, showered, shaved, changed his clothes, and at ten minutes to eleven was seated at the head of the boardroom table, waiting for the others to arrive. He had not stopped to talk with anyone, not even Rick, fearful that if he did, everything pent up inside him would escape in a premature explosion.

Throughout the entire flight he had thought of nothing but Charlie Quigley and of the forces, apparently rampant, that had impelled this fine gentleman, this four-decade veteran, this utterly faithful keeper of the books, to call it quits. All because of greed. That was the only word for it. It was like a progressive disease, induced by the stock issue, intensified by ascending numbers, made virulent by rumor, and climaxed by widespread hallucinations of baronial houses, expensive cars, and twilight years of pampered ease.

What the hell had started the epidemic? Any talk of a subject as important as possible acquisitions should never have gone beyond the doors of the boardroom, not even to the executive committee, let alone to the lower echelons. So there had to have been a leak. He could not believe it could have come from the long-term members—they'd always been tight-lipped. That left J.J. and Sara. He immediately eliminated J.J. The man was too circumspect, too sensitive in his awareness that an indiscreet word could often send a tremor through the financial community. All right, then, Sara. She was outspoken, influential, closest to the rank and file. As the newest member, she might not yet be inhibited by the need for secrecy. It was easy to imagine her dropping a word here and there, inadvertently perhaps, while enthusing over the agency's potential for continued growth. So be it. In a few minutes he'd put a stop to all this nonsense about takeovers. The agency had enough problems without taking over someone else's!

Promptly at eleven the members filed in, welcoming Brooks and remarking on how fit he looked. He made a point of singling out Charlie Quigley, taking him aside, placing a hand on his shoulder, to say quietly, "Charlie, we'll talk later. I think you'll be in a more receptive mood after you hear what I say to the board." Quigley, his wrinkled face pained, started to apologize for being such a nuisance, but Brooks cut him off and they joined the others. Brooks gazed around the table: Rick, Jamison, and Sanchez on his right; Jacoby, Sara, and Quigley on his left. Their expressions were identical, mouths slightly pursed, eyebrows slightly raised, the look of a theater audience when the curtain begins to ascend.

"This meeting will be brief," Brooks said. He turned to Rick. "Does everyone know why we're here?"

"Yes. To discuss the question of acquisitions."

"Did you explain my position?"

"No." Rick smiled. "I thought you could do that a lot better than I."

"At least I'll be louder. All right. First let's make sure I've got this straight. From what I hear, there's a rumor all over this shop that we're about to branch out by taking over other agencies. Is that right?"

There was a nodding of heads.

Rick said, "It goes beyond the shop, Brooks." He took from his lap a folded copy of *The New York Times*. "Here's a line from this morning's business notes: 'The word on Wall Street is that Madden and Associates, the big Madison Avenue advertising agency, is considering a takeover of competitor Thornley and Babson.'"

"Now who the hell planted that?"

Jacoby's gleaming head stretched from his white collar. "It may have come from Thornley and Babson."

"Why, for godsake? We haven't even talked to them."

"It's not really so strange. They would like some agency to make them an offer. Somehow they heard that Madden and Associates might be interested. By publicizing that, they hope to start some bidding. Meanwhile their stock is enhanced. Yesterday it was up a point, and this morning it rose another three-quarters."

"All on rumor? And that raises a point." Brooks scanned their faces, his eyes lingering a fraction longer on Sara's. "Has anyone here mentioned a word about this outside this room?"

All replied negatively, Sara's voice rising above the others to state flatly, "Absolutely not!"

"Anybody got an idea how it started?" Brooks glanced at Jacoby.

Jacoby arched his small frame and stroked his gold watch chain. "I believe it to be a spontaneous reaction. Consider the events. Some months ago this agency offered shares to outside investors. The investors responded eagerly, providing you with large amounts of liquid capital, a surplus of cash, which, of course, must be invested. What more logical way to invest it—or so market analysts would think—than in the business you know most about? The people who advise Thornley and Babson on financial matters would have been remiss if they had not pointed this out. That could be the source of the rumor. Once started, your employees would be bound to hear of it. As with most rumors that seem to promise great personal benefit, it would quickly become accepted as fact."

"I suppose that's the answer. What's our stock doing?"

Rick said, "Up a quarter yesterday, a half this morning. It now stands at just over fifty-one. The market index is down more than five points."

"You see," said Jacoby, smiling, "your stock remains bullish despite a general sell-off. The item in the *Times* has apparently fueled further speculative investment."

"If I issued a statement that there's absolutely no truth to this takeover business, the stock would drop—right?"

"Not necessarily. It might simply remain for a while on a plateau. Meanwhile you could expect pressure from investors to make good on the rumor."

"For Christsake, J.J., you're saying they'll try to call the shots?"

"I'm afraid they have that right. In the final analysis, the shareholders are the owners of the business. It's a two-way street. Once you accept Wall Street money, you must also accept much of their advice on how the business should be run."

"But I've done that. We've restructured management, changed our cost-accounting system, cut operating costs. That's okay, I go along. But when people who, for godsake, don't know good advertising from bad, who wouldn't know how to sell a can of beans, when they tell me to go out and buy another agency, they're going too damned far."

"Naturally, as chief executive officer, you have the right to refuse."

"You're damned right I have!" Brooks jumped to his feet. "Listen, let's make sure there's no doubt about my position. I'm sick up to here with all this student government. Technically, maybe it's true the agency belongs to the stockholders. But only technically. In fact, with your help, *I* run it. I've run it for over forty years, and Charlie Quigley, who's sitting there wondering if he's working for a lunatic asylum, he knows I've run it successfully. I didn't start with a one-room walkup office and build it into a half-billion-dollar company just so I could hand it over to a bunch of get-rich schemers whose only interest is in how many bucks we're making. Well, I like bucks too. But I want to make them on a sound basis, and that basis is to give our clients the best advertising, the best service they can find anywhere. And that's how we'll attract more business, more bucks, the same as in the past." He stared at them and sat down. "Now, are there any questions?"

There was silence. It was Sara who finally spoke. "Brooks, I'm sure we all agree that the market shouldn't influence our decisions.

So suppose we forget the market and consider the acquisition of Thornley and Babson strictly on its merits."

"What merits? The kind of advertising they do—all corporate-image stuff—is outside our experience. With a few exceptions—Transcon, for one—we're a package-goods shop."

"Don't you think that's a plus? Neither they nor we would have to resign an account because of a conflict. And we'd be extending our service to our present clients who also do corporate advertising."

"Sounds fine, but it won't work. To do the job right, we'd have to send some of our own staff over there. And we can't afford it. What with all this tightening up, we're stretched too damned thin right now."

Sara persisted. "You don't think we should at least talk to them?"

"Can't do any harm," Jamison said, lighting a cigar.

Sanchez nodded, his face sullen.

Brooks's self-control snapped. "Goddamn it, I just don't seem to be getting through! I'll say it for the last time. We're not interested in takeovers, this one or any other, now or in the future. And to make sure everyone understands that, I'll put out a statement this afternoon to our employees and to the press." Again he stood up. "Anything else?"

There was nothing else.

Alone with Brooks, Charlie Quigley smiled ruefully. "Well, you can consider that our talk. Anyway, it's what I wanted to hear. Suppose we forget about the resignation."

Brooks grinned. "What resignation?"

"Something I dreamed, I guess—a nightmare. My friend, once your statement goes out, there'll be a lot of moaning and groaning around here."

"I won't hear it. Tonight I'm catching a plane back to France."

24

THE NEXT DAY the stock of Madden and Associates, sixth on the most-active list, dropped two points.

Phoning Sara that evening at home, Harry Dalton's deep voice smacked with satisfaction. "Just what we expected. The overall volume went up, the market stayed steady, and your stock took a licking."

"I never thought I'd be glad to lose money."

"It's all on paper, and you'll lose more. J.J.'s sure the sell-off will continue. It's at forty-nine now. It should keep on sliding until it hits at least forty."

"Then you'll move in?"

"We will if we think Madden's ready to talk sense. Right now, that seems likely. His statement in this morning's *Times* should have run in the obituary columns. He was telling Wall Street, telling his own people, that he wasn't having it with their kind of growth. To investors, being *against* growth is like being *for* dying. Did you get any feedback at the office?"

"I never heard such bitching. A few talked about unloading. But most of them were saying that, by God, something should be done. Why see their profits melt away just because of a Stone Age board of directors?"

"They blamed it on the board?"

"Oh, they meant Brooks. But it was easier, and safer, to lay it on a group and not mention names. I made it clear that I was against the decision, that I was for taking over any reputable agency we could get our hands on. I didn't say that to everyone, only to the guys with some clout who I'm pretty sure won't turn me in."

"Good. That puts you on the side of the angels."

"Sanchez and Jamison are no angels. After what happened yesterday, they must be ready for murder. At lunch last week, they both told me that the stock should eventually hit a hundred. That's if we went ahead with acquisitions. The way they said it, I figured that's when they'd cut out, both multimillionaires."

"They'll get there. All they've got to do is hang tough."

"What really bugs them, I think, is that Brooks didn't even put it to a vote. He just said how it was going to be and that was it. If there'd been a vote, we'd have swung it."

"No, you wouldn't. You'd have Madden, Bradley, and Quigley against you. Three against three, which would kill it."

"You're forgetting J.J."

"He'd have abstained. At this point, if he voted with you, Madden would be suspicious as hell and would come out fighting. He'd break his ass to discredit J.J."

"But he's done nothing illegal," Sara said.

"He never does—that's why I picked him. But he's a world-class manipulator. Anyway, he can't take a chance on tipping his hand. If he did, Madden would go right to the stockholders and he'd probably convince a majority that this outsider was the tool of the Devil. And he'd have them thinking he'd corrupted you and Sanchez and Jamison."

"Who's corrupted? We're just standing up for the stockholders, trying to do what's best for the agency."

Dalton chuckled. "That's how to look at it. All right. Until we're sure we've got the muscle, J.J. will play the part Madden assigned him—the disinterested counselor, the man who wants very little for himself."

"How long before we get the muscle?"

"Soon, I think. The pressure's got to come from the people who, whether Madden recognizes it or not, really own the agency. That pressure's already started. In a week or so it should be ready to blow."

"Look, I've got to hang up. There's someone at the door."

For a moment he didn't answer. Then, without inflection, he said, "Sure. Talk to you later."

There was no one at the door. But it was true she heard a ringing. It came from inside her head, echoing in her ears, accompanied by a frantic heartbeat and panicky breathing. It had happened twice before, within the past six weeks, the second attack frightening her into seeing her internist. But they were nothing like the attacks that had preceded her operation—no nausea, no fainting, no explosions or bursts of lights, only the ringing, and the hammering in her chest, and the panting, as though she were about to suffocate. Had she been examined at the hospital since the tumor was removed? Yes, three times, the last two months ago. No, she hadn't seen Dr. Kloster, he had been away, lecturing, she thought, but it had all been routine, conducted by a resident who asked her how she felt (just fine, she said), looked at the scar, checked her eyes and reflexes, and that was about it.

What about her personal life, everything okay there? That again! Oh, yes, she enjoyed her job and had been very successful, in fact had been given her own—

"Great. But I said personal, not business." The nice smile, the boyish, ruddy face, the pleasant brown eyes. "Like, how are things between you and that lucky guy you live with?"

"That broke up."

"Oh? Whose idea was that?"

"Really, does it matter?"

"It would if you felt rejected, if you've been brooding about it."

"Okay, then, it was his idea. But it wasn't exactly rejection, not as though he was tired of me. And I don't brood about it. I'm much too busy." Why must she feel so indignant? This man was a *doctor*.

"Have you seen him since the breakup?"

"Almost every day. He works in my office. Our relationship is very friendly."

"I see."

"What do you mean, you *see*? That's doctor talk! Translated, it comes out you don't know what the hell is wrong!" she said, only half-jokingly.

He looked startled, then gazed at her calmly, saying nothing, as though waiting for her to burst into tears. She didn't, feeling cold and unrepentant.

Then—oh, so professionally—he started using words like "tachycardia" and "hyperventilation" and "syndrome" until she was ready to grab his stethoscope and jerk it around his throat.

"Look, Dr. Corbett, would you lose your license if you talked like people?"

After a brief, reflective pause, he continued, firmly and somewhat coldly. "The symptoms indicate intense anxiety. The usual treatment is psychotherapy. I recommend it. But first you should have a thorough physical examination at the hospital. Also, Dr. Kloster should be consulted."

She glared at him.

"I'll be glad to make the arrangements," he said.

"No, not now. I can't spare the time."

"One day, that's all."

"I'll call you."

He looked at her skeptically, nodded, and wrote her a prescription for Valium. Leaving, she was surprised at how much better she felt.

Now, gasping for breath, her heart palpitating wildly, the ringing inside her skull turning to a steady buzz, she lurched to the bar and poured a straight bourbon. Downing it, she held herself still for a minute, then, feeling the drink bite and grip, walked cautiously to the bathroom and gulped two Valiums. She soaked a towel with hot water, wrapped it around her stiffened neck, returned to the living room, poured another shot, and brought it to the sofa, stretching out on her back. She closed her eyes, moving only to sip the bourbon— this was the last one; she knew that booze and tranquilizers could be a lethal mixture—and tried not to think.

But the thoughts charged in, vague at first, then clarifying as the sedation took effect. What was happening to her? Nerves. This time she was sure of it, as sure as the certainty she'd seen in Dr. Corbett's brown eyes. Still, she'd been sure of it once before, only to be traumatically contradicted by a stupid slob of a thing clinging to her brain. All right, then, she'd have the physical, talk to Kloster, remove all doubt that the tumor had been destroyed root and branch.

So that would leave her with merely an emotional problem. Merely? My God, that could be worse than a tumor! Endless exhausting visits to a shrink. Never knowing when this invisible terror might strike—at a meeting, in a restaurant, on a crowded street. But no, not if she took the Valium, took it as a preventive instead of as a cure, took it before leaving for the office, before going to lunch, before a meeting, before facing a crisis. To hell with psychiatrists. She'd just pop a little pill and she'd be up for anything.

Besides, it wasn't as though she didn't understand her problem. It was, in a word, Rick. Here it was March, almost eight months since he'd left her, and she hadn't so much as shared another taxi ride with him, or had lunch or a drink with him alone, occasions when she might have gained some insight into his marriage and perhaps extracted his feelings for her. Oh, those feelings were still there, she knew that, revealed in a covert glance, in a smile that he forgot to make impersonal, in a hand half-raised to touch her shoulder and quickly withdrawn. But there had been nothing direct—no lingering handclasp, no lapse into reminiscence, no teasing old joke— nothing she could use to open it all up so that she could shamelessly reaffirm her love and thus perhaps compel him to reexamine the choice he had made. It was all so damned corporately fraternal, just two fellow workers who respected each other and worked well together and were careful never to imply a licentious thought.

Why wouldn't she suffer from nerves, from anxiety? If a nymphomaniac was confined to a convent, wouldn't she freak out? Well, she was no nymphomaniac, but she was a highly sensual woman—if Rick only knew—and she couldn't just clamp a lid on it, pretend it didn't exist, and not expect it to erupt in some crazy way. That, and the tensions of her job, all her maneuvering with Harry and J.J., her proselytizing of people like Jamison and Sanchez, and her constant concern for her image, all of it exciting, sometimes damned near orgasmic, was brutal on her nervous system. It hadn't been so bad in the days when she went to the singles bars and picked up a sexy stuntman and spent the night in his apartment or some sidestreet hotel. Those forays had exhilarated her, set her up for days, like no mood pill could possibly do. But that was all over now, ended on the day The Vardon Group began. That sort of thing was just too risky—she'd become too well known, she might run into some ad exec or client and the word would streak around that Sara, the magnificent Sara, was whoring around town, and there would go her image, along with any hope of ever getting Rick back.

So she spent her nights alone, deprived even of the company of people she worked with because she ranked too high above them now and it was thought she traveled with the rich and the celebrated—which, ironically, only added to her prestige. All those bright, vital unknowns she saw every day would be astonished to learn that the brilliant, glamorous Sara Vardon had nothing better to do than dine alone in ordinary restaurants, go to the movies, watch television, read novels. And they'd be appalled to discover that her sexual pleasure was exclusively self-induced, with none other than Rick Bradley as her fantasized lover.

Probably some of them assumed she was having an affair with Harry Dalton, especially after she'd gone off with him to shoot a second batch of commercials in Los Angeles, where she'd had dinner with him twice and they'd done nothing but discuss tactics for manipulating the agency. Rick would not be one of them, thank God. He thought Thea Roland was Harry's one and only, apparently unaware that the man could not be bound by any woman. Maybe that was why she herself had resisted Harry (who, God knows, was attractive as hell and probably fantastic in bed), fearing that at best she'd become just another Thea, sharing him with all the dumb, sexy broads that happened along. No, it was more than that. Harry could turn her on until her ears lit up and she'd still never let herself be, like Thea, enslaved by him. But he'd expect her to, which would be just as bad, maybe worse. He'd try to order her around in that half-contemptuous manner he used on Thea, and she'd tell him to get lost and that would finish the great working relationship they had. The only way to combine sex and business with Harry would be to have power and know how to use it. Then he'd know damned well that this was not just a toy he could play with and take apart, not a Thea who seemed to thrive on abuse, but an independent woman who came on recklessly and extravagantly only when that was exactly what she wanted to do.

Enough of this self-analysis. She understood herself, that was the important thing. Once the agency business was resolved and she knew where she stood with Rick, good or bad, she'd kick the pills and cope on her own. She didn't need any psychiatrist to tell her, at seventy-five dollars an hour, why she was often miserable. As for the physical exam, that was something else. There she might be dealing with something that could not be rationalized, a residual speck on her brain that would do nothing but grow. Nonsense, of course, but . . .

She called Dr. Corbett the next morning.

She went to the hospital two days later and again was subjected to the same frightening tests that had preceded her operation—the drawing of fluid from inside her skull, the injections into her neck arteries, the sectional photos of her brain by a CAT scanner—plus all the bodily insults of a routine physical examination.

She did not see Dr. Kloster until late afternoon when, still in her hospital gown, she was lying in bed watching television. She snapped it off as his tall figure, clad in a dark business suit, ambled through the open door. He seemed very casual, his smile amused, as though reacting to a joke, his greeting facetious. "So you missed us, just couldn't stay away."

Didn't he know that she was sick with dread? "Please, doctor, no light bedside manner. Is the verdict in?"

He sobered, his fine hands rising in an apologetic gesture. "It's in. You've been acquitted."

"You mean—"

"You're clean, totally clean. The slob hasn't returned and he hasn't got any sisters or brothers or even a distant relative. And your general physical condition is excellent."

"Thank God." She realized she'd been holding her breath. She let it out in a long sigh.

"So if that's what's been worrying you into a breakdown, forget it."

She stirred uncomfortably. "I gather you talked to Dr. Corbett."

"Yeah. He told me your symptoms. Right then I figured the trouble wasn't organic. But we had to be sure. Now we are. If your attacks continue, what you'll need is a different kind of doctor."

"A psychotherapist."

"That's what Corbett recommends, and I agree."

"I'll think about it. First I'll try handling it myself."

His thick eyebrows met in a frown. Then he shrugged, sat down, and smiled. "I've been keeping track of you in the papers. As that cigarette ad used to say, 'You've come a long way, baby.' Your own exclusive setup. Member of the board of directors. How did all that come about?"

She relaxed, feeling on firm ground now. "I guess it started when I was in here recuperating. I had plenty of time to think and I decided I wasn't getting nearly the credit I should for the work I'd been doing. My God, they used to call me Sara Sunshine, like I was a Red Cross worker."

"So you became more assertive?"

"Uh-huh, just like the men." She grinned. "The new Sara Vardon."

"Ruthless?" He continued to smile.

"When necessary. You know the saying, 'Do unto others before they do it to you.' "

He was silent for a moment, then said, as if to himself, "I wonder . . ." and let the words hang.

"Wonder what?"

"Oh." He blinked at her. "This new assertiveness, this change in the way you deal with things—I wonder if that could explain your emotional attacks."

"How?"

"Well, as you said, it's totally unlike the way you used to act, and that could produce stress."

"Not with me. I thrive on it."

He made a face. "You see? That's why I'm not a psychiatrist." He got up and said offhandedly, "Corbett tells me you're living alone now. I hope that's not getting you down."

She felt as though the eyes that had once peered into her brain were doing so again, this time seeing not a tumor but a printout of her forlorn state. She turned her head away, conscious of a thickening in her throat, and of her hands fretting the hem of the sheet.

"I keep very busy," she said.

Corbett was right, thought Kloster as he strode down the corridor, the seizures were emotional in origin, probably triggered by the loss of her lover and the compensatory compulsion to achieve great success. Whatever it was, the cure was beyond his competence. He was a neurosurgeon, concerned only with aberrations that could be seen, if not by the naked eye, then almost always by X ray.

He turned into a room, empty except for counters and cabinets and an illuminated rack covered with X rays. He moved along the row of films, staring at each, then stopped before one and drew out his barrel-shaped glasses. He thrust his face close, feeling his eyes bug as they focused on the site where the tumor had clung. No problem there. His hand had been steady, the scalpel had cut clean, the shallow wound had healed and vanished. His gaze crept farther on. And there it was, unrecognized by the technicians because it seemed so much a part of the fissured, jellied mass, known to himself only because his hand, jolted by a tremor, had put it there.

It was a crescent scar, smaller than the white tip of a fingernail. That it was still visible after eight months indicated the penetration had been deep.

Kloster yanked off his glasses and stood back with a feeling of helplessness. How he wished he could tell her about it, if only to make her aware that if she behaved eccentrically she would be blameless. But he could not, even if he was willing to risk a malpractice suit. Telling her would only increase her anxiety without offering any hope of remedy for the effects the incision *may* have caused, her transformation from shyness to aggressiveness, her blithely professed ruthlessness, her seeming amorality. Kloster knew no more about the region his knife had accidentally assaulted than he did about the black holes of the universe.

Besides, he thought wryly, why would she want a remedy? Aggressiveness, ruthlessness, amorality—weren't these the qualities that distinguished the ideal corporate executive?

25

SARA WAS LATE for the board meeting, having closeted herself in her office until she was sure the Valium was working. She apologized as she slipped into the chair between Quigley and Jacoby, across from Jamison and Sanchez. From the chairman's seat, Rick forgave her with a smile. There had been a profound silence as she entered, and there was silence now, growing ominous as the heads turned toward Rick.

"As you all know," he said, "this meeting was requested by J.J. The only thing I know about the subject is that it's urgent."

There was a note of reproach in his tone, Sara thought, as though indicating that he should have been briefed. That had been deliberate: it was important, Harry had told her, that the meeting be held before Rick could consult with Brooks.

"I'm sorry Brooks could not be present," Jacoby said. "Am I correct that he is now in Paris?"

"Yes," Rick said. "He'll be back in a few days."

"I'm afraid this is much too serious to wait."

"All right then, suppose you get right into it."

Jacoby grasped the lapels of his dark jacket and bowed his shiny head. "I will be blunt. Reliable sources inform me that there is widespread disapproval of the way this agency is being conducted."

Rick leaned forward. "Wall Street sources?"

"Yes. Their disaffection was, of course, expected. Ten days ago, when this company issued a public statement committing itself to the status quo, naturally there were bearish growls on the Street.

This was immediately reflected in a sell-off of the stock. Today it stands at just over forty, a loss of more than ten points in less than two weeks of trading."

Sara heard Quigley's soft snort of disdain. Across the table, Sanchez stared sourly at the table. Jamison's rumpled face, impaled by a cigar, was impassive.

"As usual," said Rick, "Wall Street overreacted. The stock will turn around, with or without their blessing."

"I believe you are right. All things considered, I'd say the stock is now very much underpriced. It should attract support from investors whose eyes are always peeled for just such a situation. But that would be a slow process. Meanwhile, present shareholders will become increasingly restless, particularly those who are employees of the firm." He paused and his gentle eyes swept their faces. "I understand you've been made aware of their discontent."

"Discontent?" said Jamison. "That's an understatement. They're ready to man the barricades."

"It's all over the shop," said Sanchez.

Sara simply nodded. Rick and Quigley exchanged grim looks.

"If something is not done, and done quickly," said Jacoby, "I fear for the consequences."

"What consequences?" Rick said.

"The shareholders might very well demand a complete change in management."

Sara said, "Certainly that wouldn't include Brooks. After all, this is his agency."

Jacoby gave her his benign smile. "Forgive me for contradicting you, Sara, but this is not his agency. We must remember that it belongs to the shareholders. They have the power, if they wish to exercise it, to elect any management they want."

"This is nonsense, J.J.," Rick said, his voice harsh. "You're talking as though Brooks would just stand aside and let it happen. Brooks is a fighter and he's a salesman. He wouldn't wait for any vote. He'd canvas the stockholders and he'd sell them on his way of thinking. He'd convince them that it's a hell of a lot better to grow soundly— from within—than to inflate the stock temporarily through take-overs that we're in no position to handle."

"I would agree with you, Rick, if it had been done earlier."

Rick looked at him. "I'm surprised you didn't advise it."

Jacoby's eyebrows rose in a look of contrition. "Yes, I should have suggested it. But then Brooks was going off on all these trips and I guess I miscalculated the urgency of the matter, and didn't have the heart to interfere with his pleasure." He shook his head ruefully. "That brings up another problem. Unfortunately, these well-deserved vacations have worked against him. He is viewed by many as an absentee chief executive."

For a moment, no one spoke. Then Sara said, "Dammit, that's not fair! I'm sure he knows everything that's going on and contributes to the decisions. Isn't that right, Rick?"

Rick hesitated before saying, "We keep in constant touch."

"Then can we assume," said Jacoby, "that he knows of all this adverse reaction?"

"Not entirely. I saw no reason to upset him about something I was sure was temporary. I wasn't aware that the situation had become as critical as you seem to think. I'm still not convinced of it."

Jacoby glanced at Sara, then at Jamison and Sanchez. "From what I've heard here," he said gently, "I'd say that many board members agree with my estimate. However, I urge you to investigate and satisfy yourself as to whether or not I am simply being an alarmist."

"I intend to," Rick said. "I'll also phone Brooks and fill him in on this meeting. Knowing him, he'll be back in the office as soon as he can get a flight."

Jacoby tugged at a fringe of hair, then dropped his hand in a gesture of futility. "I'm reluctant to say this, but it must be faced. I'm not optimistic that Brooks's presence here will discourage the mounting opposition. In fact, I fear he will only aggravate it."

"You mean the opposition is aimed at Brooks personally?"

"Regrettably, yes. It is understandable, of course. Brooks alone is blamed for the decision to reject a program of outside expansion."

"Look, I covered that. He'll go to the stockholders and he'll win their support. You can bet on it."

"The odds, I think, would be against me. It is painful to say so, but to many investors Brooks is seen as old-fashioned, out of touch with the way a business must operate today in order to achieve substantial growth."

"That's b.s.," Sara said. "But if that's the image, maybe it can be changed. Suppose he agreed to go ahead with making acquisitions. Wouldn't that—"

"Now you're talking," Sanchez said.

"Wouldn't that kill the rebellion?" Sara went on. "I'd think the stockholders would parade him up Fifth Avenue."

Jacoby smiled sadly. "Ordinarily, perhaps. But not"—his gaunt face turned grim and his head thrust forward—"not when he is opposed by an organization determined to take over the ownership of this agency."

They stared at him.

"Are you serious? Are you stating a fact?" Rick asked.

"I am. Now you know why I felt such an urgency to hold this meeting. The facts are simple, easily understandable to the least informed investor. A large, highly reputable company is prepared to make an offer to your shareholders to acquire Madden and Associates. At present, my sources tell me, the figure being considered is fifty-five dollars a share—fifteen points higher than its present price. Payment would be made either in cash or through conversion to stock in the parent company."

Sara gaped at him. "Fifteen more points for every share!"

"That would be the initial proposal. I believe that, shrewdly handled, the figure could be pushed higher."

Jamison, cigar poised, and Sanchez, squinting through his dark glasses, had tensed forward.

Rick's steady gaze seemed to probe Jacoby's face. "Who is this great benefactor?"

"Interestingly enough, it's one of your clients—Transcon Airlines."

Sara jerked back as though struck. "My God! Harry Dalton!"

"That's right," Jacoby said. "I'd forgotten that you create his television commercials." He turned to Rick, who was recovering from his astonishment. "And you supervise the account. Tell me, has Dalton ever intimated any interest in acquiring the agency?"

"I don't deal with him directly. Everything comes through his ad director, Jim Westbrook." Rick looked at Sara. "How about you, Sara? Has Dalton ever suggested he wanted to get into the agency business?"

"Never. All he ever talks about to me is how he's going to look on the tube." She appeared to think. "But wait, there was something he once said. I was only half listening, but I think it had to do with putting together some sort of conglomerate." She shook her head. "I don't recall the details, if there were any."

"He's already well on his way," said Jacoby. "He's got the airline. He has substantial interests in hotels and motion pictures. Apparently he thinks that an advertising agency, which could be expanded to include many allied services, would complement his other enterprises. Also, I suspect it would benefit his tax position."

"You're absolutely sure of this?" Rick said.

"I'm sure that the offer is being formulated. That came to me from a confidential source in the Wall Street house he does business with."

"Do you know Dalton?"

"I've met him several times. He's quite impressive. Based on his record, I'd say that when he goes after a property he'll spare nothing to get it."

"That sounds like you think he'll succeed with us."

"As the situation stands now, I don't see how he can fail. I suggest we look at it. Your investors have been disillusioned. They feel they have been deprived of legitimate gain by the obstinacy of the highest-ranking executive officer. Then into this nest of dissatisfaction walks a man admired as a war hero, as a rugged individualist of unquestioned integrity, as a bold entrepreneur who has transformed small businesses, notably Transcon, into hugely successful enterprises. This man, Harry Dalton, says in effect, 'Gentlemen, I am prepared to increase your wealth dramatically, in two ways. First, I will pay you far above the market price for your stock. Second, I will give you the opportunity to associate with an organization dedicated to constant expansion, constantly increasing profits, in which you will share. Now I ask you—' "

Charlie Quigley's fist banged the table. "That's enough!" He stood up, flicked a silver forelock from his eyes, and glared at Jacoby. "Now you listen to me." His gaze swept contemptuously across the faces of the other directors. "All of you. I've got something to say and I'm going to say it only once and then I'm going to get the hell out of here."

"Go ahead, Charlie," Rick said.

"It's just this. I've been listening to a lot of loose talk about a man who's not here to speak for himself. He's been called things like 'old-fashioned' and 'out of touch' and 'obstinate,' and it's becoming plainer and plainer that the feeling here is that if he wasn't around, everything'd be just fine. Well, let me tell you something. If it wasn't for Brooks Madden, none of *you* would be around! No, Rick, goddammit, don't interrupt. I know you said he was a fighter and a great salesman, but that's not enough. Not by half, it's not enough!"

Rick sat back, staring morosely at Quigley as though examining his own conscience. Glancing at him, Sara felt a surge of anger. Why must Rick defer to this bookkeeper who knew no more about advertising than its arithmetic?

"I'm not about to go on and talk about how a penniless kid started a two-bit classified agency and turned it into a worldwide company billing close to half a billion dollars. But what I've got to remind you of, and God help me if I don't, is the *way* he did it. He did it by being the best damned merchandiser in the business. He did it by always being straight-out honest with his clients. He did it by making this shop the best in town to work for, by being fair and kind and understanding. Why, for Christsake, before going public he even gave up a chunk of his stockholdings so more people could share in the bonanza! He gave most of his life to this agency." He paused, pushing back his chair. "That's the man you're talking about, the man I've known and worked for and loved, yes *loved*, for more than forty years. That's the man you're putting down like he'd been sent in by those slide-rule management consultants and isn't it too bad he didn't work out."

"Look, Charlie," said Jamison, "no one's denying—"

"Of course no one's denying! How the hell can you? And why deny it when it's a whole lot easier just to forget. And that's what everything in me says you're getting ready to do. Why worry about

Brooks? Hell, he's rich, why not turn him loose so he can enjoy himself before he dies? You'd be doing him a favor. And, oh yeah, let's not overlook how, with him out of the way, you'd be helping out your own bank accounts. Fifteen more bucks a share, bang, just like that. Just for kicking Brooks Madden goodbye and kissing Harry Dalton's ass!"

"Charlie," Rick said, "sit down and let's discuss this calmly."

Quigley moved toward the door. "You be calm. I like myself better mad. And I'd rather not be here while you commit a capital crime."

"What are you talking about?"

"Murder. If you dump Brooks, it will kill him."

He went to the door, yanked it open, and stalked out.

There was a bristling silence.

Finally Jacoby said, "I must say I admire his loyalty. I must also emphasize that his estimate of the situation is greatly distorted."

Rick looked at him wearily. "J.J., I don't think any more should be said. Not until I've talked to Brooks."

The meeting was adjourned.

Harry Dalton grabbed his phone, heard Sara's voice, and asked her to hold on. He crossed the office and shut the door—in Thea's face as she was about to enter. "Later," he said, and went back to his desk.

"Go ahead, Sara."

"Harry, I've been trying to reach you all afternoon."

"I've been with the Wall Street wizard. You know him—he likes to play cloak and dagger."

"The limo bit again?"

"Yeah. His secretary called me and I had to take a taxi to the Upper West Side near the river, then sneak into his black Bentley. Next I'll be wearing a wig."

"So you heard about our meeting."

"Practically verbatim. The guy has total recall. He even recited Quigley's bleeding-heart speech."

"Okay, then you know what I know."

"More. Our friend was with Bradley when he phoned Madden in Paris."

"How did he take it?"

"Madden's a tough old bird. He didn't moan or swear or reach for the bottle. He just started barking orders. Investigate this, check into that, then—the clincher—get hold of this guy Harry Dalton and tell him he wants to have a talk."

"You'll see him?"

"Sure, I'll see him. But only if he's with his board of directors."

"What if he refuses?"

"He won't. He'll know that if he does, I'll break the stock offer to the press."

"When does he get back?"

"Tomorrow afternoon. And this time it won't be any fly-in–fly-out trip. He'll stay and dig in."

"Why so sure?"

"For one thing because Maria's coming with him."

Sara hung up the phone, left the drugstore, and stepped out on Madison Avenue. It was a few minutes past five, the time signaled by the mass exodus from her office building across the street. She paused on the thronged sidewalk, undecided whether to go back to work—she usually stayed until six—or to flag a taxi and go home. Both prospects produced an inner groan, inimical as they were to the excitement pulsing through her, the sense of anticipation announcing that she was about to become the center of a great happening, perhaps as early as tomorrow, when Brooks would return.

And to add to her buoyancy, there was the first breath of spring—it would arrive officially in a few days—borne down the avenue on a light breeze that had picked up the scent of the green grass and budding trees of Central Park. It was so damned nostalgic, evocative of those days in the after-work twilight when she would prance into the Elysee bar hoping to see Rick and, later, when they had become lovers, rush home to be kissed and fondled and mated. Oh, no, she could not face the office with its dimmed lights and its sheathed typewriters and its maintenance crew banging about, nor the apartment with its deafening silence and its frozen dinners and its shattering memories. Instead she would walk, perhaps stop to eat at some impersonal place like Schrafft's, a place where a woman alone would not be accosted and, more crucial, not be tempted to gratify her surging libido.

The decision made, she turned abruptly, and gasped as her shoulder cracked against the chest of an oncoming figure.

"Oh, I'm sorry!"

"That's okay," the man said, and started away. Then he stopped, came back, and said, "For Christsake!"

She stared at him, startled. He was dark, thick-haired, his body seeming taut and well built.

"I *said* I'm sorry," she said.

"Well, goddammit, I'm not!" He gave her a white grin. "Jennifer! Jennifer Ralston!"

She opened her mouth to protest his mistake, then closed it as her mind shaped a memory. A singles bar, that first night she had gone to one, right after the Transcon presentation. . . .

"Eddie Baron," he said, and grasped her shoulders and drew her back to the plate-glass front of the drugstore.

"Well," she said, and gave a tentative smile. White shag carpeting . . . sexy stereo music . . . a huge bed with purple sheets. . . .

"Jennifer, you look terrific. Where've you been? You're not in the phone book. You didn't go back to where we met—I asked."

"Well, I was away a lot."

"Three times I cut my throat, three times I lived." He was grinning, talking in that extravagant way that had rushed her to his bed. "You better grab me while I'm still alive. Let's have a drink."

She was thinking fast. Jennifer Ralston, that's who she was now. Free-lance writer, always traveling. Leaving tomorrow, in fact. When in New York, she stayed with a girlfriend and her husband. They expected her for dinner.

"How about over there?" He was pointing across the street.

The Elysee! My God, Sara Vardon and this macho stud at the Elysee! "No, not there. Really, I've got to—"

"Okay, we'll get a bottle, sit on the curb, brown-bag it. Anything so I don't lose you again. Sweet Jesus, how I thought about you! Crazy. You drove me crazy. Oh, those days in the asylum. The electric shocks, the ice-cold baths, the bitch we called Big Nurse."

She was laughing nervously, feeling his breath against her cheek. Glancing past him, she saw two people she knew crossing the street into the green light. Oh, what the hell. . . .

"Let's just walk a bit," she said.

The action started even faster this time: one double scotch at a bar, then a half-block walk to his art deco apartment, then another scotch, a tumblerful that looked like tea, but only half imbibed because by then they were furiously engaged in a pre-mating ceremony marked by clothes flung all over the room. It was a while before they made it to his king-size bed. First there were the chairs, the couch, the floor, to receive their contorted imprints, muffle her cries, absorb the dampness that seemed to sluice from her loins.

He was different from before. There was no need to instruct or encourage or guide. He knew all the things she wanted, when to tease, when to linger, when to pressure. He was in charge, in total control, withholding himself until there was not a pore of her body that remained unravished. And then, when she was sure she had been drained to a quivering emptiness, when she lay on the white shag rug like a patient dying on the operating table, he rose to a crouch, grasped her beneath the arms, and dragged her from the room and into his bed, where he activated her once again with the measured precision of a carpenter driving in a spike.

Again it went on through the night, abating only for brief convalescent naps and trips to the bathroom. And again, when her eyes opened to the gray morning light, she felt renewed, invigorated, euphoric, a state that seemed in no way related to the durable sex machine whose back she now faced.

Silently she slipped from the bed, crept to the living room, and gathered up her scattered clothes. She was dressed, handbag slung over her shoulder, about to approach the front door, when he walked in. He was wrapped in a red velour robe, his hair finger-combed, his eyes like dark, bright marbles.

"Oh," she said, "I was trying not to wake you."

He smiled and lit a cigarette with a gold lighter. "Why? So you could disappear again?"

"Oh, I'd have called you."

"Like you did before?"

"I told you, I've been away. My job keeps me traveling."

"Bullshit, Jennif—I mean, Sara."

She froze, suddenly wary, suddenly frightened, suddenly loathing his smug smile. "What did you say?"

"Your name. Sara. Sara Vardon. The girl who lives on East Sixty-third Street."

Her heart gave a pump. "Why, you—" She unslung her bag and started to open it. "You looked in my wallet!"

"No, I looked at these."

Her head snapped up and she saw that he was holding several newspaper clippings.

"Sara Vardon," he said, speaking slowly and in a tone of awe. "Appointed veep of Madden and Associates, a great big advertising agency. Appointed to the executive committee. Appointed head of her own special outfit. Appointed to the board of directors." He grinned, pocketing the clippings. "Now that's real progress—only in America. But, believe it, I'm not all that surprised. Class, that's what you've got, real class."

"You bastard."

"Hey, you're talking to your lover."

"So, you didn't just happen to bump into me last night! That was no accident!"

"Hell, no." He dragged on his cigarette. "Like I said, I've been keeping tabs on your career. I'm a fan."

"And you know my address."

"Sure, it's in the phone book. A nifty brownstone in a classy neighborhood."

"What! You've been *following* me!"

"Well, you know, I had to see if I had any competition. It looks like I haven't. You eat alone, walk alone, watch TV alone. And unless you're keeping some guy under the floorboards, you sleep alone."

248

"Now look, you—"

"So I've been thinking. I figure what you need is some steady guy who really digs what goes on under that lily-white skin." He smiled. "You know, a guy who's not pushy, who you have on the side, and who you never have to worry will louse you up with those fancy Madison Avenue executives."

She was flabbergasted. "Now wait just a minute."

"Think about it. A secret lover, always at the ready, pistol cocked. No more lonely nights."

She gaped at him. The guy was serious. Did he actually think that she, Sara Vardon, would commit herself to a character who looked like a cheap movie gambler?

"Eddie, you're having delusions. Now let's get this straight. It's been a lot of fun but now it's over. Finished. We won't see each other again, not ever. Is that clear?"

He stubbed out his cigarette, then came to her, locking her in his arms, lazily stroking her buttocks. "Tell me that in bed, baby."

She tore away, sprang to the door, and flung it open. As she slammed it behind her, she heard a burst of laughter.

26

THE DAY AFTER he arrived in New York, Brooks Madden, flanked by the other directors, sat facing Harry Dalton in the agency boardroom. Brooks, though inwardly furious, had managed a civil greeting, not only because Dalton was an important client but also, as J.J. had emphasized, because he was simply an aggressive businessman exercising his legitimate rights in the free-enterprise system. He should no more be faulted than should Brooks if he were to make an unexpected offer to purchase a local bakery.

"Thank you for coming," Brooks said. "I'm sure you know why we invited you."

"I do." Dalton smiled wryly. "A rumor. Wall Street's as bad as Washington, D.C."

There was a ripple of laughter.

Rick said, "This rumor is different. It seems to be true."

Dalton gave him an appraising look. "Not officially. As I said on the phone, we need a little more time to work out the details. But I can confirm that we're preparing to make a bid for your company."

"We're here to listen," Brooks said.

"All right. We plan to offer your shareholders a price substantially above the market value for their stock."

Jacoby hunched forward. "Substantially? Can you be more specific?"

"I'd rather not. But let's say in the neighborhood of fifty dollars a share."

Jacoby smiled thinly. "My information places the figure at fifty-five dollars."

Dalton eyed him, as though resenting his presence. "Sorry, Mr. Jacoby, but I can't be responsible for your sources. The fact is, the stock keeps slipping. It was down another point yesterday."

"It will come back."

"Maybe so, eventually. Personally, I don't care all that much whether it does or not. I'm not getting into this because of the numbers on a quote board."

Jamison jabbed with his cigar. "Maybe I'm stupid. Are you telling us you'd lay out a huge sum to buy up stock and then not give a damn about getting your investment back?"

"No, I'm simply saying that my reasons have nothing to do with pushing up the stock. No question, that would happen. But *why* it would happen is the only thing that interests me."

Sara smiled at him. "Okay, let's have the commercial."

Dalton gave her a fatherly look. "This time I'll need more than thirty seconds." He ran a hand through his black curls and gazed around at the others. "I don't know how much you people know about me, but in case you haven't heard, I can't keep my big hands off a business I think I can make grow. It was that way with the airline. That started with a few beat-up planes and a small group of airmen who'd never flown or serviced anything but fighters and bombers. I don't have to tell you what that nothing of an airline is today. The only point I want to make is that I got my kicks by building, making the airline grow. Sure, I made a lot of money, including money from the stock taking off, but all that was secondary. Building it, beating the competition, that's all that really mattered."

"I'm sure we all admire your achievements," said Jacoby, "but this is a different proposition. You knew airplanes and presumably you knew the airline industry."

"Meaning I don't know advertising. I give you that, although I don't think it's all that complicated. It's a business and I know how to run a business." He scowled and thrust out his jaw. "Look, I didn't come here with my hat in my hand to apply for a job. I was asked to come and I agreed because I thought I owed it to the people who handle my account to explain what I have in mind for this company."

"Go ahead," Brooks said. He sat back and grasped his lapels.

Dalton's eyes flared at Jacoby. "I suppose I should have expected a certain amount of hostility here. To some of you, I probably look like a pirate out for plunder. If that's the case, I'd better start by saying that what I've got planned can be of great financial benefit to everyone in this company. That includes the people sitting at this table."

"Yes, of course," Jacoby said soothingly. "The stock offer would—"

"The stock offer's just the beginning of the profits you stand to make. The important thing is the agency's potential for growth. Let me give you an example of what I'm talking about. You all know of Dentsu, the Japanese advertising agency. They're the biggest in the world, billing well over two billion dollars. That's about eight hundred million more than J. Walter Thompson, the second biggest. All right. Now how did Dentsu get to that position? Mostly it was due to the booming Japanese economy, which increased advertising expenditures. But another consideration was the agency's eagerness to expand. They're no longer just a Tokyo agency. They also operate in New York, Chicago, Washington, Los Angeles, San Francisco. And in Melbourne, Honolulu, Bangkok, Hong Kong, Singapore, London, Paris."

Dalton looked hard at Jacoby. "A two-billion-dollar agency, Mr. Jacoby. Would you say that whoever was responsible for that knew the advertising business?"

"Very definitely."

"Not going in, he didn't. The credit belongs to a guy named Hideo Yoshida. He was a nobody who came from a small town in the southern island of Kyushu, and knew less about the advertising business than I do."

Jacoby's eyebrows arched in surprise. He said nothing, but his look of interest intensified.

"Yoshida revolutionized advertising in Japan. And the way he did it would be pretty much the pattern I'd use for revolutionizing

Madden and Associates. I'd start with acquisitions here in New York. I'd open offices in more U.S. cities and then buy out or merge with the best local agencies. I'd do the same thing overseas, concentrating on the countries that now import your clients' products, then moving to those that eventually will—China, for example. I estimate that within five years the billings would triple, reaching somewhere around a billion and a half dollars."

There was a stunned silence. Dalton paused for a few moments, then went on. "Assuming I'm right, the value of the stock would naturally increase tremendously. In fact, the mere announcement of such plans should start it jumping. But for many of you, and for your employees, the rewards can be even greater—bigger jobs, bigger bonuses, bigger payouts from profit-sharing."

Charlie Quigley, who had been doodling morosely on a yellow pad, scraped back his chair. "Let me get clear on one thing, Mr. Dalton. Who'd be running the agency—this one, Madden and Associates? The people who are here now or people you brought in?"

"That's a good question, and one I can't answer now with any certainty. But I will say this much: I'd retain every member of the present management who enthusiastically endorses my program."

There were furtive glances at Brooks.

"I think that's only fair," Dalton said. "It would be against my interests and the interests of the whole organization to have in authority people who are opposed to what I've outlined."

"What about the rest of the agency?" Sara asked.

"It would stay as it is. There'd be no interference from me in the day-to-day operations. My job, almost exclusively, would be to seek out and, with expert advice, evaluate opportunities for expansion. I'd also help negotiate the deals and use whatever influence I have to bring in new clients."

Again, silence. Dalton looked at his watch. "That's about all I can tell you right now. When it's finally worked out, I'll submit a formal proposal in writing."

"You've been very cooperative," Brooks said. He cleared his throat to erase a tremor. "You've given us a lot to think about, a lot to discuss."

Dalton stood up. "I hope your thinking will be positive. That would spare us a lot of grief when it goes to the stockholders."

After he left, Brooks was aware that no one was looking at him. They were studying the ceiling, or the pictures on the walls, or the reflections in the polished table.

Finally Charlie Quigley said, "The hell with him, Brooks. If he wants a fight, we'll give him one. And we'll whip him."

No one spoke.

"Let's think about it," Brooks said. "I'll get back to you when I know where I stand."

He knew where he stood, knew it when he had contemplated their bemused faces, knew it now, sitting alone behind his closed office door, knew he would remain implacable whatever the cost. He was against it, mentally and emotionally and professionally against it, ferociously against it, as he would be against a burglar he caught ransacking his home.

And that's what Dalton was, a burglar. It made no difference that he was breaking no law—in fact was supported by it—he was a burglar nonetheless, seeking to take what was not his, a living entity created by the sweat and the brains, and yes, the enormous pride of another man. What did Dalton know or care about the hope, the frustrations, the drudgery, that had formed the foundation of this great company? Memories wheeled through his mind. Soliciting ads for furnished rooms and getting slammed-door rejections. Hoarding loose change in a jug for office supplies. Post-dating checks to pay the rent. Rearranging the reception room furniture to hide the threadbare carpet. Paying for media space with due-bills on the cheap hotels they handled. Sweating over the books on bright summer weekends. Trudging through stores, factories, warehouses. All for a dream—not of wealth, not of leisure, not even of security —a dream of something that a janitor's kid had never known but was determined to acquire and bequeath to his family: respectability.

That's all he had wanted. And he had achieved that long ago, through sacrifice, dedication, force of will, and, above all, integrity.

People respected him, trusted him because he kept his word, told the truth, competed fairly, was fiercely loyal to his employees and clients. These were the qualities associated with his name, the name of his company. These were the abstract things that in fact formed a far more solid basis for success than London-made suits and glib rhetoric and lavish dinners at "21." These were the things he had impressed upon the agency, *his* agency, as a personal watermark—irremovable, eternal reminders that in a predatory business, there was nothing so disarming as simple decency.

And now the integrity of this company, this projection of himself, was about to be assaulted by a corporate buccaneer interested only in extending his power to gratify an insatiable ego. To him, Madden and Associates represented no more than a stack of chips in a coldblooded, high-stakes game that had but one objective: to be the biggest. So the pragmatists would take over—not right away, but eventually—the men who believed that whatever worked was worthy, who would not hesitate to split commissions with clients, bribe foreign officials, effect mergers by seducing agency targets with dollars and stock options. To hell with quality, to hell with camaraderie, to hell with the sentimental notion that a company should be known as a good place to work. Be the biggest. Be number one. What else mattered?

If the takeover succeeded, he would, of course, be unceremoniously dumped, along with Rick Bradley and Charlie Quigley, loyalists who could not "enthusiastically endorse" Dalton's grandiose schemes—and Jacoby, who, uncharacteristically, had exuded hostility. That would leave Sara, an avowed expansionist, and Jamison and Sanchez, whose avarice had been painfully evident. With those three as a nucleus, Dalton would round out the board with his own henchmen, leaving no one in the hierarchy to utter a word in support of the agency's traditional values.

There must be a way out, *had* to be. A man didn't just stand by and watch his life's work go down the tubes.

He got Rick on the phone.

"J.J.'s here, Brooks. We've been going round and round on this thing. Shall we come in?"

"I'll come to you."

Entering Rick's office, closing the door, he looked at their somber faces and became aware of a pervasive gloom, reminding him of the times he had sat in a hospital anteroom, waiting for his wife to die.

"J.J. thinks Dalton holds all the trumps," Rick said.

"Listen, it just looks that way. Wait'll I get to the stockholders. Wait'll I tell 'em how this agency began, how it was built, how it's run. They'll see that what they've got now is a solid, growing investment, not a crazy dream that's just so much pie in the sky. Believe me—" He stopped as he saw Jacoby sadly shake his head. "All right, J.J., let's have your opinion."

J.J. rose from the sofa, one hand stroking his bald head. His gentle eyes were troubled. "There is no doubt in my mind, Brooks, that you would present a very effective case. I'm sure that the great majority of stockholders would agree that your stewardship of the agency has been more than admirable."

"Well, then—"

"But that's the past. What Dalton is offering is the future. Consider the glowing picture he painted. A worldwide communications network, the centerpiece of a dynamic conglomerate. An agency that within a fairly short time would triple its billings, causing the stock to soar. Would the average investor doubt that a man like Harry Dalton, a man renowned for success, could bring it off? I regret to say I don't think so. You yourself know how convincing Dalton can be, for that is exactly why he is used in the commercials for his airline."

"Are you saying we should just roll over?"

"Oh, no. I think you should fight him."

"Even though you say we'd lose?"

"I was speaking then of a head-on battle." Jacoby sat down, his frail body seeming to squirm inside his black suit. "There is another option."

"What?"

"Preemption. To put it more plainly, you could beat Dalton to the punch."

"I still don't get it."

Jacoby regarded him unhappily, started to speak, then, with a helpless gesture of his hands, looked at Rick.

Rick slapped his desk. "I want no part of this, J.J. I said that before and I say it again."

"Dammit," said Brooks, "speak up! If you know of a way to block Dalton, I want to hear it."

"As you wish," Jacoby said. "But perhaps it would entail too great a sacrifice."

"Tell me."

Jacoby told him. When he had finished, Brooks stared at him like a man who had been sentenced to death.

That night he told Maria what Harry Dalton had said at the meeting. On the walk home he had rehearsed how he would handle it, and so was able to speak unemotionally, his manner appearing almost indifferent.

"My, how you've changed," she said.

"Changed?"

"On the plane you sounded like you were about to have Harry neutered."

"Well, I've had time to think."

"And?"

"I'm still thinking. There might be a way to head him off." He could not tell her of Jacoby's suggested counterstroke, not while it was still churning inside him like a lethal poison.

"Would it be terrible for you," she asked, "if Harry's offer was accepted?"

He forced a smile. "Not as long as I have you."

"You have me. Depend on it."

But later, in bed, he did not have her. Despite her provocative murmurings, her eager stroking, her bodily artistry, he was unable to achieve erection.

And when he finally gave up trying and she sought to console him, speaking in a tone that seemed to him maternal, he knew she was aware of how intensely he feared for the company that had given him his identity.

Three days later the story appeared on the front page of *The New York Times* business section:

Brooks Madden has retired as chairman and chief executive officer of Madden and Associates, the giant advertising
agency he founded.

The board of directors named executive vice-president
Rick Bradley, 35, to succeed Madden.

Replacing Bradley as second-in-command, with the title
of president, is Sara Vardon, 25, acclaimed along Madison
Avenue for her creative brilliance.

The company said yesterday that Madden, 64, was stepping down to allow himself more time for personal interests. He will remain a member of the board and will be
elected chairman emeritus.

In a letter to stockholders announcing the changes,
Madden stated: "This is the proper step to take in view of
our decision to pursue an aggressive program of expansion,
which has my complete support. As a first step, we have
begun talks with Thornley and Babson, a highly respected
advertising agency, for the purpose of acquisition."

Bradley, a graduate of Harvard Business School who has
been with the agency since . . .

Brooks let the paper fall to his desk. He started to get up but his
knees gave way and he fell back in his chair, breathing heavily. The
shock of seeing the story in neat rows of type was almost as great as
when he had heard the proposal from the lips of James Jacoby.

At first he had been too aghast to appreciate the logic of it. The
revered founder gracefully stepping aside in a statesmanlike transfer
of power to the two dynamic executives he had so carefully
groomed—one a brainy, handsome young man, schooled in management, liked and admired by everyone, the other an even
younger woman, charming and beautiful, but with a mature creative
talent that was the delight of clients and the envy of the industry.
What better team to generate the enthusiasm, the energy, the
support necessary for a vigorous program of expansion? Yes, expansion, to preempt Harry Dalton's plans, beat him at his own game.
Not, of course, to that visionary extent, not nearly that much, but
enough to satisfy the shareholders that the company really meant

business, enough to reverse the stock's downward plunge. Unfortunately it could not be done if Brooks remained in office. He had come to personify to the stockholders a no-growth philosophy, a cautious paternalism that prevented the grown child from venturing farther out into the world. But of course the child would still need to be warned against pitfalls, still need occasional restraint, still need the benefit of the father's experience. And so it was imperative that Brooks stay on, effaced perhaps from the minds of investors but as influential within the agency as he had ever been, even though he might choose to absent himself at frequent intervals. Also, there was always the possibility that at some propitious time in the future he could, if he wished, reclaim his full authority.

For an instant, he recalled, he had felt a blinding hatred for Jacoby, a rage triggered by the fleeting thought that this Wall Street wizard was deliberately employing sophistry and doomsday prophecy in order to force a resignation that would somehow serve a selfish purpose. But reflection told him that this was nonsense. Jacoby owned very little stock, aspired to no position within the company, was universally respected, and was independently wealthy—all the qualifications of a disinterested counselor. He could have no motive other than his obligation as a conscientious director to recommend what he considered best for the company.

No, it was not Jacoby, nor even Dalton, who had cut him down. He had done it himself on the day he agreed to go public. If he had remained adamant in his opposition, there would have been no dilution of his authority, no pressure from Wall Street or management consultants to expand, no internal discontent. But he could not have remained adamant without risking the loss of executive personnel and a number of key clients, losses that would have gutted the agency and eroded its power to attract replacements.

What had incited his people, particularly the executive committee, to become so suddenly obsessed with the desire to open up Madden and Associates to any and all investors? It was not as though they had just discovered a new and easy way to get rich. They had known that for years but had always yielded without protest to his refusal. And then it was as though a Pied Piper had come tootling down the aisles, gaining followers at every door, mesmerizing them into joining their voices in a persistent demand for gold. That's when it happened. That's when he had surrended the fort and begun his march to oblivion.

Well, so be it. At least now the agency was in a strong fighting position to lick Harry Dalton. Once that was done, and he was sure it *would* be done, they could move firmly ahead, not in a way he approved but guided by capable, trustworthy hands that would keep the company's integrity intact. Rick would be a great chief executive officer, honest, fair, decisive. And Sara, well, she was young and had a lot to learn about management, but there was no denying that naming her president was dramatic proof of the agency's commitment to creative excellence. If he'd had any doubts about her loyalty, they were removed when she fiercely informed the board that she would battle Dalton right down to the wire and the hell with his account. Yes, they'd be fine, just fine, and he himself would be around to assure the continuance of his own principles. The agency would still reflect the character of the man who had given it birth, christened it with his name, raised it to maturity.

His biggest regret, aside from his own downfall, was the resignation of Charlie Quigley. He had anticipated that, but was unprepared for the aching sense of loss, like the loss of a brother, when Charlie, tears welling in his eyes, made the irrevocable announcement. Forty years. My God, had forty years gone by? How little time was left, how quickly he would use it up. But forget that. This was now. Charlie would have to be replaced, not only as treasurer but also on the board, preferably by a prestigious outsider, Jacoby had suggested, which would give the agency even more leverage in the contest with Dalton. Probably Jamison and Sanchez would also be getting out, remaining only until they felt sure that the new management's actions would escalate the stock. Time enough to consider that later.

He sat back in his chair, hands clasped behind his head, and tried to think of himself as elder statesman. The term disgusted him. It was a euphemism for a man whose fires had burned out. God help me, he thought, as his mind flashed to the lovely, sensual woman who had been cheated by his impotence. But that was only temporary. It would come back, stronger than ever, just as soon as . . .

The phone rang. It was Jacoby.

"Brooks, I have good news."

"The stock is up?"

"Almost three points, in active trading."

"Fine. Just as you predicted."

"But that's not why I called. I have just learned something of much greater interest."

"I'm listening."

"I confess it is more than I dared hope." His gentle voice slowed, became sardonic. "It seems that Mr. Harry Dalton no longer likes the competition. He has decided not to make an offer at this time."

"I'll be damned!"

Jacoby chuckled. "Not you, Brooks, not you. In fact, you've been blessed."

"And you did it. J.J., I don't think I'll ever question your judgment again."

Jacoby hung up the phone and allowed himself a broad smile of self-congratulation. True, Harry Dalton had conceived the grand design and Sara Vardon had contributed cleverly to its execution. But it was he, James Jacoby, who had formulated the procedure, analyzed every maneuver, foreseen every reaction.

Now they were precisely where they had planned to be. The rest should be easy, carried along largely by sheer momentum. He frowned, recalling Dalton's harsh humor as they sat in the back of the Bentley. "Well, J.J., how does it feel, stealing a half-billion-dollar outfit?"

He had been offended. After all, everything they had done had been quite legitimate—and constructive. The agency would now go on to become the colossus of the industry.

Ridiculous to think they were stealing. They were creating a work of art.

Book Three

27

PRESIDENT!

The word resounded through Sara's head as though shouted by a crowd, while she smiled and waved from a gilded balcony. She was beautiful, powerful, adored by her subjects—and ready now to reconquer the elusive man at whose side she would stand.

Oh, there was no doubt of it now. Rick's look of pride and affection after the board had voted. His hug that lingered beyond politeness as his chest pressed against her breasts. His kiss on her cheek, light and casual to the onlookers, but erotic to her as she felt the quickening of his breath. It was still all there, pristine and lovely and portentous of fabulous things to come. She must continue to be patient, though, allowing time for them to settle into their new jobs, to form a close working relationship, to become dependent on each other, their thoughts and actions intertwined. And then someday, some golden evening in the after-hours seclusion of his office or hers, the chemistry would erupt into a glorious fusion.

But she would not think of that now. This was a night to get high, literally high, flying with Harry amid the stars as they circled above the city, drank champagne, gloated over victory. It was all so right, so much more exciting than her suggestion on the phone that she sneak up to his office for a drink or meet him in an out-of-the-way bar. That, he had said, would hardly be fitting for one who had just attended her own coronation. And besides, this was no time to risk being seen together. But his "I just happen to own a nightclub located about thirty thousand feet up" clinched their plans.

Standing now before her full-length bedroom mirror, she gave a final pat to a curve of dark hair while admiring the snug fit of her beige silk dress. A date, she actually had a date! And on a Friday night, a time when she usually went to a movie to forget the empty weekend ahead. What's more, she was being picked up by a uniformed chauffeur who would usher her into a long black limousine and drive her to the airport to be met by one of the lords of creation! She laughed and went into the bathroom and took two Valium. The doorbell rang as she swept into the living room.

In the limousine, gazing at the back of the chauffeur's black-capped head, she contemplated the moves that lay ahead. First, Quigley would be replaced on the board by a man recommended by Jacoby. Then, when Jamison and Sanchez retired, which they had privately informed her they would, two others would be appointed directors, people who could be controlled. Together with herself and Jacoby, that would make five directors who thought alike and would vote alike. Surely Rick, new as chairman, installed because of the sudden commitment to expansion, would look with favor on the progressive proposals of such an overwhelming majority. Eventually, perhaps within a year, would come the great moment of decision—whether or not to accept Harry Dalton's new offer to merge with his burgeoning conglomerate. This time the terms would be simple—an exchange of shares in Madden and Associates for higher-priced shares in the parent company, with the expectation that the stock would then soar. Harry would gain complete control of the agency without having laid out a cent of cash.

There would, of course, be protests from Brooks, but by then he would be out of it, retaining only his honorary title. His voice would be lost in the acclamation of the majority. And Rick? Would his loyalty to Brooks compel him to wage a lone battle against the takeover? She thought not. Rick was young and ambitious and would be a fool to deny himself the chairmanship of an even bigger, faster-growing agency. And she would be there, softening him, persuading him—all right, brainwashing him.

And when that was all done, she would get her supreme reward—the presidency of the whole conglomerate, second only to the board chairman and chief executive officer, Harry Dalton. She would be Rick's superior, a position he would not resent, so flattered would he be by her subservience as a lover.

Once again, life would be beautiful.

At JFK, the limousine veered away from the main terminals and came to a stop outside a Transcon maintenance hangar. Alighting, Sara saw Harry's large figure, dressed in a light sport coat and slacks, pacing the tarmac. As he turned and approached, illuminated by the overhead spotlights, she noticed that his eyes were melancholy, his mouth grim.

Greeting her briefly, he said, "The Lear's laid up for repairs. So that flight's canceled."

She felt a twinge of disappointment, but said, "What the hell, I've been flying for days. How about a bar in the terminal? Or would that be too conspicuous?"

He thought a minute. "I know of a dark one. Let's try it."

She started to walk back to the limousine, but it had disappeared. She looked at Harry, who was ruefully shaking his head.

"I'd told John to take a few hours off," he said. "And the Jeeps are all locked up for the night."

She gazed toward the airport, almost a mile away. "I guess we could hike it."

"No, you'd bust a heel." He looked around, to where a jumbo jet was parked, its lights on. Finally he smiled. "There's our answer. What good is owning an airline if I can't enjoy the merchandise?"

"You mean you'd fly that monster?"

"Christ, no. But there's plenty of liquor aboard, music, a comfortable lounge."

"Terrific!"

He took her to the first-class section, then up the small circular stairway to a lounge furnished with richly upholstered sofas and chairs and a crescent-shaped bar. Going behind it, he made them each a scotch on the rocks, then, without drinking, excused himself and went back down the stairs—to the lavatory, she guessed. Returning to where she sat on a sofa, he picked up his glass, raised it ceremoniously, and intoned, "To the president, present and future."

They clicked glasses and she grinned up at him as he stood stiffly erect and sipped his drink. At that moment she heard the clamor of engines. Startled, she moved to get up.

Harry grasped her shoulder and dropped down beside her. "Don't panic. I spoke to the pilot. He's just taxiing to the main terminal."

"To pick up passengers?"

"No, this is a standby. We won't be disturbed."

They settled back and drank as the plane bumped along the runway. Glancing out, she saw a hive of lights, flashes of wings, the snaking brilliance of approaching cars. Then she forgot about the world outside as they reminisced over the events that had brought them so far, so fast. She was curious about Jacoby. What did he get out of all this?

"I'd say about two million dollars. Maybe more if he hangs in."

"Wow!"

"Not cash, though. Well, going in, there was a small retainer. But what he's really investing in is the future. Once I officially take over the agency, he'll get a big block of stock in the parent company. A gift, but it will be rigged to look like a normal transaction. By giving it to him after the merger, it'll simply look like he's invested in his own organization. Perfectly natural. No one would question it."

"Machiavelli lives." She finished her scotch. "Harry, have you thought of a name for the new company?"

"Not yet. But it should be some sort of umbrella name that covers everything—the airline, the agency, the resorts and movies, and whatever else we pick up."

"Right. I've got just the one—Dalton International."

"You sold me. Let's get refills and drink to it."

She followed him to the bar. "It says it all in two words," she said, smiling. "Your name, which stands for success, and 'International,' which shows the range and—" She stopped, tensing as the engines revved to a roar and the walls of the cabin vibrated.

"Just clearing the exhausts," Harry said. He finished pouring the drinks and they started back to the sofa. "Look," he said, "let's quit the shop talk and get to something more exciting."

She halted, turned to face him, feeling her hand grip hard on the glass. Well, the man was certainly direct enough. So he shouldn't mind if she made things quite clear, pleasantly.

"This is about all the excitement—" She gave a sudden lurch, spilling a few drops of her drink. Her voice rose above the engines as she completed the sentence. "—I can stand."

A grin strutted across his face. "Is it? Try looking out the window."

She swung around, knelt on the sofa, and peered out. Lights, traffic, terminal, were dropping away as though drawn by a magnet.

"Harry!"

"You called?"

"For Christsake, Harry, we're *flying!*"

"That's what planes do."

She stared at him. "You knew! You asked the pilot—"

"Not asked, told. I'm the boss, remember? And it's not just a pilot, it's a crew. A crew I can trust."

She sank down on the sofa, her mind spinning. "That business about the Lear—that was bullshit, wasn't it?"

He shrugged. "It seemed too insignificant for the new president. I figured she deserved Air Force One."

"And we're the only passengers?"

He nodded. "Cozy, isn't it?"

"You're insane!"

"Correct." He sat and faced her. "I'm insane enough to think we ought to seal our partnership."

Her heart was drumming and she felt a ripple of warmth along her thighs. It was the shock of finding herself airborne. It was the excitement of her leap to power. It was the thrill of just having a date, riding in a limousine. No, it was more than that. It was Harry's eyes promising unexplored pleasures, those eyes, bold but surprisingly tender, drifting down to arouse her breasts (why hadn't she worn a bra?), to inflame the core of her sex, then up, back to the confusion she knew was revealed in the slackness of her face. Her mind quickly erected a fragile defense. This man was some twenty years older than she was. It would be like doing it with her father! But that was no defense at all. Her mind seemed to spin backward in time, and she suddenly felt girlish and demure and anxious to please.

She sought to dismiss the feeling with flippancy, sticking out her hand and saying brightly, "Fine, we'll shake on it."

He took her hand, and then, with a whip of his wrist, took all of her along with it. Her body stiffened against his great bulk and her lips closed tight against the bruising impact of his. She gave a wriggle of resistance, then, her virtue asserted, she forsook hypocrisy and came on to him with thrusting hips and openmouthed hunger.

Then he changed. He became gentle, undressing her as he would a child, touching her delicately, kissing her neck and her shoulders as she used to kiss a doll. She was dismayed and disappointed. This, she thought, would never do. Naked, she knelt on the floor and shucked off his shoes and socks. Rising to a crouch, she unzipped him, unbuttoned him, helped unclothe him, then began to bathe him with the warm dampness of her mouth. He stirred, sighed, then suddenly electrified into the Harry Dalton of his familiar image—a bull, a relentless aggressor, a giant of a man who took and took and took. But still he could not surpass her lubricious drive, her frenzy, her physical dominance that incited her to straddle him, to buck and pump and cry out in his ear.

He was a different Harry Dalton when they sat quietly drinking, clad in white silk dressing gowns procured from a closet. Though he told her how lovely she was, his words and manner could have applied to a few romantic kisses on a moonlit terrace. There was an uncertainty about him, revealed by inquisitive glances, a look of abstraction, as though he was not quite sure who this strange creature was, this cool corporation president he had created, this astonishing sensual being who had urged him on with the raw rhetoric of sex.

"I shocked you," she said, smiling. She was still on a manic high, wanting him again, impatient for his desire to regenerate. She felt his equal now, awed by his genital power, but not by the power of the man himself. She was not and would never be another Thea, a fawning slave. She was herself, Sara Vardon, an independent woman who, in yielding to the great Harry Dalton, had exploited him for her pleasure. He had taken nothing from her inner self and therefore nothing from Rick.

He smiled back at her, but without humor. "I'd give it an eight on the Richter scale."

"Shall we try for a ten?"

"We shall. As soon as Mother Nature permits."

"Maybe I can give her a nudge." She dropped her hand between his legs.

He gazed at her quizzically, then stood up. "First let's get something out of the way."

She parted her dressing gown. "You mean this?"

"No, I mean Rick Bradley."

She started, felt blood surge to her cheeks. "Now why would you bring him up?"

"Why not? You used to live with him."

A huskiness gathered in her throat. "So you heard about that. Who told you?"

"I don't remember. It may have been Westbrook. Anyway, what about Bradley?" He stood over her, like a building about to fall.

She felt a wave of anger. "Harry, you'd better understand something right now. You don't own me. I don't have to answer questions about Rick or anybody else."

She relented when she saw his stricken face.

"But I will," she said. She must not betray even a suspicion of her feelings, lest Rick, like Brooks, become a victim of Harry's power to destroy. "That ended some eight months ago. It ended because it had to end. Rick has a wife and son. He needed them and they needed him. It's as simple as that."

"You haven't seen him since?"

"Not outside the office. In the office, we work well together and we're friendly. Nothing else. Now does that satisfy you?"

He stepped back. "It does."

She stood up, smiling. "Prove it."

He reached out and slipped off her gown.

Later there were caviar and lobster and goblets of champagne, eaten and drunk in a euphoric haze, accompanied by the pervasive instrumental show tunes of Arlen, Porter, and Hammerstein, and by the humming rhythm of the engines driving them aimlessly through the black sky. They descended to the main cabin and he set up an old movie—*Casablanca*—but they left while Dooley Wilson was playing "As Time Goes By," preferring their own playing, which sent them back to the lounge for consummation.

They piled cushions on the floor and slept, then were jarred awake as the wheels crunched to a landing and they heard the hurricane roar of the reversed engines.

As they dressed, Sara peered out a window, seeing only darkness and a distant cluster of lights. So they were back at the hangar and somewhere nearby would be John, the chauffeur, and the limousine that would return her to her apartment. It was long past midnight, late enough perhaps for Harry to abandon caution and come to her bed. She was satiated now, but knew that her desire would soon be rekindled by erotic flashbacks mixed with dismal thoughts of her silent, empty rooms. On the ride to the city, she would tempt him into passionate agreement.

Downstairs in the main cabin, there was no one in sight. But the huge curved door had been thrown open and stairs wheeled up. Harry took her arm as they stepped out and paused on the top platform. She felt a warm, scented breeze touch her cheek and, looking out, saw the dark spikes of slender trees swaying against a purple sky. She dropped her eyes and glimpsed the silhouette of a limousine, different from the one she had ridden in earlier. The chauffeur standing beside it was not John.

She stared at Harry. "Where in hell are we?"

"Not hell," he said, eyes glinting. "Paradise."

She gave her head a shake.

"The natives call it Barbados," he said.

The house—his house, a hideaway that few people knew about —was nestled against a hillside in a grove of cabbage palms and bearded fig trees. There were only five rooms but they were large, deeply carpeted, furnished in rattan covered with multicolored cloth, the walls decorated with huge West Indian paintings. Glass doors opened from the living room onto a cantilevered terrace, below which a flagstone path flanked by tropical shrubs led down to a sugary private beach.

"It's not real," Sara said. "None of it's real. You must have dropped acid in that last drink." She felt stunned, emotionally unbalanced, a condition that had grown progressively more acute as they sped through Bridgetown, the capital city, the harbor undulant with swaying masts and rocking schooners, and on to roads splitting fields of sugar cane, past torchlit resorts resounding with jazz and disco, and finally here, to a white terrace, silver now with moonlight flashing like diamonds across the onyx sea.

"Yes, it's unreal," he said. "And that's why I bought this place. Reality can get damned depressing. When it does, I hop down here and play Robinson Crusoe, the elegant version."

"Does that happen often?"

"A few times a year. I never stay more than a week."

"And aside from that, the house is empty?"

"Sometimes I loan it out, for business reasons. A married couple, Barbadians, take care of it."

"They're here now?"

"No, I phoned and told them to take the weekend off."

"You had everything all planned, didn't you?"

"Everything."

"What if I hadn't cooperated, back in the lounge?"

"Well, I'd have saved the company a hell of a lot of gas." He grasped her shoulders and turned her to him. "You're the only woman I've ever brought here."

"Not even—"

"*Especially* not Thea." He said it as though her presence would somehow be corrupting.

"Tonight I'll believe you," she said. "In fact, tonight I'll believe anything you say."

"And do anything I want?"

She stroked his chest. "Anything."

"Fine. Let's take a bare-ass swim."

They swam and splashed in calm water that was like warm silk, strode the white sand to where huge rocks rose like black peaks of buried mountains, swam again, then wrapped themselves in blanket-sized towels, returned to the house, and brought mugs of mulled rum to bed.

They made love slowly and lazily this time, the urgency replaced by a lingering fondness that allowed them to savor the subtleties they had ignored in their previous gluttony. And then they fell asleep, abruptly, simultaneously. They slept as though they had peacefully died, eclipsed by eternal oblivion. They slept until the sun rose hot in the blue-denim sky and stood poised overhead. For a while they lay awake without speaking, hands clasped, aware of the polite chatter of birds and the scent of jasmine and bougainvillea. Then he exploded a laugh and she joined in, no need to ask why.

At the side of the house there was a pool dug from coral rock and encompassed by lush foliage. There, dressed in short cotton robes, they ate papaya at a small wrought-iron table screened by giant philodendrons. They swam, baked naked in the sun, made love on thick blue mats joined in the shade, dozed, drank, talked trivia, and drifted mindlessly through the long, languorous afternoon and into the sudden night.

The next morning, waking early, they packed a hamper with cold chicken and ham left by the housekeepers, added two bottles of white wine, and took off in a small sailboat moored on the beach. Handling it expertly, Harry caught a westerly breeze and sailed far out, then circled back and anchored in a blue-green lagoon overhung with palms. They swam, snorkeled, drank wine, joined bodies on a strip of warm sand, then ate ravenously and languished in the dark purple shade.

And on it went, Sara caught up in a hypnotic ambiance of exotic sights, sounds, and fragrances, her mind delightfully disoriented, overwhelmed by sensation. Only once did she think of Rick, a blurred image of him comically dressed in a Madison Avenue suit, replacing Harry at her side. She felt a fleeting regret but no disloyalty. After all, this weekend adventure was no more than a celebration of hard-won victory, perhaps someday to be repeated but of no lasting consequence to him or to her. Harry would return to his Thea and his ever-changing stable of bedmates, and she would resume her pursuit of Rick, enhanced by her position of virtual consort. She did not deny that being with Harry was far more than a sexual fix, totally unlike the sheer animalism perpetrated with Eddie Baron, but it was not to be compared with the glorious union she envisioned with Rick.

Meanwhile there was the feeling of wonder, of exultant hearts, sentient bodies, a sense of awe at being miraculously transported to this Caribbean wonderland.

Late that Sunday afternoon it drew to an end, again with the chauffeured limousine, the quiet ride through Bridgetown, thronged now with tourists, the waiting jet, again with no one visible, the roar of engines, and the wistful gaze down and back as the green, pear-shaped island dwindled to a speck and vanished.

It was about ten o'clock when John chauffeured the limousine to a stop in front of her apartment. During the four-and-a-half-hour flight back to JFK they had at last been too exhausted to do more than play lightly at love. They had watched two movies, she falling asleep midway through the second. The ride to the city was even more subdued, her head drooped on his shoulder, his manner strangely detached. The letdown, she thought, the crash from their sun-drenched tropical high to the depths of a misty night whipped by cold March winds.

She was surprised when he suggested coming in for a nightcap, then realized that he was being gallant, not wanting the idyllic weekend to close on a dismal note. Leaving the chauffeur to wait, they entered her dark apartment, where, snapping on lamps, she felt a surge of gratitude and relief at having this big, confident man present to slay the ghosts that preyed on solitude.

Midway through the second brandy she took him to her bed, the first man to have shared it since the night preceding her collapse in Bloomingdale's. Again, as he had at the start of their first mating, he handled her gently, undressing her as though she were a helpless child. This time she did not interrupt, but stood quietly in the glow of the night light, smiling contentedly, feeling valued and secure. And when he finally took her, with a steady, controlled energy, she felt no need to surpass him in aggression, but was instead delighted only to respond and yield herself to a long, slow, all-encompassing climax.

Later, at the door saying good night, she was aware of his small, secret smile—a self-satisfied smile, she thought, as though he were relishing some inner triumph. He had gone and she was about to take off her robe when she guessed its significance. Harry Dalton had annexed, or so he must think, the domain that once belonged to Rick Bradley.

She paused, shocked, confused as to whether she had been exploited, Rick insulted.

The doorbell rang.

So he had forgotten something. Good. She would keep him for a few minutes, somehow make it clear that this was her territory, that he must not go away believing she was now his possession.

She opened the door. A foot jammed against it.

"Surprise," said Eddie Baron.

28

HE WAS INSIDE, back braced against the door, before she could do more than gasp. Her hands went up as though to ward him off, but he simply stood there, arms folded across his camel's-hair coat, smiling an old-friend smile.

"Thanks for waiting up," he said. "It's not every girl who'd—"

"Get out!" Instinct told her they were the wrong words, said in the wrong way. Her brain, confused by fear, flashed a jumble of signals—fight, scream, flee, phone the police—all of them goads to violence.

"Hey," he said, smile unwavering, "I've *been* out. I don't like out. It's too damned cold." He moved toward her, opening his coat. "So what you should do is say, 'Eddie, why not sit down and have a nice warm-up drink?' "

She backed off, her brain now receiving but one message: appease him—talk to him, find some way to induce a peaceful exit. But don't let him near your bed. Good God, never again with the likes of Eddie Baron!

"Come on, Sara, let's hear it for Eddie."

She halted and forced a weary smile. "Eddie, why not have a nice warm-up drink?"

His black eyebrows twitched in surprise. "Now that's the Sara we know and love."

Following her into the living room, he shrugged out of his coat, revealing a corduroy jacket and open-necked navy shirt. He tossed the coat on a chair, looked around, and settled his gaze on the small corner bar. He went to it, saying, "I'll pour. Sit down, sit down, make yourself at home."

She remained fixed in the center of the room, feeling less vulnerable with her feet planted on the carpet. She was suddenly conscious that beneath her white robe was nothing but skin.

Two brandy glasses sat on the bar, left there when she and Harry had been galvanized to bed. Eddie picked one up, swirled the remains of the drink, then sniffed it.

"Well, well, brandy. Just what I had in mind." He found the bottle and drew the stopper.

"None for me," she said.

"Dr. Baron prescribes it. Purely medicinal. You're all uptight. You're as white as your robe." He raised the glass he had sniffed. "This the one *he* used?"

"What!"

"This glass, did he drink from it?"

"Look, what's the difference who—" She took a breath to steady her voice. "There are clean ones in the back of the—"

"Hell, no. I want to be able to tell my friends I drank from the same glass my hero drank from."

Her heart seemed to flip. "Eddie, what are you talking about?"

"Harry Dalton—who else? Head honcho of Transcon Airlines. The guy who talks to me on the tube like I'd be a dumb shit if I didn't fly his jets."

She thought of grabbing a lamp and breaking his skull. But only her jaw moved, flexing until it hurt. She kept her voice level. "So you saw him."

"Him and his fancy chauffeur and his block-long limo. Great, just great. Like watching a movie." He shook his head in mock disbelief. "Imagine Eddie Baron, that schmuck from Flatbush, having the same woman as Harry Dalton. I tell you, Sara, there's nothing like living in a democracy."

She felt a sense of foreboding. Easy now, she thought, play it cool. If only her smile wasn't so tight, as if it were pasted on. "Eddie, I'm afraid you've got it all wrong. Mr. Dalton happens to be a client, a *business* client, nothing more."

"And business is good, right?" He poured the drinks, his expression sardonic, eyes bright with mischief. "You take off with him Friday night, you come back with him Sunday night, and he comes in and stays an hour. Now that's one hell of a lot of business. But I guess, you being president now, you've got to—"

"Shut up, Eddie! Just shut *up!*" She was trembling with rage, clenching it like a fist in her stomach, where it mingled with apprehension.

He sauntered up to her and handed her a drink. She took it without thinking, needing it.

"Don't be so sensitive, Sara. Eddie understands. Believe it, you'll never in your life find anyone as understanding as Eddie Baron. So relax, drink, enjoy."

She drank half the brandy. "I don't like being watched."

"Hey, that's too bad. Because I'm the world's number-one Sara-watcher. Like, I came by here Friday night, thinking maybe I was mistaken you ran out on me. And again I came yesterday. And this afternoon. No Sara. But old faithful me, I don't give up easy. And I'm smart, too. Sunday night, I said, that's when she'll be back. Why? Because Monday morning she's got to look all bright and beautiful when she's got her ass parked in that big president's office."

"Damn it, Eddie, what do you want with me?"

He dropped his jaw and popped his eyes. "You ask that? After all we've *been* to each other?"

"Look, I'm terribly tired. Please just finish your drink and—"

"*You're* tired! Jesus, I've been standing out there so long, my feet are bleeding in my socks. Let's sit."

He took a chair. She went to the sofa and sat stiffly on the edge of a cushion.

"That's better," he said. "Now tell me something."

"Tell you what?"

"How long you been getting it on with Harry Dalton?"

She jerked forward. "Goddamn you! I told you—"

"Yeah, business. But isn't that business—letting your client ball you?"

"No! That's not the way—"

"Back to my question—how long? I'll make a guess. Not very long. If he'd been slipping it to you when I last saw you, you wouldn't have stayed in my pad. Right?"

She knocked back her drink, the glass clicking against her teeth. Her mind teemed with obscenities that must not be spoken.

"And now, all of a sudden, he makes the big play. The chauffeur, the limo, maybe a trip into the wild blue. Christ, the guy must be nuts about you."

She snorted in disgust.

He plowed a hand through his thick hair. "I wonder what a guy like Harry Dalton—a big wheel—probably could get any woman he wanted—I wonder what he'd say if he knew that the one girl he was nuts about had been fucking Eddie Baron."

She stared at him as though he'd threatened to kill her. The rage seemed to leap into her throat, strangling speech, forcing a panicked breathing.

"You've answered me," he said. "He wouldn't like it." He licked brandy from his lips. "And if your pals in the office knew about it, I guess they'd be kind of embarrassed. You know, the new prez shacking up with a nobody like me. They might even be pissed that you put out for a big client like Dalton."

She had sensed it at the beginning and now it had been spoken: she, Sara Vardon, president of Madden and Associates, creative superstar, was targeted for blackmail. And such an easy target. Oh, not the threat of Harry being told about this slimy creep who sat with eyes glinting, lips curled in a smug little smile. No, somehow she could handle that with Harry. But her "pals" in the office— Brooks and Rick—my God, that was something else! One word, even the slightest suspicion, that she and Harry had been lovers and her whole career would crash. Brooks, who'd taken his own fall, who'd had his beloved agency snatched from his hands through direct and indirect pressure from Harry Dalton, would dig and dig until he'd come up with enough to make her the Judas of the advertising world. Goodbye job. Farewell Madison Avenue. And Rick . . .

"Don't look like that, Sara. Like I said that morning you shot out the door, I'm your secret lover. And that's how we'll keep it. All you've got to do is maybe once in a while make me happy."

"How?" She was desperate for time, time to gather her wits and get this creature out of her house, peaceably.

He laughed. "How? Hey, look, you know how. Man, do you know how!" He shrugged. "Of course, now things are a little different. Now I'm the guy you sort of have to depend on. So I'd say you'll probably want to show your appreciation."

"You mean with something besides sex?"

"Well, sure. Sex just makes us even—you get off as much as I do. I was thinking of a gift. Nothing big. Nothing you can't afford."

"Like what?"

"Well, I've had my eye on a real sporty little job. Baby, you'd love it."

"A car?"

"Not just any old car. A Porsche. Blood-red. Wire wheels. Sun roof. Loaded with extras."

"On you it would look good, Eddie."

"Now you're talking. But it wouldn't be just for me. It'd be for both of us. We could take trips, get out in the country."

"I bet you'd even let me drive."

"Anytime, anytime. There's just one problem. This dealer, he won't take checks or credit cards. It's got to be cash, all cash."

"How much?"

"Twenty grand, counting everything. But you'd only pay half. For you, ten grand's just walking-around money."

"Oh, sure. But yes, I can swing that. It'd take a few days to raise it."

"Sara, I've got to be frank. I just can't believe that you, the president of a huge company, need all that time to raise a lousy ten grand. How about tomorrow? You know, start the week right."

"All right then, tomorrow. I'll meet you at my bank."

"No, not there. That's a little too public. We might run into one of your big-shot friends. Tell you what. I'll phone you just before noon. You have the money and then we'll figure where to meet. Okay?"

She stood up, knees quaking. "Okay, Eddie."

He rose, grinning, and came to put his arms around her.

"Please, Eddie, not tonight. I'm really exhausted."

He halted, frowning. Then his grin returned. "Sure, sure, I understand. That Harry Dalton, he must be hung like a horse."

"Good night, Eddie."

"Till tomorrow, love."

She didn't see him to the door.

Ten thousand dollars! Did that arrogant stud actually think she'd walk into her bank, cash a check for ten thousand dollars, and then just hand it over? Yes, he did. He really did. And for two reasons. One, he was a psycho. She was sure of it. Maybe not crazy enough to be committed, but inside that well-shaped head there was a cracked fitting, a minuscule flaw that urged him to believe he could blackmail her into financial and sexual submission without fear of consequences. He was like the rapist who deludes himself into thinking that the woman he has violated yearns for a repeat performance.

And then there was his second reason for confidence. He had seen it in the sudden distortion of her face, the fear that if he talked, she would be ruined. Ruined with Harry Dalton was all he had been sure of. But he'd find out about the other, her perilous position in the agency. He'd find out because once she yielded, the extortion would go on and on until he knew as much about her as she did herself.

But she wouldn't yield. Not now, not ever. Before she'd allow him to own her, bleed her, degrade her, she'd . . .

She'd what? Kill him? The thought startled her. Not because it frightened her, but because it didn't. Her only concern was being caught, jailed, disgraced.

She needed to talk to someone. Someone who was powerful, shrewd, experienced. Ironically, that description fitted the very man whose name Eddie Baron had used to terrorize her.

"Harry, I know it's late but I just had to call you."

"Glad you did. I was back swimming with you in the lagoon."

"Oh, God, if it were only true! Harry, something happened right after you left here. Something terrible."

"You're all right?"

"Yes, for now."

"Good. As you ad types say, take it from the top."

She reported it all, omitting only the sex (which she knew he would assume) and changing the original meeting place from a singles bar to a party. Harry listened in silence. When he finally spoke, his voice was calm.

"All right. First—and this is important—there's something you've got to do."

"What?"

"Not worry."

"But—"

"The rest I'll handle. I've got his name—Eddie Baron. Do you know his address?"

She gave it to him.

"That's all I need. Now go to bed. Dream you're in Barbados."

"What will you do?"

"You'll know in the morning. I'll call you at eight."

It was one of those nights when she was conscious of nerves seething beneath the surface of her skin. When her brain seemed to harden and press against the back of her eyes. When the joints of her shoulders and knees and ankles felt stiff and arthritic. When her mouth was cottony and her throat dry and she reached again and again for the glass of water, twice accompanying it with Valiums from her bedside pharmacy. It did not seem that she slept, but she knew she had because of the bizarre dreams—oedipal, supernatural, phallic—often trapped into remembrance by startled awakenings. Always she was a child of about twelve, once dressed as her mother and curled up lovingly in her father's lap; then running naked past familiar houses, her face painted like a whore's; then reaching out for Rick, only to have him dissolve in her arms; then Harry, standing outside her bedroom door, armed with a long rifle; then Eddie Baron, his thick black hair suddenly turning into a mass of wriggling snakes, like the head of Medusa.

She crawled from her bed with the first light and took a scorching shower, switching it finally to breathtaking cold as a scourge to lingering demons. She popped another Valium, washing it down with steaming black coffee, and was sitting in the living room, fully dressed, having a third cup, when the phone rang.

"Did I blast you awake?"

"No, I'm having coffee. I've been waiting for your call. Did you—"

"I did. Sara, you can forget about Baron—totally forget."

"Thank God. But how do you *know*?"

"I had him checked out. He's a small-time hustler. Until today he was working a boiler-room scam, soliciting for a phony charity. Before that, he dealt dope, peddled hot cars. He's used to getaways. This time he'll make his longest trip—to L.A. or Miami."

"He told you that?"

"He told it to a couple of guys who work for a friend of mine, a friend I don't talk about. These guys are large and well built and they have absolutely no sense of humor."

"Harry, you've got to tell me what happened. I've got be sure."

Reluctantly he told her. And as he did, she visualized the two large, well-built, humorless men striding up to Eddie Baron's door just a few hours ago and pounding on it furiously. She saw Eddie jerk awake in that huge purple-sheeted bed and hustle down the short hall, cursing all the way.

"Who the hell is it?"

"Police."

"Cut the shit! It's five A.M.!"

"We spotted a suspect sneaking into this building. We're checking out all apartments. Open up."

"Well, goddammit, he's not here!"

But he opened the door, to the length of the chain.

"You really cops? Let's see a badge."

One of the large men flashed a badge. Eddie unfastened the chain. The door slammed open and a heavy shoulder butted into Eddie's chest and sent him reeling across the white shag carpeting.

"Jesus Christ, what the hell . . . hey, you guys aren't cops!"

"Right, Eddie. Now just sit down like a nice boy and we'll have a quiet little talk."

One of the large men drew a gun and fondled it as he explained the reason for their visit. It seemed that Eddie had made a mistake, a simple error of judgment. It was okay to shake down some rival hood, or maybe even a pimp or a pawnbroker, but not some innocent young woman who had a number of very important friends. Maybe Eddie hadn't known about these friends, but now that he did, he obviously had to back off, really back off, as far as, say, Miami or Los Angeles.

Sorry, but the promise that he'd never try to see her again or cause her any trouble just wasn't acceptable. He might be tempted into forgetting that promise, and then they'd have to break his legs, and if that didn't work, they'd have to include his arms and maybe rearrange his face and even chop off his genitals. Fine, Eddie, we're glad you're convinced. But just to be sure, let's shake on it. No, all I want is a finger. This one. Well, I'll be damned. Now look what I did. . . .

"My God, Harry, you mean he *broke* it—his finger?"

"The middle finger."

For days she twitched when a phone rang, constantly looked over her shoulder, ducked into doorways when she saw men she thought resembled Eddie Baron. Then the dread was suddenly removed, again by the intercession of Harry. He'd assigned a "connection" in Los Angeles to hunt down Baron and report on his activities.

"He's in Hollywood. Works for a photo studio, hustling mothers for pictures of their kids, which he submits to producers—he says. I doubt if he'll ever set foot in New York again. Not even if he wins an all-expense trip on a game show."

Her relief was immense. "Thank you, Harry. I wish there was a way I could repay you."

"How about tonight?"

"Oh, I wish I could, but I'll be working late."

"Now tell me the real reason."

"Okay, but you know it. After that scare with Eddie Baron, I think we should cool it for a while. It's too damned risky, Harry."

He was not offended. "We could take a motel room at Coney

Island and decorate it with palms. But all right. I'll call you in exactly two weeks."

"You sound like that's some special day."

"That's when I get back from Germany, Munich. There's a group over there doing interesting things with film. I'm flying out in the morning."

"You do get around, don't you. Well, have a good one."

"I will. Oh, by the way, I'm going alone. Not even a secretary."

Before she could speak, he said goodbye and hung up.

She sat gripping the phone. Was Harry implying she had replaced Thea as his mistress? If so, she'd just have to straighten him out. A sometime playmate, fine, but never the total lover that she had for so long reserved for Rick.

Hanging up, she wondered if Thea knew of her weekend affair with Harry. It didn't matter. Thea would surely dismiss it as simply another sexual interlude in his promiscuous career.

And that, of course, would be the truth.

29

NOW SARA'S DAYS, and most of her nights, were crowded with meetings. There were meetings to apportion Rick's and her duties —Brooks always present, ostensibly to offer advice, but saying little and looking haggard and distracted. It was decided that The Vardon Group would be dissolved as a separate unit, with Sara becoming director of creative services for the whole agency (unchallenged by Lou Kahn when he was told she would restrict herself to reviewing only new and major campaigns). There were meetings to discuss the progress of negotiations with Thornley and Babson, which Rick was handling, supported only in body by Brooks. There were meetings on the stock (it had risen close to its old high), meetings with the executive committee, meetings with clients and prospective clients, meetings with account executives, meetings with the committees on finance, personnel, employee benefits, meetings with people who had problems or ideas or who just wanted to win points with the new president.

It was ironic, thought Sara, that the higher she rose and became more deeply immersed in administration, the less she contributed of the very thing that had propelled her to eminence—creativity. There was no room in her mind to conceive a commercial, no time to offer more than broad suggestions, no incentive to demonstrate her talent. The result was a sense of loss, as though she were being deprived of some sort of psychic nourishment. But she shrugged it off as a small price to pay for the status she had achieved, for the feeling of being a catalyst to all those around her, for the sheer excitement of power.

But the price was suddenly inflated on the morning Rick dropped into her office and casually suggested that she replace herself on the Transcon account.

"So," she said, smiling, "you think I'm doing a lousy job."

"You know better. The campaign's a smash. But the pattern is set and it should be easy for someone else to step in. As things are now, you're too busy to be taking off on these shooting excursions."

She made a pretense of checking her desk calendar. "The next shoot is two months away."

"I know. But we'd want the client to know well in advance."

"Have you mentioned this to Westbrook?"

"Hell, no. I wouldn't do that before talking to you."

"How do you think he'd take it?"

Rick took a chair. A shaft of sunlight brightened his blond hair, accentuating his tan and the taut hollows of his cheeks. What a beautiful man, she thought, and was struck by an impulse to shut the door. But she ordered her mind back to what she sensed was coming and thought how to play it.

"I've got to level with you," he said. "Westbrook would take it as a signal that we're ready to call it quits."

"Oh, I don't think—"

"Sara, forget modesty. Dalton chose us as his agency only because of you. In fact, though you've never said so, he offered you his account to start your own agency."

"So?"

"So the instant he hears you're cutting out, he'll charge in here and demand that you be put right back."

"And if I'm not?"

"We're sure he'll take his business to another shop."

"We? Who's we?"

Disconcerted, he shifted his eyes from her face. "Naturally, I discussed this with Brooks."

"Then it was Brooks's idea?"

"Yes, but—"

"Brooks Madden! The straight-shooter! The upfront guy who

never shades the truth! Rick, I just can't believe he'd use a trick like this to dump a client, even Harry Dalton, who I know he hates. The Brooks I knew would face right up to him and tell him he was resigning the account."

Rick seemed to examine the carpet. "Okay, Sara, you're right. I hate to say it, but this isn't the Brooks you knew." His tone became defensive. "He's crushed. He's confused. And why wouldn't he be? He's lost control of his life's work, lost it because of one man—Harry Dalton."

"But he can't bring himself to kick him out?"

"No, because he doesn't want it to appear that it has anything to do with the attempted takeover. He feels that would make him look small and vindictive—'not respectable' is the way he put it."

"He thinks this way is respectable?"

"As I said, he's not himself. He thinks that by forcing Dalton to make the move, we'll come out looking like the injured party. That's out of character. The old Brooks wouldn't have given a damn how we looked. Sara, the man needs help. One way I can help is to treat him as though he still has authority. Whenever possible, I want to go along with his suggestions."

"That's understandable. So you felt you had to agree to this one."

"I didn't commit myself. I said I'd hit you with it and get your reaction." He smiled. "I gather it's negative. That leaves two choices: either we directly resign the account or we keep things as they are. Want to vote?"

"I vote for things as they are. Rick, do you realize that the Transcon commercials are the only creative work I do? I think it's good for me and good for the agency to keep my hand in. Besides, we only shoot two or three times a year, so it's not all that time-consuming."

"Then that's it. But if you don't mind, I'd like to let Brooks down easy. Dalton's in Europe now, so I'll simply say we want to wait until he gets back and then see how the situation develops. The way we blocked his offer, there's a good chance he's already decided to fire us."

"I doubt it. Harry Dalton doesn't let that sort of thing bother him. To him, it's all in the game."

He looked at her quizzically. "I guess by now you know a lot about him."

She was suddenly wary. "Only as a performer. He's always been very cooperative."

"He hasn't—" Rick stopped, as though he'd bit his tongue. His face flushed.

She managed an amused look. "Hasn't what? Come on to me?"

He recovered, smiling, but not before she caught the flicker of concern in his eyes. "Well, it's no secret that he's quite a womanizer."

He was jealous! She masked her elation with a shrug and a tolerant curve of her lips. "I suppose that's unavoidable. He's a very attractive man."

He blinked. The remark, as intended, seemed to have stung. He made a throwaway gesture and got up, saying, "Sorry, Sara, it's none of my business."

Looking up at him, her eyes declared that it was very much his business. "Then you don't want an answer?"

"Forget I mentioned it." He paused, flashed her an intense look, then said, "I'll tell Brooks you want to stay on the account." He nodded, smiled perfunctorily, and abruptly left.

Let him wonder about Harry, she thought. Let him visualize them together, the voracious satyr and the maiden who was no longer shy. Let him imagine the unimaginable—the two of them romping on the bed that once was his.

Anguish, vanity, curiosity, should soon do the rest. She need only provide a plausible opportunity.

She contrived to pass him often in the halls, always giving him a somewhat distant smile, hurrying on when he seemed inclined to linger. She avoided going alone into his office, instead conducting what business they had on the phone, her voice impeccably professional. At meetings that they both attended, she sat as far from him as possible, addressing her comments to the group. She managed several times, at the end of the day, to occupy the same elevator as he, escaping in the downstairs lobby without bidding him good night. Once, as she was leaving the building, she ran into him and

Brooks about to enter the Elysee for a drink, and they asked her to join them. She declined, saying she must get home to receive a long-distance call.

When he phoned late one rainy afternoon, just as she was about to leave, she was unprepared for his "Sara, I've got to see you."

"What about?"

"Our basic new business presentation. As you know, we're revising it. I'd like you to look it over."

"You caught me on my way out. Suppose we meet first thing in the morning. I think Lou Kahn should be there."

"He's here now."

"I see. Well, I wish I could—"

"Okay, let's make it nine A.M. tomorrow. I'll be working on it tonight and it should be in much better shape then, anyway."

Hanging up, she cursed herself. She had become so fixed in her aloof attitude that she had automatically rejected a rare opportunity. She sat at her desk, stared for ten minutes at the rain whipping the windows, then called him back. She would tell him that she had rearranged her plans and would join them. Now her only concern was for Lou Kahn to be the first to leave.

She got Rick's secretary. Sorry, he was not around, presumably had left for the day. Probably, Sara thought, he and Lou had gone down to the Elysee for a drink before resuming. Good. She'd join them.

It was six-fifteen when she entered the bar, only to find a few people, all strangers. She walked to the rear and peered into the restaurant section—no one but two waiters. Feeling ridiculous, she compounded it by returning to the lobby and taking the elevator to Rick's floor. His office was dark. The maintenance men had started their rounds. About to leave, she saw the door to Brooks's office burst open. Brooks stood there for a moment, seeming to sway. Then Rick appeared behind him and began helping him into his coat.

Sara swung back to the elevators and caught one going down as she heard the approach of footsteps.

She was out on the puddled sidewalk, flagging down a taxi, when the two men came out of the building, Rick holding Brooks's elbow in a firm grip. A Yellow splashed to the curb and the driver threw open the back door. Sara signaled to Rick to join her. He did, propelling Brooks ahead of him and into the rear seat. Sara squeezed in and shut the door. Rick gave the driver Brooks's address and the taxi crawled into the rainswept traffic.

Rick, next to her, said calmly, "Thanks, Sara. It's no night for walking." He glanced down at her and his eyes rolled sideways to indicate Brooks, then back as his head gave a little nod.

She didn't need the cautionary gesture to know that Brooks was drunk. It had been evident in his glazed eyes, slack face, erratic gait, and now in the reek of scotch. Apparently he had spent a good part of the afternoon depleting his private stock.

"All come my place," he said through labored breathing. "Have drink with Maria."

"I'll come up," Rick said. "It will be good to see her."

"Sara too. High time they met. Hi, time, wha's your hurry?" He chuckled and they joined in.

"Thanks, Brooks, but I can't," Sara said. "Another time."

"Okay, rain check. Lis'n, that's pretty funny. Rain check. Rainin' like hell out there."

He lapsed into somber silence, twice broken by incoherent mutterings directed at some inner drama. He was asleep when the taxi pulled up at his apartment building. With his hat mashing his ears and his coat bunched around his neck, he looked, thought Sara, like a wino passed out in a cold doorway. Rick massaged his neck and slapped his cheeks lightly, bringing him to semiconsciousness. "Lis'n, I won't do it," he said, his voice broken and somehow remote. "Goddamn, tha's final." Rick thrust across him, got out on the street side, and hefted him to his feet. Steadying him with one hand, he handed a bill to the driver with the other.

"You go along," he said to Sara. "I'll take it from here."

"No, I'll wait. You'll need a ride."

"I'll manage. Many thanks. Talk to you in the morning."

Before she could protest further, they were gone, Brooks listing precariously against Rick's shoulder, feet seeming snarled in an invisible net. She turned her glance on the driver, whose broad Latin face was contemplating her without expression.

"Where to, lady?"

"We'll wait," she said.

"Sorry, I'm due back in the shop. Already I'm late."

She reached inside her purse, drew out and handed him a ten-dollar bill.

"So we'll wait," he said, and cut the motor.

Sitting there tensed against the damp chill, her mind went back to the day Rick had brought her home from the hospital. Was she now headed for a repetition of that scene, again to emerge the humiliated loser? As the meter ticked away, it seemed apparent that this was not the night she would find out. Probably Rick had been invited to stay to dinner. Why not? His wife was not expecting him; he was supposed to be working late.

"Look, lady, I can't stay no longer."

"Just a few min—"

And then the door clicked open and he was there, grasping the hand she extended to bring him in beside her. As the taxi sped away, his hand remained in hers and he gave her a grateful smile.

"Thanks for disobeying orders," he said. "I called for a cab but they were all out. I thought I'd pick one up on the street."

"You did." There was no aloofness to her now. The elation that had erupted when he appeared was vivid in her indigo eyes, her curved lips, the glow of her skin. She let her body slump so that it moved almost imperceptibly against his.

He seemed not to notice. "Brooks packed it in as soon as we got upstairs. I had a quick drink with Maria. She's really worried about him, Sara."

"You mean he does this often?"

"Oh, not in the office. Usually in some bar, alone. I gather she's had to come for him a few times. It's so goddamned sad."

"Why doesn't she get him away?"

"She's tried but he won't budge. He keeps saying we need him during this transition period. But I don't think he really believes that. He just can't bear to think that the agency's no longer his. So he drinks, and for a while he has delusions of making a triumphant comeback. Like Napoleon at Elba, Maria says."

"Have you talked to him about it?"

"No. I thought it was just something he had to go through before adjusting. But it's a lot more than that. He's sinking into a full-blown depression. Maria's urged him to see a psychiatrist but he refuses. Now I'll see what I can do, as soon as he dries out."

He sighed, shut his eyes, and rested his head against the back of the seat. Looking at his haggard face, she let her hopes recede. His mind was so filled with the tragic figure of Brooks that there was no room for her. She was no more than a temporary confidante, unsought, joined to his thoughts only by ugly circumstance. Preposterous to have believed that mere proximity would destroy the last of his resistance. She edged away, sitting up straight and staring ahead. Then her gaze was drawn back to his face and she saw that his eyes were half open and focused on her.

"I'm almost home," she said, as though to explain her withdrawal.

"Ah, Sara," he said, and suddenly he half turned, touched her cheek, and drew her against his chest.

She was startled into rigidity. But only for an instant. Then her whole being seemed to disintegrate, all of her pouring into him, her legs, arms, hips, breasts, and face sliding against his, her mouth yielding its inner richness and transferring to him her warm, quickened breath.

It did not stop. It could not stop. Until—

"Look, I gotta take off." The driver's voice.

"We're here?" Rick's voice.

"Mister, you *been* here."

In the living room there was no specter of Brooks, or of Harry Dalton or Janice Powers or a little boy named Scott. There was no talk of anguished nights or searing jealousies or of what they had become or where they were going. It was as though their awful separation had been excised, thrown away, and the past and the present spliced to form a seamless continuity. Clasped together on the sofa, he spoke to her as he had on that day long ago when he astonished her with her confession of love, murmuring endearments, admiring her sweetness, her gentleness, her capacity to please.

Dazzled by victory, caught up in mindless euphoria, she was only subliminally aware that his words were meant for a Sara preserved in nostalgia—the ingenuous, plastic Sara dedicated to his pleasure and self-esteem. And now, insidiously, she began to metamorphose into a clone of that long-ago girl, unconsciously piecing together fragments of her former self, concealing all that was different beneath patches of memory and remnants of emotion. Again she appeared as the starry-eyed, small-town copywriter enchanted by the handsome, debonair Mr. Manhattan.

But there was no way to conceal her erotic need. It had lived too long inside her, a fantasy enhanced rather than diminished by solitary gratification. Still, she proceeded with the old discretion, slipping her hand beneath his jacket and stroking his chest, then letting her hand descend and, as though innocent of premeditation, press gently against his loins. He responded slowly, almost reluctantly, she thought, as though fearful to leave the romantic cocoon he seemed so intent on weaving. Then, as he came erect, his whole body seemed to sigh and he half turned, grasped her hips, and swung them toward him and into him, hands then lowering and infiltrating her skirt to caress her thighs, then rising to slip beneath her lace bikini.

It was going to happen here, she thought, here on this narrow sofa, and with their clothes on, and with an aftermath that would be awkward, even ludicrous, the act somehow defiled by the sound of a closing zipper. Oh, no, not this way, not like two pubescent lovers rutting in the back seat of a car!

"The bedroom," she whispered.

She felt his muscles tighten, sensed the sudden gap between them, both physical and emotional, saw, as his head drew back, the negation in his eyes, and knew intuitively that he suspected the bed had been tainted by the presence of an alien body.

"*Our* bedroom, Rick. I've never shared it with anyone else." She could say it honestly because at that moment it seemed true.

His face relaxed. He took her hands and, rising, drew her to her feet. Then he kissed her eyes and her mouth and said, "You go ahead."

She wished he had swept her up in his arms, rushed her through the door, flung her on the bed. But no, it must be played out in the familiar way, she nakedly awaiting him.

In the bedroom she lit the two small bedlamps, then quickly undressed, taking wicked pleasure in strewing her clothes on the floor. She was lying straight out under the sheet when he entered, his lithe body stripped to his shorts. He slipped in beside her, snapped off his lamp, then reached across to hers. Impulsively rejecting the anonymity of darkness, she caught his arm and clasped it across her breasts. He sank back on the pillow, squirmed to pull off his shorts, and scuffed them to the floor with the heel of his foot. It was all so reminiscent, she thought, and so predictable. She would be fondled, caressed, kissed, he the controlled aggressor, she the shy respondent, too inhibited to do more than synchronize with his movements while in the missionary position.

She felt a surge of rebellion, and as he came toward her, she expressed it by flinging off the sheet and rising to her knees. As she looked down at him, flaunting her breasts, undulating her hips, the fragile fabrication of the girl she had been vanished. The tip of her tongue licked on a shameless smile, which she crushed on his mouth, her lips then leaving to join her exploring hands, her body twisting, turning, thrusting, dispelling his dismay and drawing him into the hunt. Now it was as she wanted it, wild and reckless, a tangling and thrashing of limbs, an oral and tactile ravishing, a pandemonium of lubricious pleasure—until he exclaimed "Sara! Sara!" and grasped her shoulders, pinned her on her back, split her thighs, and plunged forward for the final impalement. But before he could penetrate her, it happened—a sudden catatonic rigidity, a warm, viscous fluid spurting against her inner thighs, and, from her, an involuntary cry of frustration.

He rolled away, groaning, one arm cradling her head, the other draped across his face. There was a long silence before he said, "Rick Bradley, the great lover. I'm sorry, Sara."

"Don't be." She said it automatically, politely, as a defense against the resentment chilling her desire.

"That never happened before." He gave a short hollow laugh.

"But then I never knew a woman could be so damned exciting. Sara, you're wonderful."

She felt appeased, and optimistic. "So are you."

"Until." He snorted in self-disgust.

"It doesn't matter." She felt an odd satisfaction. She was being compensated for the humiliation he had once made her suffer. Now she was in command. His failure had obligated him. She turned her head and smiled against his cheek. "Just remember that you owe me one."

He laughed again, an authentic laugh, and said, "I can't wait to pay off."

"Oh, yes, you can. You'll wait exactly twenty minutes."

He shook his head. "You flatter me."

"I flatter myself. Now stay where you are and I'll get us a brandy."

When she returned he was sitting up, hands behind his head, gazing meditatively into space. Remorse? she wondered. Or was his mind replaying the tempestuous scene, perhaps awed and shocked that she, his innocent Sara, could be so depraved?

She sat facing him as they drank, his eyes averted from her unrobed figure, his manner restrained, as though they were being observed in some public place. But she was brazen now, teasing him with her touch, bending to kiss and breathe warmth along his chest, grasping his hand and flicking the palm with her tongue. Fifteen minutes, not twenty, was all it took to arouse him again, to incite him to reach out greedily and bring her into him, to repeat with variations all the delightful insanities that had precipitated his failure. But this time he did not fail, even though it was her body that finally dominated, breasts and buttocks exuberant, mouth ravenous, every muscle and nerve quaking in a delirium of joy. He stayed hard until the finish, climaxing with her as she squealed and shuddered through a long orgasmic convulsion.

She looked down at his face. "Wow," she said.

He smiled.

But there were no smiles as they sat sipping another brandy in the living room, he fully dressed, she in her white robe.

"Sara, I don't know how we're going to handle this."

She was wary of discussing it. His loss of passion would have reduced the incentive to make a commitment, and he might fall back on the conventional morality that decreed fair play for everyone concerned, which was not the way the world worked. If he must anguish over his responsibilities to his wife and son, let him do it alone. Let him do it when the memory of this night inflamed his mind, stirred his blood, when it demanded him to return, not for a few hours but for thousands of days.

"Why not let it simmer," she said. "We can talk about it another time."

"I can't just let you—" He threw out a hand in a despairing gesture.

"Do what? Become the quote other woman unquote who's always writing to 'Dear Abby'?"

He looked at her miserably. "You deserve more than that."

"What do I deserve?"

"You know the answer to that."

"Yes, of course." She smiled wryly. "But it seems that position is filled." She couldn't resist adding, "Satisfactorily, I presume?"

He expelled a breath. "That's just it. There's nothing wrong with it. It's what I expected. But—"

"Let's not talk about it." He had practically said what she wanted to hear: life with Janice Powers was a drag. "Look, why push it tonight? There's plenty of time. Whatever you decide, no matter what, I'll accept."

He took her hand and gave it a grateful squeeze. "Still the same lovely Sara. I was afraid you'd changed, but you haven't. He paused and added, "Not basically."

She recalled her demure look and used it.

30

THE PACKAGE, addressed to Brooks Madden and sent special delivery, arrived at four o'clock. It was no bigger than a book, which Maria Corliss assumed it was until she gave it a shake and heard it rattle. Better than if it ticked, she thought, which struck her as being not at all funny. Why would anyone want to kill Brooks when he himself was doing such a thoroughly successful job of it?

She placed the package on the coffee table (noticing that it was postmarked Grand Central Station and, oddly, bore no return address) and went upstairs to the bedroom—*her* bedroom, hers alone, which for weeks Brooks had not entered. Her isolation had been neither sought nor imposed, it had simply happened, the way married people stop kissing each other good night, or one starts going to bed while the other stays up to watch television. That she could have handled. In fact, with the aid of the right scent, spectacular Hollywood lingerie, and a few R-rated words, she could have quickly reversed it. But what did you do with a man who constantly came home half smashed and sat silently in a chair, maintenance drink in hand, eyes staring into space. Well, first you tried to start a conversation.

"Darling, I've been thinking about Phoenix. The desert's gorgeous in the spring."

"What? Oh. Yeah."

"I was looking at the weather map this morning. Eighty-four and clear. How about that?"

"About what?"

"About Phoenix."

"What about Phoenix?"

"I think we should go there."

"Can't. Sorry. Too much to do."

"Come on, the agency can spare you for a couple of weeks."
Silence.

"Think about it, Brooks. Please think about it."

"What?"

"Phoenix."

"What's in Phoenix?"

"You and beautiful me. *All* of me, batteries included."

He answered with a head shake, another trip to the bar.

There had been weeks of such scintillant dialogue, uncommunicative, exasperating, heartbreaking, always aborted when she so much as approached the forbidden territories of business or sex. Earlier she had jumped in boldly, saying he should be damned glad he was out of the pressure cooker, saying that now he could enjoy all the fun he'd missed as a young man, saying that if he didn't see it that way she'd find the best shrink in New York and personally cart him to the couch. That had been the first and only time he'd exploded at her. Listen, goddammit, he wasn't about to be told how and what he was supposed to feel about his work or that he should just run off yelling to hell with all of you. And as for this other thing, what for Christsake was she saying—that he'd lost his marbles? Well, okay, maybe he'd misplaced a few, temporarily, but he sure as hell didn't need some Park Avenue head doctor with a picture of Sigmund Freud on the wall to help find them.

"What about the other problem?"

"What other problem?"

"The one Masters and Johnson keep talking about." She was mad too.

"So you want to bring that up."

"How I'd love to!"

He stared at her, speechless.

"Oh, Brooks, dearest, I'm sorry. Me and my hilarious wit."

He made himself a drink and took it to the den. He was still there, passed out in a chair, when she came down in the morning.

Now it was really the pits, especially when she would awaken at some godawful hour, step out on the balcony, and see him sitting below, gazing into a whiskey glass. They were polite to each other, even cordial, but no more intimate than two strangers. There were times when he demonstrated his need for her—when he was afloat at the Biltmore bar or the King Cole Room at the St. Regis and he would phone and say, hey, come on down, miss you, want to talk to you, and she'd throw on a slinky dress and rush to meet him, only to discover he was no longer being served, and her only talk was with the returning taxi driver who bitched about how lousy everything was and she wholeheartedly agreed.

She'd probably have left him before this if she didn't understand what he was going through. She'd had a bitter taste of it herself back in the early fifties, when the casting calls stopped coming and the deal-makers at Chasen's and the Polo Lounge started getting astigmatism. Then the only ones who contacted her were the cheapie producers who optioned almost any property they could for almost nothing, hoping to package it with a name actor and a name director and thus make it bankable, which almost never happened. And if it did, the film usually died in the provinces. It was a humiliating experience, made worse when she got offers to do commercials for denture creams and laxatives and support hose. She'd probably have ended up peddling tract houses in the San Fernando Valley if she hadn't lucked into foreign relations and married a rich Greek who thought she was still a star because in his country that was what she was.

Well, marriage was no way out for Brooks, because he was already married—to the goddamned agency. What he couldn't see, refused to see, was that his dearly beloved had filed for divorce, in fact already had the interlocutory decree. After a proper grace period, it would be final and he wouldn't even have custody of his colonial furniture. She could only hope that before that happened, he'd face the dirty realities, as he always had, get himself together, and realize that he couldn't resuscitate a dead dream with infusions of boozy fantasy. Until then, no one could help him because he wouldn't let anyone into his tortured mind, including Maria, who, of all people, should have been relied on to lick his wounds, massage his ego, restore his optimism.

And so she was leaving him. Not for good—that would be intolerable—but long enough for him to get some perspective on their relationship and perhaps make a reasoned choice between the company that had forsaken him and the woman who never would. She would wait in Phoenix, how long she didn't know, and would monitor the situation through calls to Rick. If Brooks continued his slide, she'd come back, share his misery, do her best to cushion the final crash. But now she could only stare at the half-packed suitcases, the shoes cluttering the floor, the hangered dresses laid out on the satin spread.

"Oh, shit," she said, and slumped on the bed, crushing a Givenchy creation, and let the tears flood down her sculpted face.

She was showered, made up, combed, but still in her dressing gown when he arrived. It was shortly before six, much earlier than she expected him, implying that he had sacrificed his pit stop in order to be on his best behavior on her last night before flying to Phoenix. He was taking her to dinner and then to the theater, an evening arranged, she suspected, to preclude any more private talk. They'd already talked and he, in his distraction, had not questioned her explanation that she merely wanted to check on her property and at the same time get some sun. It frightened her to think that perhaps his ready acceptance indicated he was glad she was going and didn't care if she ever came back.

He faked a smile but, as usual, avoided kissing her by making a small ceremony of getting out of his coat and placing it with his hat on a chair.

"I won't be long," she said. "I've been through makeup and now I'm in wardrobe."

"No rush, it's early. Make you a drink?"

"Fine, but leave out the ice. I'll add it later." She started for the stairs. "Oh, the mail's on the coffee table. There's a package for you, special delivery. It came late this afternoon."

"Who from?"

"There was no return address."

As she mounted the stairs, she glanced back and saw him examining the package. He held it to his ear and gave it a shake.

"Shall I call the bomb squad?" she said.

"Probably from the office. Film reels, I think."

"Films?"

"Yeah, the latest commercials. I haven't been at the screenings lately, so I guess they're keeping me posted. I'll run 'em when we get back." Beyond the living room there was a den equipped with a projector, a screen, and a tape deck. Several times he had surprised her, shocked her really, by bringing home prints of her old movies.

Reaching the balcony, she looked down. He was at the bar, pouring. As she turned to enter the bedroom, he downed a shot of straight scotch.

She inspected herself in the full-length mirror, tawny hair carefully feathered against her cheek, eyes made smoky and spiked with expensive lashes, mouth artfully enriched; her dress was dark green silk, sequined, clinging, racily décolleté. Who would ever think that the restored ruin in the glass was fifty-eight?

She would—and did. Inside she felt desiccated, uncertain, fearful, just plain old. But he wouldn't know that. All he would see, if he noticed at all, was the image, and perhaps that would be enough. With luck, it would be etched into his eighty-proof brain and in memory he could undress it, idealize it, maybe feel twinges of lechery that would propel him to a phone. "Listen, I'll be out on the next plane!"

My God, she was hallucinating.

Okay, you're on. The final performance, the grand entrance.

She swept out to the balcony, head high, smile slowly forming to acknowledge the applause—an appreciative grunt would be just fine.

He was not in the living room.

Apparently her audience had gone to the bathroom. She gave a what-the-hell shrug and slowly descended the stairs, smiling and nodding and waving her hand as though responding to a standing ovation. Then, as she reached the last step, she made a witch's face and thumbed her nose.

Her drink, iceless, was on the bar. She plunked in two ice cubes, stood there for a moment listening for the toilet to flush, then gave up and went to arrange herself on the sofa. Setting her drink on the coffee table, she saw it was littered with torn wrappings. So that was it: he had decided to screen the commercials. God help her, his dumb business had followed him home, preempting their precious time with spiels for hemorrhoid-relievers, sweat-stoppers, drain-unpluggers. She turned back, paused in the hall leading to the den, fine-tuned her ears, and heard the whir of the projector, interrupted at intervals by the rumble of voices. She returned to her drink, drained it, went back to the bar for another.

This one she took down the hall, hesitated at the closed door to the den, then gave a sharp knock. She heard the sound snap off, then nothing, and then his voice, hoarse, peremptory, almost belligerent. *"Come in!"*

She thought of opening the door a crack, apologizing, saying she was ready, then scurrying away. But one look at him was enough to trigger her alarm system and she flung the door wide open and stepped inside. He was sitting on the edge of a brown leather chair, body knifed forward, eyes transfixed by the blank screen. Gripped in his hands were two sheets of white paper. Beside him, on a lamplit table, stood an untouched drink. He looked like a man who had experienced the Apocalypse and witnessed the Second Coming.

"Brooks, are you all right?"

He gave his whole body a shake, like a dog startled from sleep. "For Christsake," he said, his tone more awed than angry.

"What is it? Tell me, what *is* it?"

He rose slowly, turned, and seemed to look through her. "I've been a goddamned stupid fool."

She looked at the screen, at the papers clutched in his hand, presumably scripts, finally at the projector. It seemed obvious that the commercials had produced a revelation: he, Brooks Madden, son of a janitor, had dedicated his whole working life to manufacturing garbage. What she was observing was the sudden destruction of pride.

Now his eyes were focused on her. "Sit down, Maria. I want you to see this stuff."

She sat.

"Then I want you to cancel your flight."

"What!" Hope rose inside her like a warm breath.

"We'll reschedule it in a day or so."

"But—"

"I'm going with you."

"Brooks, what's this all about?" Rick said.

"I can't tell you on the phone. You wouldn't believe it. You'd think I was drunk or crazy. Probably both. Just get the board together. Ten A.M. tomorrow."

"I'll call them tonight. But on such short notice, they'll think it's an emergency. They'll ask what it's all about."

"Listen, just tell 'em I have an announcement to make."

"Right."

"And call Charlie Quigley. I want him there."

"But he's no longer—"

"*Ex officio.* I want to see his face."

"Okay. Now I think I know what you're up to."

"See you tomorrow."

Ringing off, Rick smiled. The man hadn't sounded either drunk or crazy, just a bit manic. And why not? Obviously Maria had at last convinced him to chuck the agency business entirely and spend the rest of their lives exploring the world.

"Hello, Sara?"

"Rick!"

"Hope I didn't interrupt your dinner."

"Are you kid— Oh, you can't talk?"

"This'll take just a minute. Brooks called. He wants a meeting of the board at ten tomorrow morning."

"*Brooks,* calling a board meeting? What for?"

"He wouldn't say. Only that he had an announcement to make. My hunch is he's decided to retire."

"What makes you think that?"

"For one thing, he asked that Quigley be there. I just talked to Charlie. He agreed that Brooks must be packing it in. Two old buddies retiring at the same time. Brooks is sentimental, you know."

"There goes another gold watch. Sure, I'll be there. And Rick—"

"Yes?"

"We've got to talk. How about tomorrow, after work?"

"Fine. Thanks, Sara. See you at the meeting."

Leaving the phone, she returned to sit in front of the portable TV, the image of Walter Cronkite dissolving to one of Rick, his face bland as he hung up the receiver and joined his wife and son. The words "comfortable" and "contented" sprang to her mind and she felt an odd uneasiness. A comfortable, contented life—wasn't that what Rick had always wanted? Wasn't that why Janice Powers had moved from the action scene, chucked her career, become a hearth-side wife and mother? Wasn't that why, here in this apartment, Rick had spoken to her as though she were the old winsome Sara, the girl with small-town values, uncursed by ambition, subordinating herself to the achievements of her lover?

But that Sara was gone, or at least had faded beyond recognition, replaced by a mature woman fully conscious of her worth and determined, as much as any man, to exploit every ounce of her potential.

Could Rick abide such a woman? Oh, in bed, yes—great, terrific, mind-blowing. But what about the day-to-day Sara who now reveled in the amoral corporate game with its maneuvering and manipulation, its hype and its ploys, all somehow justified, not only by personal success and the accumulation of money but by something beyond self, the building of an enterprise awesome in its size and might? Could Rick, the MBA from Harvard Business School, the charismatic manager rather than the bold innovator, the man dedicated to established systems and conventional wisdom, could he even grasp such a concept? And failing that, could he accept those people, like herself, who were willing to commit their lives to the structuring of empires, or would he view such people contemptuously as freebooting opportunists motivated only by greed?

Right now those questions were of urgent importance. They must

306

be settled quickly because, with Brooks retiring, his prestige and influence no longer a factor, Harry Dalton would not wait with his plan to take over the agency.

Tomorrow evening, before they took each other to bed, she would subtly test Rick's reactions to the great days that were coming.

She was in her bed asleep when the phone blasted next to her ear. She twitched, gasped, rolled over, and blinked at the small illuminated clock on the night stand. Just past midnight. Now who . . . ? My God, not Eddie Baron!

The phone seemed to shriek. She placed a hand on it and, when it shrieked again, picked it up very gently. One identifying sound of that evil voice and she'd cut it off. Then what? She had no Harry Dalton to turn to. . . .

But she did.

"Everybody rise," he said. "His lordship has arrived."

"Harry, my God, you scared the hell out of me!"

"Sorry, but I told you I'd call today."

"You *told* me? When?"

"When I left for Munich. I said I'd call you in exactly two weeks. Five minutes ago the two weeks were up."

"Where are you?"

"JFK. I just landed. In less than an hour I can be there, belting your brandy."

"Oh, Harry, I can't. I've got an important board meeting in the morning and—"

"Be a no-show. You feel spent, exhausted, you can't even get out of bed. I'll make it all true."

"No, I've got to be there." She told him about Brooks's apparent retirement.

"For Christsake, I figured him to hang tough, live to fight another day."

"He's hanging, but not tough. More like on the ropes. Getting dumped really knocked him out."

"Frankly, I'm sorry. He's one of the decent ones—too decent.

Anyway, that should revise our schedule. Let's discuss it. Say when."

"I'll call you tomorrow."

"Good. Right after your meeting. I'd like to hear what Madden had to say."

"Right. And Harry—"

"Come in."

"I'm glad you're back."

She was. It was like having an armored knight guarding her door.

When she turned out the light she closed her eyes and slept like a child.

31

BROOKS WOKE at six. He'd had five hours of dreamless sleep and felt charged with energy, his mind clear and clicking. There had been no farewell dinner (only soup and a sandwich brought to the den by Maria), no musical comedy (only excited conversation followed by deep, solitary thought), and no attempt at sexual reunion (he was not ready to risk it, and at midnight she had gone to her room, completely understanding, even joyous).

Now, dressed in his favorite dark suit, sitting at the kitchen table scorching his mouth with black coffee, he reviewed all they had discussed and every aspect of the scenario that he, brooding alone, had planned. His only fear had been that the morning would bring doubt and indecision. But no, his belief in what he was about to do was still intact, his confidence undiminished. He need only caution himself to remain calm, controlled, avoiding even a suggestion of bitterness. Olympian, that was the stance, a high-level figure whose self-possession would, in itself, emphasize the enormity of the wrongs committed against him.

He left before Maria wakened, first taping a note to the refrigerator door ("ONWARD! Love, Brooks"), and, ignoring the empty taxis, strode down the avenue, swinging his briefcase in the April breeze. He reached his office at seven-thirty, went directly to the boardroom, opened it with his key, and arranged everything as he wanted it. Then he sat in his old chair at the head of the long polished table, adjusted his expression as he thought it should be—cool, equable, judicious—and mimed a few opening remarks to the imagined members. He smiled, mockingly and at himself, reminded of the countless rehearsals he had forced himself through prior to new business presentations. If only he'd had the spontaneous grace of Rick Bradley, his climb to the top would have been so much less awkward.

Shortly after eight he left the building, walking crosstown almost to the East River, where he stopped at a hole-in-the-wall eatery to be served coffee and Danish by the proprietor, Olaf, a man he had known for thirty years. Coming back, he cut down to Forty-second Street, continuing across Madison and Fifth to Bryant Park, behind the Public Library. He stood there for a while, gazing across the street at the site of his old walk-up office, the low gray building now replaced. He recalled the soiled, double-hung windows that had borne the gold-leafed legend, MADDEN ADVERTISING.

It all came flooding back to him, the smells of age, the summer heat, the pet mouse that lived in the woodwork, the peeling paint, the rebuilt typewriters, the scarred oak furniture, the patched brown-linoleum floor, the sputtering hotplate.

Then, his identity reestablished, he hurried away and returned to an air-conditioned tower of aluminum and glass, a world of paneled walls, plush carpeting, and furnishings of burnished wood and buttery leather.

He was standing alone in the boardroom when, at a few minutes to ten, James Jacoby arrived, smile and handshake warm, manner all charm and elegance as he closeted his black cashmere coat, homburg, and malacca stick and turned to express his pleasure at how fit Brooks looked. Then came Charlie Quigley, white hair slicked back, lined face relaxed as though he'd been retired for a year, eyes inquisitive, one giving a quick wink to signify advance approval of what was coming. Pete Sanchez and Ed Jamison were next, the former whipping off his dark glasses so that Brooks could see the sincerity in his eyes, the latter bluff and hearty and favoring Brooks with a ham-handed backpat. Finally, there were Sara and Rick, entering together but Rick seeming to lag behind. Greeting them,

Brooks noticed that Sara's hair was combed more conservatively, her makeup less vivid, a look appropriate for a newly elected president.

Smiling at him, Rick said, "This is your meeting, Brooks." He glanced around. "I move you sit at the head of the table."

"Hear, hear," said Jacoby, and the others murmured their concurrence.

Brooks did not protest. Lowering himself to the soft leather, he was aware of the contour formed by his back, the hollows imprinted by his buttocks, and he could not help thinking that this, the chairman's chair, was his chair, the seat of his surrendered authority, molded over the years by his flesh and bone. And now this smiling group (they looked as though they were attending a party!) was facing him attentively—Rick, Jamison, and Sanchez on his right; Sara, Jacoby, and Quigley on his left—waiting for him to announce that never again would he take a chair, any chair, as a member of this body.

"Meeting will come to order," Rick said. "Unless moved to the contrary, we'll dispense with all business other than the purpose for which this meeting was called." He paused. "I turn it over to the chair. Brooks?"

Brooks sat up straight and smiled apologetically at the assemblage. "Thank you for coming. I hope you'll forgive me for giving such short notice. The reason for that is I wasn't able to see things straight until just last night. Now, as they say, I can tell it like it is. But first, if you'll bear with me, I'd like to take a few minutes to go back a bit in time."

Their eyes—all except Rick's and Charlie Quigley's—seemed to glaze over. Christ, Brooks thought, they must be thinking, now the old bastard's going to reminisce about how he started this great agency with a box of letterhead, a book of stamps, and lots of shoe leather.

"Relax. I won't take you back to the Dark Ages when I was a kid peddling ads for furnished rooms." He paused as they laughed politely. "No, what I want to review is *recent* history, starting with when the agency went public." He looked at Jacoby. "J.J., it was just about then that you joined the board. I remember having to twist your arm before you'd agree. Even so, I don't think you'd have come aboard if you hadn't seen that we were pretty desperate for a man who knew his way around Wall Street, and in fact knew everything worth knowing in the world of high finance. I'm sure I speak for everyone here in saying that we felt damned lucky to get you."

As the others nodded agreement, Jacoby held up a restraining hand. "You are much too generous, Brooks. However, I must say I've enjoyed great satisfaction in what little I've been able to contribute."

Brooks smiled. "Okay, be modest. But considering why I'm here, I think it's only right that I mention some of those 'little' contributions."

"Please abstain, Brooks." Jacoby's bald head seemed to recede into his crisp white collar. "I'm quite embarrassed as it is."

"Well, J.J., it's my meeting, so I'm afraid you'll just have to be embarrassed some more." Brooks's eyes swept around the table. "I think we all should be reminded of what J.J. has done for the agency. An example. When the stock first shot up and we couldn't figure out why, he was the one with the answer. There was a rumor on Wall Street, he said, that we were about to take off on a great period of growth. And the reason, he pointed out, was not just because the agency was sound and had a good track record. A lot more important was the fact that we had a highly publicized creative star who gave us an exciting, glamorous image. Take a bow, Sara."

Sara flushed and shook her head in self-deprecation.

"Of course, we knew you were a star, Sara, or we wouldn't have elected you to the executive committee and then set up The Vardon Group. But with J.J. emphasizing how valuable you were, some of us began to think that still wasn't enough, especially after the management consultants J.J. hired recommended that the creative department should be represented on the board of directors. So we elected you a director, which was a damned sensible move. I guess you could say that J.J. was sort of your sponsor."

He thought he saw a glimmer of puzzlement in Sara's eyes, a sudden wariness. Then she turned away, bowed elaborately to J.J., and said, "Sir, I thank you."

Jacoby waved it off, not looking at her, his gaze fixed on the tabletop, either in meditation or embarrassment. Brooks went on.

"Yes, a sensible move. The fact is, J.J., I can't think of a single recommendation you've made that wasn't sensible, logical, good for the company. Take the way the crisis with Harry Dalton was handled—"

Rick cut in, "I'd say you deserve a lot of credit for that, Brooks."

"Thanks, but that's not so. Listen, if it'd been left to me, I'd have started one hell of a stockholder fight, and I'd have lost. Let's recall the situation. Here's this war-hero flying ace, this tycoon, this maverick, who, because he's a client, thinks he's got a license to run the whole show. So he decides to take us over. He comes in here and tells us that he's ready to offer the shareholders a hell of a lot more than the market says their stock is worth. Plus, he's got a dream to create a worldwide agency network that eventually would be even bigger than that Japanese outfit, Dentsu, and that would be the major partner in a huge, growing conglomerate. That makes pretty exciting listening, whether the listener owns a hundred shares or a hundred thousand. There was no way we could beat that offer, no way at all."

Jamison said, "But Brooks, old fella, you did beat it. You made the great Harry Dalton turn tail."

"Wrong, Ed. Again, the man we've got to credit is J.J. He's the one who knew how to slay the dragon."

Jacoby's head came up. "Really, Brooks, I merely suggested a possible countermove. It was you who saw its merits and made the decision to act on it."

"Still being modest, eh? The important thing is—and I don't want anyone here to forget it—it was your idea. I can't say I was exactly happy with it at the time, but I could see that, like all your ideas, it made nothing but sense." He gazed reminiscently at the ceiling. "The chief executive officer, me, the guy Wall Street had pegged as Mr. No-Growth, should step aside, give up all authority. Replacing him would be two people. Rick here, who's young, likable, and a hell of a good manager, would become chairman and chief exec, and Sara—well, there's no need to throw any more bouquets at her—she'd become president. And that wasn't all. To show the stockholders the agency really meant business, we'd announce merger negotiations with Thornley and Babson, a move I'd previously turned down flat. So that's what happened and that's why Dalton backed off." Again, he scanned their faces. "And I'm sure that all of you here—you excepted, Charlie—couldn't be more thankful to you, J.J."

"That's not entirely true," Rick said. "Like Charlie, I wish you were still the boss."

"I appreciate that, Rick. I think you may even mean it."

"I do."

Only Quigley nodded.

"Well, Rick," Brooks said, "I'd be a liar if I said I didn't want to be back at the top again. Matter of fact, only this morning I was thinking about that. I'd walked crosstown to have coffee with an old fellow I've known almost half my life. He kept telling me how happy he was about my success and wasn't it great that I still had the brains and the energy to run a business that seemed so hung up on youth. Naturally I didn't tell him that I wasn't running anything, that I was only a consultant. He might have asked what a consultant does and I'd probably have hit him with that old gag: a consultant is a guy who, when you ask him the time, borrows your watch."

Brooks laughed. The others smiled. He was conscious of feet shuffling, fingers tapping, chairs creaking. He was undeterred.

"After I left him, I walked down to Forty-second Street to where my old one-room office used to be. Standing there, reminiscing, I couldn't help thinking how cruel business can be, especially the advertising business. You know, a guy works like a donkey most of his life to build something for himself, he's loyal and dedicated, and it's only natural he begins to get a feeling of ownership, even though he's aware that the real owners are mostly people who've never so much as set foot inside the shop, the investors who've done nothing more than buy fancy certificates. Then this fellow gets some numbers on him and the young folks start breathing on his neck and all of a sudden, bang, he's out on the street. It doesn't matter that he's still as good as he ever was, no, to hell with that, he's over sixty, or maybe it's fifty, which means he's over the hill. So it's goodbye, here's your watch, engraved 'from your friends,' and maybe we can have lunch sometime."

Brooks stopped, feeling a loss of breath, a slipping away of control. Listen, he told himself, that's enough self-pity, too much. There's no reason for it, not now, just play it cool, like Raymond Burr doing Perry Mason. Now get with it, stick to your script, forget them all eyeing you like you're some lush in a bar, about to come apart and shake your fist and flood the joint with tears.

But he saw that J.J.'s look was different, a bit tense maybe, but eyes compassionate, and voice warm and gentle as he said, "Fortunately, Brooks, that's not the case with you."

"The agency needs you, Brooks," added Rick.

But from Charlie Quigley, no words, just a long searching look.

Brooks straightened, shot his cuffs, grasped his lapels, and grinned. "Well, now, I can't tell you how glad I am that you feel that way."

They gazed at him curiously.

"And I'll tell you why. Last night, as I mentioned, I did a lot of heavy thinking. And I came to a decision that, I've got to admit, surprised the hell out of me."

Their faces broke into relieved smiles. At last, the announcement.

"I decided," said Brooks, "that I'd ask you directors to reinstate me as chairman of the board and chief executive officer."

They stared at him as though he'd gone raving mad. There was a long, painful silence, broken finally by J.J. "But Brooks, my dear man, that is not possible."

"Why not?"

"Because, well, surely you must see that your stepping aside—a tremendous sacrifice, which we deeply appreciate—has restored confidence in the agency. Believe me, it wounds me to say that, but you yourself have affirmed that it is the fact."

Brooks shrugged.

"Also, others—Rick, here, and Sara—have only recently been elected to replace you. You can hardly expect them to remove themselves voluntarily in order—"

"That's exactly what I expect."

"Brooks, you must face reality."

"Listen, I have faced it. I faced it last night and confirmed it this morning." Brooks paused, cleared his throat. "And do you know what that reality is?"

"I believe I have just stated it."

"Wrong."

J.J. suppressed a sigh. "I'd be interested in hearing what—"

"The reality, Mr. Jacoby, is that you're a goddamned crook."

32

MOST OF the reaction was as he'd anticipated: Rick grasping his elbow and saying something that began with "Now, Brooks . . ."; Sara pop-eyed, her white skin flushing red; Sanchez and Jamison gaping at him, then at each other; Quigley, dear old Charlie, his face torn between a grin and a grimace.

But what he had not foreseen was Jacoby, benign face suddenly malignant, jumping up and striding to the phone in the corner, grasping the receiver but not picking it up, scowling back at Brooks and saying in a voice that belonged to a psychiatric social worker, "Mr. Madden, you are not yourself. That is understandable. You have been through a harrowing time. You are distraught and in need of medical help."

"The hell I am!" Brooks shot Rick a look of appeal. Rick glanced away, as though confirming the diagnosis.

"And I intend to see that you get it," said Jacoby. He picked up the receiver.

It was wrenched from his hand by Quigley, coming unnoticed along the wall. He cradled the phone, stood eye-to-eye with Jacoby, and said, "Now let's hold it a minute."

"But the man is obviously in need of—"

"Of *friends*, Mr. Jacoby. Why don't we just try a little friendship before you start the sirens going?" He turned, white hair now unslicked, a swatch dangling limply over one eye. "Brooks, how you feeling?"

"Charlie, I feel just fine."

"You realize you called Mr. Jacoby a crook?"

"Sure I realize it."

"You think you can prove it?"

"I know damned well I can."

"Here and now?"

"Here and now."

Quigley looked at Rick and gave a palms-up gesture. "I'd say he talks rationally, Mr. Chairman. And I'd say he's nonviolent. So why don't all of us here—his friends—listen to what's on his mind? I'd also say we owe him that."

"Ridiculous," Jacoby said. "Ridiculous and pernicious. Why should we listen to the imaginings of a man who is quite plainly ill? It is not only unfair to me, it is also unfair to Brooks. What he says is bound to cause him great remorse once he is well."

Everyone turned toward Rick.

"We'll listen," he said.

They were looking at him, thought Brooks, as they might look at a man holding a shotgun on a crowd, or at a figure standing on a window ledge.

"What I've got," said Brooks, "is an audiovisual presentation, the kind you're all familiar with. Will you please turn your attention to the screen?"

There was a shifting of chairs as they moved to face the wall at the far end of the room. On the table, midway between them and the wall, sat a compact movie projector.

Brooks pushed a button set in a narrow console beneath the edge of the table. A screen slowly descended from the ceiling to cover the middle of the wall. He hit a second button, lowering the lights.

"This first scene took place on the west side of Amsterdam Avenue between Ninety-seventh and Ninety-eighth streets. The time is midafternoon."

He pressed another button and the screen was lit by a square of white light. It jiggled for a moment, then steadied as it was wiped out by a closeup of a street sign. The camera then pulled back to a long shot of the avenue, cars and trucks speeding past blighted buildings. After a few seconds it zoomed in on a gleaming black limousine parked at the curb, held briefly on the license plate, the number indecipherable, then cut medium-close, to a side view of the chauffeur at the wheel.

The limousine was a Bentley. Brooks froze the frame.

"Would you agree, Jacoby, that this car—a Bentley—is yours?"

In the semidarkness, Jacoby appeared to study the picture. Without turning his head, he said, "I will agree that it is a Bentley."

"But not your Bentley?"

"It is similar."

"Not identical?"

"Perhaps." He still did not move, his chin remaining cupped in his hand as he contemplated the screen. "There are, of course, many Bentleys identical to mine." His tone was that of a parent indulging an obnoxious child. "There is really no way of telling without seeing the license plate, which, as you noticed, was not readable."

Brooks snapped off the projector and brought up the lights. He reached into his briefcase, which was resting against his chair, and drew out an eight-by-ten photograph. He passed it to Sara, noticing a tremor in her hand. As she presented it to Jacoby, Brooks said, "That's a blowup of the license plate. Now, in case you think it was shot separately, I'll tell you that any expert can prove it was lifted from the film you just saw." He waited until Jacoby had peered at the photo. "Is that your plate?"

Jacoby didn't answer.

"All I'm trying to establish," said Brooks, "is that your car was parked at that location."

Jacoby erupted. "What possible bearing can that have on this . . . this *inquisition*? This whole affair is becoming preposterous!" He turned to Rick and threw up his hands. "I appeal to you, must we permit—"

"J.J., we agreed to listen."

"*I* did not agree!"

"You want us to vote?" Quigley asked, and as Jacoby glared at him, added, "What's such a big deal about saying if that's your license plate?"

"Because it opens the door to all sorts of insulting questions."

"Door's already open. I'd like to see if there's anything inside."

Jacoby stared across at Sanchez and Jamison. Their two pairs of eyes—inquisitive, probing—voted against him. "Very well," he said, "yes, it is my license plate, it is my car. But why it should be in that particular location I have no idea." He paused, thinking. "Please show the film again, just the picture of the car."

Brooks cut the lights, started the projector, and froze the frame showing the Bentley.

"Yes," Jacoby said, "I recognize my chauffeur, even though his face is unclear." He tapped the table. "That must be it."

"What?" said Brooks.

"My chauffeur. Obviously, for some reason I'm not aware of, he drove to that address and—"

"You mean you weren't with him? In the back seat?"

Jacoby squinted at the screen. "You can see I am not."

"Maybe bent down?"

"That's absurd."

Rick said gently, "Why not get on with it, Brooks."

"Sure."

Jacoby, speaking quickly, offered a second thought. "Mind you, I am not stating positively that I was not in the car. You'll notice that the rear seat is in shadow and I always wear dark clothes. As for the location, my business takes me to many sections of the city and—"

"Well, let's find out," Brooks said. He pressed the button that activated the projector.

The camera panned away from the Bentley to show a taxi pulling up ahead and double-parking. A man got out and sidled between cars to the sidewalk. His face was averted, as though he was looking down the avenue. When he turned, his figure was blocked by the chauffeur, who had stepped to the sidewalk and was holding open the rear door of the Bentley. The man ducked inside. The chauffeur shut the door and strolled off. The face of the arriving man had not been revealed.

Again, Brooks halted the projector. To the camera's eye, the Bentley appeared unoccupied.

Finally Brooks said, "Would you care to identify that man?"

"I would not."

"Any particular reason?"

Jacoby snapped to his feet. "Two reasons, Mr. Madden. First, the man is not recognizable. He could be any of numerous people I do business with."

"Then it *was* a business meeting?"

"How can I possibly recall that if I don't recognize the man?"

"But you do hold business meetings in your car?"

Jacoby hesitated, then surged on. "Very frequently. The car is equipped with a telephone and dictating equipment." His bald head, gleaming in the pale light, swung back and forth as he included his rapt audience. "I think you know that I am a very busy man. To save time, I constantly use my limousine as an office. I would hazard a guess that I have met there with hundreds of men. So you see it is asinine to ask—"

"Okay, you made your point," Brooks said. "Now what's the second reason you won't say who he is?"

Jacoby's gaunt face thrust toward him like a fist. "The second reason, Mr. Madden, is that I refuse to be victimized by a man no longer responsible for his actions, a man so obsessed with regaining his position that he would stoop to hiring a detective to discredit a highly respected director of this company." Once more his head rotated. "I implore you all—"

"Why the hell would I want to discredit you?"

The head swung back. "That, I'm sure, is evident to everyone present. It was my suggestion, as you pointed out, that you step aside for the good of the agency. Therefore, in your twisted mind, I became the villain, without whose counsel and influence this board would never have challenged your authority. So I must be destroyed. Then you could persuade—"

He was interrupted by the sudden whir of the projector. Hand raised as if to slice air, he turned to the screen as the Bentley gave the first sign of interior life.

The rear door on the street side opened.

"This is twenty minutes later," Brooks said. "The footage in between was cut because nothing happened."

A hunched figure appeared in the door, head down as he stepped to the street.

"He got out that side to hail a taxi," Brooks said.

The figure turned back, slightly nodding his head. He straightened, and from inside the Bentley a face pushed forward. It was Jacoby.

The other man nodded again and turned toward the camera.

Brooks froze the frame.

The man was Harry Dalton.

There was a sharp, collective intake of breath.

Brooks said to Jacoby, "Any doubt who that man is?"

Jacoby sank to his chair.

Brooks brought the lights up halfway, but kept Dalton's image on the screen.

Jacoby, face rigid, eyes glittering like metallic chips, scanned the faces around the table. Following his gaze, Brooks found himself exhilarated by the expressions of shock and dismay, the same as he had seen on the faces of a jury when, under the relentless questioning of Perry Mason, the apparently incorruptible man on the witness stand suddenly cracks and confesses.

Rick said quietly, "You have the floor, J.J."

Jacoby straightened his tie, ran fingertips along his fringe of hair. Slowly his features transformed into an expression of melancholy. He looked at Brooks. "Would you like to continue the film?"

"That's the end."

Jacoby's eyelids descended, perhaps, thought Brooks, to cover an almost imperceptible flicker of relief. He turned off the projector and brought the lights up full.

Speaking softly, sincerely, Jacoby said, "I had thought that the meeting you just witnessed would never be revealed. But then, of course, it never occurred to me that anyone"—he flicked a glance at Brooks— "would be so malicious, so vindictive as to employ stealth to have it filmed." He paused to take a long breath, as if to check his resentment. "And once the film was made, who would think that I would not immediately be confronted with it in private and asked for an explanation? Instead, without warning and under the guise of making an announcement to the board, this man you once honored presents it here as proof of treachery."

As he shook his head in disillusionment, Quigley said, "Well, it's never too late. You can explain it now."

Jacoby ignored him. "Now, of course, it is apparent why Mr.

Madden took the time to pay tribute to me, charting many of the steps I advocated to assure the viability of this company. Though he admits they were sensible, he is now prepared to assert that they were taken as part of a Machiavellian scheme to advance the interests of Harry Dalton." He stared at Brooks. "Is that correct?"

"I'd put it plainer. You were doing your damnedest to hand the agency over to him."

Jacoby wryly worked his lips. "And yet, because of my recommendations to you and this board, Dalton withdrew."

"Sure, but you'd knocked me out of the driver's seat. The next thing would be to run over me. You'd then pack the board with your stooges and they'd vote to join up with Dalton. He'd get the agency without paying out cash, just an exchange of stock."

Jacoby gave him a look of anguish. "Mr. Madden, it is clear that you have become paranoid, delusional."

"J.J.," Rick said, "let's reserve judgment on that."

"Very well." Jacoby drew himself up and folded his arms across his meager chest. "I shall now set the record straight. The question to be answered—the only question—is why I met in secret with Harry Dalton." He smiled thinly. "The answer is quite simple. He telephoned me and requested the meeting." His hand went up as Rick started to speak. "You ask why I would accept. Again, the answer is simple. He said he wanted to discuss a way to resolve the situation and avoid a divisive battle with the stockholders. Naturally, I was interested."

"How come you didn't report that phone call to me?" Brooks asked.

"Because Dalton said the meeting must be held in strictest confidence or he would refuse to cooperate. I protested but he was adamant. Finally, I agreed."

"You also kept the *results* of the meeting in strictest confidence," Brooks said.

Jacoby peered at him resignedly. "Yes, and for a reason that will become clear." He turned to Rick. "May I go on?"

Rick nodded, his face inscrutable.

"So, as you saw, we met in that most unlikely place. Dalton reviewed where we stood and repeated his grandiose plans for the agency. I grew impatient and said that if this was all he had to say, he was wasting his time and mine. Then he made an astonishing proposal. He asked me to join forces with him and attempt to convince the board to agree to the takeover. He indicated that the rewards to me personally would be substantial."

"But of course," said Brooks, "you told him to go to hell."

Jacoby shot him a withering look. "In effect, yes. In that last scene, where my face is revealed, I am telling him that I never want to hear from him again."

"But you still didn't report it," Brooks said. "Listen, are you asking us to believe that after a guy tries to buy you off and you turn him down, you still go along with this confidential bit?"

Jacoby contemplated him gravely. "Mr. Madden, considering the depth of your resentment, I doubt that you will accept my reason for remaining silent."

"Try me."

Jacoby turned and addressed the others. "I cannot tell you how enraged I was by Dalton's proposal. Let me merely say that I vowed then and there to do all in my power to thwart him. After considerable thought, I could see but one possible solution: remove Brooks, install Rick and Sara, proceed with the acquisition of Thornley and Babson, and by thus appeasing the stockholders, disarm Harry Dalton. Which, I need not emphasize, is precisely what has happened."

"But—" Brooks began.

"Let me finish, Mr. Madden! You have accused me of despicable acts, now please have the decency to hear me out." His eyes flashed, his chin trembled, his body shook, as though he was making a supreme effort to master his righteous indignation. Gaining control, he lowered his voice to just above a whisper. "I ask you all to consider the reactions of this board if I had informed you of Dalton's scheme and then recommended the reorganization now in effect. Would you not have been at least dubious of my motives? Would you not, perhaps, have asked yourselves whether my alleged rejection of benefits to myself was no more than a ruse to win your complete confidence and thus your approval of whatever I proposed? Would there not be suspicion that I might, in fact, be doing exactly what this irresponsible man has accused me of doing—conspiring with Harry Dalton to steal this agency?"

Brooks looked around. Heads were slowly nodding—all but Rick's and Quigley's.

"I simply could not take the risk that my integrity might be questioned, that you would therefore fail to act, that this agency, so dependent for success on sensitive people, would be swallowed up by a coldblooded conglomerate." A note of sanctimony had crept into his voice. "For these reasons, and only these reasons, I chose not to speak out."

There was a breathless stillness. Then, as though choreographed, all heads swung simultaneously toward Brooks.

Brooks, fascinated, continued to gaze at Jacoby. The little man seemed to have grown a foot taller, he thought, in the eyes of the others. On their faces was the stamp of utter belief, understandable when he considered the mesmerizing sincerity of the speaker, his exalted reputation, and, above all, his apparent success in rescuing the agency from the clutches of Harry Dalton. Slick. The man was just too damned slick. He could cut your throat and convince you he'd saved your life.

Brooks got up, went to the side of the room, and stood next to a small table bearing a tape recorder. The men with their backs to him—Rick, Jamison, Sanchez—turned their chairs to face him. Across the table, Sara, Jacoby, and Quigley tensed foward.

Brooks said, "I'm as impressed as you are by that silver-tongued speech. But I've got to say I was even more impressed when I heard him speak in a previous conversation."

He pushed a button on the recorder. There was a crackle, then the whir of leader tape.

"This one with Harry Dalton," Brooks said.

A voice, unmistakably Jacoby's, burst from the machine:

JACOBY: Harry?
DALTON: Hi, J.J. Aren't you getting pretty reckless, calling me at the office?
JACOBY: Please, Harry. I must talk to you.
DALTON: Sure. Why the hell else would you phone?
JACOBY: In private. At the usual place.

DALTON: Amsterdam and Ninety-seventh? Look, one of
these days you're gonna get your hubcaps
ripped off.
JACOBY: Harry!
DALTON: Why don't we just get a couple of gorilla suits and
meet at the zoo?
JACOBY: Harry, it is extremely important.
DALTON: Can't do it today. I'm up to my ass in—
JACOBY: There has been a break.
DALTON: You mean Madden bought it? He's moving out?
JACOBY: Correct. But we can't talk—
DALTON: You're a goddamned genius, J.J.
JACOBY: We must meet to discuss it.
DALTON: Right. I'll be there at three.

Brooks pushed the off button. In the stunned silence, he looked
across at Jacoby. The man who had puffed himself into a giant had
suddenly shrunk. He was slumped in his chair, his sagging chin
drawing his mouth into sullen lines, his eyes glowering at the
recorder as though at a monster.

"The detective," said Brooks, "is not only good at shooting pictures from a van, he's also an expert at tapping telephones."

Jacoby arched his back, tried painfully to expand his chest. "A
frameup," he said weakly. "The voices were faked."

"I don't think even you could sell that to anybody," Brooks said.

"It is illegal. It would not be admissible in court."

"We're not going to court. We'll settle it right here."

There was a knock on the door. Brooks strode to it, noticing from
the corner of his eye the looks of awe.

He opened the door a few inches. It was the receptionist. As she
spoke to him, Rick came up.

"Show him in," Brooks said, adding, as the door closed, "He's
late."

"Who?" Rick asked.

"Harry Dalton. I phoned him before the meeting."

33

AS HARRY DALTON strode into the room, Sara felt the hard lump inside her begin to dissolve, the corded muscles relax, the fear subside. The Valium, choked down dry with saliva when Brooks first cut the lights, was finally working. Never in her life had she endured such tension—not with her mother, not with the rapists, not with Rick when he said he was leaving her.

From the moment Brooks turned on Jacoby and called him a crook, she knew intuitively that this was no booze-brained fool who fancied he could elicit guilt through pure shock. This was the old Brooks Madden, shrewd, dynamic, and disciplined, confident he could back up his outrageous accusation with hard facts. Jacoby, she had been certain, would be crucified, a conviction that remained unwavering throughout his specious eloquence.

That left only her own personal agony. Would Jacoby, once exposed, drag her down with him, perhaps inadvertently? Or, if not that, was it possible that Brooks, through his detective, had compiled evidence implicating her? Her mind argued that he had not or surely she would have been included in the indictment. No, Jacoby had to have been the only target, logically selected because only he had the prestige and the influence to mold the agency's management to accommodate Harry's ambitions. Her own part—her maneuverings to a position in the executive suite—could only be seen as the actions of an aggressive, talented woman determined to achieve parity with men.

Still, she was ravaged by fear.

Until now, as the Valium . . . but no, it wasn't those stupid little yellow crutches that were producing this tranquillity. The effect was much too sudden, the terror they had been assigned to subdue much too intense.

It was Harry, big and solid and self-assured, standing inside the door, thick black curls quivering as he nodded a cool greeting, then his eyes catching hers, prompting a small half-mocking bow, as if to say, at your service, my dear. Harry was here, her tough, fearless patron, the man who had abducted her to a tropical paradise, who had treated her as a child and as a woman, as lover, playmate, partner, the man who had freed her from the bondage of blackmail. Harry was here, bringing her a sense of peace and security.

And now he was saying to Brooks, "As you see, I got your message." His eyes flashed to the screen, then moved to the accusing faces of Jamison, Sanchez, Quigley, coming to rest on the forlorn figure of Jacoby, who considered him with a sort of furtive ambivalence, as though uncertain whether he was friend or foe.

Brooks regarded him blandly. "Glad you could come."

"I hope it's worth the trip. What the hell is all this about your meeting being crucial to my future plans?" Again, he scanned the faces at the table. "Anyway, it looks to me like the meeting's over and you've just voted to commit mass suicide."

"Far from it," Brooks said. "Have a chair and we'll give you a quick review."

Jacoby shook himself to his feet. "I refuse to sit through this again. Harry, Madden hired a detective to follow me."

Dalton, walking down the opposite side of the table, behind Jamison and Sanchez, paused, face expressionless. "And?"

"He shot pictures of you and me meeting in my car."

Dalton continued on and dropped into a chair, beyond Sanchez, leaving an empty one between them. He gazed across at Jacoby. "How'd I look?"

"Not very good," Brooks said. He and Rick were now seated.

Dalton ignored him, concentrating on Jacoby. "That's all? That we met? Didn't you tell them what it was all about?"

"I—"

"You bet he did," Brooks said. "For one thing, he claimed you offered him what amounted to a bribe to join up with you so you could take over the agency. He said he turned you down flat and gave us reasons that I can't even play back, they were so complicated, but that made him look like Jesus Christ and you like the Devil."

Dalton kept his eyes on Jacoby. "Now why would you do a thing like that, J.J.?"

Jacoby, appearing exhausted, eased himself into his chair. "I was trapped. There was absolutely no other choice."

"Because they had us on film? Hell, why not say we were playing backgammon?"

"Be serious, Harry. The only way out that I could see—"

"Was to lay it all on me. From the look of you, you didn't convince anybody."

Quigley said, "Oh, he convinced us all right. I'd have voted for him for Pope."

Jacoby stared down at his hands. "Harry, Madden also has a tape of us that—"

"The car was bugged?"

"No, my telephone. The conversation was the one when I called you to say that Madden had decided to get out. I asked you to meet me."

"You suggested wearing gorilla suits and meeting at the zoo," Brooks said. "Want to hear it?"

Dalton turned to him. Looking from one to the other, Sara saw that there was no clash of eyes, no hatred, no indignation, no contempt. In fact, they seemed to share a strange rapport. Was it because each, in his own way, was a builder, each risen from poverty, one the son of a janitor, the other of an itinerant union organizer, each fiercely independent, dogmatic, driven.

"No, Mr. Madden, I recall that conversation very well." Dalton smiled briefly, as though in grudging admiration. "All right. You seem to have the cards. How do you want to play 'em?"

"I want a letter from you stating that you have absolutely no interest in acquiring this agency, now or in the future. If you should someday change your mind, I'll circulate that letter to the stockholders as evidence that you can't be trusted."

"You'll have it in the morning."

"I want a second letter, this one acknowledging our resignation of your account. The letter will be written by me, but signed by you. It will make clear that we fired you because we could no longer tolerate your ideas on advertising. The letter will be made available to the trade press."

"Accepted."

Brooks looked around the table. "I assume no one, not even Mr. Jacoby, will ask for a vote on that."

They shook their heads, Jamison muttering, "Hell, no."

Sara looked hard at Harry. He appeared no more daunted than if he'd lost a hand in a small-stakes poker game.

Brooks reached into his briefcase and brought out a sheet of paper. "Now, Mr. Jacoby, it's your turn. Another letter, this one already typed. All it needs is your signature."

Jacoby, hunched over as though struck by a chill, gave his head a negative shake. "I will not sign anything that in any way incriminates me."

Brooks cocked an eyebrow. "For a genius, Jacoby, you're pretty goddamned stupid. Listen, with what I've got on you, I could fix it so you'd have to sell your limo, pawn your watch chain, and use your malacca stick to spear papers in the park."

Jacoby attempted a sneer. "I told you, the material you have would not be allowed in court."

"I'm not so sure of that. Suppose I went to the press and accused you of being a thief and a cheat and a liar. You'd have to sue me, because if you didn't, people would believe it. Okay, is there any court in the country that wouldn't allow me to back up my charges? Hell, the court would demand it. So what you've seen and heard here would become public property. How about that?"

A flush rose from Jacoby's neck to color the skin of his bare skull. His mouth dropped open, snapped shut.

"But I'm not going to the press and I don't want any part of the courts. And I'll tell you why. No question that I'd win, that I'd ruin you. But I don't like the price. Knowing you, knowing what a slippery, lying bastard you are, you'd somehow use it to dirty the agency. And that's only half of it. The other half is that I don't want everyone knowing what a dumb son of a bitch I was to hire you and kowtow to you and lick your hand while you were stabbing me to death."

"Now see here—"

"*You* see! Listen, if I ever hear of you saying one word against me or this company or anyone working here, as God's my judge I'll forget what I just said and run you right off the continent. Now, have you got that?"

Jacoby looked like a man struggling to cap an inner volcano. His eyes bulged, his body rocked, his fists pressured the table.

"I'd say he's got it," Dalton said.

"In that case," said Brooks, "I'll be magnanimous." He half rose and shoved the sheet of paper down to Jacoby. "That letter contains only two lines. It simply states that because of compelling personal reasons, you are forced to resign as a director of Madden and Associates."

Jacoby's eyebrows jumped in disbelief. He edged the letter closer and stared at it. He gazed back at Brooks as though suspecting a trick.

Then he whipped out a gold fountain pen and scribbled his name.

Dalton got up slowly, his expression sardonic. "Can I assume that these ceremonies are concluded?"

"Not quite," Brooks said. "There's still one loose end."

Dalton sat down. "Name it."

"Sara Vardon," Brooks said.

Sara felt that the floor was falling from under her. She seemed to be plummeting through it, head spinning, breath cut off, heart beating wildly. Then there was a bodily numbness and a sensation that all of her faculties were concentrated in her eyes, swelling from their sockets. She tried to speak but the words were strangled in her throat. She had only a blurred notion that Harry had lurched forward, that Rick had cried out, that the others had suddenly petrified.

Brooks lowered his voice. "Sara, I suppose there's some excuse for you. You're young and impressionable, and I can see that a big operator like Dalton here could stuff your head with a lot of crazy ideas. God knows, he had the opportunity when you were off together shooting commercials. He was a client—you, personally, made him a client—and, what the hell, aren't we always saying we've got to keep the client happy? Also, you're ambitious, have a right to be, and being a woman, it's only natural you'd cut some corners just to stay even with the men. But—"

"Brooks, what the hell are you talking about?" It was Rick, voice rising almost to a shout, tanned face mottled, smooth blond hair tousled into stalks.

"But," Brooks went on, "you also have a brilliant mind, always showed good judgment, at least around here. So I've got to figure you knew exactly what you were doing when—"

"Brooks!" Rick said again.

"—when you decided to throw in with these two pirates and grab control of the agency."

Dalton banged the table. "Leave her out of this, Madden! Anything Sara got in this agency was damned well deserved."

"Right. That's why you picked her as your inside partner. Same reason you picked Jacoby. Two hotshots who had all it took to make it on their own—admired, respected—so who'd ever think they'd sell out to a wheeler-dealer like Harry Dalton?"

"Sara had no part of this. You're just fishing. You think because she was on my account, I must have corrupted her. Guilt by association. Christ, Madden, get off it."

"I wish I could."

"That should be easy, because you don't have a shred of evidence. Look, you had a tail on Jacoby. Now tell me, have you got any Mickey Mouse movie that shows him meeting privately with her?"

"No."

"Damned right you don't. How could you when there never was any such meeting? Okay, next question. You had Jacoby's phone tapped. Any tapes of conversations between them?"

"No."

"So all you've got is suspicion. Suspicion based on the fact that Sara and I took a couple of business trips together and that I once offered her Transcon if she'd start her own shop. Back off, Madden. There's not another person at this table who'd buy that as evidence."

Sara expelled a long, slow breath. Harry was getting away with it. That deep, positive voice. That attitude of disdain, even arrogance. That great dominating look, which alone was enough to crush dissent. She felt her mind steady, her muscles relax.

Rick was staring at her, eyes imploring. "Sara, is what Brooks says true or not?"

She looked at him blankly, not answering. A strange coldness swept through her.

He sat back, seeming to guess she was in shock.

"I'm afraid you made a mistake," Brooks said to Dalton.

"*I* made . . . Look, you're the one who—"

"You said Jacoby's phone was bugged. It wasn't. It was *your* phone."

As Harry jerked back, eyes incredulous, Sara's repressed fear escaped in a visceral spasm. She felt the blood drain from her head, plunging her into gray darkness. *Oh, my God, don't faint, please don't faint!* She sucked in air, held it, did it again, and the threat receded.

"You're lying," Dalton said. "My offices are posted with guards day and night."

"The detective outsmarted them," Brooks said. Again, he reached into his briefcase, bringing out two reels, one larger than the other. He placed them on the table.

A look of uncertainty crossed Harry Dalton's face. He erased it by massaging his jaw. "You're bluffing," he said.

Brooks gazed at him silently before saying, "Give it up, Dalton. You can't protect her any longer." He turned to Sara. "Listen, Sara, I'd rather not humiliate you any more than I have to."

She sat stiffly, primly, eyes shifting to the anguished face on his right, Rick's face. Was this the end for them? The thought produced no emotion. Something inside her seemed to have died.

Brooks tapped the reels. "So I won't use these. I won't, that is, if you'll agree with what I say is on them."

He paused for a response. No one spoke.

"I have a recorded conversation between you and Harry Dalton on the day you were elected a director. You asked him to look for your picture in the next day's *Times*."

"Oh, Christ," Dalton said. "Why the hell wouldn't she want to impress her client?"

"Sara, you said how surprised you were. Dalton, however, was not at all surprised. He said he'd used his influence to have you elected."

"So what?" Dalton said. "I've always said she's the smartest person you've got in the shop. Why wouldn't I—"

"You said you worked it through Jacoby."

"Again, so what? You know, now, that Jacoby and I—" He stopped, waved a hand.

"Were plotting a takeover, right? Then why in hell would you want Sara to know that you could give orders to Jacoby?"

Dalton stared at him grimly.

"Unless, of course, Sara was in on it."

"That doesn't prove a damned—"

"That's one conversation. There's another. Dalton called you at home, Sara. He said the stock had dropped a couple of points. You both were happy about that because you figured it would continue to slide and then Dalton could, as you said, 'move in.' You talked about the reaction in the office, about strategy, about—"

"Goddammit, Madden, I can—"

"Explain it? Try it and I'll hit you with another! And another!" Brooks lunged forward, finger jabbing. "And then I'll take you to the movies. I'll show you your limo picking up Sara at her door. I'll show that limo coming back, this time with both of you in it. I'll show you going into Sara's apartment. And if that doesn't grab you, I'll show you some bedroom scenes—"

"Shut your goddamned mouth!" Dalton was on his feet, towering over the table. Now there was no empathy in his eyes, no respect, only hate and contempt.

Brooks said quietly, "I think you've answered for Sara."

Sara said nothing, felt nothing. It was all a preposterous dream of figures haranguing each other and she was not really a part of it, only an observer viewing it with wonder from a great distance. Unconsciously she rose, turned, and stood behind her chair, hands resting on the cool leather back.

Dalton glanced at her, then stared at Brooks. "Madden, I used to credit you with decency. I was wrong. You've got no more decency than a hyena."

For the first time, Brooks seemed to falter. He looked away, gnawed at his lip, rubbed his bright cheeks. Then he pushed back his chair, ignored Dalton, and gazed up at Sara.

"You can write your own resignation, Sara. Handle it any way you want, so long as it's on my desk tomorrow."

Sara seemed not to hear.

Dalton started around the table.

"For godsake," Rick burst out, "they're two of a kind! Thieves!"

Dalton stopped as though he'd hit a wall. His face twisted in disgust. "Thieves? Who the hell are *you* to talk about thieves!"

Rick stood up, facing him.

"Bradley, did it ever occur to you that *you're* a thief?"

"That's nonsense!"

"You think so? Ask yourself, did you ever *make* anything, *build* anything? Did you ever do a goddamn thing on your own that took guts and sweat and imagination? Christ, no! Let some other guy do that. Let him work his balls off and get the ulcers and the flak from the competition and the pressure from the bankers. Then when he's made it, when he's got something big and profitable going, you walk in with your hothouse education, your Harvard Business School bullshit, and you grab a big chunk of the action. You don't add anything, you don't go for the big play. No, all you do is not make waves, not upset anyone, know when to talk and when to shut up and whose ass to kiss. And, oh, yeah, we mustn't forget how important it is to have a good tailor, a good barber, a good address, and see that the headwaiter at '21' knows you by name. Add it up, Bradley, you're a thief, a gentleman thief."

"Get out of here!"

"I haven't finished. Now ask yourself, what kind of a thief is Harry Dalton? I'll tell you. I create something that wasn't there before. And once it's solid, I expand it, add to it, even if it means pushing some slow-movers out of the way. The result, like it or not, is progress." He paused, lips curling in scorn. "And the people who are in it with me, I back up. Not like you, Bradley. When Madden, the guy who built this agency from ground zero, who put you where you are, when he was getting busted, where the hell were you? Where else but on the sidelines, playing it cool, not saying a god-damned word. That was the way to handle it, wasn't it? After all, Jacoby was making all the right moves. All you had to do was sit back and the top job would fall right into your lap. In my book, that makes you as much of a thief as anyone else in this room."

Rick stood there, silent and still, face livid and beginning to sag.

Like a melting wax figure, Sara thought, as she moved toward the door. From the corner of her eye she saw Jacoby gathering his coat, hat, and stick from the closet.

"Finished?" Brooks said to Dalton.

"Madden, I'm never finished. But if you mean am I leaving, yes."

When he turned to join Sara, she was gone.

34

HARRY DALTON slammed down his phone. Again, no answer from Sara's apartment. And she was not in her office; the secretary had said she'd left for the day. Now, at three in the afternoon, he could only think that she had gone into hiding, perhaps to brood alone at a dark table in an empty bar.

So they'd been licked, pulped. But what the hell, you didn't lie down and count your wounds. You bounced back. You looked around for a new territory to invade, hoping the inhabitants would have the good sense to escort you to their throne.

Now Madden was back on his, as chairman and chief executive officer, with Bradley replacing Sara as president. Reporting it to him, Westbrook, who had heard it from Bradley when he learned that the agency had fired Transcon, couldn't suppress his resentment. What was going on? Why wasn't he let in on anything? Well, said Harry, it had been a big surprise to him, too—especially Sara Vardon's leaving—but forget it, they were better off. Westbrook's cherubic smile had returned. Westbrook was another lackey, three grades below Rick Bradley.

So, he thought, let's get it over with. Write the goddamned letter, so unnecessary, promising to keep his big hands off the agency. He pushed a button. In a moment, Thea Roland hurried in.

She was all smiles, all blonde sleekness, all dressed up (yellow silk, lots of cleavage) to get undressed. Suddenly he felt sorry for her, this confidential secretary in whom he hadn't confided, this lover who lately hadn't gotten any loving. Then, as she sat and crossed her polished legs, grasped her shorthand book, and flashed a square-cut diamond, his sympathy vanished. Christ, he had her living like a duchess.

Still, he felt a need to talk, tell her the whole mixed-up story. Going in, Jacoby had insisted that she be kept entirely in the dark. ("Why risk that she might unwittingly reveal something?") He had not protested, if only because it would spare him from putting up with her prickly relationship with Sara. Now it didn't matter.

But first the goddamned letter.

He dictated quickly, pausing only to growl over the key sentence: "Therefore, you have my absolute assurance that at no time and in no way will I attempt to acquire Madden and Associates."

Looking up from his desk, he saw that Thea's eyes were rounded in surprise. He gave her a grin. "Like to hear about it?"

"God, yes. I've been dying to know why you've been so secretive."

He reported it all, from the time he had coached Sara into the executive committee to the devastating scene that morning in the boardroom.

She shook her head in amazement. "Harry, I'm sorry. You must feel crushed."

"Bloody but unbowed. The fact is, Madden deserved to win. The guy's one hell of a fighter. That I knew. What never hit me was that he'd think to hire a detective to bug my phone."

"Not to mention the movies."

"Yeah, of me meeting Jacoby."

She looked at him archly. "Not of Sara?"

He studied her face, that smartass expression that said you couldn't fool Thea Roland. No way, she knew the score. Knowing what she wanted—to lock the door, shuck her clothes, incite him to sadistic sex—he was struck by revulsion. He felt no desire, only a dull anger.

"Yeah, also of Sara," he said.

"And of course not alone." Her tone was sardonic.

Yes, she wanted him brutal. "Shit, of course not alone. I was one of the stars. Terrific scenes. Going into her apartment. Drinks in the living room. Then the heavy stuff—Christ, there was a camera planted in the bedroom! Great performances—"

"Really, Harry." Her eyes glittered. She licked her lips.

"—scene after scene of rampant sex."

She covered her ears, pretending to be shocked. But he could hear her breath, see her eyes glaze as her imagination took over.

"That's how it was," he said. He could feel his scowl, as though it had been stamped into his face. "Isn't that what you wanted to hear? Doesn't it turn you on?"

She dropped her hands but remained silent. A salacious smile hovered about her mouth. Her gaze was fixed on something in space. He knew what it was—two bodies banging the hell out of each other. She turned the look on him.

"Harry," she said, "it's all over now and you've still got me. Forget about Sara and her Rick Bradley."

"Bradley? That's finished, has been—"

"I suppose. Bad enough hearing she tried to rip off the agency. But then, seeing you two together—"

"Let's drop it."

"—and then seeing himself with her in the very next scene. Well . . ."

A chill washed across his back.

She looked at him and seemed to recoil. "All right, Harry, I won't say another word."

"Type the letter."

"Right away. I'll have it in a few minutes. Then—"

He had stalked away and was gazing out the window.

He scanned the letter, inked his signature, placed the pen back in the holder. From beside him, she leaned down, half exposing her breasts, exuding her scent, and reached to pick up the paper.

"Leave it. I want to read it to Madden." He pointed to the conference table at the far end of the room. "Get on the phone over there and monitor the call. I want a record of it."

When she was seated and had picked up the phone, he placed the call. He was put right through.

"Yes, Dalton?"

"I've got the letter you asked for. I thought I'd read it to you."

"Go ahead."

Dalton read the letter.

"Fine. That's what I wanted."

"It'll be sent over today." Dalton paused, glanced at Thea, saw she was taking it down in her book. "By the way, Madden, I'm sorry I blew up."

"I got a bit carried away myself."

"It was those movies that got to me. I'm not much for X-rated films."

"Listen, I'd never have shown them to the board. Maybe to you and Sara, but no one else."

"Sure, and I know why. Bradley'd have had a hell of a time explaining. In fact, he might have been booted out along with Sara."

Silence. Then, "So Sara told you about that, uh, incident."

"Right, Bradley's big bedroom scene."

Again, silence. When Madden spoke, his voice was gritty. "I destroyed that part, Dalton. And if I ever hear that you so much as—"

"Nobody'll hear it from me. Look, as far as I'm concerned, none of this ever happened."

Ringing off, Dalton shoved back his chair and watched Thea coming toward him. Consternation twisted her face.

"I don't get it," she said. "You say you saw the film. But the way Madden talked, he didn't show it."

"He described it."

"Oh, I see."

"No, you don't. He described the scene *I* was in." He paused. "That's all."

She stopped in the center of the room, eyes blinking rapidly. "But, before the call, you told me—" She shook her head in confusion.

"About Bradley and Sara in bed? No, I didn't. That item came from you, and I quote, '. . . and then seeing himself with her in the very next scene.' Unquote."

"But Harry, that's what you *said*." Her voice was shrill.

"I couldn't have said it because I didn't know it. You heard Madden. He'd destroyed the scene with Bradley and he wasn't about to mention it to a soul."

"Then . . . then I must have imagined it."

"Sure. You imagined I *said* it. But what you didn't imagine was that the scene was originally there, on the reel. You knew that for a fact when you sent it."

She snapped back as though struck. "Harry, what are you talking about?"

"The awakening. For Christsake, Madden never hired a detective. *You* hired one. *You* sent those tapes and films to Madden with a letter—unsigned, I'm sure—telling him every move in the game. *You*—"

"Harry, I didn't. You're wrong! Oh, you're *wrong*, Harry!" Her face had turned paler than her hair.

He contemplated her in silence, wondering how in hell he could have tolerated her for so long, this whore, this procurer, this panderer to all that was selfish and mean and vicious in himself. Yet it was he who had made her that way.

"Admit it, Thea. It might make me go a lot easier on you."

"I can't admit what I didn't—"

"All right, then." He got up. "You've had it."

"Harry, no! Look, okay, I did do it. But I had to. I was losing you, Harry. Losing you to Sara. I knew it that day, here in the office."

"What day?"

"The last time she was here. And then, after she left, you just about raped me. I'm not complaining, Harry. It was wonderful. But it wasn't me you were having. It was her. I was desperate. I knew I had to do something to stop her. Oh, God, Harry, I couldn't lose you!"

"You have."

"Oh, no, no, please!"

"I'll give you exactly one hour to clear out. And never come back. You're fired."

"What! But you said—"

"That I'd go easier on you. Right. You'll get six months' severance pay. You'll get your cut of profit-sharing for the full year. If you want it, you'll get a letter of recommendation. That's it."

"Harry, you can't *do* this. I . . . I won't *let* you!"

He stepped toward her. "You'd rather be thrown out?"

She gave him a stricken look, turned, bolted through the door.

Brooks cradled Maria's head on his shoulder and stroked her tawny hair.

"Well," he said.

"Not just well. You were sensational!"

He grinned. "That was my second victory today."

"But not your last."

"There's more?"

"Oh, my, yes." She reached under the sheet. "It's only five in the afternoon."

35

SHE HAD DASHED OFF her resignation, fled the office, walked the streets, wandered through Saks and Bloomingdale's, stopped for two drinks at the Plaza, sat in Central Park, hiked to her apartment, stared at her front door, then retreated, and kept walking toward the East River.

And now she stood where it all began, at the iron-railed walkway, with cars whizzing past on the adjacent expressway, tugs and barges lazing down the river, the Queensboro Bridge arching to the south. And the bench where she had sat and heard the tall, blond, elegant man and his interminable preamble to the astonishing words, "I love you, Sara."

She was surprised that the memory evoked neither nostalgia nor bitterness. Instead, she was swept by a sudden gratitude for all that Rick had given her—a sense of belonging in the glamorous mainstream of New York, of being cherished as well as admired, of being protected against the cruelties she had suffered in adolescence.

But that had been the old, insecure Sara, a person she now recalled as some blurred figure in a faded photograph. This woman she had become—confident, self-possessed, assertive—could never again be so emotionally dependent.

Nor could she ever be happy in the life which she had once thought so desirable, that she foresaw for Rick. Eventually there would be the showplace mansion in Connecticut, kids romping on a manicured lawn with a playful dog, the commute to the city with friendly, pink-faced men, a day of cajoling, stroking, mediating, then home in the bar car to a wife smiling at the door, cocktails at the ready, children shouting, newscasters on the tube capsulizing the world, and too much dinner. On weekends, golf and tennis and parties (same bland faces, same happy chatter, same sneaky passes), and of course the local theater group, Janice at last the star she had never been.

My God, what would Harry Dalton say!

But he'd already as much as said it, there in the boardroom, face to face, savaging not just Rick but all the people who created nothing, built nothing, merely greased the wheels, people who depended for happiness on a multitude of small satisfactions. Too harsh, maybe, but exactly the way Harry felt. Harry, with his implacable ambition, his huge appetites, his disdain of the ordinary, his relentless pursuit of ever-possible dreams.

Harry could never have stomached the sedate, guileless girl she used to be, the Sara Sunshine she might still be, had it not been for a stupid slob of a tumor snipped from her brain by the sure hands of Dr. Vance Kloster, who probably never suspected that he'd worked a miracle. Harry had never known that pitiful other Sara, only the woman she had become—the woman who was so much like himself!

"Two of a kind," Rick had said. "Thieves!"

But they didn't have to be thieves, not if they were together, really together. Oh, they could break a few rules, cut some corners, shove aside the drones, but they didn't have to steal, not if they were joined as a single force.

She was shaking now, as though a cold motor inside her had suddenly kicked over and was throbbing with heat and energy.

She reached into her bag for the Valium, then threw the bottle back. Who needed it? And why destroy such an adrenaline high?

What she needed, fast, was a telephone.

She turned from the railing and started to run.

"I'm sorry, Mr. Dalton has left for the day."

"Thank you. I'll try him at his hotel."

"I'm afraid you won't find him there."

"Oh?" If it had been Thea, she'd have suspected a runaround.

"He went to the airport."

Please, don't let him be with Thea.

She saw him as she slammed out of the taxi. He was alone, still in his business suit, hands shoved in his pockets as he strode to his Learjet warming up on the tarmac.

"Harry!"

Her shout was swallowed by the revving engines.

She raced toward him. "Harry! Harry! Har—"

He turned. Stood there. Grinned.

"I'd given you up," he said.

"Oh, no, don't ever do that! Harry, I just discovered something fantastic."

"About Bradley? That you don't really give a damn about him?"

"How did you know?"

"I saw it at the meeting. Hell, Sara, there are a lot of Bradleys around. Every woman has had an idol she's worshiped."

"Okay, I outgrew him. Now I'm as old as you."

"Or as young."

"Right. Where you going?"

"Up. Just up." He motioned toward the sky, deep blue in the twilight. "Anytime someone kicks me in the belly, I rise above it."

"Take me with you."

"You think I'd let you stay?"

"The offer still holds, Sara. Just ask and you can have my account, start your own shop. But I hope you won't ask."

"Why not?"

"Because I want you out of the ad business. I want you with me, making movies, supervising the resorts, using that great brain."

"What about Thea?"

"She's out of it. I'll brief you another time."

"But I don't know anything about movies or—"

"I'll teach you. In a week, you'll be teaching me."

"Well, I did say in my resignation that I was leaving to pursue other interests."

She gazed out the window, saw a pale moon, stars beginning to brighten.

"Christ, let's stop talking business. It's champagne time. Or brandy might be more fitting, the hero's drink."
"I'm drunk without it."
"You'll need it to keep warm."
"I *am* warm."
"You may not be when you come out from behind that dress."
"The zipper's in the back. Would you mind?"
There was no sense of time.

"I see lights, Harry. Are we about to land?"
"In a few minutes."
"Damn. I wish it could go on forever."
"It will."
The plane circled, descended.
"That doesn't look like JFK."
"It isn't."
"Then where—"
"Barbados," he said.

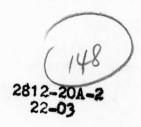

2812-20A-2
22-03